Pra

Fenella's Fair Share

Fenella Woodruff, boldly navigating 21st-century singledom, is a brilliantly sharp-tongued comic creation. She's happy playing den mother to her immature flatmates, until dishy divorced Martin joins the menage and disturbs their precarious dynamic. With a warm wit reminiscent of Alan Bennett and Victoria Wood, Chris Chalmers has created a heroine to cherish, for all her flaws and flummoxes.

Suzi Feay, book critic and the former literary editor of *The Independent on Sunday*

Fenella's Fair Share

A Novel

By the Same Author

Dinner at the Happy Skeleton
ISBN 0993323987

Five to One
ISBN 0993323960

Light From Other Windows
ISBN 099329362X

The Last Lemming
ISBN 0993323944

And for children:

Gillian Vermillion—Dream Detective
ISBN 0993293689

Fenella's Fair Share

A Novel

Chris Chalmers

ROUNDFIRE
BOOKS

London, UK
Washington, DC, USA

CollectiveInk

First published by Roundfire Books, 2024
Roundfire Books is an imprint of Collective Ink Ltd.,
Unit 11, Shepperton House, 89 Shepperton Road, London, N1 3DF
office@collectiveinkbooks.com
www.collectiveinkbooks.com
www.roundfire-books.com

For distributor details and how to order please visit the 'Ordering' section on our website.

Text copyright: Chris Chalmers 2023

ISBN: 978 1 80341 547 5
978 1 80341 564 2 (ebook)
Library of Congress Control Number: 2023936561

A CIP catalogue record for this book is available from the British Library.

Design: Lapiz Digital Services

UK: Printed and bound by CPI Group (UK) Ltd, Croydon, CR0 4YY
Printed in North America by CPI GPS partners

We operate a distinctive and ethical publishing philosophy in
all areas of our business, from our global network of authors to
production and worldwide distribution.

Contents

For R.H. with love.

Part I:

No. 4, The Ridge

Chapter 1

Take it from me, sharing a house with people twenty years your junior is like having children. It requires the same cat-herding skills, if not the dutiful sense of affection.

It is rare we are all home on a Thursday evening. If we are, Ethan and Georgie are more likely streaming something in their rooms than gracing the communal areas. Another aspect of sharing that makes me feel my age. However, the unwritten constitution of No. 4, The Ridge requires the presence of all housemates to vet potential new residents, which amazingly we managed on the two nights it took us to conduct interviews last week.

Result: (eventually, and with a little finessing from me) Martin.

Tonight he moves in, and I am happy to form a welcoming party of one. I get home from the Picture Gallery by seven and he is due at seven-thirty. Just time to change out of my work skirt and blouse, administer an evening puff of White Linen and make a sandwich. Yet, when it comes to it, the bread knife stalls over my crusty cob. I put lettuce and hummus back in the fridge and pour myself a glass of juice instead.

He is ten minutes late when his Fiat pulls up at the kerb. Since none of us owns a vehicle he could have parked in the drive, but it pleases me to see him wait to be offered. The driver's door slams in the shade of the silver birch and there is a chirp of control locking. Martin is alone, though a single suitcase and sports holdall hardly warrant extra hands. I have the front door open before he can negotiate the bell.

"Travelling light?" I observe matily.

"Hello again, Fern!"

He smiles and puffs his cheeks. A quizzical glance upstairs says he is keen to ditch the bags.

"It's *Fen*, actually…" I wave away his apology. "You remember which bedroom, don't you?"

When Javier gave notice I considered switching to that room myself. In some ways it would suit me better than the master, with its draughty shower and box of tricks for satellite sport I never bother with. But the prospect of the communal bathroom, with shared hand soap and endless wiping of the loo seat, is too much like living in halls.

Martin is back down in the time it takes me to pour an orange juice for him. Once he has re-parked the car, I show him the neat corner cupboard in the hall for hanging his jacket. Like everything I have seen him wear, it is good quality; a designer-take on a donkey jacket, fashionable yet appropriate for a man in his forties. The same goes for those not-too-snug jeans, and the fleecy top he pulls over his head as he settles on the settee.

He takes the proffered tumbler and I wonder what he makes of me. I like to think my good posture, honey-tint bob and Zara separates mark me out as the house authority-figure. Not that I'd claim such a thing.

"Nice to be here," he says. "You home alone?"

I try to look as if I haven't noticed. "Yes. Often the way. Ethan and Georgie are always out and about."

Martin nods, then launches into a query about his references for Mr Burnside. He seems a little agitated, which is to be expected. Getting divorced must be deeply unsettling.

"… But he said how only one could be personal. The rest have to be from a previous employer, or a professional, so I'm struggling a bit. Being freelance, I don't tend to work in places very long, so—"

I sympathise. "A doctor will do. Or if you have a solicitor, you could…"

Oops.

He chuckles away my discomfort. "Don't worry, it's not a sore subject! Good idea, I'll call him tomorrow." He slurps from the glass. "You been married yourself?"

Abruptly I feel the oddness of sharing the evening with a complete stranger.

"No, actually." I lean for the remote and turn the television down a notch.

"Don't blame you. Tell the truth, if I had my time again I dunno if I would… I don't mean I regret the kids. Far from it. But Trudie's my second. Wife. So if anyone should know better…" He tuts. "Perils of marrying a younger woman!"

I let this sink in, then ask if he has eaten. Say I'm making a sandwich and offer him one, unless he has brought food with…

"A sandwich isn't a meal!" he crows. "Hey, I passed a chippy on the way. How about I zip out and pick us up a couple of fish suppers?"

While he is gone I resist the urge to peek in his room. Busy myself warming plates and rinsing the house's oddly shaped fish knives. I blob ketchup into a ramekin then check the cupboard for tartar sauce… That bottle of Sauv Blanc on Georgie's shelf would go beautifully with fish. But it's not chilled, and anyway the risk of getting caught booze raiding on Martin's first night feels unwise. Any them-and-us scenarios, youngies v. oldies, are best avoided. I open a bottle of my own less-suitable Shiraz.

"You should have said," he offers, tucking into the steaming plate on his lap. "I'd have stopped at Tesco."

"Doesn't bother me if it doesn't bother you," I say, halfway down my glass already. "A bit uncouth I know, but I rather like red wine with fish."

He dabs a chip into the dish of ketchup on the coffee table. The dollop I transferred to my own plate hasn't registered.

"So," he says between chomps. "Stands to reason we'll all be getting to know each other while I'm here."

Which is amenable, and as misguided as I'd expect from someone new to house-sharing. I am tempted to launch into my own potted history… After all, isn't unpicking the tapestry of one's life over a bottle of wine what first evenings are for?

He has other ideas. "Go on, tell us about the other two. What have I let myself in for?"

This puts me on the back foot. The particulars of my own life are one thing, third-party gossiping is another. Disloyal somehow, albeit to people I suspect feel no allegiance to me. Also potentially embarrassing, when it reveals I've spent years living with people I hardly know. Still, a shame to burst his bubble…

"Well, Ethan's a nice chap. He's been here the longest, after me. Does something techie at London Transport. He has explained it, but I'm lost in seconds. Computer modelling or something. All to do with getting passengers round the system with the minimum of bottlenecks—if you will!" I refill our glasses, laughing at my own joke. "And Georgie works at St Gulliver's. The homeless charity. Very commendable, though I don't know how she does it. Puts heart and soul into her clients when half of them don't want helping at all."

Martin wipes a prong full of batter round his plate. "I thought she was something like that."

My fork hangs in mid-air. "Did you?"

"I can always spot a social worker. My wife's area."

Interesting… From what he said at the interview, I saw him with some ball-breaking businesswoman, all high heels and big opinions. My slightest of probings opens a vein:

"Trudie's the Acting Head of Social Services at Wandsworth Council. So not in the muesli-jumper brigade any more, but I know the look. Works like a dog, too. Her boss left at Christmas and she's in line for the big job. In fact that's how the problems started…" He is studying his few remaining chips. "All began as a joke of mine: Mrs-Head-of-Social-Services, neglecting her own kids… I'm no comedian, I should know better. Then, what with me being freelance, she thought I should adjust my Work-Life-Balance." Air quotes, either side of his plate. "Said if she was working more hours, I should work less."

Suffused with the wine, I find the details of his domestic life captivating.

"—Thing is, when you start turning down work in my business, the phone stops ringing. So we agreed on a compromise. Get an au pair to help out in term time, long as I stay at home in the hols."

"Sounds a fair solution," I say cautiously.

"It does. Except, soon as I'm halfway through a job and tell them I need half-term off, my name's mud. The au pair was happy doing the extra week, but Trudie wouldn't have it. Guilt, obviously. Feels bad unless one of us is at home with the kids…" He swallows. "Sorry, you don't want to hear all this."

"No, I do… I mean, it's fine. I just—I wish I could help."

He waves a speared chip. "Cut a long story short, we've got very different ideas about parenting. Among other things. Irony is, now she's on her own she's working longer hours than ever. Says she'll only take the big job if it's part-time or a job-share. Fat chance of that! Meanwhile, the Council's got the perfect excuse to drag their heels appointing anyone. And there you have it. Stalemate."

I hear myself sigh. Both the rocky maritals and the work/life conundrum are achingly familiar. Luckily, as the seasoned viewer of a hundred television dramas, I know exactly what to do: stay calm and offer comfort as the situation plays out.

"Anyway," I say brightly, "I hope you'll be happy here. I've always found this house very calming. It has an odd way of attracting people looking to—regroup."

"Yeah?" says Martin. "Was that you, when you moved in?"

I smile. "Sort of. It was all a bit of an accident really…" My story can't match his for three-part-drama appeal, but his eyes say *continue*. "I had a little flat of my own, near where I work… One bed, garden, no issues with the upstairs neighbour. I bought at the top of the market, then thought I'd made a huge mistake when the prices slumped. Of course, it clawed back its value and all was well." I allow myself another slosh of Shiraz. "Then my financial adviser convinced me we were on the brink of another crash. Said I should ride out the dip all over again, but I couldn't face the flat being an albatross round my neck." This sounds wrong. "Do I mean millstone? Anyway, the flat upstairs got burgled and that was that—I took the plunge. Pastures new."

Martin nods slowly. "You bought another place?"

"No. I sold up, invested the lot in what my adviser calls a 'sound-yet-diverse-portfolio', and moved in here."

I can see he is mystified. People often are, which grates given my own crystal-clear logic at the time. A bit of post-rationalisation usually does the trick:

"I needed a change. Been living on my own too long. On the verge of turning into a nutty cat lady! The world opens up when you're around other people, don't you find?"

Another nod, signifying nothing.

"I've never lived on my own," he says. "Ever. At home with my folks till I got married, then sharing with a mate when that went Pete Tong. Didn't see myself settling down again, I can tell you. On course for being the oldest swinger in town, till I met Trudie! Kids, you see. It dawned on me I wanted them after all, which I never did with Stacey." He puts his glass on the table. "Funny how things work out."

Fascinating: the mess people make of their lives, when they fail to avoid the pitfalls as I have! Oh, I take my hat off to anyone who can do it; make a go with a significant other, the pluses outweighing the minuses… Yet all too often, marriage is a battleground from which few emerge unscathed. Take my mother—deserves a medal for putting up with Father's moods for forty years! Not that it stops her trying to root out a man for me; a contradiction I have never resolved and a grey area between us (getting greyer all the time, like Mother).

"I know what you're thinking," says Martin. His glass is empty too. "But don't worry, those days are behind me. I won't be turning this into a house of ill repute!" Sharing out the slops of the bottle, I wonder why I'm not thinking this at all. "See, my priority's my kids, full stop. So when your Mr Burnside twisted my arm about signing up for a year—well, I couldn't do it."

Now this is news. In all my time at No. 4, The Ridge our landlord has contracted tenants for a full year, minimum.

"How did you...?"

He shrugs. "I told him my situation. How I'm looking for a stopgap, till Trudie and me sort things out and I can get a place big enough for the kids. He was pretty reasonable, as it goes. Especially when I offered to up the rent..." He raises a weary eyebrow. "Anyway, by the sound of it you've got him eating out of your hand!"

I am fogging again. "Have I?"

"He said, if I'm Fen Woodruff's choice, that's fine by him. Says how he really trusts your judgement." He gestures to the back garden. "Then he mentioned his wife."

"Did he?"

"Said how he wants this to be a happy house, for her sake." Martin twirls a finger over one ear. "Is he a bit, er—?"

They often ask that. "I'd say he's *spiritual*. Not in the Ouija-board sense, but I think he still feels a bond with her. Here."

Putting down his empty glass he slumps back on the settee. Is about to say something else when he discovers an intriguing morsel snagged on a side tooth.

"You'd—*hrrgh*, sorry! You'd think he'd move her to where he's living now, wouldn't you? If he's got a thing about her?"

9

"True. But an annual visit seems to suffice." I can't resist the smirk; "And perhaps the second Mrs Burnside isn't *quite* so keen?"

His laugh covers a burp. "Fair enough. Each to their own, eh!"

Which is a very sound attitude in my opinion. I, or rather we have chosen well... I am wondering whether to suggest another bottle when Martin slides his empty plate over mine and reaches for my glass.

"Right. Dishwasher, or do I slop and you dry?"

This time I am smiling, though I can't quite hold his eye.

A body language expert, analysing yours truly, would identify 'Looking away from a man before he looks away from me' as my *modus operandi*. One I am slightly ashamed, but also wary of. It suggests weakness of character, as well as weakness of a different kind, since it only arises in the company of a man I find attractive.

And I know from experience what a nest of vipers that can be.

Chapter 2

No. 4, The Ridge is no one's idea of an architectural gem. Its red brick and elephant-grey slates hail from the 1970s. The uPVC windows, which look like sash but aren't, are less elegant than those of the houses opposite, giving us the better view. Other bonuses include proximity to Wimbledon town centre. Train, tube and Little Waitrose are six minutes' walk, while a heart-pumping march up the hill brings you to Wimbledon village. The town's gamine alter-ego offers overpriced boutiques and restaurants with napkins, in contrast to our sedate, suburban sprawl.

The house has four beds, two baths (one en suite, mine) and an extra loo downstairs. There is an unspectacular kitchen and open-plan living area with adequate storage for all the tat renters accumulate. Decor is neutral throughout and, aside from the odd stud wall, it is a solid, comfortable place to live. In my eight years, I have grown quite attached. Though that doesn't stop me thinking our landlord has been rather lucky.

Mrs Burnside arises, so to speak, whenever we interview candidates for an empty room. She is a topic to tick off, like the joint account for bills and importance of mastering the thermostat, and can be useful for thinning the field. Occasionally, a would-be tenant will get cold feet. That said, the presence of a grave in the back garden, with its raised plinth and stylised obelisk, can also work the other way. One young woman, heavy on the eyeliner, was a shade overenthusiastic on spotting Mrs Burnside's anthracite slab. I fielded three follow-up calls, one after I'd already told her the room had gone.

For more suitable candidates, Mrs Burnside is of fleeting interest. Something to spark the curiosity then forget. When we showed Martin the vacant second bedroom, his reaction was perfect... Straightening up from a manly check of what would soon be his radiator, he glanced down at the garden. Georgie, Ethan and I waited, the penny-dropping moment always one to savour.

"Well," he said with a shrug. "Seen it all now..."

After that, he stayed for a second cuppa and we had a laugh about it. Martin's interest in Mrs Burnside was on a par with the space allocation of the fridge: polite, if a mite perplexed anyone should think a man burying his wife in the back garden warranted a lengthy explanation. Her plinth—tall enough to make an impression, low enough to discourage the resting of drinks—is just another fixture. One I have personally grown quite fond of, occasionally filling her silver flower holder with fresh-cut stems when I've a mind to.

Ever keen to avoid friction, I keep Martin's rolling quarterly agreement with Mr Burnside to myself. Georgie was quick to bemoan the length of her contract when she moved in. She likes to play the metropolitan nomad, beholden to no one, despite the fact she has been here three years. On the Sunday before Martin moved in, she, Ethan and I were in the living area. I had called a powwow to make a decision re the room. Javier left weeks ago, and it was testing our landlord's good nature to leave it empty much longer, an urgency lost on the others. Georgie had made it plain she wasn't keen on any of the candidates; Ethan showed virtually no interest in the interview process at all, implying he'd happily leave the decision to us in a way that made me wonder if he truly sees this place as home.

Of course it is different when you're young. Or youngish, in Georgie's case. She is thirty this year, three years older than Ethan, yet her wardrobe leans towards the studenty. Skimpy leggings and baseball boots; slash-neck tops worn with one shoulder protruding, like she rolled out of bed and fought off marauders en route to the kettle. Her current posture, cross-legged on the settee, reveals a ladder in one thigh guaranteed to catch the eye of any man but Ethan.

"Well," I say, since someone needs to start the ball rolling, "I vote for Martin. Anyone else?"

"Cool, yeah," nods Ethan, deep in his mobile. "Which was he?"

The Japanese half of his parentage has not instilled a sense of formality. Ethan is as casual as the tee shirts that cling to his skinny frame. Left to him, the room could be let to a grenade-rattling jihadi through sheer indifference.

"The freelance graphic designer," I remind him, trying not to sound peevish. "Seemed like a nice chap."

"That's it," he nods without looking up. "Older guy, splitting up with his wife. Yeah, he was sound." His thumb finds a link and takes his attention with it.

That's a majority vote for Martin; though I have learned not to railroad the house into doing things my way. "How about you, Georgie?"

She sits back, risking further revelation by hosiery.

"I don't know. I mean, I know we said another guy'd be best, but I'm thinking did we get lucky with Javier? Martin's got kids and—well, he's a bit *blokey*, isn't he?"

At this I am lost. I cannot see how his children are an issue, since the policy at No. 4, The Ridge is strictly adults-only. As for her other objection: is it ageist, class-based, or an allusion to Martin's machismo? All dubious to my mind... Seriously, if working with the homeless hasn't taught her appearance is no gauge of character, what hope is there? The most likely reason is that Georgie has an issue with men, though I can't be sure. This is not the sort of household where relationship hinterlands are laid bare. But she has always been cagey about her love life, any casual liaisons conducted strictly off-site.

Being selfish for a moment, I will admit Martin's age is part of his appeal. Next March marks my own half-century, and I have always been fifteen or more years older than everyone else living here. According to the Property pages, Single Mature Adults are a growing demographic in the rental sector.

Mostly unwilling, unlike myself, not anticipating a return to communal living till they parked their Zimmers in front of the snooker with all the other old dears... But if that's the trend, why not reflect it here? Isn't there a logic to evening up the median age?

Oh, I pride myself I can get along with anyone, of any generation... But if I learned one thing from my attempts to up the in-house camaraderie (old-school Scrabble Night was an utter failure) it's that others focus their lives beyond these walls. So if this is just a place for them to bunk and bathe, isn't that more reason I deserve a buddy? Someone else who sees the benefit in keeping the landline?

On top of that, Martin strikes me as a practical sort. Good in a crisis like a leaky pipe, or when the pilot light blows out and no one can read the note in the boiler cupboard. From his palace in the Cotswolds, our landlord isn't bad at getting things fixed, but there are times a seasoned hand could solve the problem on the spot. I wonder how to flag up the good sense in having a man about the house without sounding like I'm casting aspersions at Ethan (which I wouldn't dream of, even though it's justified). This calls for cunning, and a cheeky flex of the rules...

"Okay, Georgie. We need to get a shift on though. FYI, I'll be out the next couple of nights, so can I leave initial meets to you and Ethan, then catch up with whoever you favour after that? If they're fine with you I'm sure they'll be fine with me..."

My tactic pays off. Georgie also has plans for the next few nights, probably genuine in her case. Whether that, or the utter panic on Ethan's face at the prospect of being saddled with a grown-up decision, she backs down:

"We can give Martin a go, I guess..."

As if changing housemates were as easy as changing shoes!

And so it was for the first time ever that I came to be sharing No. 4, The Ridge with someone broadly my own age. Which, after eight years, seems only fair.

***

Aside from being disappointing, the potential brevity of Martin's tenure is also a nuisance. While it is nice to know Mr Burnside respects my judgement (uncharitable reading: it saves him a truckload of bother) I'd prefer he stuck to his contractual guns in future. Filling vacancies is a chore I can do without.

Still, it was as well Martin took control that first evening. Diverting us to the washing-up meant a second bottle of Shiraz stayed on my shelf. We switched on the telly instead and watched the last, indecipherable episode of a spy drama set in Damascus. All to the good. Neither Georgie nor Ethan showed their face before we turned in, and an inebriated Fen Woodruff might have said something unwise.

For the upshot was this: Martin has a certain woodland charm. His neat build, clear hazel eyes and chestnut thatch peeping over his open-neck shirt bring to mind the denizen of a more comforting world. One where security lies on a bed of grass, within a moss-lined tree hollow. That he is on the shorter-side of average (generous estimate: five foot seven) reinforces the effect. But since that's an inch taller than me, it is not an issue.

Consequently, in the fortnight since he arrived, I have been self-monitoring: analysing my feelings, to see if they are valid or just the product of an under-occupied mind. My work, in the marketing department at Dulwich Picture Gallery, is currently dull. We are between exhibitions and Derek, my limp if largely harmless boss, is pulling his weight for once, which makes me prone to fixate. It is a trait I've been aware of since I was thirteen: cooped up at home with a leg in plaster, convinced the new young milkman was leaving messages in the way he arranged the silver-tops. Girlish lunacy in retrospect, but this time the foundations are strong. I am a mature woman, seasoned by life—and there *is* something adorable about Martin.

He has old-fashioned qualities. Like the way he asks how I slept if we see each other at breakfast. Also, he wears quality pyjama trousers (Emporio Armani in duck-egg blue) accompanied by a vest in white or cream, I am fairly sure for modesty's sake. I glimpsed him once in the small hours, popping down for a glass of milk. That snapshot of flesh through his closing bedroom door was proof Martin passes the night bare-chested.

He is neat in his habits, as Mother would say. Cleans up after himself and never leaves clothes in the communal areas. He is excellent at ironing too—the sign of a man used to a preoccupied wife and small children (Freya eight, Nathan six; I have made notes). I sense that living here is doing him good. He is fitting into the house-share routine admirably, and exhibits little of the turmoil I associate with a disintegrating marriage. Beyond the odd silent barrage of texts, nothing furrows his brow as he watches TV or contentedly reads his newspaper. Personally, I am almost fully digitalised. Happy to keep abreast of events from my iPad, if reluctant to relinquish the glossy indulgence of my *Marie Claire*... Yet something about a man at peace with his paper, a sensible distance from a roaring fire, never fails to warm my cockles. Alas the flues of No. 4, The Ridge were blocked up long ago.

On this particular morning—a Saturday in May—the living area is warm from the sunbeams glancing in like undipped headlights. It is Martin's third weekend which, if it follows the pattern, will see him disappear on Sunday to visit his children.

He lowers yesterday's *Guardian* and tosses a glance at the ceiling. "Those two must have had a big night."

Whether Georgie is home is anyone's guess, though I am fairly sure I heard Ethan's floorboards creak as I warmed my weekend croissant. The remaining pastries are still in cellophane, ready to tempt Martin after his morning jog, though this part of his routine is fluid. He is still in pyjamas and shows no sign of swapping his slippers for Nikes.

"You never know with them," I sigh affably. "I've learned not to keep tabs on the comings and goings in this house." Does that make me sound judgmental? "There's croissants if you fancy. I'll only throw them out..."

His dense hairline jiggles behind his paper. "I won't thanks, Fen. Watching my figure."

I say nothing, though his usual breakfast of a hefty bowl of Frosties with token sultanas suggests otherwise. Martin is blessed with a naturally athletic physique. An average man his age would require more than a weekly trot round the Common to stay in such pleasing shape. Pâtisserie aside, I have on occasion offered my services on the catering front. He is no great shakes in the kitchen; ding-meal curries and casserole pots-for-one suggest his wife does the cooking. So on evenings when we've been home alone (never Wednesdays; more child time) I have taken to over-catering. I enjoy cooking for others, even surreptitiously... Will casually mention I can't eat another mouthful of homemade moussaka or shepherd's pie. Insist it's never the same reheated, and won't he save me the bother of transfer to Tupperware?

If the younger contingent have plans for tonight, I will offer to cook for Martin and me. Georgie and Ethan are often out on a Saturday. She is part of a meagre-sounding social set, who imbibe rivers of booze then summon Asian delicacies via Deliveroo. What Ethan gets up to I can't say. I see him with a circle of friends as nerdy as he is, flopped out on beanbags, discussing vloggers through a cyber-hail of incoming messages.

Whoops—Talk of the devil.

"Morning, guys!" he calls, cantering downstairs.

He looks tousled but wide awake by his standards, in baggy boxer shorts and a green tee shirt that is new to me. Martin

17

doesn't flinch as he disappears into the kitchen, but I suspect something is going on. Ethan rarely eats breakfast, yet eggs are being cracked and plates taken from the cupboard. His coffee machine, used once on his birthday then left out for Georgie and me, is being loaded with tinfoil capsules.

He reappears, smiling beneath his immaculate black fringe. "Sorry, Fen, can I have a slug of your milk?"

The next I see, he is teetering upstairs with a laden tray, all of which passes Martin by... Not wishing to bolster my image as the house busybody, I say nothing. Return to my shopping list, where half a dozen items languish frustratingly in brackets, depending on the viability of dinner à deux.

An hour later, I am making a second coffee when there is more movement above. Ambient aural swirls, the soundtrack to Ethan's getting-up routine, cut abruptly and I hear two voices with none of the tinniness that signals his chats on FaceTime.

Ethan has a guest!

Chapter 3

I am back in the living area, ostensibly reading *Marie Claire*. Martin is deep in the Sport section, showing no sign of going for a jog or shower. I sense impending awkwardness... Wonder whether to say something and give him a chance to make himself scarce, when the brush of door on carpet says it is too late.

Two pairs of feet process downstairs. Ethan is still barefoot, the other wears sturdy lace-ups. Our overnight visitor is shown straight to the front door. I assume this is flashpoint-averted, until a low laugh and inflected murmur suggest further delay. A moment later, an unknown young man strides into the room. He is lanky and black, smiling with the fine-featured nonchalance of one who feels quite at home. He is Ethan's age or thereabouts, with jeans cropped aggressively above the ankle. His denim jacket has a psychedelic design, half motorbike, half sunset. And underneath is the tee shirt Ethan was wearing earlier.

"Soz," says the lad. "Forgot my—"

He reaches under the coffee table and pulls out a khaki fisherman's cap. Inside is a smartphone he slips into his pocket, simultaneously patting the cap onto his head.

Martin looks up from his paper. "Wotcha. Wondered whose those were."

The young man glances at Ethan who is standing on the threshold.

"Sorry, yeah... Cass, this is Martin. And that's Fen."

"Hey," nods Cass, winking in my direction.

For an instant we freeze, like actors missing a cue.

"Cool jacket," says Martin, returning to his paper.

Ethan whispers something about a train, and with a wave Cass is gone. But not before more titters on the doormat. There is the sound of lips colliding, a shrug of chafing cloth. After the front door closes Ethan charges upstairs with a yell of "Okay if I use the shower, Martin?"

"Go for it, mate."

Are his words just a little clipped? I am torn between my innately liberal nature and a desire for Martin to feel comfortable in his own home. In my old flat-sharing days, someone like Ethan would have trod carefully, to avoid embarrassment for himself and others. Unlike the ones I remember from the Eighties he doesn't come across as resoundingly gay, though that only serves to compound the problem. In those days, any man with a tattoo was a homosexual or a sailor; now you're lucky to find one without. And in the interim the gays have gone mainstream, while so-called metrosexuals revel in the kind of bodily refinements—hair gels, piercings, self-tans—that would have mortified my father… But that is not Martin. Tarring him with the brush of my childhood, in Surrey untouched by the Swinging Sixties, is doing him a disservice.

That said, it feels wise to check. I flip a glossy page as I frame my words:

"Well, that's a turn-up. I can't remember the last time Ethan had a mate kip over!" Martin grunts but his paper doesn't move. "Seemed nice enough, anyway… Though I suspect we only got an introduction because he forgot his hat!" I am freewheeling now, not sure how to stop; "At least we were here! Don't know about you, but I'm not keen on the idea of strangers wandering in and out. Though Ethan may know him well, in which case—"

"Doubt it," says Martin. His face appears in a valley of newsprint. "Looked like a shag to me."

"Oh. Do you think? Yes, I suppose."

I turn pages without looking. He disappears again.

"Good on him, I say," says Martin.

"Yes," I swallow.

A minute later he folds his paper and yawns, in the way I find endearing: mouth agape, lips curled over top and bottom teeth at once.

"Had him down as the quiet one, Ethan," he says. "Bit turned in on himself. Nice to see him doing something normal."

I nod. "He can be a bit of a loner. Spends forever in his room, but they all do nowadays, don't they? On their phones or whatever."

"Yup. Saying that, most the gay guys I know put it about like buggery—'scuse pun! Got sex on tap, what with Grindr and all."

I feel my colour rising. Of course I know it goes on—using apps to track down sexual liaisons like a branch of Boots. As a rule, my eyes glaze at the thought of anything more complicated than Facebook. I even delegated the Picture Gallery's Twitter feed to one of the new girls in my department, conveying it as a reward not a chore I was glad to be rid of.

"I don't know if Ethan's like that, exactly. He goes out with friends now and again, I'm pleased to say. That's probably where he was last night. It's not like he makes a habit of... casual partners."

Martin is smiling. "Whatever. I've sat in meetings with guys I thought were checking their emails when they were really on the pull. Lining up a lunchtime quickie, with some bloke round the corner!" He tuts. "Life of Riley, your gays."

He almost sounds envious. This sex-tracking app has a straight equivalent, the name of which escapes me. The girls at work are always talking about it, details modified for office ears.

In my day, gays were 'other', living and loving by different rules. More promiscuous, certainly. Ghastly diseases aside, they seemed to skitter through life free of the responsibilities that weighed on the rest of us. Not that I'm judging—I got on well with the ones I've met over the years. But now their rules seem to be universally adopted, and not just style-wise. Back then, the unspoken truth was that gays had an easier time if they passed as straight—today it's virtually the other way round! Eye-popping tattoos, shaved heads, even the most elaborate hairdo assures you of nothing about a man.

What disturbs me is that Martin appears more attuned to Ethan than I am. I've done my best to coax him out of his shell. Offered him the odd glass of wine, though Ethan isn't much of a drinker. We chat when we cross paths. Swap tales of our office tribulations and whatever spanner the travel gods threw in the commute today... Yet he seems more at ease with Martin than he ever does with me.

I am stereotyping obviously, but my reading of the gay/straight paradigm is this... A gay man's feminine side means he can be expected to relate to a woman better than a heterosexual man. It's a sliding scale, with gay and straight men at either end and women in the middle. (Lesbians will be on there too somewhere, or possibly that's a different scale.)

Anyway, now I'm wondering what all this says about me. I turn the page on a spread of moody A-list makeovers...

Or does it say something about Martin?

He is scratching his stubble. Designer or not, there is something comfortingly un-edgy about those pyjamas, and his vest with the loose thread, worn for more days than is strictly hygienic.

No. It doesn't.

Martin is a family man, through and through. It was pressure of the work/life balance that caused ructions with his wife, nothing more.

I am scolding myself for jumping to conclusions as he stands from the settee. Stretches once, fingers laced overhead like a diver set to spring. Scratching an armpit, he peers at his Fiat in the drive.

"Best give her a wash-down... What Saturday mornings are for, isn't it?"

Our family don't do divorce, which may or may not be a bad thing. My parents steered doggedly through thirty-nine years of marriage, until Father's heart attack ten years ago. He nipped out to the greenhouse to water his tomatoes and never came back. By the time Mother shuffled to the bottom of the garden, he was gone. Slumped on a stack of fertiliser bags with a curious robin hopping between his slippers.

Mother's mother was a Methodist, who drummed the sanctity of marriage into everyone. The sacrament was an inescapable bond which Granny manipulated for as long as she was alive, and to a palpable extent thereafter. It was only after Father passed away that Mother questioned whether it was fair on either of them to endure marriage as long as they did. A dichotomy made thornier by the fact their final years together were when her illness took a grip, and she could least have managed without him.

Multiple Sclerosis is a sentence I would wish on no one. Though the day Mother relinquished her adapted Nissan I fielded her call with a sense of relief, since it also meant the end of her unheralded swoops on No. 4, The Ridge. Barring short-distance manoeuvres with a walking frame, she is now confined to home. A social as well as physical handicap she takes with stoic grace.

So followed a shift in our mother-daughter dynamic. Now, on birthdays and holy days when I take two trains and a taxi to her home in Oxted, my sense of duty is lightened by the fact I am seeing her on my own terms. On the return journey, after three hours in the claustrophobic bungalow, I can feel satisfied Mother's needs are being catered to, at least for now. Twice-weekly visits from a diligent cleaner, deliveries from Sainsbury's and the support of two neighbours who unaccountably vie for the privilege of being at her beck and call—all spare me more than a modicum of guilt.

Her illness has also wrought a change in Mother I did not anticipate, by exposing a generous streak I struggle to accept. From small beginnings (offloaded crockery, Father's watercolours of donkeys on the beach at Cromer) the gifts have become more substantial. In some, there is a sense of setting things straight. As if she believes the end is nigh, though with her type of MS that's statistically no more likely than anyone else approaching eighty. Other gifts smack of a last hurrah: the working-through of a bucket list, like the time she hired a car and driver to take us to the gardens at Wisley. The latter waited patiently in the car park, smoking under a copper beech, while I wheeled Mother round the ornamental trellises. She regaled me with how she and Father used to come here for horticultural inspiration. But her real enthusiasm she saved for the shop, where the purpose of our visit became clear.

Mother wanted a magnolia. Mother has always wanted a magnolia, as I remember from childhood. Her favourite shrub was an endless source of friction between my parents, and on spring days-out I would watch from the back seat for the approaching shock of ivory or rosy-hued blossoms. The sight of them, swamping the boughs like scallop shells, never failed to make her sigh and him jab the accelerator. Father's view on magnolia was unwavering: once shed, their leathery apparel was a gardener's nightmare, one he would not tolerate. A week of blowsy beauty did not justify the labour of clearing them up, nor their slimy residue if left to lie... This pig-headedness he took to the grave. For a while Mother and I were regular visitors at the crowded plot adjacent to the knave of St Cuthbert's. One day, seated on a bench two mossy angels from Father's slab, she chewed on her cheek and said:

"It's a pity they jam them in so, Fenella. We could have planted a little tree over him…"

That she finally acquired the shrub of her dreams that day at Wisley said something had changed. At first I feared senility kicking in along with everything else; an impression our driver seemed to share. His ciggy-hand stalled an inch from his lips as I trundled Mother gingerly back to the car. Two sacks of compost lay across the arms of her wheelchair, while the sapling itself sprouted from the yarn-handled carrier slung over my back like Robin Hood's quiver. The driver took the lot without a word, jigsawing them into the boot and leaving me to transfer Mother from chair to passenger seat… There was not enough daylight for planting out when we got home. But the next time I was over, the magnolia occupied a corner of the lawn, courtesy of the neighbour Mother dragooned into planting it where she could see it from her chair.

The truth is, she was locking down the things that matter. Wistful dreams can no longer wait another day. Her new television, the size of a beach towel, has a pixel clarity that earns experts on the *Antiques Roadshow* an upbraiding for the state of their cuticles. And, despite her infirmity, her dream-catching is not confined to home. Once a fervent emailer, Mother's fingers now respond too sluggishly to the signals from her brain. Hence the old-fashioned paper brochure that arrives at No. 4, The Ridge, alerting me to her globetrotting ambitions. Her wobbly hand on the redirecting label reads:

JULY OR AUG? WILL CALL TO DISCUSS.

Inside is a range of cruises to all corners of the world: Atlantic crossings and Mediterranean tours, direct from Southampton; a circumnavigation of Australia and a voyage around Cape Horn, both requiring long-haul flights.

I am agog. The brochure is packed with sights I have mooned over but never truly expected to see. Partly cost, partly because I'd never allow myself to indulge in such extravagance alone. And, since Mother is unable to travel solo, I can only assume it is an invitation.

"I don't remember you mentioning cruising," I say, when she calls the landline that evening.

"I'd never really thought about it. It was something Bill said."

This refrain, along with 'something Kath said', has become more frequent since Mother's sphere of influence shrank to include her two eager neighbours. Friends of many years' standing and both also widowed, they live a few doors apart. Mother has given each keys in case of emergency, though seems happy for them to pop in regardless. Their visits rarely cross which suggests a level of collaboration, yet she takes pleasure in playing one off against the other. It is Bill, retired accountant and dab hand in the garden, who has sparked this latest idea.

"His sister-in-law uses a chair... He says she and her husband are regular cruisers because everything's so accessible. Lifts and ramps all over the ship, and you can get an adapted bathroom. Then when you're in port, most of the excursions are wheelchair-friendly. Unless it's something ridiculous, like potholing... Have you got the Sabre Line brochure there?"

She directs me to page fifteen. From the sound of slowly flipping pages, she is looking too.

"How about that? Eight nights to the Norwegian fjords. And that ship — it's a floating city!"

The *Diamond Sabre* does look beguiling in the photo. It is docked beneath a precipice in an emerald green fjord, as sleek and incongruous as a steam iron on a snooker table. In contrast to the early days of cruising, I know modern liners are constructed to an ever-increasing size and sophistication. This one, with its crystalline windows and tiered balconies a dozen deep, could probably plough through an iceberg and cube it for cocktails. You need to look closely to see the rows of lifeboats, camouflaged against the paintwork.

"Wow," I say. "But won't it be full of..." I draw back from the next words like they're hot.

"*Old people?*" finishes Mother. "*You mean the over-fifties, Fenella? I think we'd fit right in, don't you? You've only a year to go yourself!*"

I change the subject. "What about seasickness? We'd be at sea a long time. What if it's choppy?"

"*That's you, you're worried about!*" she scoffs. "*Remember that coracle in Hunstanton? I'll be fine, long as I keep my brakes on. Besides, the blurb says most of the sailing's done at night. You wake up in a new fjord every morning. Imagine that!*"

I am still frowning as I scan the itinerary. "Well, there's a whole day when you leave Southampton. And another on the way back."

"*Good! I think that'd be lovely. We can stroll round the deck and take the air—decide where we're going for our dinner. There's four different restaurants, and a theatre. And prices are all-in, barring booze. Go on, I'm offering to treat you!*"

So that's clear. I don't know what to say.

On the day I graduated from Exeter, my parents made it plain my priority was to get a job and stand on my own two feet. In the intervening decades I did exactly that, without resentment. Had I children of my own, the same rule would apply. All of which makes me wary of how to respond.

"I can pay for my own holiday," I say, instantly regretting it. Mother and I have made one trip in recent years: a Eurostar break to Bruges. We went Dutch, so to speak, and the trip was not a success. A dearth of disabled toilets, plus cobbles, cobbles everywhere, ruined what should have been a relaxing weekend. After that I lost the urge to chaperone her anywhere more taxing than the garden centre.

"Don't look a gift horse in the mouth, Fenella!" she snaps. *"Besides, you know I can't do it on my own."* A sniff travels down the line from Oxted. *"They sail once in July and twice in August, so when suits you? Assuming you want to see the Norwegian fjords..."*

I do. I always have. This, as every year, I have been putting off planning a holiday, since nothing exposes the reality of singledom like a public breakfast-for-one... And if Mother insists on dipping into her savings, well, why shouldn't I benefit, rather than the saintly Kath or Bill?

"Thank you, Mother. It looks wonderful. Can I check with work and call you tomorrow?"

Chapter 4

That was a distraction technique. I needed a moment to analyse the potential ramifications of a week at sea with Mother... In my position as Marketing Coordinator at Dulwich Picture Gallery, I take my holiday when I damn well please. I answer only to the ineffectual Derek and, whilst it is better one of us is in situ at all times, I know for a fact he is hiking in the Camargue in September. This gives me a free rein all summer, though I'll tell Mother we need to go in August... My best friend, Avril, often gets tickets for the tennis in July and it's a shame to miss it.

Dulwich is a leafy enclave of South London not unlike Wimbledon. In fact, as I trundle through my commute, I can fool myself the entire journey is borderline bucolic if I shut my eyes through Tooting, Streatham and Herne Hill. The Picture Gallery itself is a raw-brick extravagance by Sir John Soane and dates from the early nineteenth century. Its collection of Old Masters, from the Tudors on, is regularly supplemented by more modern works basking under the gleam of Soane's innovative glass roof. Thousands of visitors enjoy its airy calm every week, oblivious to us beavering away in the East Wing.

My job covers everything from overseeing publicity to liaising with schools over pilfered headphones. The following day, my morning is back-to-back meetings and a brainstorm re our forthcoming Escher exhibition, the largest ever mounted outside the Netherlands. The afternoon I spend checking proofs of the next catalogue. A task I am wise to spin out if I want to leave on time; the busier I appear, the less chance Derek will offload his diary into mine and nip off to the Oval for the cricket.

The rest of the marketing team includes Cheryl, Derek's P.A., and two new recruits, Tash and Millie. They are replacements for a couple of long-servers, respectively put out to grass and relocated to an arts collective in Cornwall. I am still feeling my way with the new girls, in my role as their line manager, mentor and reluctant confidante when it can't be avoided. A case in point: the Friday before last, when the boss insisted on drinks at the local pub.

Others were invited, but the gathering soon dwindled to us four women and him. This was Derek's cue to stump up for a third bottle of Chardonnay, then make an excuse about collecting his dachshund from the vet... I watched him go with dread. When alcohol and female colleagues mix, a male presence has a way of keeping a lid on things, particularly one as sobering as Derek.

As his Saab departs in a spray of gravel the decibels at the table rise. The new girls have morphed from strangers into bosom buddies in a week, and Cheryl is embroiled in their banter, which switches seamlessly from the best place to buy a sandwich to the shag-ability of the pub's barmen. Tash and Millie giggle like the schoolgirls they were a few years ago, and Cheryl follows suit, spitting particles of dry roasted peanut across the table with each guffaw. She is overweight and unhappily married, a pairing I have observed goes together like poverty and cheeseburgers.

As glasses fill again, one particular barman has become the object of scrutiny. East European, with hair as dense as a shoe-brush. He moves confidently, manipulating optics with one hand and passing back change with the other. At one point he levers himself onto the bar top, pirouetting on a denim-clad knee to reach a bottle of something obscure. The thickness of his eyelashes would suggest mascara, were that not at odds with the rest of him. The unironed sleeves of his tee shirt, unshowily slack around mango-sized biceps, suggest a man indifferent to his appearance. His easy smile clinches it for the girls, and breeds speculation he is in fact Spanish.

"I've always had a thing for Latinos," says Tash, the more boisterous of the two. "Italian, Portuguese, whatever... All down to my first snog, I reckon. In Ibiza aged thirteen, when my parents went off on a pedalo. How 'bout you?"

Her new friend, who has shaken off the mousey demeanour of her first day in the job, sits forward on her stool.

"I like gingers, I don't care what anyone says. Ed Sheeran or that guy who did the long jump." Millie shrugs, as Tash says something demeaning I miss. "So? All the more for me!"

They laugh, and so does Cheryl who has finished her wine and is looking round for more. She and I are veterans of many a departmental jolly, endured through gritted teeth in my case and increasingly misty vision in hers. Her tolerance for alcohol is low, at odds with her appetite for it when she has a night off from the kids. Tonight she is loosening up dangerously. I am on the verge of saying goodbye before anyone pours her another, when Cheryl pipes up:

"Your turn, Fen. What's your type?"

Eyes turn in my direction. I wish I'd nipped to the Ladies when I had the chance. I cross my legs in a way I hope looks relaxed.

"Oh, I always think it's rather demeaning, pigeon-holing men like that. I mean, I wouldn't appreciate anyone saying I'm a particular type of woman."

Lips purse and chins twitch... Well, if I'm that easily categorised I have no wish to know how! My instinct is to raise the tone. Point out that, in my experience, the old adage of 'handsome is as handsome does' is entirely true. But, given the tenor of the evening and the flushed faces across the wine-smeared table, it's a losing battle. I take the easy way out:

"Tall, I'd say. Tall is always nice." And with that I swipe up my bag and make a beeline for the loos.

All twaddle, of course. But then it is precisely none of their business.

***

Under normal circumstances, the prospect of a cruise in the third week of August would be enough to make any summer slip by. As it is, my attention is focused at home, observing the trials of our new housemate with an empathetic eye. Martin's wife, Trudie, is being difficult about the children. The solicitors aren't helping, losing papers and going on holiday at the wrong moment. Chances of a calm termination to the marriage look slim.

"Bitch!" yells Martin at the clematis, loud enough to lose me the thread in my Margaret Atwood.

It is a sunny Saturday afternoon in the garden. No one else is at home, and it's safe to assume he hasn't spotted greenfly. I refresh the screen of my Kindle. I do not condone expletives in the garden, but in the circumstances it may be justified.

Martin hasn't noticed me under the patio umbrella. The mobile drops from his ear. He dials angrily, then changes his mind. As he turns I switch the angle of my chin, to suggest reading not watching from behind my sunglasses. Fists thrust at the pockets of his shorts.

"Sorry," he says, taking a breath.

I look up slowly, pretending to finish the page. "Trouble?"

"Should have expected it now we're getting to the nitty-gritty. Trudie's being an arse. Wants to settle everything on what I could earn, not what I do earn!"

He and I have had one or two chats of late, over wine when Ethan and Georgie weren't around. In the last couple of weeks I have sensed him riding the divorce-proceedings bronco with greater trepidation. What started steadily is now swinging in all directions. Martin's world is dissolving, and there is little I can do but nod and offer sympathy. Be there if he hits the ground with a bump.

"What does your solicitor say? Aren't there rules about that? Laws, I mean?"

He shrugs. "I'm dealing with his number two. Fat lot of use she is! Says she's tried contacting him, but guess what—He's not reading his emails in Bali!"

He strides over and slumps in a patio chair, elbows on the slatted table, head in his hands.

"Now Trudie's getting funny about me visiting. She knows I like to go over Wednesdays, and that's been fine. She stays over with a mate so I can tuck them in, do breakfast and the school run. Only now it's not convenient. Says it has to be Thursdays, and I work late Thursdays! I dare say there's a law about that too, but till Larry Legal-Pad gets back from his private beach club..."

My fingers grip the Kindle. I long to console him. Lay a hand on Martin's meaty shoulder and tell him he deserves better than a woman who plays games with his children. But there are boundaries. He and I share a house. Nothing more.

Leaning out of the shade he squints in the sunlight. He is wearing flip-flops and a short-sleeved football shirt. I am usually wary of men who wear their club's colours off the terraces, but since knowing him I have become oddly attuned to the West Ham livery. The claret and blue (how he laughed when I called it maroon!) is enough to make my heart skip when spotted on others. At least on Martin it's flattering, unlike most of the men who waddle off the train on match days, yodelling up the platform and clapping in unison like it's a skill. As with those women who squeeze into fashions meant for waifs, a mushrooming belly has become a display item for both sexes.

I have an idea. Controversial, possibly unworkable, but worth a try...

"If it was just once, would you like to have the children to stay?"

Martin shades his eyes as he looks my way. "Goes against the rules though, doesn't it? Georgie put me straight on that the day after I moved in. I get the impression she sees enough of kids at work."

I brush his words aside. "That's more a guideline than anything set in stone. If only we had a camp bed or similar..."

He perks up. "Not a problem. They can have my bed! I'll take the cushions off the sofa and kip on the floor. The kids'll love that. Be like when we went camping!"

It is a relief to see him smile. Such a lovely smile, almost film-star quality... Martin could be a model if he were a bit taller. More cable-knit than Calvin Klein admittedly, but with his jawline and those shoulders...

"Leave Georgie to me," I say.

I slide the sunglasses up my nose and pretend to go back to my Kindle.

It is the next afternoon before we women of the house cross paths. On Saturday Georgie went shopping on the Kings Road with a friend, never to return. For someone who works with the homeless and claims exemplary Socialist principles, she has a lot of friends in Chelsea. Her finances are a mystery. A mid-level job in the charity sector can't pay a fortune, yet somehow funds a lifestyle verging on the profligate.

Martin has slunk off to the West End for a consoling pint with a mate. Ethan emerges from his room at intervals, to make herb tea and Ryvita sandwiches. The sun, in typical British fashion, is making sporadic appearances, so I am in the garden taking a hoe to the borders in a light sweater.

I don't look up as the clunk of the front door echoes through the house. When I do, Georgie is on the back step, sucking a lollipop like a comic-strip minx. She is in the clothes she wore yesterday. And she is not alone.

"—It's nice enough," she is saying. "Not Hampton Court, but we've got a statue of sorts..."

She and the young man cross the lawn to examine Mrs Burnside. He makes a thing of peering at the plaque, reading every word. I carry on hoeing. It is another unwritten rule of

No. 4, The Ridge that housemates do not automatically qualify for introduction. In the presence of outsiders we are invisible, like servants in one another's household. The only exception is if a guest is likely to be a regular visitor.

"And this is Fen," says Georgie.

The young man smiles despite a lollipop of his own, and does a sort of salute over the obelisk. He is wearing creased fawn chinos, and a tee shirt with a V-neck so elongated it suggests torture by spin drier.

"Wotcha," he says cheerily.

I smile back, waiting for more. Instead they turn on sneakered heels and scamper indoors. His name is Lorenzo, though despite the raven locks and their shorter, curlier cousins on proud display beneath his Adam's apple, he is as Italian as a Tesco pizza. By four o'clock I am tired of making myself scarce; there is little to do in the garden since Martin turned out to be an enthusiastic mower.

In the living area, Georgie and friend are facing off from either end of the settee. The television is on (a retired Indian couple, downsizing to a converted forge in Tring) but neither is watching. Contrary to his scruffy attire, Lorenzo is very well-spoken. He lives in Ladbroke Grove, works in the City and, judging by their conversation, he and Georgie share a whirl of friends. They come across as new acquaintances with much in common, not least an obvious mutual attraction.

Georgie's pearlised toenails are in Lorenzo's lap. Their torsos remain leg-length apart, yet they make no concession as I take the armchair. They are giggling over an incident of the previous night. Someone called Nico, mistaking Swedish accents for Geordie and trying to interest two girls in the finer points of Newcastle United versus Spurs. As their merriment grows, the toes on Lorenzo's thigh take on a life of their own, clawing at the crotch of his chinos like a child excavating a sand dune. It is an awkward moment, but not an unfamiliar one.

Among the sum total of nine bodies with whom I have shared this house, I have witnessed various displays of intimacy, and am perfectly sanguine about it. I can't expect everyone to conduct themselves with the dignity I do. But if the current crop are going to start bringing home their *beaux* (potentially *belles* in the case of Martin only) isn't it reasonable they should go upstairs, rather than paw at one another in the open-plan?

I sit my ground. Fix my eyes on the couple on TV, as they ponder the letting potential of a derelict shoeing shed. I have standards; I think we all felt more comfortable when I stuck a calendar over the silver S, M, E and G on the fridge door... But I am no stick in the mud, not by a long chalk. Yet, as the longest serving resident of No. 4, The Ridge, I resent being made to feel a gooseberry in my own home.

It takes two appearances from Ethan and the return of a russet-cheeked Martin, swaying slightly as he is introduced to Lorenzo, to convince Georgie they'd be better off elsewhere. Lorenzo looks sheepish as he bids, "Cheers now," to me and "Cheers, mate!" to Ethan and Martin. Valedictions that sound fake delivered with public-school plumminess, and reveal he has not retained our names.

Still, this is quite a day. That's the matter of Georgie's proclivities put to bed once and for all (so to speak)... Having missed my chance to broach the issue of visiting children, I spend the next half-hour flicking between channels. At eight o'clock Martin takes a shower while Ethan, who was also out last night, makes cheese on toast.

"Having an early one," he says, flashing me a comic-weary expression. "Night, then."

He plods upstairs with his plate.

I wonder if Martin is freshening up to go out again. All these comings and goings have put me out of sorts. They remind me I have spent the entire weekend at home, bar a drop-off at the dry cleaners. I have a mind to see what's on at the cinema...

Whipping out my iPad, I am searching for a film that might also appeal to Martin, when he reappears in jim-jams and a zippered hoodie.

"Needed that," he says. His still-damp hair is darkening the hood. "Me and Adrian ended up on a crawl of our old haunts. Nightmare! He's a bad 'un, Adrian…"

I slip away my tablet and go back to clicking the TV remote. He chuckles;

"I see Georgie pulled!" His face is unjudging, and impassive to the onscreen parade of sitcom repeats and body-shock documentaries. "Turning into a right old hotbed of vice round here, eh?"

"Mmm," I smile, trying not to raise an eyebrow. "It can be a bit like the *Big Brother* house at times."

The comparison makes sense the more I think about it. What must Lorenzo think of Martin and me, housemates almost old enough to be Georgie's parents? Perhaps nothing—and certainly not at the moment. By the sound of it, the pair of them are making use of the shower. Which, along with the designer rucksack that disappeared upstairs with Lorenzo, says he is here for the night… I settle on a noisy period drama. With guns.

"Anyway, I'd say this rather works to your advantage." I nearly said *our* advantage. "Be a mite churlish of Georgie to deny you a sleepover now. Wouldn't it?"

Chapter 5

The matter of Martin's children is resolved two evenings later.

No. 4, The Ridge has its own WhatsApp group, which I view as one more example of the niceties of communication usurped by a colder medium. But in this instance it is a godsend. Alone in the living area, with *EastEnders* playing out in the corner, I direct-message Georgie:

> **Think Mart too proud to ask, but sense he could do with having children over? A one-off obvs. Perhaps coordinate on a night convenient to you if it's a bother?**

A pause. Long enough for two smashed glasses and an unlikely declaration of love at The Vic... I have my counterpunch prepared: an oblique reference to Lorenzo, who left a mess in the communal bathroom on Monday, and slopped enough coffee on the worktop to drown a small dog.

> **Sure. Bless. Tough on him, poor thing. Don't know when I'm around this week so do whatever. Gx**

Well, well. It must be love!

The sleepover is arranged for Thursday. I have half a mind to go out and leave them to it. Arrange dinner with Avril with whom I am long overdue a catch-up. It will be odd for Martin's children, coming to stay with Daddy in a house full of strangers... Then again, if Ethan or Georgie are here, trooping around the house with all and sundry, isn't it better I am there to add a little homely stability?

Whilst I like children in small doses, I am spared the yen for motherhood that ruins so many lives. Any regrets I have, re failing to meet Mr Right in my fertile years, are more for the waste of my sexual peak than desire for a baby. Children are like pets: a sweet diversion when borrowed for an afternoon. But full ownership is akin to waving life goodbye. An early menopause snuffed out any danger of a latent hankering, and that was that.

So, on Wednesday evening I make a cake (chocolate sponge, orange icing). Baking gives me a melancholy rush of nostalgia. It's something I did when I lived alone, though for others more than myself. My fudge almond brownies were a trusty fallback on birthdays, and my pineapple upside-down cake a sure-fire hit at parties. Always accompanied by a leading supermarket bubbly, lest turning up with baked goods alone smacked of insolvency... Odd, but now I have housemates who would happily trough on the fruits of my labours, I rarely get the urge. A shared kitchen is not one's own. My baking tins are stowed in the cupboard beside Georgie's pasta maker, still in its box with one unsettling hair trapped under the half-price sticker. Indeed, pre-Martin, any cooking for more than one brought back the dolefulness of school camping trips—the group vegetable-peels and washing of utensils in bowls of grey water. But since his arrival I am baking again, prone to displaying flapjacks in lidless Tupperware with a note:

HELP YOURSELF, I'M STUFFED!

Midweek works best. At weekends anything sugary is wolfed by Ethan and Georgie as they roll in from their night before. So, wise to Martin's comings and goings, I leave out buns, sponges and flans a few minutes before he gets in. It has become our little joke: my incompetence at judging the size of a batch; him saying he can always take them into the office tomorrow, then winking as he mimes stuffing two in his mouth at once. He is particularly partial to my orange-iced chocolate sponge, which

I hope runs in the family, though I toss off a batch of peanut butter cookies just in case. Then I remember every other child has a peanut allergy these days... The lid will stay firmly on until I've checked with Daddy.

On Thursday evening, Georgie is a no-show, but Ethan and I are in the living area when Martin pulls up in the drive. Treating the arrival with his usual interest, Ethan barely looks up as two small figures in elasticated anoraks tumble in with Daddy. Martin is carrying their overnight bag.

"Say hello to Fen and Ethan, Freya. You too, Nathan."

The girl mumbles. The boy stares. Ethan nods, and I grin what I hope is playfully as Martin unreels them from their coats. Of the two, the girl looks more like him. Both have his wide hazel eyes, but the boy's hair is fair, of a shade that will darken with the years. They follow him upstairs and down as their belongings disappear. Nathan trails him to the kitchen, while Freya hops up on the settee with a thin paperback, oblivious to the lifestyle chat on TV. She is unfazed by Daddy's new home.

"Good book, Freya?" I ask.

She nods, solemnly turning a page. She is halfway down the next before she replies.

"It's about a little girl who can see what people are dreaming."

As a premise it sounds dubious, but I can see the appeal to an innocent mind. The cover features two children menaced by a dragon. Ethan, social obligations complete, returns to his earbuds and the game on his phone. Since Martin and Nathan are doing something involving chopping and filling the kettle, I turn down the TV and slip in beside Freya.

"I used to love reading when I was your age. Still do, actually."

She is busy with an illustration of a drowning kitten being rescued by a Scottie dog. I persist:

"*The Lion, The Witch and the Wardrobe* was my favourite. Do you know that one?"

At this, bright eyes lift from the page. "We've got the audio book. Is that the one with the goat-man with the furry chest, like Daddy?"

I twitch involuntarily. "It may be..."

With that, I am stumped for more to say. Freya seems happy in this world of her own. Which, as the pages turn, moves from a pirate galleon to outer space, then the perils of climbing through an impossibly large bunch of flowers.

"Dinner time, Freya!" calls Martin from the kitchen.

She puts down her book and trots to the breakfast bar. I wonder if they are this well behaved at home, or eat off laps in front of the telly like their father... I listen out for the scrape of plates that signals an end to what smells like spag bol, then saunter into the kitchen to make a cup of tea.

"Well, I don't suppose anyone's got room for my chocolate-orange cake!"

A pause. Martin looks awkward.

"I don't like chocolate," says Freya lapping a morsel of Bolognese off her finger, "I like marshmallows. And Nathan's had a strawberry mousse, and he's only allowed one pud a day cos the dentist said."

Martin chuckles. "But it's very kind of you, Fen. Isn't it, kids? I'd love a bit if it's going begging..."

Peanut butter cookies save the day. The children chatter away with one each as I serve up slices of cake onto side plates. I take mine in the other room, then realise I didn't make tea. Wonder if I need to wait for the children to go up before I pour myself wine instead.

"One of your cakes?" asks Ethan, unhitching himself from a cityscape of lobbed incendiaries and burning cars. His eyes are hungry.

I reach for the remote. "On the side. Help yourself."

Once the dinner things are in the dishwasher, the children return. They are lively in Martin's company, cavorting on the settee and panicking briefly over a forgotten sock. Homework has been done at school, which leaves an hour before bed to do whatever children do.

When Nathan catches sight of Ethan's mobile he is over at his chair, peering with a little-boy curiosity even the thickest skinned can't ignore. For a six-year-old, he has a remarkable grasp of the covert surveillance and assassination techniques vital to the game. With Daddy's permission he takes control of the device. Until, from his position on Ethan's knee, he is coaching our resident geek on the best tactic to avoid poison gas.

Martin and Freya are giggling over her book... With jollity to the left of me and guerrilla warfare to the right, I am pig-in-the-middle. On the verge of sneaking out, in the guise of putting cake away but actually for a swig of red, when Freya says:

"Is it true you work in an art gallery?"

I sit back. "I do, as a matter of fact. In Dulwich. Do you know that one?"

Freya considers. "Is that in Trafalgar Square?"

"Erm, no."

"Is it the one by the river with the big chimbley?"

I shake my head.

"Have you got any nice pictures in your gallery?"

"Well, I think so. What sort of pictures do you like?"

From under Martin's arm Freya leans forward. "I like horses best. And battles. Especially battles with horses, as long as they don't get hurt."

"I like those, too. We have a few. One in particular, though it's not on display at the moment." A flash of inspiration. "Perhaps you could come to my gallery one day? I'll show you some of my favourites!"

Freya's eyes light up. "Like a private tour?"

I nod.

She is agog. "Like Ariana Grande, when she went to Hamleys and they locked all the doors to keep the tourist children out?"

"I suppose. Actually we've got something else on soon you might enjoy. Do you like puzzles?" Freya does. "It's an exhibition by a man who used to draw impossible things. Staircases that go on and on forever, and hands that draw themselves. Would you like to see that?"

Unhooking from Daddy's elbow, she bounces off the settee and grips my chair-arm.

"I'd *love* to see that! I love impossible things. That's why I like dreams, because then you can do anything. Fly if you want to, or ride horses under the sea..."

Martin smiles. "Careful, Fen, you'll have a friend for life there!"

Uninvited she clambers onto my knee. "What I really like are horses in winter time. When it's all snowy and you can see their breath... I saw a picture like that in a gallery once. Mummy bought me the postcard and I drew it again and again, but I couldn't get the breath right. It should look puffy like smoke, but mine looked puffy like marshmallows. Are you good at drawing horse's breath?"

While Freya runs upstairs for her sketch pad, I give Martin a look of amiable apology. But if he is annoyed to have his time with the children hijacked by strangers, it doesn't show... He watches contentedly as his daughter returns to my lap; where, with a fuchsia-pink felt tip, she demonstrates the problem of capturing equine exhalation. I grimace as the pad is passed to me and a lime-green pen wedged in my fingers. I follow her lead, drawing a passable horse's head, happy to be spared the leg arrangement... The bulging eyes and flaring nostrils earn a giggle, though my rendering of breath is met with silence. It's more discharging fire hydrant than gasping horse.

"My daddy's a brilliant *draw-rer*," says Freya, in lieu of an opinion.

"I know," I say. I don't, but it stands to reason for a graphic designer.

"You should put his pictures in your gallery. He's very good at space rockets." She is back at her drawing pad, one little heel drumming testingly on my shin. "And tigers."

Squeals of delight at an explosion, audible from the shared earbuds on the next chair, spare me more discomfort.

"Come on, you two!" says Martin. "Bath-time. Freya, you're first…"

Later, when the children are in bed and Ethan has withdrawn to his room, Martin and I are drinking wine. I am hoping I acquitted myself well.

"Lovely children. I do hope they sleep alright, strange bed and all."

Martin crosses his stockinged feet on the coffee table. "Take a bomb to wake them once they drop off… How come you're so good with kids? Freya thinks you're brilliant."

I try not to look surprised. "I don't know. But who wouldn't be, with those two? I nannied a bit at uni. Then there's all the school parties at the Gallery. I get roped into the odd presentation for my sins, to field their endless questions…"

That sounded demeaning but Martin doesn't seem to notice.

"Anyway we might take you up on that—pop over to Dulwich sometime. I'd like my kids to have an appreciation of art. Don't want them growing up like those plonkers on quiz shows… Ask them to name a great artist, and all they know is Banksy!"

I had seen myself taking Freya round the Picture Gallery alone. Stopping at the cafe for an apricot slice, then stepping into the magical, behind-the-scenes world of the restoration department, where a snowscape by Stubbs is currently getting a thorough clean. But I like the idea of a foursome too, with Martin and little Nathan. We could pick a quiet morning, keep to the main gallery and arm the children with factsheets, then leave them to it while we grown-ups immerse ourselves in art... Martin hasn't expressed much interest in my job, but he'll have a designer's eye for sure. Will bring a fresh perspective to my appreciation of pictures I haven't glanced at since my first week in the job, when I made a point of viewing the entire collection over successive lunch hours. I imagine us brushing shoulders, heads inclined like courting grebes, as he explains the lavish use of pigment in a Reynolds, the play of light in a Constable...

"That would be fun," I say, careful not to imply I'm taking his suggestion as a cast-iron promise.

He levers his feet off the table and leans forward to top up our glasses. "Talking of your gallery, I finish up at work next week. Be kicking my heels, so if you need any help with your brochures and stuff... Design, layout, finished artwork—I'm your man!"

The wine catches the back of my throat, like a first taste of unruly red, not a smooth agreeable white. This conversational shift unsettles me.

"Oh right. Well, we're pretty staffed-up at the moment, but good to know. Little jobs have been known to drop on my desk out of the blue."

He sniggers pubescently. I re-run my words and titter.

"Really, Martin—your mind!"

His feet return to the table, revealing a hole in one sock. Companionable silence reigns as we watch the news. Flotsam-clinging refugees pass before my eyes. I am torn between a gentle thrill that he and I are getting on so well, and a notion I am being played... As the night wears on, I watch his reflection in the black of the window. At one point the fingertips of his hand slip contentedly under the waistband of his jeans, the first of his two habitual resting postures. The other involves hooking a finger over the neck of his tee shirt and scratching his chest hair audibly. Both are distracting, and both leave me dry at the mouth.

Twice he looks over, catching my eye with a smile that suggests nothing beyond face value. At quarter to eleven he stands... I assume our evening is over, or he is going to check on the children. Instead he uses the nylon cable of Mr Burnside's very twentieth-century pulley system to close the curtains. Sits back down again with a sigh, his eyelids drooping through a documentary on surrogacy among Sunderland benefit cheats.

I bide my time. Finish my wine as I wait for his breathing to switch from heavy-rhythmic to the low-whistle that says he is asleep. Then I tiptoe over, wobbling slightly as I lay a hand on his shoulder. Rest it there for as long as I dare, before shaking him gently.

"Martin—Come on, I can't leave you down here."

His eyes snap open, dewy-clear even at this hour. He yawns, chin sinking into the olive-skinned pleats of his neck, a rare posture in which he looks less than deeply attractive. His knees creak as he rises. I turn off the television and collect glasses while he snatches our still-warm seat cushions off the suite.

"Night then," he says, yawning again. "You'll lock up, Fen, yeah?"

I nod then smile sadly, as he lumbers upstairs to make a meagre bed on the floor beside his children.

Chapter 6

Sailing day is the third Saturday in August. We are casting off, or whatever cruise liners do, at 11am.

I am sleeping at Mother's the night before, so say my goodbyes to No. 4, The Ridge at bedtime on Thursday… Make my escape with my wheelie Samsonite next morning, skipping breakfast since I have no wish to run into Martin again. Our leave-taking was warm and well-meant, and his kiss on my cheek could be devalued by further goodbyes. At work, I catch myself touching my face more than once.

When I wake up on Saturday in Oxted, the air of a military operation takes hold. Whatever hand-to-hand combat settled which of Mother's acolytes has the honour of conveying us to Southampton, the victor was friend Bill. As he slams us individually into the rear of his Renault Scenic, I half expect him to produce a peaked cap from the glove compartment. Barrelling down the M3, his attentiveness starts to pall: his constant checking that Lillian is comfortable and her seatbelt doesn't dig. Three times before Basingstoke mint imperials are proffered over his shoulder; I wonder at the spell she cast to keep him under her thumb.

"Let me, Fenella, I insist!" says Bill.

This, on arriving at the Queen Elizabeth II Terminal, as I go to erect her wheelchair in the car park. At the barrier, Bill is affronted when a lackey says he may proceed no further. Flustered, when two more take charge of the cases and Mother's walking frame. As I wrestle the wheelchair grips from his grasp and we say goodbye, he is virtually lachrymose. Twenty paces on, his reflection in a shiny advertising hoarding is still waving.

"I'd be lost without Bill," says Mother, before adding enigmatically, "Though I daresay a break will do us both good."

Check-in is smooth. The counter is staffed by mature employees in ironed slacks. People not unlike Bill himself, the kind who volunteer at hospitals. Security is lower-key than I expect, and our mustering point more relaxed than the airport equivalent. There is similarly a distinct lack of youths in track suits asleep across the modular seating.

"Different sort of crowd on a cruise," observes Mother, peering round as far as her chair allows. "Plenty of people-like-us."

Calculating an average age of sixty-five, I find this less appealing. Even so, my heart is light at the thought of eight days at sea, and the dramatic vistas awaiting us... Eventually, we are called upon to board. It is only at the top of the gangplank, as another rather unfit flunky in a polo shirt relinquishes control of the wheelchair, that I remember it won't all be effortless relaxation. Mother's mobility and her body weight have been moving in opposite directions of late. Another reason hale-and-hearty Bill is useful for outings.

"Push, Fenella!" she says. "We're blocking the road!"

Avoiding thick carpet is the key to easy driving. It says something for the ship's organisation that three thousand passengers boarding simultaneously does little to hinder us. In five minutes we have tracked down our room on Deck Eight.

"Oh. No chandelier."

Mother doesn't look too disappointed. We've had many a chortle over the arch tone of cruise-liner parlance. In the brochure every cabin, however small, is referred to as 'a stateroom', evoking the grandeur of yore. Without consulting me she has upgraded us to an Oceanview Suite. This amounts to an extra living area in our neatly appointed room, with a settee and smoked glass coffee table partitioned off from the beds by a panel holding the second flat-screen TV. Sliding doors lead onto the balcony, an amenity denied anyone opting for an innocuous sounding but coffin-esque 'Interior Stateroom'.

For now, our view is of Southampton quay, with its cranes and monumental warehouses that service floating towns like *Diamond Sabre*. The timetable I saw at check-in suggested ships come and go on a daily basis. Yet, while this may be travel on an industrial scale, the promotional puff promises a veneer of luxury. Time will tell... A knock at the door I hope is our luggage turns out to be a small, empty-handed steward. Filipino or similar, he is impeccably dressed in the crew-livery of aubergine trousers and a jacket with Nehru collar.

"Good afternoon, *Misses-es* Woodruff! I am Marco, your personal butler..." This is the form of address, delivered in a soothing tenor, he will use for the duration of the voyage. Unfailingly with a nod and a smile, as he passes us in the corridor or delivers Mother's afternoon tea and biscuits; "...An' I am *a-bail-able* for you twenny-four hours a day!" he concludes implausibly, pointing out his extension on the phone list. He also demonstrates the minibar, the heating/ air con, and reminds us to use hand sanitiser, dispensers of which pepper the public areas with a frequency once given to ashtrays.

"Well," says Mother as Marco backs out, soundlessly closing the door. "Our own personal butler. Whatever next!"

I am consulting the glossy free-sheet he left behind. It is called *Sabre Says* and contains details of all of today's onboard activities, plus menu highlights from the four high-end restaurants. There is also a reminder about dress code.

Mother sniffs. "Are you going to help me onto the bed, Fenella, or do I summon Marco?" Her feet are already off the footplates. "I think he'd struggle a bit, don't you?"

On the dot of four-fifteen the blare of the horn reverberates through the aft decks. Mother and I watch from the balcony as *Diamond Sabre* sets sail. Neither of us is soppy enough to wave at the sprinkling of anonymous well-wishers on the quay. Woodruff women are not given to public displays of emotion.

Mother leans on her walking frame, her chunky-knit cardigan done up to the neck. Over the course of many phone calls re suitable cruise attire, we agreed it would be breezy at sea. And August or not, we are heading north. Bergen, our first port of call the day after tomorrow, is on a par with the Shetlands. Even in her sprightlier days, any latitude higher than Birmingham would see Mother reaching for her thermals.

"Warm enough?" I ask, chiding myself for being so hard on Bill.

She nods and smiles wistfully. Her cheeks glow as the choppy depths of the Solent appear between us and the shore, and the coastline grows broader and smaller and further away.

"You know, Fenella, there were times I thought I'd never go abroad again. So much easier to stay at home when you can't get about. Doesn't stop you wishing, though."

She has never travelled a great deal. Not when I was a child, nor even when I'd flown the coop. The oft-pontificated-upon foreign climes that Father saw in the Merchant Navy seemed to kill his urge for more. So, when I was home from Exeter or attending Sunday lunch, Mother would draw pointed attention to the postcards on the mantelpiece from Frank and Beryl Prescott. The Danube or the pyramids; Lake Garda was a favourite for a while, which she eventually visited with friends when all suggestions fell on deaf ears... My parents perennially ended up in the New Forest or, if Father was pushing the boat out, Norfolk. Anywhere further than a two-thermos drive from Oxted meant he'd dig his heels in and spend the money on the greenhouse. All of which tells me this trip is another reflection of Mother's sense of mortality. I put a hand on her arm and squeeze.

"Mind you," she says before I can say a word, "this is your holiday too. You needn't be at my beck and call, you know. Leave that to Marco... I'll look at the excursions, do a couple with you if they're step-free and don't involve cobbles. Otherwise, you can park me up somewhere with a nice view and I'll be fine. Understand?"

"Alright, Mother. Thank you."

She eases her arm away in search of a tissue. "Now get me out of this cardigan and into something alluring. I want to see round this ship!"

Passing through Reception on Deck Five, I pick up a fold-out map. Navigating the acreage of decks, from our stateroom to the restaurants to the shopping mall and back again, will take a while to master. The public areas are opulent, bordering on glitzy. Reception fills an entire half of the Atrium—a yawning chasm in the heart of the ship, at the base of which lies a central plaza. According to the itinerary, this palm-fringed salon is also a venue for on-board activities from BMX biking to Zumba workouts. I can't decide if it is magnificent or the most vulgar thing I've ever seen in my life.

"It's like Las Vegas!" roars Mother.

She knows to project in her chair, since speaking at midriff level in the wrong direction won't always reach my ears. But she's right: the mosaic floors of the ship's communal areas are awash with cream and crimson curlicues befitting an emperor's palace. The distant ceiling, ever more striking as we rise in one of six crystal elevators, boasts a light installation like a flying saucer. There is something Vegas about our fellow travellers, too. Pristine white pumps and high-waisted safari khakis, indeed the full gamut of smarter leisurewear, greet us at every turn. Many waistlines also look American, though I am yet to hear the accent among the passengers. The crew, by contrast, are as cosmopolitan as can be, and sport the flag of their homeland on their name badge. They are immaculately groomed to a man and woman, like airline cabin crew without the ready-baked skin.

We are thinking about a coffee stop until we see the time, and opt for an aperitif instead. The velvet-swagged entrance to Overtures, an inviting lounge bar, looms at just the right moment. It is almost empty. We take a table by the window, with a view of the deck and gun-metal seas beyond. I have barely settled Mother before we are presented with menus by a smart if unpronounceable Hungarian. The cocktail options are daunting. Using the principle of ease and economy we adopt when lunching at The Jade Rickshaw in Oxted, we plump for two of the Day's Special.

Mother watches the barman slosh up our Strawberry Sea Breezes with surgical concentration. "He'll need to get quicker about it if there's a rush on..." But by the time they arrive, in highball glasses with ice and a sculpted berry, she is too engrossed in the passing cavalcade to notice.

"Bottoms up, Fenella," she says.

I tut, but can't suppress a smile. "Bon voyage, Mother..."

Multiple Sclerosis means her grip is not as sure as it was. Chopsticks were the first to go, followed by scissors. She takes her glass in both paws, like Winnie the Pooh holding the honey pot. It is a bonus that cocktails come with a straw. Mother takes a mighty suck before lowering her glass to the table.

"I wasn't sure I'd feel like a drink, but isn't it calm? You'd hardly know we were moving..."

On this level the sensation is imperceptible, any hum of mighty engines lost to the early-evening hubbub. My cocktail slips down like milkshake leaving a solid strata of ice, and I feel devilish enough to order another round, particularly at the promotional rate. Cash is verboten here. Anything not included in the fare—alcohol, excursions, goods in the boutiques—can only be purchased using the plastic card that doubles as our room key. Yes, it would be all too easy... Then I remember Mother's medication, and the notorious cocktail-kick that creeps up on you from whatever spirits seep between the professionally packed ice. She looks down at her pleated skirt and the shoes she travelled in.

"Look at us! Knocking back cocktails and we're not even dressed for it." She claws at the cuff of her blouse. "Ten past six."

Five minutes later I am reversing her towards the door, one hip narrowly missing a faux parlour palm. While our backs were turned two more tables have filled, and in the corner a girl in spangles is setting up a microphone and what looks like a synthesiser on wire legs. Mother digs the deck plan from her handbag. Bars are dotted all over the ship, including one either side of the Casino.

"We can try another tomorrow," she says. "Help us get our bearings..."

At the lifts a steward in braided epaulettes insists on pressing the call button. He stands aside as we enter. Joao's badge says PURSER with a Brazilian flag. He bids us a polite, "Ladies, please to enjoy your first night onboard," and alights a floor below ours.

No. 4, The Ridge, Martin—even Mother's bungalow this morning seem long ago and a good deal farther away than just past the Isle of Wight... I have a suspicion I am going to enjoy cruising. The fetters of life are off, and as she says it *is* my holiday too. Perhaps I'll pop out later when she is in bed. Take a turn around the deck, or have another drink.

Why not?

Chapter 7

Mother is an anomaly. Her MS diagnosis came late in life, when the niggling symptoms attributed to arthritis were revealed for what they were. She has fought it all the way, with the help of an interested specialist and a nurse who does home visits when she is not up to attending clinic. In the early years, my father, a man who rarely engaged with anything that didn't suit him, stepped up to the plate. He retired from his job in the Civil Service and dedicated his last six years to making her as comfortable as possible. As the specialist warned, the progressive nature of MS means we can expect a series of tipping points as the disease takes hold, till managing it becomes the focus of Mother's life. I suspect this time is approaching.

After our Bruges experience, I was apprehensive at the idea of eight days confined with her. Yet by day two we have both slipped into the onboard routine, eager to revel in all the possibilities on offer. Our first-night dinner was a triumph. The staff could not have been more welcoming, and our Thai waiter and waitress made a charming fuss of Mother. My notes re her disability evidently made it through to the maître d', since we were allotted a perfect table in the Koh-i-Noor Restaurant, with room to manoeuvre if she wished to transfer to a padded taffeta dining chair.

The restaurant is both plush and relatively cosy, a neat trick for a space the size of a football pitch. The menu offers an acceptable choice of courses and, aside from an overemphasis on the supplementary wines, I can't fault it. I catch Mother looking round at the other diners. She would have a better view if we swapped places, but her way of commenting on people in earshot makes me loath to suggest it.

"I think we're a bit overdressed, don't you?" she says, straightening the lapels of her daisy-print bolero jacket. We smile tongue-in-cheek over what we have vowed will be a single glass of Sancerre. The dress code seems open to interpretation. True, there are no flip-flops, and any jeans sporting a rip are encrusted with enough diamanté to embarrass a Fabergé egg. But here and there smart-casual has been taken lightly. Spaghetti-strap tops abound, and sports jackets few and far between. With two formal dinners to come we can but hope standards rise.

"Have you noticed, Mother? Hardly any children."

Aside from a couple of toddlers in high chairs it is adults all the way. Odd, considering it's the school holidays, and the onboard array of swimming pools, ball pits and trampolines at every turn. But then Norway is not Florida. I can't imagine even nice children like Freya and Nathan hankering to cruise the fjords when they could be firing paintballs at Goofy, or whatever it is you do at Disney.

Three tables away, partly obscured by a pillar, one man is bucking the trend. An inch of white cuff peeps from the sleeves of his tailored jacket. He is wearing cufflinks and yes, a tie. His companion is not visible; but from the way he concentrates on his dinner (eyes down, switching to mid-distance as he chews) they are a couple with little left to say. I estimate he is in his mid-sixties and as well preserved as he is turned out. What the papers call a silver-fox; a term they apply to any actor, and improbably football manager, deemed to have kept his sex appeal without resorting to hair dye. This one is not my type, though there is something intriguing about him, and a little sad. Holidays have a way of helping couples paper over the cracks.

"I don't think I can manage the *marrons glacés*," says Mother, breaking the spell.

She has finished her lobster which looked like a well-fed crayfish, and its accompanying salad apart from the capers. Our little waitress smiles at the empty plates as she clears away. It is not until we take another look at the menu and Mother decides she will have pudding after all, that I glance back at the table by the pillar. It is empty.

Another quirk of her wretched illness is that Mother feels most energetic at the end of the day. She is chatty after dinner as I get her into bed, and still as we turn out the light, passing positive judgement on our first day at sea. Whether it's this or the soporific effect of the sea air, I no longer have the urge to go walkabout after all.

Tomorrow is a sea-day, which means no landfall for twenty-four hours. The lengthy serving time of breakfast, not to mention unlimited room service, means we have nothing to get up for. Sharing a room with Mother brings home the constraints of her illness, things I vaguely recall from our conversations but have never fully processed.

Next morning, all is laid bare. Just getting out of bed takes her forever. She will eventually need one of those divans that shunt you to the vertical. But for now, and here, she soldiers on, shuffling into the seated shower with her walking frame. She is gone a very long time.

"I'm fine, go back to sleep!" she yells, when I ask again if she is alright.

I turn on my side. Pick my mobile off the side cupboard, then remember there is no signal at sea. Mother reappears in the clothes she took in with her, immediately changing her mind about the right belt for these shoes. Once I sprint through my own bathroom routine, it is almost eleven when we leave the cabin.

There is still more to explore. But weeding out the places of no interest (I shall not be hitting the gym, and neither of us is a gambler) we soon have our onboard stamping ground mapped out. We settle for brunch in the Blue Moon Court, a glorified self-service cafeteria offering everything from vegetarian sushi to a pancake station. The option to queue up, queue up and queue again are a boon to passengers of a mighty appetite. As the week wears on, I realise this is their eatery of choice two, sometimes three times a day. Many diners here are clinically obese, which implies they see all-in cruising as a safe space to indulge. Some I suspect don't go ashore at all. They are here for the catering: the abundance, and the sense of acceptance.

We do a circuit of the Promenade Deck to work off our brunch burgers, figuratively in Mother's case. After twenty minutes at a medium shunt we are back where we began, outside the Explorer's Lounge. Here, two couples in fleeces occupy sunbeds, taking the air and any Vitamin D bestowed by the milky sunlight. The men look bored and the women are talking:

"Oh, *we* did Antigua with Sea Spray Deluxe," says one. "Lovely beaches if you can dodge the hawkers... We always opt for Sea Spray over Sabre if poss. It's the service. Can't do enough for you!"

The other woman's reply includes a shrug. "I know—food practically thrown at you on here! Shocking. Plus I've started golf, and Sea Spray have a driving range and their own professional. We're doing Sydney-Hong Kong in October. I've set my heart on teeing off in both harbours..."

I park Mother far enough away to enjoy the view in peace. Competitive-Cruisers is a subset of passengers I have already identified, along with the Mawkish-Marrieds and Shameless-Scoffers. Across the balustrade lies the North Sea, uninterrupted but for a drilling rig stubbed up on the horizon like a lost chess piece. Once the foursome move off in search of the pharmacy (the lady golfer needs a lip balm) there is no one on deck for fifty metres... I lean on the rail and breathe in the brisk air. It feels good to be away from the traffic and pace of the city, even if it means being away from Martin. I am fairly sure Norwegians don't do air pollution, so the week is sure to be a tonic... As views go, this one is bleakly dramatic rather than beautiful.

Scudding icebergs of cloud, flat-bottomed and worthy of a Turner, bleed greyness into the water; a lone seabird, all wings at this distance, is the only living thing. And while the swell is negligible, I am grateful for whatever tonnage of steel keeps us from it. That's a lot of water, and I don't like to think how deep. Cruise liners seem impregnable nowadays, but out here you do wonder...

Mother's feet are on the low railing as she rummages in her bag for mints. I help her, and it is only as I straighten up I notice another elbow. It belongs to a portly man in sunglasses. A fringe of hair dances around his pate, like seaweed in the current. He nods me a smile and lifts the binoculars off his chest. Pushing up specs, he focuses on something that might be another ship. Mother has noticed him too.

"I can wheel myself away, you know!" she proclaims on the breeze. "Make myself scarce, if you want to be alone..."

"Shush, Mother!"

I feel myself turn puce. Her ideas about 'the right sort of chap' have been making my toes curl since I was seventeen. In her view, a woman without a man is like a hat without a head. She has never embraced the idea I might actually enjoy my independence. On visits to the bungalow, I am lucky to make it through our lunchtime TV quiz without being matched to one of the resident pundits. *("He's divorced, you know. And he's the arty type. I bet he loves exhibitions...")*

Binoculars Man is embarrassed or too engrossed. I catch myself second-glancing to check my initial assessment... Brown sandals, beige socks. He is no Martin.

"Ready to go in, Mother? It's the Captain's Champagne Welcome at five. You'll want to freshen up first."

"I'm enjoying the view, thank you, Fenella. I've not been on the open ocean since—"

"It isn't the ocean, it's the sea. Come on, you'll be sick of it in a week, and it is a bit grey."

Stowing her mints she shuts her handbag. Then with a last look at the waves she submits to being propelled through the sliding doors.

"I worry about your soul sometimes, Fenella. I do..."

We eschew cocktails in favour of a free glass of fizz in the plaza after the Captain's speech. Now the traditional champagne spectacle is over, a team of nippy stewards are deconstructing what is left of the teetering pyramid of glasses. The Captain's words were corporately ignorable, and we had a poor view anyway.

"We could have done with that stepladder, like the woman from Ipswich," observes Mother, referring to the excitable passenger who volunteered to pour bubbly at the apex.

Dinner passes without incident. Some diners are awkwardly sharing tables, so I am relieved when we are led to the same place settings as last night. Our Australian maître d' confirms it is ours for the week, "on account of the other madarme's *mowbility* issues..."

Tonight, Mother goes out like a light. I lie in bed listening to her breathe, and try to detect a sensation of nautical movement. I have just calculated there is another six hours before she starts clattering about again, when the ship's gentle vibration lulls me to sleep.

Chapter 8

"If it's Monday, this must be Bergen!" chuckles Mother.

My eyes open on her tottering carefully from the bathroom in her walking frame. This time, she has washed and dressed without waking me. It takes me a moment to connect her words to the subtle change in cabin ambience: we are at a standstill.

As her free hand works the curtains, the view across the balcony suggests another container port. But here the warehouses are brighter, the corrugations crisper, in a way that says, "You Are Now In Scandinavia." I throw back the duvet and almost skip to the bathroom. Today has an air of long-ago birthdays: promising treats and surprises, or at the very least something new.

Over breakfast I scan the new edition of *Sabre Says* that was thrust under our door in the night. It features tips on what to do in Bergen, and today's entertainment schedule for those staying put.

"There's a traditional old quarter which looks good," I say, by which I mean flat. "Art galleries and King Haakon's Hall. That's beside something called the Rosenkrantz Tower. No mention of a lift…"

The forecast is for 19°C of hazy sun. A shuttle service from the quay to the city's historical heart begins at half-past ten. Last call to board is at 5pm, which gives us a full day to explore. I suspect Mother will have had enough in a couple of hours, after which I'll be free to explore on my own. By the time I have queued for her third piece of toast and fetched our things from the room, all exits are thronging with passengers eager for dry land.

"How long's this going to take?" grumbles Mother as we find our mustering point. Salvation appears in the form of Enrique from El Salvador, waving a diamond-shaped plastic card.

"Priority Access please!" he smiles, handing it to me. "This is yours to *juze* for every disembarkation an' shuttle. It mean you please go to fron' of queue."

He takes charge of Mother, leading me past the waiting droves. At the bottom of the ramp he sees us onto the first in a line of specially equipped buses. Inside, she and I are greeted by conspiratorial nods from three more pairings of chair users and carers. Once we're all strapped in the bus pulls away.

"That was very seamless," says Mother, twenty minutes later.

We are drinking lattes outside a coffee shop in Bryggen, the old quarter. I am still reeling from the price of two lukewarm mugs. The bus dropped us all at the edge of what a wooden hoarding identified as a World Heritage Site. From there we rolled down the pavement in a dissipating procession, to a string of eighteenth-century timbered houses with pitched roofs. Now converted into boutiques and artisanal cafes, Bryggen's pristine red and ochre facades suggest a backdrop Norwegian viewers will know from their period TV dramas. But with its view of the clean, bustling harbour, it is a winner with Mother.

"Shall we carry on this way," I ask, indicating the meandering street. "Or find the museum?"

She opts to keep going. Past the moored sailing boats with their wires clinking on masts, till we reach the terrace's last four-storey frontage. It is an art dealer, with paintings within and emphatically simple driftwood sculptures in the window. I am about to swing her round to go back when Mother spots something she likes.

Inside, the shop is overheated, as if anticipating a less-than-hardy clientele. She examines a tiny cormorant, whittled from an L-shape of black-stained flotsam. Everything else on display has the same unfussy clarity. *Naive art*, my boss would call it, but then Derek favours works that make a splash. To use another of his unlovely expressions, 'getting bums through the door' of a public gallery is a very different job from selling art.

I find myself gravitating to the rear of the shop where a pair of canvasses dominate. One is an Edwardian family: mother, father and two children, eating at a table in the garden. The other is a woman in a long dress, feeding swans on a riverbank. They are by the same artist and share a chilly, ethereal quality, as if viewed from beneath the surface of a pond. They could be trite in a different palette, but something about their subtle rendering in greens and yellows draws me in. I am wondering what Martin would make of them, when an American voice behind me says:

"Someone's been studying Sven Richard Bergh!"

It belongs to a tall, vigorous-looking man with grey hair and a hat tucked under his arm. He looks familiar though I can't place him. Then I notice the cufflinks.

"I don't know him," I reply, peering at the laminated card between the frames. "Or... *Per Johansen.*"

The man steps in beside me. "Swedish. Late nineteenth, early twennieth century. Famous for his portrait of Strindberg, and another work called *Nordic Summer Evening.* Masterful, his way with dappled light..."

My eyes are on the picnicking family though I want to look at him. Men who strike up random conversations are not my favourite thing, though the setting makes it less intimidating. It reminds me of launch parties at work, where engaging with strangers—journalists, potential sponsors—is a necessary evil.

"I'm not up on Norwegian art," I say, turning slightly. "Except Munch, of course."

No one in the shop looks to be with him. Mother, who has moved on to more scrimshaw, is facing away a little too pointedly, making a show of not listening. The American gentleman changes tack.

"So, how are you enjoying the *Sabre*. Neat enough tub, right?"

"Yes, I... It's our first cruise, so we weren't sure what to think. Marmite, you know."

He doesn't.

"—Whether we'd love it or hate it... You can't know until you try."

He smiles. "Gotcha. Yeah, cruising's not for everybody. But once you get in the rhythm..." He turns abruptly. "And how are they treating this lady?"

Mother pretends to be oblivious.

"Eh? Oh yes, nicely thank you." Her eyes give him the full up-down-up-again assessment. "You're on our ship too, then?"

"I am. In fact, I need to get back." He pats his jacket pockets. "Got a call to make, and of course I forgot my phone."

In an awkward manoeuvre the three of us leave the shop together. The fedora goes back on the man's head, and before I know it he is pushing Mother at an easy pace down the well-maintained pavement. He has plenty of small talk, all charming. This is clearly not his first time in Bergen.

"Haakon's Hall's up that-a-way, though you'll need a cab. Not sure you can access every level, mind. But this is Scandinavia, so they're pretty hot on that sorta thing."

At this moment Mother spots a mobility scooter coming the other way. The rider is a lady in a sequinned tee shirt. Her handbag is in the front basket and her husband is ambling along beside her.

"That's what I could do with," she says, clutching her bag to her lap. "There's a lot of those contraptions on the ship, Fenella, have you noticed?"

Bill's sister-in-law was right: cruises are popular with the disabled. In less than two days, we've seen every manner of walking aid and chair. Some motorised, some with canopies to shade sensitive skin. Even one with a detachable drip.

"I've suggested a scooter before, Mother. You said it was a slippery slope. That you'd never get on your feet again."

She shakes her head. "I know, but for holidays. When there's things to see and a distance to go. Easier on the pusher too, wouldn't you say, Mister—erm?"

"You're no burden to me, ma'am," says the gentleman. His manicured hands rest easily on the grips. "And the name's Jessop. Irving Jessop. Pleased to meet you."

Before I can say a word Mother has introduced me, which makes me feel about eight. Two minutes later we are back at the bus stop sign with its three-funnel liner silhouette. At the end of the harbour wall, the next shuttle is coming into view.

"Well now, I'll say good morning," says Mr Jessop. He tips his hat and joins the queue behind a couple in slacks.

Mother and I carry on, though we haven't decided where. I feel a return of the sensation in my lumbar region that ebbed while someone else did the heavy work. But if a little backache is the price of my holiday, it's a fair one.

"What a nice man," says Mother, taking out her sunglasses.

The low cloud that spoiled the view of Mount Floyen as we arrived has evaporated, revealing a funicular railway. Halfway up the heavily wooded slope, two carriages on parallel tracks encroach from opposite directions.

"See," she continues, "I said there'd be our sort of people on this holiday."

I don't know what she means, but I can guess.

"Yes well, don't get too excited. I doubt we'll see him again. There's three thousand people and fifteen hundred staff on our ship. Population of a small town."

She tuts. "Not very observant, are you? He's sitting along from us in the Koh-i-Noor."

"Mother! You made out you didn't know him from Adam."

I can't see her face but I know her lips are pursed. "There are times, Fenella, when it behoves a lady to play dumb. I appreciate it doesn't come easily to all of us…"

I stop pushing. "I am on holiday, so you can drop the matchmaking right now. Apart from anything else, he's probably nearer your age than mine!"

Mother lifts a hand. "I wouldn't dare... Look, there's the tourist office. Why don't you go and ask if there's wheelchair-access on that cable car? We'd get a grand view from up there."

I leave her parked on the edge of the pavement as, breathing heavily, I cross the street.

It can be a mixed mercy Mother's illness is purely physical. She is as sharp as a tack when it suits her, and prone to make her presence felt just as intensely...

Chapter 9

The fjord sightseeing begins in earnest the following day. I go to bed dreaming of verdant cliffs, towering over crystal-clear channels as deep as the sea.

Not to be. On Tuesday, the thrill of waking to another new vista is tempered by drizzle as I pull back the curtain. Geiranger Fjord looks as ill-tempered as its name. A cataract, tumbling down the glacier-carved granite, suggests an elemental shortcut from slate-grey sky to leaden sea. According to the blurb, this is the most spectacular fjord of all, its abandoned mountain farms a photographer's dream, which all sounds a bit *Blair Witch Project* for me. Similarly, I have no desire to pose on the rocky overhang that is another unmissable landmark. Not since I read about a recent spate of fatalities among gap-year Instagrammers, swishing their Nikes off the edge of the world.

As it is, Mother wakes with a headache. On top of the doomy skies, which are forecast to last till afternoon, it puts her off exploring her first fjord for another day. Luckily it is Marco to the rescue, who gamely delivers us breakfast-in-bed, even though we missed the midnight deadline for ordering.

As I emerge from the bathroom, Mother looks stoic in her bed jacket, propped up with an extra pillow.

"Don't worry about me, Fenella, I'll have two Anadin after my toast," she yawns. "Then a nap usually does the trick. You go ashore. I can find my own way to the lifts, or get Marco to bring me another cuppa..."

This is her brave face. At home, she and her walking frame rarely venture further than the garden. The idea of Mother, rolling out of the lift onto the wrong floor and getting lost, is not something I want on my conscience. As it is, I don't like the look of this weather either. I decide to stay on board for now, give it an hour and take a turn about the deck.

"I'll be back after your nap," I say, "to see how you're feeling..."

My step has the slightest spring as I shut the stateroom door. Our long, long corridor extends to a distant room-service cart in one direction and further than I can focus in the other. Across the central divide containing the lifts lies a parallel corridor of doors, replicated on two decks above and three more below. It is not just Mother who could lose her bearings here.

I take the lift down to the free barista station in the plaza, and am soon sipping a cappuccino from an ideal vantage point for watching our microcosmic world go by. Undeterred by the elements, droves of passengers in rainproofs are heading for the exits. By the time I drain my cup, the glittering Atrium is the emptiest it has been. Two purple-suited stewards in special gloves polish the rails around the walkway; by the Rolex concession, a few desultory onlookers gather for a demonstration of origami towel-animals. These creations, left playfully in every room during dinner, are the work of Marco and co, as they pop in to set chocolates on pillows and give en suites their final primp of the day. Returning from the Koh-i-Noor, we have so far been greeted by a puppy, a dolphin and last night, thinking we'd been forgotten, an impressive gibbon dangling from the curtain pole by one dexterous arm. Mother was so delighted we took a photo.

I could sit here all morning, drinking the ship's very acceptable coffee. Those pastries look enticing too... I remember my waistline and decide to take the air instead.

Outside, the rain has eased. More stewards are mopping puddles from the timbered deck. There is no denying one feels cosseted on a cruise liner, which explains why they are such a hit with the old and infirm. From the balustrade, I watch a handful of stragglers marching down the gangplank. At the end they must brave a photo opp: two loons in horned helmets with integral blond plaits. This feels at odds with rest of the cruise experience—even from here, the passengers' discomfort is palpable... I do up an extra button against the Nordic summer breeze, and saunter in the opposite direction. To my mind, animals deftly sculpted from towels and wags in plastic Viking hats sit either side of a good/bad taste divide. But, as revealed by the currency-pricing on the cocktail menu, the headquarters of Sabre Line are in California USA. And, whilst there is no onboard McDonald's, nor Mickey Mouse marching a meagre cohort of children to glee club, the fingerprints of Uncle Sam are here if you look.

Hah! A case in point: I pause at the notice, bolted to one of the empty Jacuzzis that dot the open decks. Under the cruise line's signature crest are the words:

PERSONS IN ANY FORM OF DIAPER
ARE **NOT PERMITTED** IN THE
RECREATIONAL POOLS AND SPAS

I cannot decide which is more astonishing: what it says, that it needs to be said, or the total lack of irony. For all America has given the world, there are times when its influence makes me despair. It feels unkind to connect such tone-deaf brashness with someone as cultured as Mr Jessop. Surely he would baulk at a sign like this?

Further along the walkway, I pass a fully clothed gaggle on deck chairs, drinking coffees and chatting over paperbacks. The cover of one *(THE LOOK SHE GAVE YOU)* features a woman peering down a stairwell. Someone else has a *Harry Potter*, and I try not to shudder. In my opinion, any adult unashamed to be seen reading a children's book should be fed Lego till they're sick.

Which reminds me, I still haven't broken out my Kindle from the bedside drawer. So far, seeing to Mother has filled any time not taken up with onboard distractions... I scan the onshore panorama. Beyond the unappealing pontoons and chalet-style buildings of Geiranger itself, the sun is starting to make the fir-swathed rocks and pea-green water look inviting. But there will be plenty more spectacle tomorrow. Perhaps I'll have time to read later, after all.

For now, I settle for one last bracing circuit of the deck before I go and see to Mother.

"So. How 'bout that?"

The smile playing round Irving Jessop's lips is of a father watching his children on Christmas morning. From the moment he gave us his stiff little wave in the Koh-i-Noor last night, it was obvious something was afoot. He would not be drawn; just asked us to meet him at the starboard entrance on Deck Four at nine-thirty this morning. By insisting on changing her blouse twice, Mother has made us late.

"Where on earth did you get that?" she asks, mouth agape.

"Ain't what you know," says Mr Jessop, "it's who. Now, this is strictly against the book, so you gotta be comfortable with this thing or it's me who'll be walking the plank..."

The invalid scooter is orange with a black vinyl seat. Its tapering front and chunky rear compartment give it the look of a single-seater golf buggy. I am as shocked as Mother.

"Mr Jessop, you're a magician! Did you organise this in Geiranger?"

He laughs. "Nope, strictly canoe hire-only back there. But I happen to be on very good terms with one of the ship's maintenance guys. You'd be amazed what they got stowed away on here. It's been repaired, but he assures me it zips along like a dream."

Mother is quivering. For all her enthusiasm, the scooter is making her uneasy.

"I haven't driven in years, Mr Jessop. Or ridden a bike. Do you need lessons for one of these things?"

"You do, ma'am. And I am at your service."

He wheels her close enough to see the controls, then hops into the seat himself with the confidence of a cowboy from the Old West. "My wife spent her last eight years on one of these things. Kept her part of the world till her last few months, God bless her..."

"Oh," says Mother.

"I see," I say.

"This is a newer model, but the controls haven't changed any. Ignition's here, just like a car. And this dial sets the pace... Then you flip the throttle this-a-way to go forward, and that-a-way to go back."

"I can't see myself wanting to go backwards," says Mother. "Where's the brakes?"

"No need, Lillian. Just take your hand off the throttle and it slows to a stop."

I can see this turning awkward: Mother is torn between fear and gratitude at this extraordinary gesture. But she is proud, especially in front of strangers... How do I extricate her without offending her new friend?

She is halfway out of her wheelchair before I can say a word. "Come on, Fenella. Give me a hand!"

Mr Jessop demonstrates swivelling the seat through ninety degrees for easy mounting. I fluster as she climbs aboard, but the way he is pressing his forearm to her lower back, using his weight to steady her, confirms his experience. Only one or two passers-by witness what feels like a pivotal moment in Mother's dotage. I want to whisper she needn't do this—that we can thank him but say we are fine as we are...

A moment later, squeezing the throttle, she is away. Off down the broad avenue of deck at a pace, operating the controls by paddling fingers. Mr Jessop and I watch her go.

"She's a natural," he says. "Look, I hope you didn't mind me muscling in. But when your mom said she wanted a scooter, it reminded me what a lifeline it was for Francine when we were on vacation."

"No, I... It's terribly kind of you! It's just—I wouldn't want Mother using it unless she's absolutely comfortable. Her illness causes a lot of stress, and the point of this cruise was to give her a break from all that."

Mr Jessop smiles sadly. "Multiple Sclerosis, right?"

"Yes. How did you... Did your wife—?"

He shakes his head. "Parkinson's Disease. But I practised medicine for thirty-nine years—consultant cardiologist—so I know MS when I see it."

I swallow. Mother and I were trying to guess his profession only last night. She plumped for oil magnate, me attorney. I find myself paying more attention to what he is saying.

"Up to you, of course," he shrugs. "And for as long as your mom can get along without it, she should. It's use-it-or-lose-it with MS, as I'm sure you know. But I tell you, those contraptions are a blessing. If she's never used one, maybe you can think of this as a test run. She'll know what to expect if she decides to get one."

It is a sobering thought. I tend to glaze over when Mother voices fears about her future. Not being heartless—I just can't see the point in expending energy on things beyond our control. From what I've read, the progress of MS is unpredictable. We'll face the challenges as they arise, roping in the services available... But for now, there is no denying what Mr Jessop says makes sense.

Forty metres down the deck Mother executes a slow turn, indicating politely to a steward with a tray full of tumblers.

"Sound advice, Mr—sorry, is it Dr Jessop?"

The morning sun in his eyes causes him to squint through a distinguished crinkle of crow's feet. "Please, Fenella, call me Irving."

He is a very nice man. Of the kind that means I haven't the slightest problem holding his gaze as I reply;

"Thank you. I will. And you can call me Fen."

Chapter 10

Mother's enthusiasm for her new toy is making me wary. The next day's free sheet describes the terrain around Olden as *'limited-access friendly with some restrictions outside the village'*.

"I'll be fine!" she insists. Her gaze is on the settlement of wooden buildings nestled around the quay. "There'll be a coffee shop, and a craft shop I bet... Look, there's someone in a chair now, going up that hill. I'll make short work of it in this thing!"

But Irving and I are agreed; she needs someone with her until she has mastered the scooter. When he offers to accompany us ashore "just while your mom gets the hang of it", I am relieved.

The sheer immensity of the fjord landscape is only apparent a distance from the ship. We chat, the three of us, strolling on the quayside, Irving's hand never far from the scooter's handlebars. At the first shop selling cable-knit sweaters I look back down the valley. Before we docked, the pilot executed an achingly gradual three-sixty degree turn, so the ship is now facing down-channel for our departure. Another smaller cruise liner is moored on the other bank, but even the towering box-shaped stern of *Diamond Sabre* is dwarfed by the surrounding crags.

It is seven hours before we need to be back on board. I yearn to stride out and join the straggling line of sightseers meandering over the hill... Olden village promises venerable churches and glittering streams. There's even a glacier somewhere. But before we go further Mother detours into the knitwear shop, almost colliding with a couple who nod and say something encouraging in another language.

"Careful," I cajole. "You're in charge of a lethal weapon there..."

Like the ramps and disabled loos that were everywhere in Bergen, the shop is laid out with aisles wide enough for a scooter. Mother is in her element. In my childhood she was a fervent shopper, with ever an eye for a bargain. She dearly misses a day at the sales and relishes any retail opportunity, even if it's only looking. I watch patiently, not wishing to be churlish. But Irving is scratching his ear behind a stack of Fair Isle gilets. I should take charge and let this poor man get on with his holiday.

"If you want to get going I'm sure I can—"

"No, no," he smiles. "Don't worry about me. I've seen Olden many times. It's beautiful but it doesn't change any."

I am fingering fisherman's socks, wondering if they would suit Martin. Irving has made one or two references like this, and my curiosity is piqued.

"Mother and I were wondering where you live? America is so vast and—"

"Here."

"Sorry?"

"Well, here today—Gone tomorrow, as they say!"

"Oh. Right." I take this to mean he is the meditative type, living in the moment. Not my thing, but each to their own...

"I mean, I live aboard ship."

I stop in my tracks. Mother heard it too. She reaches into the scooter's pannier for a tissue.

"The cost of a decent retirement community back home would make your hair curl," says Irving. "Francine and I did a lotta cruising over the years. It helped her to relax, getting away from the city. Which was Boston, since you ask... I'd see the change in her, soon as we stepped aboard." A hand goes to his eyes and I look away. "Always Sabre Line or Cunard, and one way or another we racked up a truck load o' loyalty points." He slips a hand into the pocket of his weatherproof jacket. "When she passed I was ready to sell up and move somewhere smaller. But then, with all the deals they offer their best customers, I realised I could spend my time travelling the world for less than the price of a condo in Santa Barbara."

"What a wonderful idea!" says Mother. I agree, though I am already thinking through the pitfalls.

He shrugs. "I get my meals cooked to gourmet standard... Don't have to make my own bed or even a cup of coffee. Dry cleaning and the odd bottle of Pinot Noir's all I ever pay for. There's even a mini-hospital on board—please God, I never need it."

"Isn't it lonely?" I ask.

Irving smiles. "With thousands of new sailing buddies every other week? Nope, can't say it is." His eyes are on a polystyrene mannequin in a bobble hat. "I'll admit, it's not the life I anticipated, but it feels right for now. Whenever I'm someplace we've been before, it brings back a bit of Francine. And that way I remember her happy, not as she was in her last year. At home."

Mother sniffs; I wonder if I have something in my eye.

"Anyways—I got a proposal for you ladies." He skirts the display and leans on the scooter's backrest. "Madam, how about I escort you to where I can promise the finest view of the fishing boats a-coming and a-going." Mother looks intrigued. "It also happens to be right beside a cafe that serves the finest *Solskinnskringle*—that's custard pastries to you—in southern Norway!"

She looks at me. "I'd love to. What about you, Fenella?"

Irving winks. "Then I was thinking your mom and I could take a look around the other shops. Maybe go back aboard for a spot of lunch, if we've had enough of the fine fresh air by then?"

"Oh, I don't know," I bluster. "Mother might prefer me to tag along. I mean, it all sounds lovely, and I was reading about the fishing boats only this morning..."

"Mother might prefer to make up her own mind!" she barks with a smile. "Honestly, Irving, you'd think I wasn't here, the way she speaks for me!"

She takes the mobile from her handbag, checking for the stylus she uses to tap out messages. "I can text if I need you.

Otherwise we'll see you on the ship. For cocktails." She nods to her new factotum. "Lead the way, Irving. There's a custard fancy in this town with my name on!"

He waves goodbye as they negotiate their way out. As they cross onto the wooden walkway, I hear Mother say "...*wonderful daughter, but a terrible liar. Fenella's always hated fishing. Ever since her father hooked a jellyfish off the groyne at Cromer...*"

Chapter 11

The village of Olden is laid out on one straight road running perpendicular to the sea. Once I'm over the hill, *Diamond Sabre* is out of sight. But even on *terra firma* it somehow works its magic, making thousands of bodies disappear. Surely most passengers have disembarked on a cloudless day like this? Yet the village is almost empty.

Birds twitter invisibly. The air is sublime, with a purity that cuts through the occasional waft of Nordic farming. At home I rarely think of the pollution that plagues London, so much of it insidiously odourless. But as I follow the gentle slope away from the sea, there is no denying this feels like the cradle of creation. There is a crispness you can see as well as smell. I keep to the pavement though traffic is negligible. A single tractor rumbles by as I reach a scattering of hillside homesteads, neatly spaced like the display in a toyshop window. They are brightly painted with cosy-looking hideaways in the eaves, and if lanes connect them it isn't apparent. It feels as if nature still holds sway here, and only man's primmest efforts earns a place.

Fifteen minutes later, I reach the first of the map's two churches, high points on the trail for today. One would seem adequate for a village this size, though it plays its part judging by the sea of gravestones. I wonder what the orderly Norwegians would say about burying someone in your own back garden... The layout of the church is cruciform, with whitewashed walls and a slate roof of the colour I associate with Florence. Inside, eight or ten tourists have taken pews to gawp at the minimalist interior. Ropes, snaking down from the central bell spire, are trained over structures at the end of each row like antler-inspired hatstands. The church's altar, and adjacent loin-clothed trio, suspended in a symphony of suffering, are irresistible to the camera clickers. I take one discreet photo and wander out to the car park.

I am taking in the view when one half of a couple from the ship follows me outside. He is on his mobile, which is unaccountably switched to speaker. I have no wish to listen, but I don't have a choice.

"Pete, I'm dialling Darren in... Darren, you there?"

His accent is educated Yorkshire. The call is about a trade deal in Asia. It sounds confidential, yet despite the red vein pumping at the neck of his Pringle knit he seems relaxed. Too blissfully on holiday to worry about a random woman or eavesdropping mistle thrush. The man has his back to me, but knows I am here. I am about to leave him to it when, blatantly and at length, he breaks wind, a sound like ripping canvas. He continues speaking without missing a beat... Horrified, I stomp across the gravel. Refuse to let him catch my eye with his good-natured nod, which offends me even more. How can a man who takes sophisticated holidays be such a graceless pig?

I like to think he wouldn't do it in front of his wife, but who knows? As I turn out of the car park, pristine fjord opens up around me and I find myself yearning for Martin... I wonder how things are at home, by which I mean things with him. GMT is an hour behind. He will be at work now, thinking about his lunch with one eye on the clock.

I sigh. So much majesty to immerse oneself in, and the prospect of another impeccable evening aboard *Diamond Sabre*... If only he were here, and we were enjoying it together! How proud I would feel, being escorted around the ship by Martin... Hopping ashore, seeing sights new to both of us, secure in the knowledge a romantic dinner awaits. All followed by a return to the haven of our stateroom — setting for our passionate lovemaking, to the imperceptible swell of the sea...

Simultaneously, I find myself longing to be at the coffee table of No. 4, The Ridge. Just the two of us, sharing supper in front of the telly, chewing over the day or whatever weighs on his mind. It is not a place Martin would recognise as remotely significant—yet to me it means everything.

How on earth, I ask myself, has it come to this?

With Irving in Overtures. Come and join. M

The text arrives as I unlace my walking boots. The second church (less dour, more ornate) and a little light off-roading beside a stream has left me ready for a snooze. Eking out nuances from Mother's texts is pointless, but this could be a plea for rescue.

Sliding the balcony door I spot a brace of carrier bags on the settee. She has been back to the room. I am tempted to investigate but my hands are grubby. Outside, I am about to give my boots a mud-shifting clonk on the rail, when I remember the balcony below and leave them on the floor to dry.

By the time I have changed into a long-sleeved tee shirt and made my way to Deck Six, Mother and Irving are on their second Mojito. Whether it is the alcohol or a day of bracing air, she is positively glowing.

"Fenella, there you are! We were just saying we should have ordered a jug. Irving, ask them to bring another..."

"I'll look at the menu actually, Mother," I say, by which I mean the Day's Special. Edging round the scooter, which is parked behind the table as proudly as a new bike, I take a chair.

"So, what did you make of Olden, Fen?" asks a smiling Irving. "Magical, right?"

I agree. I am about to draw a comparison with the Lake District then think better of it. "And what did you two get up to?"

"Oh, we had a lovely time," chimes Mother. "We watched the boats go by, then a bunch of men on those paddle-board things, didn't we, Irving? They looked like Jesus walking on the water! Then we had a scout round the shops. He was very patient, but I wanted to get a present for Bill. And Kath, cos she's watering the garden."

"Your mom's quite the shopper," says Irving.

"Happy as a pig in you-know-what!" chuckles Mother. I suspect this is her third Mojito.

Irving is unfazed. "Just as well, because I had to leave your mom for a while to speak to my broker." He pats the phone in his pocket. "No escape from this darn thing on dry land. Most ungallant of me, I know."

Ha! I am tempted to say there's a lot of it about... Though I am quite sure Irving manages to tend to his investments without losing sphincter decorum!

Mother slurps when her straw hits bottom. "You should speak to him about your portfolio, Fenella."

This earns her my disapproving look. "We are on holiday, Mother. And so is Irving."

Mr Jessop looks faintly embarrassed. "Okay," he says, levering himself from the low armchair. "Time for my nap. I'll let you ladies enjoy your evening. See you at dinner maybe. Ah, here's our man."

The waiter arrives with my drink and more honey-roast cashews. By the time he has settled both on coasters and taken Mother's order of a St Clements (straw, no ice) Irving Jessop has gone.

"Really, Mother! Can we not discuss my financial arrangements with someone we hardly know?"

She shrugs. "I just thought it might be useful. You've never a good word to say about that financial adviser of yours. And Irving's doing alright, isn't he? Sailing the world in the lap of luxury. Whatever he's doing with his money, we could all use a bit!"

We fall silent until her drink arrives. Mariano pauses to remove a spent lime wedge and adjust the angle of the nuts.

"All I'm thinking is, it might be nice for you to get to know each other."

"Mother—"

"He's good company, being so well travelled."

"If you think I—"

"And he's on his own, Fenella! Like you!"

This is too much. "Mother, how many times have I told you, I do not need your input in my private life?"

"I don't know anything about your private life!" she huffs. "I just assume there might, possibly, be room for someone else. Seeing as you never say you're courting..."

That word!

It has stalked me since I was twelve years old. First, as something shameful and forbidden, for which I was too young. Then as something I might, then really ought to be considering... How I long for the day when I can make an announcement that stops Mother's prying for good! I like to think it may not be too far off...

"You're very grouchy, Fenella. Did you have lunch?"

"Yes," I lie. "A ham sandwich."

The rum in my drink has gone straight to my head, not helped by an empty stomach. I feel guilty for snapping. She is only doing what mothers do.

She senses it and steers clear. "We came back on board for ours. Well, when I saw the prices in that cafe. I liked his *Solski*-whatsit doughnut. But it seemed criminal, forking out for pizza or those funny herrings when it's all free on here." Mother peers into her orange and lemonade. "Not that Irving didn't offer to pay..."

I fire her a look. But her attention is focused firmly out on deck.

Chapter 12

Irving gives us his gentlemanly wave as we take our seats in the Koh-i-Noor. During dinner I am careful to avoid his eye, in case it encourages more interaction. Mother looks subdued, her gaze firmly on her plate.

After cocktails we took the scooter to the room so she could switch to her chair for the evening. The restaurant is less spacious than the bar, and I had visions of her careering into chair-backs, like a child taking a pedal car into church. It is now stowed none-too-snugly in our hanging space. A nuisance, if we are keeping it for the week, but worth it.

We stick to our customary glass of wine. Only I have pudding, and by the end of the meal a pall has descended. As I wheel Mother across the Atrium's mosaic floor, something in the set of her shoulders, her grey hair almost white at the scalp, makes me feel cruel.

"Do you fancy the show tonight, Mother?"

The ship's impressive theatre is rotating three revue-style productions over the week. So far neither *Broadway Bonanza* nor *Soul Train Sensation* has tempted us into the wheelchair spaces. *Hound Dog Heaven: A Tribute to the King* may be more her thing.

"Actually, I think I'll have an early night, Fenella. Don't let me stop you though..."

By the time I get her to bed I have missed curtain-up. I am not a fan of Elvis, but I am curious to see the auditorium if only to report back to Avril. My best friend, a dyed-in-the-wool theatre buff, has warned me not to expect much from the productions; a step down on the touring shows at my local theatre, and a small step up on holiday-camp vaudeville.

Loitering outside, the pound of hoofing and the opening chords of *Blue Suede Shoes* seep through the padded doors. The interior, shown in the brochure as crimson-carpeted including the walls, can wait for another night. It is half-past eight, and I am mulling another complimentary cocktail when I feel a hand on my shoulder.

"The stage door's on Deck Three if you're queuing for autographs," says Irving Jessop with a twinkle. His tie is still immaculately knotted. Most of the male diners had loosened theirs by the end of the meal.

"Oh, I don't think it's really me. I prefer straight theatre as a rule. We get very good Ibsen in London."

I am grandstanding and have no idea where that came from. Avril and I once toiled through Act One of *The Master Builder*, got tipsy in the interval then sneaked out for tapas in lieu of Act Two.

"Okay. Then the *Diamond Sabre* dance troupe may not be for you. They do rather cater to the lowest common denominator. Talking of which, did you see the Gallery?"

He is gesturing to the glass doors across from yet another bar. An artist's easel stands inside, propped with a palette and two glistening, gouache-tipped brushes, as if the owner has stepped away for a change of smock. Whenever I pass here a leggy, efficient-looking girl with an iPad is on the threshold, ready to pounce. At first I was intrigued that the ship boasts a gallery, till I realised it was just a ruse to part passengers from their money, not a venue of merit. Keen to avoid non-essential expenditure, I have given it a wide berth.

"Come on," says Irving. "It's a hoot."

I am not sure I want to spend my hour of freedom like this, but can think of no reason to decline. The activity programme thins out in the evening when most passengers are happy to amuse themselves. Tonight's highlights include a showing of *Ghost* at the on-deck cinematorium, with knee-rugs and hot chocolate. Then there is the nightly LGBT meet-up ('Unhosted') in the Library Bar, and an opaque-sounding gathering that, according to Irving, is the code name for an AA meeting. A trot round the exhibition feels the least dismaying option.

He holds open the gallery door that is, for once, unwomanned.

"I'd be interested to hear your professional opinion," he says, still twinkling.

That he is amused puts me on my guard, but I soon see why... Without exception the work is atrocious. I recognise none of the artists, which this time is not down to gaps in my knowledge. The perpetrators of such cloying, greetings-card style creations are unlikely to be known by anyone except their mother. Moulded gilt frames are everywhere, and each cluster of canvasses is professionally hung and flatteringly lit. Yet, like the chocolate mousse I've learned to bypass on the Blue Moon Court buffet, appearances belie any real substance.

A set of seascapes look like they were daubed by an eight-year-old. Floral still-lifes are everywhere, as is, inexplicably, the Grand Canyon. There are at least three renditions—possibly four, though the title, *Pudenda, or Paradise*, suggests not... I am perusing this when the door-girl appears. But instead of launching into her spiel, she hands us both a glass of something sparkling with an exhausted smile and teeters back to her desk. The empty flutes she scoops up along the way suggest a recently disbanded soirée.

Still she says nothing as we pass her perch, where she upends the last of a bottle into her own glass. On top of everything I have drunk this evening, the bubbles go straight to my head... Something about this girl—serene and immaculate, getting resolutely sloshed at the end of a mind-numbing day—is making my mouth twitch.

Rounding another display, the work of a lady from Pennsylvania tips me over the edge. Irving, two paces behind, takes a second to cotton on. I can barely stifle a gale of laughter as he too sees the funny side... It is a marine epic: on a beach, a small boy is building a sandcastle while out to sea foaming waves coalesce in the form of a gigantic pup, looming from the deep. This colossal canine Neptune looks set to trigger Sandcastle Boy into a frenzy as soon as he looks up.

This art is not naive, it is plain hideous. I try to control myself long enough to examine the other two paintings in the group. One features cloud-form chihuahuas, the other sand dunes, whipped up by a tornado into a troupe of dancing palominos. The label on each reads a mouth-drying $8,999.

Irving is first to get his snigger in check. "We really shouldn't, beauty being in the eye of the beholder and all. I guess they convey a certain..."

"Nerve?"

"I was gonna say confidence, but yes. Let me tell you, this is pretty typical of the stuff you find in cruise ship art galleries. They mostly all have one."

"Really? Good grief." My voice drops to a whisper. "I could do better myself. As a curator, I mean. I can't paint for toffee."

We move on to the final display: geometric hedgerows, through which Pierrot-heads pop macabrely at intervals. He peers at another label.

"They certainly add a premium for showing them here. Guess they think people are more likely to blow their bucks on an investment while they're living the dream!"

"You think these are investment pieces?"

"Nope, I don't, but then I wouldn't buy 'em. It's all kidology. Charge enough for stuff and someone's gonna think it's worth it."

I wonder if he is giving me a cue. Livid as I am at Mother for bringing up my portfolio, I wouldn't mind picking his brains. If Irving plays the investment game, he is surely winning.

"I don't think I'd trust my own taste. I mean, I know a bit about art, obviously. But I've been in it long enough to know people ascribe quality to the oddest things. You're talking to the woman who organised an exhibition of Haitian owl-pellet jewellery..."

Irving knocks my elbow and I return the nudge. This is the most relaxed I have felt all week. Mother is easy company, but she's still Mother at the end of the day.

"Doesn't matter what you got an eye for," he says, "long as you got it for something. When I gave up my cardiology practice, I purchased one or two artworks that turned out not to be the wisest move. Now I leave the investment decisions to my broker... You dabble in the stock market too, right?"

I laugh self-consciously. "In a small way. Like you, I leave it to the professionals." I have no wish to expose my hazy grasp of my own portfolio to someone rich enough to sail the world in luxury.

We are nearly back at the doors. There's one last canvas to cast an eye over, by someone who at least has more technique than the others. It portrays a middle-aged couple in chain-store leisurewear. Compositionally, it could be an homage to *American Gothic*: careworn woman on one side, stern-looking man on the other. But behind them, instead of a clapboard homestead there's a retail superstore; and the man's hand clutches not a pitch fork but a plastic yard brush. The price tag around the brush head, and the polythene carrier bags cutting into his wife's track-suited elbow, seem to make sense of the title: *The Seven Dollar Itch*.

It reminds me of a Beryl Cook, in the way it presents the mundane as ineffably heroic. My own taste is fairly classic. Modern art has its place, though much of what qualifies nowadays is a church too broad for me... Take this acrylic. It has its merits, but such glorification of the banal feels out of place in a gallery. An opinion I recognise for what it is: snobbishness. Were this a pair of eighteenth-century labourers, or a cloche-hatted waif crawling home from her shift at the munitions factory, I wouldn't question it. But because it's contemporary it opens up the baggage of my prejudice—and apparently my xenophobia.

"Hot darn—Mom and Pop are a-shopping' at the mawl!"

My attempt at a Southern drawl springs out of nowhere. The booze has loosened my tongue as well as my manners... One can be too relaxed in somebody's company, and this is overstepping the mark.

"Shades of Grant Wood, for sure," says Irving, appearing not to notice. "Another artist unafraid to reveal their influences."

My mind casts around for something safe. It alights on the man in the painting, who reminds me of the flatulent oaf in the church car park. Not a story I am about to share. And yet—

"Do you ever find yourself wondering what keeps couples together?" I ask. "I mean, a portrait is a snapshot, nothing more... But for me, here the artist is saying, 'Look at these two— this is their life.' Trapped in a tedious relationship, reduced to shopping for mundanities in matching leisure suits!" A snort of laughter escapes me with a shudder. "I can't think of anything worse, can you?"

Chapter 13

These words prey on my mind for the next day and beyond.

Nag, the way it does when you know you let your standards slip. Partly my insensitivity to a man who has lost his wife; more sheer boorishness, for belittling the kind of relationship I aspire to more than anyone. I made myself look bitter in front of Irving, and it hurts.

I have begun to anticipate the end of the holiday. Too much freedom can be as suffocating as none, and the pressure to enjoy oneself wearing. Six days away from home feels like a fortnight, and even this behemoth of a ship has started to feel claustrophobic. Not literally, with its bounteous fresh air and endless marine horizons. But socially, inside the tight bubble of obligation where I find myself with Mother and Mr Jessop. All unspoken, of course.

I am equally vexed by the fact it bothers me at all. Wealthy or not, Mr Jessop is hardly a catch. All the men I have ever found alluring broadly kept pace with my age. There is not a hint of frisson between us, and if Mother thinks otherwise that's her stifled imagination. Or vicariousness—I suspect she is warming to Mr Jessop herself... What kind of widow she would be, merry or otherwise, if her illness didn't plague her is hard to say. At nearly eighty, she shows no interest in the opposite sex: which, after forty years with my father, makes perfect sense. Add ten years a widow, and Bill and any other men in her circle are convenient acolytes, nothing more.

Mother married relatively late with me onboard, which doesn't suggest the most considered, or even voluntary of unions. Photographs of her pre-marriage show a vivacious young woman, verging on the glam: half a head taller than her friends, inclined to mini dresses and cheeky displays of décolletage when away from Granny's reproving eye. Despite MS and the intervening years, she is discernibly the same woman, perhaps more now than she has been for decades... Living with Father seemed to suck her dry of *joie de vivre*—a state of affairs which paradoxically showed signs of reversing in the last three years of his life, when her diagnosis manifested in fumbled plates and stumbles on the stairs. Father, an inveterate tutter, curbed his exasperation and became protective, almost affectionate towards her, in ways I had never seen. If anything, it was when they were happiest. But since then, I've never suspected Mother of hankering for another male presence beyond the sort she can send to Sainsbury's.

It transpires my misgivings about Irving may be shared. The next day's port is Flåm, a chocolate-box village at the end of mighty Sognefjord. Mother and I disembark and pass the day without sighting him; no surprise, given the mustering hordes. She doesn't mention Irving either, as her scooter cruises the steeply sloping pavements. The views down the valley are as majestic as ever. Sognefjord, longest and deepest of them all, is a name I remember from studying North Sea fisheries for Geography O-level. Or was it glaciation?

Flåm meanwhile is famed for its mountain railway, which meanders over ravines and waterfalls. According to the video playing on the cable channel during Mother's bathroom hour, it offers fairy-tale views of snowy plains in winter, reduced to drifts dotted about like discarded tissues in summer. The train ride looks appealing; there is a hint of the Von Trapps escaping the Nazis about the green carriages, like mobile munitions boxes. But when I try to book at the desk in the ship's plaza, the last tickets have gone. Mother and I settle for a stroll up the hillside, which the gradient quickly turns into a hike, making us ever-more grateful for the gift from our thoughtful friend.

An hour later, the brow of this particular hill leads into a park, where the trail loops through weatherproof artworks. We stop for a breather beside what looks like the silver death mask of a wild boar, hovering spectrally against a backdrop of moss. Across the path is an installation of nature's own: a tree stump, being devoured by toadstools like a flock of dun-coloured butterflies. Once the only other walkers amble round the bend, we are alone in the eerie glade. I lean on Mother's handlebars as our eyes are drawn to the panorama and the ship berthed far below. The upper decks are swathed in wisps of low cloud like frozen smoke. 'Ethereal' doesn't do it justice.

"You forget there are places like this, don't you?" says Mother. "When you're busy with your own life..."

She is not given to philosophising but I know what she means.

"True. In fact, this week has made me think of all the other places I've meant to go and never have. Tokyo, San Francisco. The Galapagos with the giant tortoises."

I stop; am I being heartless again? I have plenty more travelling years ahead of me...

Mother lets it go. "I suppose you have to take comfort in the fact that it *is* here—all the time, green and peaceful, doing its business. We can always come back, can't we? It's not going anywhere..." She slips a tissue from her pannier. "And they look after things, don't they, the Norwegians? A view like this in Surrey, the Council would build flats on it!"

I reach for the hand that isn't dabbing her eyes. I've forgotten how much this week means to her. Sometimes Mother's optimism puts me to shame.

We are in no rush to get home.

St Swithun's Cathedral looks doomily Gothic as we approach. High arched windows stare blankly from beneath the towers' verdigris eyebrows. A border of blood-red roses, poking out like a tongue, completes the semblance of a face. I have an urge to look out for a postcard to send Martin, though it won't turn up until long after I'm home. But I've never sent one to a housemate before, and the politics of addressing it to him-only are insurmountable. I should have bought those socks instead.

As I stride and Mother trundles, Irving is waiting at the double doors. He is in an overcoat, sensible given the moisture-laden air. His wardrobe options for every clime suggest a highly organised person.

This rendezvous is Mother's doing. There was no sign of him yesterday, even at dinner. I finally mentioned him at breakfast, saying it would be a pity not to see him before we disembark, the day after tomorrow.

I suggest we keep our eyes peeled in Stavanger, just as Mother pulls a slip of paper from her bag.

"Room 691," she reads aloud. "Just as well one of us pays attention..."

I left the phone call to her, and here we were. The prospect made me nervous, but now this feels like the right thing to do. Irving looks as relaxed as ever.

"So, what do you think of August in Norway's tropical south?" he asks with a wink. Mother shudders on cue. "I'm serious—this city has the most northerly tropical gardens in the world. They even grow cacti. Worth a look around, though I doubt we'll have time today."

The temperature inside the grey cathedral is positively balmy. It is top of Irving's list of Stavanger's must-sees, followed by the Fish Canning and Petroleum Museums, neither of which appeals to me. But St Swithun's has its merits. The Scandinavian simplicity of the church in Olden is here too, in the ranks of blond-wood chairs laid out in place of pews. The stained-glass windows are magnificent; boiled-sweet panes, muted on one wall, iridescent on the other where the chilly sunlight works its magic. The pulpit is another splash of colour, the antithesis of Lutheran austerity. Its conical *abat-voix* and the booth itself are festooned with Biblical carvings—deathly white doll-like figures in robes of ochre, red and blue. It reminds me of the

Thai temple that stands incongruously down a leafy avenue in Wimbledon village. Not the building itself, but the impromptu offerings scattered in its grounds: random ornaments and children's action figures, clustered on rocks and suspended from tree branches. Expressions of devotion that feel more like an installation by the Chapman Brothers.

"You're thinking *Toy Story*, right?" says Irving beside me.

I smile noncommittally.

"Matter of fact, it's the work of a Scotsman by the name of Smith, way back in the 1650s. Reputedly, the finest example of Baroque decoration in Scandinavia."

We are examining a larger carving of Jesus wrestling a lion when I notice Mother. She has ground to a halt at the step up to the choir stalls, and her three-point turn risks pranging an upright piano.

"Is my back wheel snagging on the carpet, Fenella?" she calls over her shoulder.

Irving and I leap to assist. "Hang on, Mother—"

I keep a foot on the edge of the crimson runner as he coaxes her fingers from the controls.

"That's the way," he says soothingly, manoeuvring the scooter back, then forward then back again, like a rancher cajoling a heifer into a pen.

"Thank you, Irving," says Mother when her own fingers are back on the handlebars. Then she is off down the nave at a confident pace, ignoring the stares of the half-dozen sitters with arms crossed or fiddling with their phone cameras. Irving smiles wryly.

"I think we're done here," I say.

Chapter 14

He is treating us to lunch and won't hear a word against it.

"I know a great little place in the Old Port. It was a favourite of Francine's."

"Bit early to eat though, Irving?" says Mother. "I got them to do me an egg and bacon bap for breakfast. It's still going down." I roll my eyes. "The ship doesn't run to HP Sauce, but I've acquired quite a taste for their ketchup..."

We are heading back the way we came until Irving indicates left.

"I hear you, Lillian. That's why I thought we'd take a little detour first..."

One more street and we are in what looks like a Conservation Area: identical white clapboard houses with red slate roofs and uniformly neat front gardens. The street lamps look Dickensian, the litter bins like they get a daily jet-wash. The pavements are narrow, which means Mother is riding on the dreaded cobbles, but even these are rendered smooth by her scooter's suspension. We pause at a plaque; the area is a remnant of Stavanger's eighteenth-century architecture prior to remodelling after the Second World War. These quaint little buildings, once working class dwellings, are now in demand from culturally sensitive urbanites.

Further along, beneath a fluttering Norwegian flag, stands a memorial to the fallen of the War: a cast-iron watchman in a peaked cap, clutching binoculars. Either side a cannon is aimed squarely out to sea, give or take an intervening cottage. With so few people about, the street feels like a film set. The lone extra a woman with a watering can, dousing fuchsias in a hanging basket.

"I could live here, it's so quiet," says Mother, taking in the pristine lawns and china figurines peeping from window sills.

"It's like an English village without the dog mess." At this she takes a corner abruptly, zooming up a side street as something catches her eye. I frown as I watch her go.

"I wouldn't worry," says Irving. "All the streets lead back to this one. Long as we stay in the Old Port we're never far from home. Look…"

Over the roofs of adjoining cottages an arc of *Diamond Sabre's* hull rises like a peering eye. The notion that it is watching us makes this pristine backwater feel more like Toytown than ever.

"You've made Mother's holiday with that scooter," I say. Right on cue she reappears from the next side road, negotiating a postbox. "Mine too, when I think of all the pushing you've saved me. It'll be a wrench when we get home. I bet she'll buy one in a month."

Irving shrugs. "I hope I didn't force the reality of her situation. It's gotta be her decision."

There is a junction a hundred metres ahead, a busier road harried by twenty-first century traffic. It seems sensible to walk that far then turn back.

"And how about you," I ask, glancing over the rooftops to where the ship's top-tier balconies have a grandstand view. "Not going home anytime soon? Boston, I mean?"

He shakes his head. "Ship turns round in Southampton, then I'm off again day after that. Capri-Sorrento-Amalfi Coast, if I remember right. Then I drop in on an old friend who retired to Sicily. After that, I believe I'm picking up a Cunard tour to Perth, Australia. Via West Africa and the Cape of Good Hope."

"Wow, Irving. You have an amazing life."

I don't mean to sound jealous. Only part of me is. I suppose everyone handles grief in their own way, and this is his. Privileged obviously, but practical if the alternative is as expensive as he says.

"Oh, I know I'm lucky. I also know I've been luckier… Sometimes I feel like a ghost, haunting all these beautiful places, looking for the wonderful times I had with my wife..." He catches my expression and smiles. "Don't pity me. No need."

Mother has done a loop at the top of the street. She zips out from the next turning, full of the joys.

"Lovely wisteria up there, Fenella! I always wanted one of those trained over the front of my house, Irving, but my husband wouldn't hear of it. Said they ate the mortar." When she is parallel to us she slows to a walking pace. "He could be a pain like that."

"Well," says Irving, "I know an Englishman's home is his castle, so I'm sure that goes for an Englishwoman too. Couldn't you plant one now?"

"Perhaps I will. Get Bill onto it... I told you about him, didn't I?"

"Your neighbour, right?"

She nods. "He's on his own. I hate to see him with nothing to do."

I give Irving a look. "Which isn't often, is it, Mother? You make sure of that."

Irving moves the conversation on. "So, what are you ladies looking forward to about getting home? I've only been to London in winter, but I guess it's leafy and beautiful in August?"

"Fenella lives in London. Just," corrects Mother. "I live in Oxted, which is what we call the Home Counties. But yes, August can be very nice, hose-pipe bans permitting... I'm looking forward to seeing my garden. Bill and Kath are keeping an eye on it for me." She glances my way; "All part of my slave-labour programme... Have I told you about Kath, Irving? She's my friend who lives the other way. Then I'll have my shows to catch-up on with the Sky box. I like my quizzes and my soaps... How about you, Fenella?"

She is not letting me escape. But what I am looking forward to—*all* I can honestly say I am looking forward to, since neither work nor anyone else has crossed my mind in six days—is seeing Martin. And even that is laced with trepidation... I have managed not to over-think him. This week has been a welcome break from my feelings, and the minefield that is falling for someone in my situation... One last day at sea, then it's back to the world of Oyster cards and shared bills. Of stray socks and wrangles over the vegetable crisper, where any passage to a happy outcome is fraught with potential embarrassment. I am about to make up something when Irving intervenes again:

"Now, who's ready to eat?"

We are at the end of the lane.

"The little place I know is five minutes away." He points to the nearest turn towards the sea. "It's called Gjøk. That's the Norwegian for cuckoo..."

As we amble on I lag behind, while he regales Mother with stories of Stavanger's resistance to the Nazis. Irving knows so much about everything and has a knack for tailoring the conversation to his listener. Mother is animated in his company, in a way I have rarely seen her with Bill or Kath. Or me.

Poor Mother. She is going to miss him.

Chapter 15

Sunday afternoon.

As I push open the front door of No. 4, The Ridge it is hard to tell if anyone's home. Weekend comings and goings mean a certain laxness of the house rule re turning the mortice lock. Not a slackening I allow myself, but one I have learned to live with. Now, walking into the familiar habitat of our front hall (the smell of indeterminate cooking, junk mail no one has thought to recycle) breaks the seal on a life I briefly left.

I lug my suitcase upstairs. My room shows no signs of trespass: the sash of my floral dressing gown is draped over the door knob at the exact angle I left it. Miraculously, the begonia on the sill is still in flower despite a reproachful tutu of wilted foliage. I have no affinity for pot plants, and asked no one to water it in case they took it as permission to snoop. Paranoia, possibly; overestimation of others' interest in me, almost definitely—but only what I would have done.

I tip a tooth mug of water over the crusted soil till it seeps incontinently into the saucer. There was little conversation on the drive from Southampton. Mother was subdued from the moment she woke in our stateroom for the final time. The palaver of packing and negotiating corridors, thick with luggage carts, magnified her gloom. Last night, as we said our goodbyes to Irving Jessop over a farewell cocktail in Overtures, I forgot to ask what to do with the scooter. Cue Marco to the rescue. Our cheery butler had been the soul of helpfulness all week, and never more than when he spied the hefty tip on the table. He was fingering the scooter's controls as he waved us off down the corridor, promising to return it to stores when the coast was clear.

On the journey home, Bill's Renault sped past towns and business parks, and a service station running the same offer on chicken nuggets as eight days before. When the boxy outskirts of Oxted came into view, I offered to do the decent thing:

"You can drop me at the station, Bill. There's a train every twenty minutes on Sunday."

He leapt at the idea, no doubt relishing the prospect of settling Mother into the bungalow unimpeded. She made a half-hearted protest—suggested I "stop for a cuppa, and a bite of whatever Kath's got in"—but I declined, to relief all round. There was an awkward goodbye, less marked than the feat of a ruction-free week of mother/daughter confinement warranted. As I sidled off the back seat, I squeezed her shoulder.

"Thank you, Mother. It's been a lovely trip. Speak soon, yes?"

Never one for elaborate leave-taking, she nodded through the window as Bill swung my case onto the pavement. He slammed the boot and got back behind the wheel without a word. This time, as the car pulled away, I was the one watching for a wave that never came.

In the rigmarole of disembarkation, any thought of lunch had gone AWOL. So, against my principles, I bought a pasty at Clapham Junction as I waited for my connection. Sitting on the platform I ate it from the bag, Samsonite at my knees like an obedient guide dog... A culture shock, this—the switch from the ship's clientele to the multicultural hubbub of the station. I manoeuvred my suitcase closer as a man strolled about in front of me before sitting down. He was wearing a mock sheepskin jacket that looked out of place in August. His saggy vest beneath revealed a chest tattoo: a tracery of script that read for all the world as *Only God Can Fudge Me*.

By the time I get home, load the machine with anything Marco hasn't laundered and make a second cup of tea, it is nearly six. I can't decide if I am still hungry, my appetite discombobulated by a ship/automobile/train combination as befuddling as jet lag.

Martin will be back later. Sunday is his day for the children. I consider throwing together something quick and delicious, half of which I can leave in case he's peckish... Is it my imagination, or does the mere prospect make my heart beat faster? Now I am here I can't wait for him to walk in. Perhaps that means it is time—today, tonight—I made my feelings plain! Subtlety gets you nowhere in this life, and it could be just the two of us if Ethan and Georgie are out enjoying their last vestiges of weekend freedom...

But the idea of cooking from scratch is exhausting. I am about to investigate my shelf when I hear a bedroom door open. My radar failed to detect life upstairs, but after a loud visit to the bathroom a rumpled Ethan plods into the kitchen.

"Hey, Fen!" he yawns. "How was your hol? Didn't hear you come in."

He tends to fall asleep at unlikely times of the weekend, a result of his nocturnal gaming habit. No danger of a hug I note, as he takes a bowl (singular) off the draining board and rattles in a helping of Mini-Shredded Wheats... He also eats cereal at all times of day, and loafs about in what I'd consider bed-wear though may in fact be a nod to his Japanese heritage.

"It was lovely, thanks."

I have yet to distil the cruise experience into the single-sentence my return to the office will require.

"Awesome," he says, disappearing into the living room.

Two minutes later I follow, with a mug and three almond-buttered rice cakes.

"Everything alright here?" I ask, kicking my feet up on the settee.

Ethan places his phone on the chair-arm, an acknowledgment that real-world interaction is unavoidable.

"Yeah, cool. So how was it? How was Sweden?"

I correct him and give him top-line. Pretend my own phone is upstairs when he tries to sound keen to see photos. His claim to envy Mother and me "yomping around the fjords in your hiking boots!" says he has never registered a single word I said about her. I let it go, more interested in hearing about here, and careful to ask after Georgie first.

"Not seen much of her, tell the truth. She was here yesterday, in and out. With that bloke she's seeing. Nice guy, Lorenzo."

An assessment open to interpretation now the cards of Ethan's sexuality are on the table... One advantage of sharing a house with a heterosexual male is that you are unlikely to be drawn into assessing the merits of other men. Some women revel in a gay friend, to talk shoes and soap operas with; someone they can count on, up to a point, for a masculine perspective. I have never wanted this.

"And how's Martin?" I ask placidly.

I wish Ethan would go back to his phone instead of looking at me like that... He is considering something.

"Yep, good... Oh yeah, we were well glad of him last week! The upstairs loo did that thing again—you know, when the cistern churns away for hours? Me and George couldn't remember what to do, and the overflow was squirting all over the kitchen roof. Then Martin came home and got the lid off." He mimes pressing down. "All to do with the ballcock!"

"Yes," I say, aware it is. Then, as if the thought just occurred, "Has he had any more overnight guests?"

It was meant to sound innocent, indulgent... Playing back my words in the pause that follows, they sound prying and possibly suggestive. But Ethan was here when the children stayed over; he will understand. Yet his crinkle-eyed response suggests something else.

"Well—not his kids, no."

He is smiling. Very nearly simpering, something I have never noticed before. I feel my own expression ossify, and in the silence that follows the image of the cartoon coyote pops into my head: shut in a deep freeze by that beeping bird, till its muzzle snaps off and shatters on the floor... I manage an encouraging look, but Ethan just shrugs.

"Can't tell you much really. Georgie saw her, I only heard them. In the bathroom."

Her? Them? *Together?*

"Tuesday morning, or maybe Wednesday. Dunno what time they got in, but they made a right old rumpus according to George. Of course she's got the adjoining wall..."

His voice tails off. I realise I am nodding furiously and stop. Am about to jab at the TV remote, when a three-note fanfare signals the end of my laundry cycle.

In the kitchen, my mind is on Fast Spin as I yank the clothes from the drum. I manage to fold everything, pile it on the worktop and erect the ironing board, all without noticing...

What floozy has Martin taken up with the moment I'm off the scene?

And what does it say that he's leapt straight into bed when he's meant to be focused on bringing his marriage to a painless conclusion? Not to mention the children! Didn't he say they were his top priority? Divorce can wreak havoc when parents pull the rug of all they know from under their vulnerable offspring!

I flick on the iron... *Is it my fault?*

Should I have made a move when I could? Our boozy evenings—laughing at the trials of life, making ribald observations re communal living—were they my chance and I missed it?

Making the first move has never come naturally to me, but that's no excuse... *I am forty-nine years old!* A shrinking violet shrivels faster than a neglected begonia!

Or is this house to blame? Am I too comfortable here, cocooned in my own little world and fooled into thinking that I set the pace? That Martin and I are two of a kind, tethered to No. 4, The Ridge by invisible bungees drawing us back, night after night?

I flick a dab of spittle at the footplate, snatch crumpled culottes from the basket, and iron.

If only we'd met somewhere else!

A works do, say. Quaffing cava, at a private view of second-string works by a major artist, or major works by a second-string artist... Would I have been so lackadaisical then? Oh, I know how it works... I've never done it myself, but I have observed others, zeroing in on whomever they fancy over the canapés. One woman in particular, long since departed, had a thing for the arts correspondent on one of the Sundays. According to office folklore, as everyone else teetered off with their goody bags she offered to show him a shortcut to the station via the canteen exit... Her underwear and a hummus-stained catalogue of *Velázquez: The Italian Years* turned up in the kitchen next morning.

Then again, didn't Martin say he had a wild streak? Imply he'd played the field between marriages? I heard it and dismissed it, because it didn't fit the narrative I built for him. Was that him giving me the green light all along?

Unable to contain my frustration, I crash through the third of four tee shirts, slamming down the iron between turns of the garment... Moving onto pedal pushers, trickily ruched at the calf, I whip out the spray gun from under the sink and blast creases vindictively.

"Fen, welcome home!"

Hands squeezing my shoulders make me yelp. I nearly drop the iron.

"Sorry," says Georgie. "Didn't you hear me come in? Oh look, typical you—back five minutes and done your washing already!"

Her head is still shaking as she takes half a watermelon from the fridge. "Go on, I'm all ears. How were the pensioners?"

Sitting at the breakfast bar in her leather jacket, Georgie gives the impression of listening as I zip reluctantly through my potted travelogue. Spooning out slivers of lucent flesh like eating a giant boiled egg, she turns the spoon in her mouth in a way I would have been spanked for as a child.

"And your mum had a good time, yeah? Bet you've got biceps like a boxer now, pushing her up those hills!"

I am weary of my own stories already, and not about to mention Irving Jessop after the pensioners comment.

"So," she says, side-eyeing, "heard about Martin?"

I return to the pedal pushers. "Ethan said he had a visitor. Is that what you mean?"

Georgie nods, tweezing a pip from her tongue with thumb and forefinger. "Fast worker or what? I only heard them chat over breakfast, but it sounds like he's known her a while."

Somehow my hands keep moving. I fold the impeccably pressed garment and pick another from the basket. *A while?*

"I mean, I guess you can't blame him, wanting to let off steam after the runaround he's had from his missus. More shenanigans from her solicitor, apparently…"

Now I feel piqued, on top of everything else. It never occurred to me Georgie and Martin were on such terms, yet they have clearly had fine chats in my absence… I thought I was his confidante, and she and Ethan merely—

"Anyway, you'll meet her if you're in tomorrow. He's staying out tonight after the kids, but they're here on Monday cos she wants to see something at the Odeon." Slipping off her stool, Georgie slides her melon carcass back in the fridge. "Not sure what. *Fast & Furious Number*-whatever's on. Could be that." She nudges me on the way out with a leathery elbow. "Something loud with plenty of banging. Highly appropriate!"

Chapter 16

It feels like I have been away a month. The office is the same and yet different.

Derek has instigated a move-around in my absence. No one has had the temerity to interfere with my desk, though it has been shunted lock, stock and keyboard wipes to a place by the window.

"He reckoned you'd like it," says Cheryl, emptying the shredder. "Nice view of the car park."

Typically there is no sign of our boss. On summer Mondays, Derek likes to diarise breakfast conclaves with his counterparts at other institutions. Their purpose is moot, and often cover for the drive up from Suffolk where he, his wife and the dachshund have a cottage.

"Morning, Fen. Nice holiday?" chimes Millie.

The department's two recent additions are sitting adjacent. Previously divided by a filing cabinet, their desks now butt up like the office-furnishing equivalent of Siamese twins. Before I can reply, Tash appears with two coffees. The girls are in instant conflab about whether she added sweeteners, before flipping to where Millie got her bamboo-and-rubber earrings. By the time Tash notices me, my holiday is forgotten.

The inbox on my laptop indicates eighty-eight unread emails. I also have four physical letters waiting to be opened, but the prospect of engaging with any of them is unbearable. I immerse myself in a clear-out of my drawers.

"Cup of tea for you," says Cheryl kindly, putting down the Lucian Freud mug that secretly turns my stomach.

I smile my thanks, which Derek's P.A. returns with a conspiratorial eye-roll towards Millie and Tash.

"Thick as thieves, those two. That Tash has got Derek round her little finger... Walked Hannibal in the park for him last week. Next thing you know, she's got a half-day to meet her sister at Heathrow. No leave form, nothing!"

Derek's dog is an occasional visitor to the office, usually when he thinks the beast is unwell. Hannibal spends the day under his master's desk like a sporadically ambient foot-warmer. He can be tempted to Dulwich Park at lunchtime to do the necessary, where he is also partial to a shared ice cream cone. I once made the mistake of walking him myself when Derek had a lunch. The wilful dachshund yanked at the leash and wrested it from my grasp entirely when he was charged by a pigeon. Hannibal made a break for the community vegetable garden; I had visions of hunting him down through the strawberry cloches. Luckily, he was retrieved by a man in wellies before he could do any damage. Safe to say, Hannibal went without his cornet.

Cheryl asks dutifully about my week off. It transpires she and her husband were once keen cruisers themselves.

"Only the booze sort," she laughs. "Back in the day. Well, rude not to wasn't it, at those prices? And plus my Eric loves his cheese..."

As the morning wears on I find it impossible to concentrate. A meeting has been slipped into my diary: the trustees of a foundation promoting the work of Micronesian artists. I find the relevant email, click the attachment and sigh... Today is not a day for canoe tapestries, indigenous or otherwise. I e-apologise and reschedule for next week.

The most pressing business on my desk are the proofs for the Escher exhibition. It opens in two weeks, and as ever printing publicity materials has gone down to the wire. The poster, A5 leaflet and catalogue-cover all feature the same image: a monochrome woodcut of dove-like birds, flying over Dutch polders. Except, as ever with Escher, it is not that straightforward. Grey patchwork fields below morph into birds above, forming a piebald flock flying in opposing directions: black into the sunrise, white into the night. His tessellation works, repeat patterns which on closer inspection are not so simple, form the backbone of the exhibition.

Something in the bottom corner of the woodcut catches my eye: a handful of tiny dwellings clustered around a cross-shaped church... Is it really only days since I was in Olden, admiring the ecclesiastical architecture, breathing air sullied only by a Yorkshireman's flatulence? On that day, a world away, my fantasies of Martin were a harmless diversion as Mother babbled on... Now this flock of birds pulling in opposite directions speaks exactly of how I feel. Look at my life and it is light one way, dark the other. All because I let my fantasies get out of hand.

I flick through the pile of glossy printouts. This is my last chance to spot printing errors. The sixty-four-page exhibition catalogue requires a good hour's concentration. Millie and Tash are sifting YouTube clips which I trust are work related. Giggling accompanies their note-taking, and the folio of Mapplethorpe portraits they turn to between clips. Derek has briefed them on next season's Queer Art Retrospective—a decision I will question if and when he appears.

A burst of Drum and Bass is the last straw. I look up from my proofs to where the pumping beats emanate: a pair of tiny speakers on Millie's desk.

"Spotify," says Tash, meeting my glare with the hint of a smile. "Derek says it's fine with him if it's fine with you..."

I say nothing. Just pick up my stack of proofs and walk out of the office.

Down two flights of stairs and I am in the East Chamber, a side room off the main viewing trail often missed by visitors ticking off the must-see pieces. The Picture Gallery is closed to the public on Mondays, so I won't be disturbed. At the centre is a spacious leather banquette like a giant's footstool. It is intended for observers wishing to pause and appreciate the surrounding bacchanals and crucifixions, and big enough to spread printouts three abreast.

I am fifteen pages through when my phone rings. The onscreen ID gives me a start. Fumbling the touchpad, I nearly cut him off.

"Martin…"

"Hello, stranger!" says his cheery voice. "'Scuse me calling you at work, Fen. You in the middle of one?"

"No, I—"

"How was your holiday? Sorry I wasn't in last night, you must be sick of giving edited highlights."

I swallow; the edited highlights I am avoiding are his. (What on earth does he want!)

"I won't keep you… Thing is, I've got a friend popping over this evening and I'm cooking a bit of dinner. Wondered if you fancy joining? Be no trouble, and after all the lovely meals you've made me…"

From the milieu of my thoughts I clutch a passing straw.

"How are Freya and Nathan? Well?"

"Yeah good, thanks… Oh, Freya got an A-star for her project on the Mona Lisa! She's dying to show you."

Is she! How nice to know I have my uses.

"Be nothing fancy. Just pasta and salad, I'm not in your league!"

I flinch, and realise I am clutching the brochure's centre spread hard enough to scrunch a corner. I try to keep the quaver from my voice:

"Georgie said you were going to the cinema? If it'll be very late, I think I'd rather—"

"Yeah, that was the plan. Turns out the film's finished… Look, if you're busy, no probs. Just thought I'd offer."

In the heartbeat I can decently wait to answer, I weigh up the merits: if Martin is seeing someone then I can't avoid her indefinitely. And I am curious, no denying it. In the way you feel drawn to test a newly sharpened knife against your thumb—Just to see...

It seems odd, him phoning me at all. Is this invitation his idea of good manners? Or does it reflect a sense of guilt, for taking up with some floozy he knows will cause me grief?

Alternatively... Is this him giving me a chance to stake my claim, before things advance too far? Has Martin realised he's dug himself into a hole, from which only the right woman can drag him free?

This glimmer of sensitivity makes me adore him even more!

"Sounds lovely," I say. "What time do we eat?"

Chapter 17

Monique. What's in a name like that?

I reach the station in time for the early train home. My carriage is packed to Tokyo-Metro capacity, requiring me to negotiate a rucksack with my bust... The girlfriend's name suggests she is French, or British with pretentious parents. But then young people re-invent themselves on a whim these days. I blame Simon Cowell.

Young people! You see, I've already decided Martin's new flame is some slip of a thing! Monique is as likely a mature woman, like myself. I scoff at my own insecurity for running in fear of youth. Take those girls at work; office juniors, yes, but already I sense the power shifting. The wide-eyed mice who crept in on Day One are now confident operators in sheer blouses... If that incident with the music weren't enough, Tash returned from her lunchtime sunshine with three buttons undone and shirt tails knotted above her pierced navel! I was going to comment (more so when the knot worked itself loose) but have learned to pick my battles... Having negotiated a lowering of the Spotify volume, her blouse swished like Bedouin tent flaps for the rest of the afternoon.

I can't remember what is on my shelf, but if there is an appropriate bottle of wine I've no time to chill it. I drop into Little Waitrose and pick up an adequate cava.

I am first home. Showering off the stickiness of commuter-dom, I run through my evening-wear options beneath the torrent. Settle on burnt orange cargo pants and a scoop-neck matelot top. Casual yet confident.

Fifteen minutes later, I am tidying the coffee table and wondering why (—What do I care if Martin's lady-friend thinks he lives in a tip!). In the kitchen, I unstack the dishwasher. Ethan is joining us for dinner, Georgie is not. I rinse a stubborn scurf of rice grains off a dinner plate to make settings for four.

As quarter past seven approaches I feel nauseous. I could have made an excuse, said I was working late, or invented an evening with Avril... Five minutes later, a key in the door makes me drop the serving spoon I am buffing and grip the worktop.

Just Ethan, sweaty in a baseball cap. He mumbles on his way upstairs.

When the front door goes again he is still in his room... Twelve minutes late I note, rearranging the frozen veg. I get off my haunches and slam the freezer, my best greeting-smile in place as they enter the kitchen. Martin has had a haircut. A bit severe, potentially remedial on a lesser man, but he can carry it off.

"Wotcha, Fen," he says, dumping a carrier bag of groceries by the bread bin. "Meet Monique!"

I take the proffered hand. It is manicured, complete with unlikely looking nails. The lines across the knuckles look tea-stained.

"*Woyyy!*" hoots Monique. "Cold fingers!"

I snatch back my hand and rub it on my cargos.

"Noice to meetcha finally! Mart says you been away on your hols—you best tell us all about it!"

The girl has the easy friendliness that often goes with Americans, Kiwis and in this case, Australians. Except 'girl' is wrong. She is probably late-thirties; two inches taller than me, and what Mother would call big-boned. Her shoulder-length fair hair is thick and well-conditioned, her mauve-ish blue eyes deep set, like a closing-eye doll.

"Before we start the traveller's tales, who's opening a bottle for chef?" asks Martin.

His single handclap implies imminent culinary labour, and he sets-to unpacking salad, spaghetti and a jar of ready-made pesto that confirms I should not expect fine dining. I am halfway to the fridge when Monique fishes a warm bottle of white from her holdall. Before I can suggest an alternative she is in the freezer drawers, rummaging for ice.

"Chardy okay for you, Fen?" she says, plucking stemmed glasses off the drainer. "'Scuse the ice, but you know what they say: *You can take the chick outta Queensland...!*"

It is poured before I can reply, ice cubes rupturing audibly on contact. She passes me a glass, sliding another across the worktop to Martin.

"Cheers, good to meet ya, Fen!"

We all chink.

After a swig, Monique says, "Actually, I might go freshen up. That okay, darl?"

A pudgy hand pats Martin's be-denimed backside on the way out, which I pretend not to see. The waft of perfume left behind conjures the girls at work. It is hot in here and getting hotter. I long to press the chilly sweat of the wine glass to my forehead. Martin, immersed in his prep, seems not to register we are alone.

"Anything I can—?"

"No-no," he says, gallantly pulling out a stool from the breakfast bar. "Take the weight off."

I would happily adjourn to the settee; let them resume their fondling over a scalding-hot pan... As I take a hefty sip, the acidic butteriness catches me off-guard. Chardonnay is low on my list of favoured grapes for being brash and obvious. Purging it from my department's hospitality menu was an action point of my first week in the job. My next words, I am slightly surprised to hear out loud:

"Well, Martin, you're a dark horse. I turn my back for five minutes and here you are with a new lady in tow!"

The wine is relaxing me; the words have no edge.

His cheeks puff amiably as he chops a pepper, one eye on the simmering pan. "You know what they say, Fen. Always the quiet ones!"

I nod, though if that were true I would be bedding half of London.

He wipes his hands on a tea towel. "Look, I know we haven't known each other long but I'll come clean. I was worried what you'd think."

"Me?"

"Well, everyone obviously, but... I mean, Christ, you know how much I've got on my plate."

The wine is also giving me a sense of detachment. It manifests as largesse;

"I can see it must be pressurising, yes. And I don't know the circumstances, obviously — no reason I should. But no one could blame you for letting off steam, Martin." I point to the roaring gas ring; "So to speak..."

He whips the lid off the pan and turns down the heat. Slides an entire pack of spaghetti diagonally into the water, then looks surprised when the lid won't fit. I locate a bowl for the peanuts he has opened and leave him to work it out.

"Look who I found!"

Monique is back with Ethan in tow. Literally, one hand around the cuff of his baggy top. His smile is awkward; our newcomer's touchy-feeliness has overstepped their acquaintance, a suspicion confirmed by what she does next.

"I won't actually," says Ethan. He burrows in the fridge for a juice, leaving Monique dangling her wine bottle over an empty glass.

"Ethan only drinks once in a while," I explain helpfully. "Got a bit more restraint than the rest of us!" I hold out mine for a top-up.

Monique, bemused but not embarrassed, tips in more than necessary.

"Hey, so I hope you didn't start your holiday confessions without me?"

She has the Australian way of giving every sentence a little kick at the end. Whether yen for affirmation or a verbal knee-jerk in fear of being met by silence, it grates on me. As it is, I have no wish to go into the detail of holidaying with a disabled parent, just to entertain a stranger. Then again, it is a way to stay in the spotlight...

"It was all very amenable, really. Lovely room, lots to do... It's the scale of the ship that hits you when you've not been on a cruise before. Like a floating resort, with all you need squirrelled away out of sight. The logistics are incredible when you think about it..."

"I was reading about this Russian oligarch," says Ethan at the sink. "He's building one with a race course, for real horses. And little submarines for underwater excursions!"

"Goodness," I say. "Well, I wouldn't want a balcony over the stables."

I am being serious, but Monique holds her nose and crows with laughter. The staccato outburst jolts Martin who is slicing radishes.

"Sorry, darl!" she says, leaning over to kiss his neck. "The only cruising I ever did was in the Whitsundays. Me and ten other seventeen-year-olds on a catamaran. Lucky if you could find a place to stow your bikini top!" She claws up a handful of nuts. "This one time, two of my mates were waterskiing off the back with a wakeboard and skipping rope—don't ask me what we were doing with a skipping rope! Anyhow, they're taking turns to kneel up on the board when Mikey snags his wrist in the rope, so when he tips over he can't let go... 'Course we're all laughing like drains and no one thinks to tell the Skip to slow down. Poor old Mikey. Got a broken wrist and a bellyful of the Coral Sea!"

Martin and Ethan chuckle at what sounds like a near-fatality. Monique remembers her manners and offers round the nuts, ending on the only other lady in the room.

"Sorry, Fen, I interrupted ya there. You were saying?"

I shake my head dismissively. "Actually, I was just thinking someone should set the table. Shall I, Martin?"

The dining area at the back of our open-plan living area overlooks the garden. Its six-setting table is more an occasional desk and resting place for goods in transit. Communal meals at No. 4, The Ridge have always been rare. My attempt to instigate Christmas dinner (crackers, party hats, small inter-course gifts) lasted a year, though I am contemplating a revival.

"Sure," says Martin. "We can eat in there if you like." He is focused on the pasta pan, bending strands as they succumb to the bubbling depths.

"Aw, d'ya think?" This is Monique. "Only we brought that movie, so I was thinking we'd sit round the telly? Eat off our laps?"

Helping herself to another slosh of wine she misses my expression.

"Who's for more Chardy?"

Chapter 18

"New Zealand?"

A thread of pasta uncoils from Monique's fork like an escaping lugworm.

"Norway," I say. "The original fjords, as it were."

Martin chuckles. His eyes flick between us, then go back to the TV.

"Uhhh," nods Monique. "Gotcha..."

Genuine or not, it is pointless responding to queries about my holiday while there is a film on. I often think how much more convivial this house would be without the tyranny of the television. By the time everyone has a tray and sits, Ethan has whizzed through the trailers and paused on the main feature. I didn't catch the title, but the thrust is clear from the opening scene: two men in balaclavas, attaching limpet mines to a Top Secret establishment somewhere snowy. No dialogue until the explosions subside... It is presumably new, though I feel I have seen it before, or at least been in the room when it was on.

I am in my usual armchair. The lovebirds are on the settee, hunched over bowls. Ethan is in the other chair, one eye on the film, the other on his phone. His fork spools and finds his mouth with only occasional mishaps. When Martin suggested eating together, this was not what I had in mind. I could have made my own better than this, and had I known it meant sitting through this film I'd have declined.

The plot lumbers on, through a snowplough chase and revelation that one balaclava is concealing a pouty, defiantly shorn woman. Ten minutes later I am in the kitchen, loading my bowl into the dishwasher. I am wondering whether I can sneak upstairs without looking rude when Monique appears with the rest of the crockery.

"Hey," she says. "Whatcha think of the movie?"

I smile, making noises not words.

"I know—bollocks, right? I told Mart they went to shit after number three. Would he listen?" Without asking she tops up our glasses from the fridge. "So what do you do, Fen? I bet he told me, but I've a mind like a sieve!"

I give her a cursory outline of my job at the Picture Gallery, not about to make the same mistake twice.

"And you?"

"Oh, I'm in production. Ad agency. That's how we met. I look after the design boys and girls. Make sure what goes out the door looks like the idea they sold in. But you'll know all about that if you're in marketing."

I nod. "How long have you been in London?"

"Four years, this time. I was here in the Noughties too, briefly. Had to head back home when my old lady got ill and Dad needed looking after." As she leans on the sink Monique glances through the window. "He's gone too now, bless him, so nothing much to pull me back."

I succumb to a flicker of sympathy as she snorts abruptly.

"I miss the old bugger, but I wouldn't want him in my back garden!"

I laugh politely. "Ah. I see you're acquainted with our fifth resident."

She raises an eyebrow. "First time I came round, Mart didn't think to mention it. Only clocked it from the bathroom window next morning. Bloody nearly gagged on me toothbrush!"

I wonder if she always travels so well prepared.

"Weird, isn't it," she muses. "How things turn out? I only took the gig at Brownlee Birkin cos they had a fire at my last place... When you're freelance, no work means no pay, so when the gig came up at B.B. I was on it like a cat on a kipper. Hooked up with Mart, second day there—he's probably told you... Eyes across a crowded production meeting and the rest is history. All cos some bozo dropped a match in the recycling!"

She offers to help as I stack the rest of the bowls in the dishwasher.

"I'll do it!" I snap. "Sorry, it's just these pasta bowls only wash if you put them on top." I gather myself. "So, do you like freelancing? I don't think I could handle the uncertainty."

Making conversation but also true. Even with my modest outgoings and a sizeable sum put away, I've never understood why anyone chooses precariousness over a steady income.

"Love it. All the rewards, none o' the bullshit. What's not to like? I been in the game too long to give a fuck for all the bloody egos this biz attracts. Used to be just the blokes but now it's the women too. I tell you, the only thing worse than a big swinging dick is a woman's brass balls swinging the other way! 'Scuse language—I get worse on Chardy..."

I follow her into the living area. She is coarse, yes, but there is not enough to Monique to truly dislike. That said, I am struggling to see what Martin sees in her. My impression of the advertising business suggests a world where the women are either funky-young-things doing the creative work, or sashaying-sophisticates wooing the clients, all Chanel suits and Jimmy Choos... But then his taste in women is a mystery. I have no idea what Martin's wife—*wives!*—are like. A little light Googling of the Social Services Department at Wandsworth Council revealed an egg-like outline where Trudie Edgar should be (still her maiden name; speaks volumes!). A rare instance when I regretted not having Facebook or Instagram, which the girls at work use religiously to slate the looks of anyone they don't know personally.

The truth is, Monique has me at sixes and sevens. On the one hand, I feel mildly heartened. If Martin finds her irresistible, then I do myself a disservice if I think I am out of his league.

On the other, I feel belittled: he has chosen a plain-speaking tart over me... But then, don't office environments generate their own microclimate, where drudgery and the thrill of subterfuge hatch the unlikeliest couplings? In that sense the odds were against me from the start: inevitably a man will seek escape somewhere dreary, rather than the secure, comforting world of home.

On screen, the blockbuster plays out in a hail of gunfire and bawled orders... When he moved in, I was delighted to discover Martin was a DVD man. My own Sony player has been an object of mirth for the younger element, Ethan and Georgie not possessing a single disc between them. Pre-cruise, he and I giggled over our reluctance to download, and I enjoyed our film nights despite his library's slant towards brainless thrills and spills.

This one is a case in point: a packing crate, blown open aboard a speeding truck, contains two Chinese corpses, one clutching a jewel of indeterminate price. A twist that elicits a satisfied nod from Ethan.

"Told you!" he gloats, meaning Martin. "If it was stuffed in the dead polar bear, why strangle the Eskimo?"

Martin grunts. Since the day I walked into this house, I have resisted the idea of a television in my room in case it turns me into a hermit. Barring documentaries in bed on my tablet, I prefer the collective viewing experience—but there is a limit. Right now, I would rather be catching up on my BBC Four Egyptology series. The presenter, Doctor Jake, has fronted numerous archaeological odysseys, all of which feature him traipsing through sandy climes before dropping to one knee in an earnest explanation to camera. He has a habit of winding up in an oasis, waterfall or lovingly excavated hammam, all of which require him to strip to his combat shorts. The trailer for this week's episode—a reconstruction of the burial chamber at Abu Simbel—features shirtless hod-carrying. Perfect duvet viewing for my weekend.

The film grinds on. None of four near-apocalyptic explosions signal the climax. If the remote were in reach I would check how long is left... The occupants of the settee, visible in my peripheral vision, engage in none of the contortions favoured by Georgie and her pseudo-Italian squeeze. Martin's hand holds Monique's chastely on his knee. Now and again her head lolls onto his shoulder, but in search of a place to rest not a neck to nibble.

I catch myself sighing, for the forensic way I observe this behaviour. Three decades of only rarely interrupted celibacy have taught me a sense of detachment. I have learned much from watching people make love (in the Regency sense); on stage, on screen and in the real world, filing away tips for when it is my turn. It is a hobby of sorts. I am like one of those diehards of the football terrace, who mentally catalogues dribbling techniques and shooting angles... The difference between me and those beer-bellied windbags is that I still intend to put my knowledge into practice.

One day.

Titles!

Music, credits—it's all over. I have no idea what happened. Though the woman with the brutal hair and lips like a boxer's ear survived to the end, loping off into the sunset in a portrait of female empowerment.

"Awesome!" says Ethan already at his phone. "Says here they're filming number eight, on location in—" he frowns; "Oo-agger-doo-goo, wherever that is." With this his mobile disappears. He yawns and rises in the armchair till his spine clicks. "Right, I'm turning in..."

I join the chorus of "Night, Ethan!", surprised to see it is past eleven o'clock; late for a school night. Monique picks up her sandals; Martin ejects the disc from my machine. Keen as I am to get to bed, I have no desire to be in earshot of any bathroom high jinks. I pave the way for staying up a little longer by saying, "No sign of Georgie yet."

"Oh," says Martin, "she won't be back. Said she's staying at Lorenzo's."

I watch him manoeuvre a yawning Monique affectionately towards the door; a parent/child role-play I have noted underpins so many lovers' games. The football fan comparison is still on my mind as, from halfway upstairs, Monique's voice says:

"So what time's kick-off tomorrah?"

Whatever our visitor gets up to in the bathroom, it gives her a second wind. It is a quarter to two. I am awake—and I am not the only one…

Ethan was right. The walls of No. 4, The Ridge have met their match with Monique. At first I think the squawk is a fox outside, but when it repeats a minute later it is clearly from within… The third time, it resolves in a trickle of female laughter bordering on manic in the darkness, followed by a volley of thumps that last for a minute. Wide-eyed, duvet to my chin like Red Riding Hood's grandmother, my woozy brain takes a moment to decode them… Until, with a vision of the leatherette bedhead that is the least attractive feature of Martin's room, the pieces fall into place.

Ten minutes later, the barrage resumes. I always thought banging headboards were an urban myth; a staple of smuttier sitcoms, unconnected to the reality of lovemaking… I have earplugs somewhere left over from the cruise, a panic purchase in case Mother snored. But they are in my toilet bag in my suitcase, which is on top of the wardrobe… I turn on my side and yank the duvet over one ear. A wave of that sinking numbness that has intruded less in recent years washes over me. It signals an instance when I feel more utterly alone than when the house is empty.

My mouth is dry, my head still muzzy from the wine. I forgot to glug my customary glass of milk before bed and consider nipping down to the kitchen, but the thought of being apprehended suffuses me with embarrassment... In the stillness of my room, this bastion of solitude to which I retreat when life's iniquities grind me down, not even my bed is a refuge. Whenever I think the cavorting has ceased there comes another thud, groan or peal of laughter... The thuds infuriate me; the laughter breeds an urge to inflict actual harm. But the groans—Oh, the groans stir me with a gnawing combination of intrigue and arousal. *Because the groans are Martin's!*

Being attracted to a man is one thing, whether for his smile or his skill at rebalancing a juddering Hotpoint... But being exposed to him, even the sound of him, *in flagrante* is a brew more heady than I can take. I have no desire to imagine him with Monique, but that's beyond my control. The pictures invade my head like pressing Play on the DVD... Will his bedroom light be on or off? The possibility of a chink beneath the door, brazen as the neon of a lap dance club, is another reason I cannot face the landing. I feel a flutter in my heart, and elsewhere, at the thought of their coupling... Of Monique's mouth, nuzzling Martin's cosily magnificent chest. Of clothing wrenched from bodies and strewn on the carpet, or suspended from drawer knobs where it landed... I don't doubt those blue pyjama bottoms are nowhere to be seen! For Martin will be a spontaneous lover—sensitive to his partner's needs. He is the kind of man who will learn and build upon every bout of lovemaking... To the good fortune of any woman lucky enough to share his bed, he is a perfectionist!

I know this; I have never seen a man iron a shirtsleeve better.

Out of sync with the soundtrack that finally falls silent, my vision rolls on. Sensual, not explicit, the mechanics of the act immaterial for the moment to resonate. So, from the bitter luxury of my spacious double divan, I give in to the indulgence... Welcome it, as I have over the years for the comfort it brings in moments of loneliness, and the diversion in a bored one.

Masturbation was never mentioned in my upbringing. I was left to discover its fears and pleasures for myself. Mother's introduction to the birds and bees amounted to a single conversation, one Saturday afternoon on the way back from swimming. It covered periods and contraception, in vocabulary that can best be described as mechanical. I knew most of it anyway, from a rare detention in Biology when I read ahead in the Third Form textbook. The only digression from the scientific in Mother's explanation was the word 'sheath', which she used repeatedly to my befuddlement. At the time, as a family we were watching a BBC adaptation of *The Three Musketeers*, and the word brought to mind Porthos played by a young Brian Blessed, for whom I had a quiet fixation... With every mention of the word, I saw him draw his sword and swish it, before flexing his torso back and forth on buckskinned thighs. An image that has stayed with me to this day, and plays an uncredited, not always helpful role in every sexual act I have ever experienced.

Ultimately, the pleasing ache rising within me meets a wave of tiredness coming the other way... Drifting off to sleep, I have the faintest sense of Martin standing over me. Indistinct at first, until the ripples settle like the surface of a pond... *He is smiling in the way that brings a little sunshine into my life at No. 4, The Ridge. A smile I was quick to claim as my own, yet now presages the heartbreak that so often comes from a wrongly jumped conclusion.*

Only... Something is different.

This is a smile in disguise. A smile that says 'All is not lost', as it teases me from behind Martin's incongruous, immaculately pomaded goatee beard.

Chapter 19

Monique likes football. Women do these days, in an evolutionary leap that is lost on me. Marketing will be to blame somewhere down the line, and I am relieved I avoided its tendrils.

Pre-cruise, in one of my flights of fancy as Martin's girlfriend, I saw myself at West Ham. A one-off indulgence and an eye-rolling capitulation to my man, just to prove I am right: that football is not for me. His team plays at the Olympic Stadium, which I remember from the London 2012 Games.

My interest in sport is niche: I enjoy ice skating when I can find it on a minor channel, and you can't live in SW19 without being swept along in the fuss around the tennis. But Avril, who can wangle tickets for almost anything, took me to the Olympic Opening Ceremony as a treat. She promised a momentous spectacle, and it was that or the Taekwondo. I chose wisely and still cherish my memories of that night when our home city was focus of the world... Shire horses and Ken Branagh in a topper; trampolinists on hospital beds, and H.M. The Queen leaping from a helicopter... Consequently, I would do my duty if required, and attend a football match with Martin. Endure ninety minutes amid the jostling hordes with their chants, clean or otherwise. And after that, I would cut him some slack. Forgive him his manly Saturday ritual of 'the match' and let him wallow in the puffery so integral to the game. The replays and highlights, the minute analysis by men with awful diction who wear ties and pontificate with their knees open.

Yet, for Monique, it is different. If she is to be believed, she has been a fan for years. Her team is Spurs, a hangover from a previous boyfriend. In her Aussie way she calls it 'soccer', but her enthusiasm for everything, from transfer rumours to the best strategy to pull back a two-goal deficit, seems genuine... As time wears on, I have no wish to be privy to more of their relationship than I can help. But with the football season underway, I am aware they have seen West Ham on three of the last four Saturdays (tickets courtesy of a chum of Martin's with a leg in traction).

It is hard to think of anything that could make me feel more inadequate... Was I a fool, to believe myself the kind of woman Martin might fall for, once the dust of his divorce settles? Or was it just bad timing? I stuck to the rules, unlike others. I could have made a play when the urge first struck—made it obvious that here, in the sanctuary of home, lies a warmer, kinder alternative to the wife he was escaping... Monique surprise-surprise showed no restraint. Did she give a thought to his situation, as she flirted in their agency meeting? Before offering herself up like a honey-roast hog on a barbie?

That woman intrudes on my thoughts too much. What *does* she offer him, anyway? It's a stretch, but I can just about see her robust charms appealing in a harsh climate. If ever there was a woman equipped to wrestle rams into a shearing position, it's her! But what does she offer him intellectually? Her job in production may call for an appreciation of design, but it will be technical not creative. Does she share Martin's love of art? When he needs more to feed his soul than an afternoon on a draughty terrace, will she join him in contemplation of London's artistic bounty? I can see them at the Tate or the National Gallery: Martin, kindling the wide-eyed enthusiasm of Freya and little Nathan, while his girlfriend stomps off in search of cut-price handbags at the gift shop.

The children! Here I hesitate. Childless as I am, have I the right to judge a father on his parenting?

On balance, I think yes. I was a child myself, blessed with an upbringing that was stable from start to finish. And, as an adult, from my dealings with local schoolchildren I have learned how they live today: the pressures of an academic system where exam grades change more frequently than the

Education Secretary... Children needed stability, and if parents can't provide it they at least have a duty to minimise the upset.

No—there is no denying it: Martin was a fool to take up with Monique. And I fear he will live to regret it!

An example arises the following Sunday. He has been out all weekend, staying over at hers in Deptford after the football. This is their pattern for home games, and I can't say I mind; the fewer animal pawings I am exposed to the better. Sundays are still sacrosanct, his day for the children. I don't know if the little ones have been introduced to Daddy's new friend but I hope not... It is early afternoon when I hear the clunk of Martin's car door. Another, then another... As I stand at the kitchen window, the air is rich with baking. I chew a blanched almond and watch a sparrow hop about on Mrs Burnside. In the living room Georgie and Lorenzo—now a sabbath fixture at No. 4, The Ridge once he has rolled out of her bed—are watching TV.

"Hiya!" calls Martin from the front door. "Don't mind us."

By the sound of it he has company, large and small. His footsteps head upstairs as whispers filter in from the hall. I peer round the door... Monique, Nathan and Freya standing in a huddle, the children cute as buttons in baseball caps and plastic sunglasses.

"Hi, Fen!" peals Freya, charging towards me.

My thighs are hugged. I pat her on the head.

"We're going to the Natural History Museum! To see the skellibobosaurus!"

Tutting from Nathan. "It isn't called the skellibobosaurus!"

"I know!" she snaps with big-sisterly contempt. "That's what *you* used to call them."

Nathan blows a raspberry.

"Something smells good, Fen," chirps Monique. She looks tired and uncomfortable in high heels, and a skirt unwisely short for a museum with an open stairwell.

"Are you baking a cake?" asks Freya. "Can I help?"

"Whoa!" says Martin coming back downstairs. "We need to get going, guys. Nathan, do you need a wee?"

His laptop is under his arm. He looks on edge as he carries it into the living area. Monique follows as Nathan scampers into the under-stairs loo.

"Daddy's got to email something for work," explains Freya. "But he always takes ages, so can we bake a cake?"

Her angelic, upturned face sets me aflutter. I can't remember the last time a child was fond of me.

"All done, I'm afraid, Freya. Can't you smell it? Mmm, lemon and almond…"

"Mmm," mimics Freya, disappointed. "Can we have some before we go?"

The cake is resting on the worktop and needs a few more minutes… I offer everyone tea in the hope of delaying them till it cools. Martin and Monique shake their heads but Georgie and Lorenzo are takers. Freya, following me round like a spaniel, wants cola.

"Haven't you had your lunch?" I ask as the kettle boils.

She nods once, lips puckered to one side. "With Mummy."

"Oh right. Is Daddy cooking tea at home tonight?"

Before she can answer Nathan marches in, wanting cola too.

"It's coming," I tell his retreating shoulders. Freya is dubious about something.

"Mummy needs to be at home tonight, so Daddy says we're staying somewhere else. Are we coming here?"

The kettle clicks off.

"I don't know," I say, pouring water over teabags. "Possibly…"

Martin wouldn't dare, surely, not without asking. Ethan is out more than he's in these days, and Lorenzo usually ambles off about eight. Even so, it's just good manners. I pour the colas and hand one to Freya who carries it carefully from the kitchen.

With Martin and Monique in either armchair and Georgie and Lorenzo monopolising the three-seater, there is nowhere to sit. A perfect opportunity for me to hunker down at the coffee table with the children. Martin's forehead corrugates as he glances up from his laptop.

"Any of you guys a wiz at TransferBot?"

Georgie and Lorenzo look blank.

"Did you try that plug-in?" Monique sounds impatient.

He tuts. "Won't work with this browser."

"So? Try another!"

I pretend to miss the look that passes between them.

Nathan slurps to a stop. "Can I have another cola, Fen?"

"Steady," says Monique. "You'll be peeing all the way to Kensington!"

"How about a small one?" I say, snatching up his glass.

Peeing! Is it just me, or does the change of initial pile on the vulgarity? (Aren't children taught to say 'wee' so they won't say 'pee'?) I sniff, unscrewing the cola cap. Another case of nations divided by a common language! I test the cake with my palm. It needs a minute longer. I haven't left enough almonds to mosaic the surface like in the photo, but a row are peeping through the crust like dinosaur bones.

Back in the living area Martin's fingers whisk over the keyboard, mission almost accomplished.

"Nice one!" He sits back as his machine gives affirmative bleeps. "Gunners made a hash of it yesterday, eh Lorenzo?"

Georgie's boyfriend looks up from her lap.

"God, yeah!" He flips onto his front so he can see Martin without dislocating vertebrae. "Back four all over the shop! Played like total girlies—*Oww!*"

Georgie removes her nail from his neck; Lorenzo rubs it better. "How did the Hammers do? Everton at home, yeah?"

And they're off... Chewing the fat and reeling off players' names like the queue at immigration. Georgie says nothing as they drown out her programme with a blow-by-blow dissection of a free kick. Monique is less forgiving, rooting grumpily in her suede-fringed bag. She pulls out a handful of vouchers and examines the small print.

"Mart, this exhibition's only free if we get there by three o'clock."

He winks, but the set of his mouth says he doesn't like being interrupted.

I feel a hand on my elbow. "Is it cake time yet?" asks Freya.

"Yay, cake!" crows Nathan, his tumbler hitting the table.

I follow them to the kitchen.

"Fingers," I warn, sliding a knife from the block. "I bet you can only manage a tiny piece, Nathan."

His protests are echoed by Freya, sparking a debate about who can eat the most. I make them wait until pieces are laid out on side plates.

"Mmm—" says Nathan. "Your cakes are even yummier than Mummy's!"

Freya nods. I cut myself a small slice.

"So, what are you going to see today? I love the Natural History Museum."

The little girl stops chewing. "Can you come with us?"

"Oh, I don't think I—"

"Yes, can you?" asks Nathan. "You can have Monique's ticket."

I nearly choke. Taking the hand from my mouth I say, "Oh, I bet you'll all have a lovely time…"

Both children go back to their plates. Freya looks crabby.

"We've seen the robot dinosaurs before. They're not as good as on telly."

Nathan agrees. "They can't chase you upstairs. And they sound like a hoover."

I am secretly delighted. The Natural History Museum I love is the one I visited as a little girl: erudite and cavernous, replete with dusty charm. I remember strolling among the dinosaur skeletons, staring into the nostrils of one macabre giant with a bony collar like an emperor's robe. My father tried to interest me in the trilobites, giant marine woodlice, the ancestors of crabs and spiders. I skipped off to my favourite Mammal Gallery instead, where beasts were frozen in the act of pouncing or nursing their adorable, dead young. I could stay there for hours, absorbing the freakishness, imagining their wild lives... Longed to unlock the cases with a key filched from a passing attendant. Press my face to the downy pelt of a lioness, or sit in the lap of the venerable old panda from London Zoo and share the bamboo he brandished like a bridal bouquet.

My most recent visit was a disappointment, an out-of-hours jolly for exhibition-sector marketers. I stood in the main foyer with thirty others, which was much as I remembered it apart from the vast whale skeleton hanging where the dear old diplodocus had been... We drank cocktails neath the shipwreck of its ribs as a student jazz ensemble tootled through Gershwin. It was only as I escaped to a side gallery with my Long Island Iced Tea that I saw what had become of my childhood haven. Touchscreens were everywhere, interactive portals replacing the faded cards of yore. Headphones for listening and apps to download, in place of anything to read for yourself! A sign of the post-millennial times, and a shift I can feel encroaching on my own Picture Gallery. One I shall resist like a lioness defending her cubs.

"When are we coming to *your* museum?" asks Freya. "You said we could..."

I look forlornly at my cake. I don't know where I stand with these children. Whether I should have anything to do with them at all now my reasons are opaque.

"I did a drawing yesterday," says Nathan, saving the day.

"Did you, Nathan? What was that?"

"A skyscraper on fire, with firemen catching babies in blankets cos they can't fly." He swallows a last morsel of sponge. "Why can't babies fly?"

"Well I—I think we'd better see who else wants cake while there's some left!"

They traipse after me as I carry in the sponge on a board. Martin and Lorenzo have moved on to QPR; Georgie and Monique are immersed in chatter of their own. Safe Sunday small-talk for people who hardly know each another.

"... can't imagine buying a place in this city," huffs Monique. "The rent I pay would get me a two-bed duplex back home. Own backyard a block from the ocean and no need for flatmates. Mental!"

Georgie glances down at her beau. "This one's a lucky sod. Likes to tell me he bought at the top of the market and how it's bleeding him dry. As if!"

Lorenzo is still talking across her thighs. I place the cake on the table, knife poised, waiting for someone to notice.

"Anyway," Georgie mock-whispers, "the repayments can't be killing him. He's got the builders in next week. Having an en suite in the master bedroom, if you don't mind!"

Her tone says this offends her principles and Monique raises a conspiratorial eyebrow. I am tired of being ignored. I also wonder if this defaming of integrated bathrooms is a dig at me.

"Well, I'd be lost without mine," I chip in. "Keeps me out of everyone's way in the morning. Now, who's for cake?" My other hand holds a wad of paper serviettes in lieu of plates. I am not about to soil crockery for people who rock up unannounced.

But Monique's mind has stalled. "I dunno—I like a separate bathroom, if you know what I mean... Show me an en suite and I think, *Why don't you just shit in the wardrobe and be done with it!*"

There is a lull in the football-talk into which her words tumble. A silent shot of teacups on TV lends them even greater emphasis. The pause feels longer than it is, shattered by a simultaneous "Urghh!" from Nathan and peals of laughter from Freya.

In the armchair, Martin's head swings slowly through ninety degrees. His eyes as they rest on his girlfriend are hard to read. I am reminded of another rare occasion when I was in trouble at school: the games mistress, spotting the nail file in my sock that rumbled me as the Phantom Netball Slasher of Cazenove School for Girls.

Martin turns to me and says, "No cake for us, thanks, Fen. It's time we went."

Chapter 20

Being single is like being left-handed. Not a problem, until others needle you into thinking it is.

When it crosses my mind, which isn't often, I think I handle it rather well, the pressure to be one of a pair. Even nowadays, when forthright independence is lauded, coupledom rules courtesy of a tide of cultural conditioning that requires feisty paddling to beat it... Oh, people talk endlessly about diversity, which usually just means tolerance for another sort of couple. Single people are still outside the tent; women in particular, and more so when they're over forty. At my age, the available categorisations boil down to *Mother or Other*. It's like Women's Lib never happened.

Monday morning is dull but dry as my train pulls into North Dulwich. Our driver is a frustrated DJ. Impressed by his own voice over the PA, he riffs repeatedly on points failures that *"definitely don't make prizes..."* The twelve-minute walk to the Picture Gallery will do me good.

I have turned over the events of yesterday ever since the door slammed on our less-than-enthusiastic museum party. Spent the rest of the afternoon in the garden on my Kindle, leaving Georgie and Lorenzo to canoodle in peace. I read a little and mulled a lot, over what possesses a sensible chap like Martin to choose a wholly unsuitable partner... Sophocles (or was it Plato?) would say it boils down to sex; the urge, like being chained to a lunatic. Well, the Greeks were right about most things, but that doesn't chime with my experience. What lovers I have had were all rational decisions, even when it's fair to say I was under the influence of alcohol. I have few regrets. Would probably do them all again, with the exception of Peter from Bridlington, who I met on an arts away-day and turned out to have a penchant for girls a good deal younger than I was... Years later, Avril spotted him in the *Daily Mail*, up in court for taking the hedonism of Tudor England too literally on one of his historical re-enactment weekends. Hellbent on excising our two-night role-play from memory, I binned that Catherine of Aragon gable-hood on the spot.

Rounding the corner at the newsagent's I narrowly miss a woman with a double buggy.

No. Love has never blinded me!

Though I sometimes feel in the minority... My theory is that men have the knack of compartmentalising. They rate women via a tick-box system which ranks certain qualities, mostly physical, above others. Hence Monique: bleached and buxom in a way they find attractive... My own father, an undemonstrative man I rarely saw out of his vest even on holiday, was a fan of the *Carry On* films—at odds with his sense of humour which, when it manifested at all, veered towards the sophisticated. One Christmas I was home from university; we were sitting up late in front of just such a comedy-classic, when it dawned on me it wasn't the jokes Father was watching for... Titillation is all very well. But in another life, was a Barbara Windsor or Joan Sims the kind of woman he'd have preferred? Been happier to make a home and raise a daughter with, than Mother?

In Martin's case, it makes sense if his motivation is lust. I can see how uncomplicated fun would appeal in his situation, and Monique is nothing if not uncomplicated. Of course it's early days; there is no reason to believe it will last. Martin will soon be immersed ever-deeper in legal proceedings, forced to watch as his perfect nuclear family detonates before his eyes. Even now, isn't he more likely to patch things up with his wife than make a go of it with some rebound floozy?

That I could live with. Those children need a mother and father.

As the park comes into view I cross to where a white van is standing at the kerb. The man inside is engrossed in his phone, the flesh of one knee pressed against the driver's window in a wet kiss... But what troubled me most for the rest of yesterday, fitfully through the night and again this morning, is the feeling of being *Other*. Little more than a month ago we were a household of happy singletons. Till one-by-one they all conjured partners from the ether, leaving me as odd-woman-out. Last night Lorenzo and Georgie disappeared for beer and mussels in Chelsea. As I settled down for the *Antiques Roadshow*, Ethan turned up with Cass who is evidently still on the scene.

"Hey, how are you?" he asked, launching himself onto a settee barely unkinked from the last brace of bottoms.

Cass is a confident young man. Able to keep his end up in conversation even when he's only met you once. He has an edge of flamboyance too, which I find reassuring. Tonight's little hacking jacket and headgear (a trilby with a violet paw-print motif around the band) suggests the kind of individuality I expect in a gay man... Ethan, who likes to merge with the crowd, appeared from the kitchen with tea and crumpets, looking for all the world like a whippet-thin version of the builders who doze on my early train.

"Cheers, buddy," said Cass, helping himself to sugar. It is hard to believe the soulmate of one so dapper wears bobbled track pants and a Jean-Michel Jarre tee shirt, though the latter is presumably ironic.

They sat quietly through my programme, with more crumpets and a shared satsuma. *More like mates than lovers*, I thought. Until a smiling Cass made a bracelet of orange peel and slipped it over Ethan's wrist in a show of something like betrothal. An hour later I was ready to follow them up to bed, double-locking the door and turning off the lights. Martin won't be back, Monique made that plain as they left. The 'somewhere else' the children are staying was her flat in Deptford, an area I have never visited in all my years in London, though it is often on the news. It looks forbidding and bristles with tower blocks, one of which is home to Monique and her flatmates. Women, I gather, who also work in advertising. I have visions of garish smalls fluttering on the balcony and strident exchanges bawled through the bathroom door... Would Martin's wife (or Martin's wife's solicitor) be happy to know her children were spending the night in a place like that? I dread to think of the sleeping arrangements, let alone what their young minds make of this whole, tawdry rigmarole. On top of this, it is term time. When will they need to be up, if Martin is to get them to Morden in time for registration? I can see it now: Freya and Nathan, bleary in crumpled uniforms, plummeting to earth in a urine-scented lift...

I am almost at the Picture Gallery gates when my mobile cheeps an alert:

Hi Fen. You home tonight? We have GOT to talk!! Gx

Georgie... I stop in my tracks. Now what is this about?

Chapter 21

"That woman!" she says, shutting the fridge. "Me and Lorenzo couldn't stop talking about her!"

The worktop is strewn with rice grains, shallots and something in a tin that looks like dog meat. Georgie picks up her wine glass and puts it down again, too apoplectic to drink.

"You know me, Fen, I'm not xenophobic. In any way. But she's so... *blowsy!* D'you know what I mean?"

I do but don't acknowledge it. I tread carefully instead.

"Monique's certainly very—bubbly."

Georgie goes back to her shallots. "Yeah, right. Talking of which, you haven't seen her pack it away. Morning after her first night here, there were *two* prosecco bottles by the bin. And *three* lager cans!"

It is not like her to snoop, though the fact she does makes me feel better.

"I suppose everyone's entitled to their fun," I say magnanimously, brushing back rice grains making a break for the floor. "Though Martin's timing *is* a bit suspect. You don't think he's going off the rails, do you?"

"Could be. I mean, it happens. I see it with families at work all the time, where the father does a bunk and none of the agencies can find him... I've got a client at the moment, lad who ended up on the street because he couldn't take the pressure of being the breadwinner at seventeen. They tracked down his dad in the end. He was working the trawlers in the Shetlands." She swigs her Sauv Blanc.

"Of course. Martin's poor children."

Georgie's eyes bulge. "Exactly! What's their mother doing, letting him cart them around like that? They're so vulnerable at that age."

I nod slowly, as if this is the first I've thought of it. It feels good to be vindicated by a professional. Even Georgie.

"Do you like Martin, Fen?"

The question comes out of nowhere. Or rather from the sink, where she is draining the tin I now see is labelled *Seitan*.

"I... Yes, I think so. Do you?"

She presses the brownish chunks against the base of the colander. "I thought I did. I guess we don't really know him, do we?"

We. Georgie and me—a team! Despite my efforts, the age gap has always made me feel an outsider. Perhaps if I—

A key in the door... Martin is due about now. I don't turn round in case he senses we're talking about him.

"Hey," says Ethan. "You guys got back just in time. Trains up the creek from Waterloo."

And with this, the scenario descends into one I do my best to avoid: two housemates cooking at once. Though 'cooking' is hardly the word where Ethan is concerned. He is a whizz with the toaster and microwave, forever claiming to have eaten a big lunch at work.

"What's that, George?" He is peering into the frying pan.

"Vegan stir fry. We've got Lorenzo's boss coming for dinner and his wife's one." She prods the glutinous chunks with a spatula. "I said I'd try out a couple of recipes. So if anyone's up for some meat-free, dairy-free, taste-free delights..."

Ethan is, for once. He tucks into a side plate of the fried rice with its surprisingly fleshy-looking sauce, as well as cottage cheese crispbreads. I forgot to defrost myself a steak pie, but claim a small appetite and make a ham and cheese sandwich instead (and another one later when no one's looking).

We take our food and carry on the discussion in the living area. I sit where I have a view of anyone coming up the drive. Now that we're all speaking frankly, I am curious to know what Ethan makes of Monique; whether he shares our unease or it's 'a woman thing'. Wheedling it out will require subtlety. He is rarely undiplomatic, perhaps a reflection of his Japanese side. The only time I've ever seen him lose his cool he was replacing the battery on a touchscreen.

"No Martin and Monique tonight?" he asks, balancing a plate of snow-covered Ryvitas.

"No," I say, shielding my mouth as the sandwich goes down. "Actually we were just talking about them. They were round with the children yesterday."

Georgie is straight to the point. "What do *you* think of her, Ethan?"

He puts his head on one side, chewing thoughtfully.

"Monique? Bit of a character, isn't she? People-person and all."

I stifle a tut. One can be too forgiving!

"We think she's ghastly," blurts Georgie. "I mean, no one can help the way they're brought up—but really!"

As character assassination goes, this is ruthless. It also conflicts with my sense of Georgie's social conscience. Her job at St Gulliver's requires the sympathetic handling of people from the wrong side of the tracks. Is this how she thinks of them too? Ethan on the other hand is PC-incarnate. I can't see him sharing Georgie's opinion, and I am right:

"Harsh, George. Live and let live, eh? A bit of brashness goes with the territory, doesn't it, with Aussies? My old Sociology teacher used to say they're so loud cos of the wide-open spaces... Not easy, passing the time of day with your neighbour when you're separated by a billabong and herd of migrating 'roos!"

She laughs. "Now who's stereotyping? I'm not saying it's *because* Monique's Australian... Though if we're talking theories, I'd say it takes a certain sort of person to turn their back on all they know and settle on the other side of the planet. I'm sure there's plenty of mousy Aussies. They're just not the ones who come over here!"

Ethan bites off a crisp corner. "Horses for courses. Anyway, people don't always choose the partners you expect. Who knows what Martin's type is... I mean, what's his wife like? Got some high-powered job, hasn't she? Maybe he likes a woman in the driving seat."

"*Fnaar!*" honks Georgie unnecessarily. She scoops an escaping morsel of meat-substitute into her mouth. "Which is fine. Whatever lights your candle. It's just... I'm probably being selfish, but when I come home at night I resent being confronted by someone so boorish. You agree, don't you, Fen?"

They are both looking at me.

"I—I think you're both right. I mean, Martin's personal choices are none of our business obviously. But yes, if I'm honest, I do find Monique a little... testing."

"Testing! It's like she's on day-release from borstal!"

"Oh, I wouldn't say—"

Georgie's eyes are popping. "You didn't hear her with Lorenzo last week! Going on about the right sort of bike saddle to avoid skiddies in your underwear. *He was mortified!*"

I am not sorry I missed this, though I am sceptical Georgie's beau is as delicate as she implies. In my experience, public-school types revel in vulgarity.

Ethan's phone appears in his non-eating hand. His concentration is dwindling, but for now diplomacy holds.

"Look, who am I to say? You've all been great about Cass coming round, and it's not like I ever asked." He could say the same about Georgie's Lorenzo, though being Ethan he won't. "But it's all part of house-sharing, isn't it? We're all grown-ups..."

I take his little half-smile to mean we are all sexually active beings. Untrue, but nice to have one's potential acknowledged... Like Ethan, I am happy to leave the topic there.

"Fair point," says Georgie. "And yeah, I hope you're okay with this, Fen. There we all were, single agents, rubbing along.

Next thing you know, it's bed-mates a-go-go and a rush on the kettle in the morning! You have been here longest — it's probably not what you signed up for."

I like to think of myself as an old-school Liberal, or someone who looks like one. I shake my head graciously.

"Live and let live, that's what I say, Georgie. We're all entitled to a private life. And it's good for me, being around you all. It keeps me—" I bite back the Y-word, "on my toes!"

The evening continues in the same good humour, with a lightness that is rare without alcohol. There is a definite sense we here present are the core of No. 4, The Ridge, and others passing through mere interlopers... I can't and won't say anything against Martin, but it reassures me to hear his choices questioned. Even Ethan, who wouldn't say boo to a goose let alone a ham-thighed emu, lets slip the truth later when the regional news runs an item on knife crime... A Muslim reporter is asking people how safe they feel walking round the capital at night. As is often the case, no one white and British seems available for comment. An East European says something without saying anything; two black girls, panicky and defiant at once, say a good deal, none of which I follow. The reporter nabs his final vox-popper outside Tesco. The young man's hair is wet from the shower; his jacket and hurriedly knotted tie identify him as one of the myriad drones who keep the clerical bowels of London moving. When he speaks, none of us can stem a titter. His accent is borderline Brisbane Redneck.

"Arrh," he says, shucking his chin. "You're pretty much okay, long as you keep your wits about-cha! Me an' me mates, if we're leaving a club somewhere dodge, we'll take an Uber. Or getta posse together and roll home in a bunch!"

"Struth, cobber!" laughs Georgie.

"Probably a mate of Monique's," sniggers Ethan, finishing his plate. "I tell you, I'd feel safe walking home with her. I bet she's got a brick in her handbag!"

Having a focus for our humour only increases the camaraderie. I have to stop myself leaping up to open a bottle. It is Monday, and even Georgie rarely drinks this early in the week; another subtle generational difference. In my first years at No. 4, The Ridge I was prone to sneaking a half-mug of the grape up to my room, in the guise of something milky and soporific. The influence of the younger element helped me to recognise this for the slippery slope it was, and I now often make it to Thursday without imbibing. That said, when Martin and I are home alone, my old habits make a comeback. One more reason I'm not sad to see him cast in an unflattering light.

"It's those pyjama trousers I can't get over!" crows Georgie. "I'm no label queen, but there's no way those are Emporio Armani!" (Ha! So I'm not the only one to take an interest unloading the washer-drier!) "Knock-off, guaranteed. I've seen them on Leather Lane Market."

"You can't blame him for that," says Ethan. "Fakes can be as good as the real thing. Cass got this cool Stussy baseball jacket for thirty quid. Why fill the coffers of the corporates if you don't have to?"

"True," nods Georgie, remembering her proletarian roots. "But he's still buying into it. I mean, he's lovely Martin, salt of the earth, but he's as tribal as the next guy. Designer, isn't he — graphics or whatever? Once they're in that world they all dress the same." She chortles again. "Right down to their flannelette nightwear!"

Still I say nothing, just rearrange the cutlery on my empty plate. If Georgie's Oxfam chic doesn't say do-gooding Boho, what does? Ethan draws the same conclusion:

"We can all fall into that trap, George. Social conditioning. In Martin's case, maybe it's rebellion too. Guys reach a certain age, get married, have babies... Next thing they know, they're sucked into Dad-World. Doesn't mean they want to spend their lives in clothes they can mop puke off." He wipes up crumbs from his plate with one finger. "What is his background, anyway? He looks pretty square to us but maybe he thinks he's a bit—*edgy*..."

He is struggling to keep the corners of his mouth down. Georgie spots it too, and a moment later we are all laughing again. Only this time I am not sure I should be. Isn't this an ageist dig and exactly what they think of me? I once caught Georgie and Javier in the kitchen, examining one of my Laura Ashley blouses like a dead eel they found in the wash-basket. A second later it had never happened, but I knew they were branding me the house frump.

All the more reason why this is novel—to feel *in* with Ethan and Georgie. Laughing about Martin goes against the grain, but it is harmless and he'll never know... My guard is slipping too. In retrospect, I should have said nothing. Let the evening pass in an easy spirit I can build on another time. As it is, my joy is more unconfined than is prudent;

"And to think, I was envious of the way you two hit it off with Martin! Felt like I'd missed something while I was away— the three of you, bonding without me." The closing credits of the news slip in to fill the silence; "I suppose I thought he was more your sort of person than I am... Which is fine. I know I can come across as a bit of a fuddy-duddy. But it's so lovely to feel—" I nearly say 'embraced'; *"included!"* (Thank God for no wine!)

Ethan and Georgie nod ruminatively, which I take as encouragement.

"—I thought, they've taken to him alright! And here's funny old Fen, odd one out again!" I don't have a handkerchief and hope I won't need one. "I suppose I've never been that good at fitting in... Partly why I opted for a house-share in the first place, take me out of my comfort zone!" I slide my plate onto the coffee table. "I'll be honest, I haven't always found it easy living here... I don't mean you two," I lie. "But some of your predecessors, well, we were chalk and cheese. You've been great. About the age gap... Funnily enough, only yesterday I was thinking about replacing the handset on the landline— *which I know* you never use! ...And I thought, 'God, Ethan and Georgie will think I'm such a maiden-aunt! I'll never be cool, like Martin.'" I sit back in my chair smiling. "Now I know better. Isn't it funny, the way things turn on a sixpence?"

They are both still looking at me. Both nodding. Which makes Ethan's words even more incongruous:

"What's a sixpence?"

Chapter 22

"Not so good," says Martin with a sigh. "It's all over with Monique."

I freeze and so does Ethan. I am at the sink, he the worktop slicing a mango.

"Oh," I say.

It is the following evening. Asking after Martin's day was pure reflex but his body language said something was amiss. He wilts visibly by the microwave, as if invisible rays are sapping his life force.

Ethan lays his knife on the chopping board. "What happened?"

Martin takes a lager from the fridge. "All came to a head at the museum." He cracks the ring pull and swigs.

I have visions of a full-blown row in front of the children and a stegosaurus. Glassy eyes watching from glassy cases as Monique throws her weight about. Thoughts of dinner evaporate as my heart does a little flip. I am slavering for details but won't pry... Another slug of lager and Martin is ready to talk.

"I should have seen it coming. She doesn't have kids, so what does she know? Nathan's got this thing about skellibobs — skeletons. Has done ever since he was two. It was a stupid place to take him, and Freya's the age where she can't help winding him up. Cue a tantrum and full-on fist fight by the T. Rexes. Of course Monique's answer to everything is a threat or an ice cream, which ain't how we brought them up... Then Security rock up, telling her to keep the noise down. It didn't end well."

He looks exhausted. His skin is shiny, lined about the eyes.

"I take the kids home to their mum then slog over to Deptford to sort it out. Me and Monique were up half the night. Not in a good way."

Ethan gives him a manly pat. "So you guys are calling it a day?"

He sighs again. "Doomed from the start, I reckon, rebound and all. Probably for the best."

I agree, but saying so won't help. When he goes upstairs to change I exchange a look with Ethan. The irony of it, in the light of what we said last night!

Any chance of a conflab is cut short by the doorbell. Ethan goes to answer, leaving the cheese knife aquiver in the cheddar like an executioner's axe.

Cass, on another unannounced visit. After a minute's muttering in the hall he appears and says hello, unpacking a brown paper sack of veg.

I carry on preparing my tuna salad, while for the second night running something experimental is created beside me… This rarely happens when one shares with singletons. Somehow a relationship breeds the desire for sensation in the kitchen.

The day was hot and evening still holds the embers, particularly in here. I am opening the back door when Martin reappears in a tee shirt, flip-flops and those shorts with the tie-waist he leaves dangling. He hasn't showered, but water has been splashed judging by the freckles on his snug-fit top, and his hair slicked back like Bryan Ferry.

"Beautiful evening anyway," he says. "Anyone fancy eating outside?"

"Cool," says Cass. "Ours'll be half an hour, but why not? Sorry to hear you've been through the mill, Martin. You bearing up, mate?"

"Yeah thanks. Can't keep me down for long!"

He shrugs heroically and I wish I'd got in earlier with the condolences. Cass's easy-going air makes him hard to dislike, but he is grating on me now. This could be his kitchen, by that way he leans a hip on the worktop as Ethan consults a recipe on his phone. He brandishes the pepper mill with the same aplomb, flipping it end-over-end like a cocktail waiter... And all the while in his hat: today, a navy peaked cap like a Greek fisherman. It will stay on for the evening (possibly all night, who knows?). Headgear worn indoors I associate with Grandma, my father's mother, who died when I was fifteen. In the decades since it felt like an impertinence, but now seems acceptable again.

"Anyway, no point crying over spilt milk," says Martin, showing no sign of slowing on the platitudes. "Who's for a glass of fizz?"

He takes a bottle of prosecco from his shelf in the fridge, a more or less permanent feature since he met Monique. *Drowning his sorrows...* He won't see today as cause for celebration even if I do.

"Snap!" says Cass, returning from the hall with his rucksack. He produces cava. "Ta for reminding me. Should be in the fridge."

"Cass is stoked cos he got promoted," explains Ethan beaming. "Deputy manager!"

His boyfriend works at the last surviving music megastore in the West End. He has evidently climbed the career ladder with the same laid-back assurance he does everything else. Before long there won't be any high street shops left but I am not about to rain on his parade.

Al fresco eating I can take or leave, but it is a lovely evening. The August sun has begun its slow-motion dip behind next door's outhouse, which leaves two long hours of slanting rays and stretching shadows. The garden is looking fine too, if I say so myself. Mostly my own horny-handed labour, including the last two mowings since Martin's weekends became hectic. The azaleas are a show and the bamboo, which never looked much, has shot up. Its foliage is the glorious lime-green of the adverts in the Sunday supps, and its black stems a dramatic backdrop for Mrs Burnside. Like primeval organ pipes.

As I busy myself, joining patio tables and unfolding garden chairs from their nook with the ironing board, my mind is turning over like an outboard engine... I feel for Martin. The rawness of a failed relationship is never easy, and after his marital break-up another churn of the emotional pot. Pressure like this can unhinge the most grounded. Set them to necking antidepressants or, if American, running amok with a firearm.

On cue, another cork pops in the kitchen. I am not sure so much alcohol is wise in the circumstances, but I am touched Martin came home to me—to us—rather than heading to the nearest boozer. He needs our support.

I go to prepare my salad dressing. Ethan and Cass are tossing ingredients in a sizzling wok, one of which is testing our collective tear ducts. Martin fiddles with the catch on the only unopened window.

"Try sucking a spoon," he says. "Works for onions."

The pungency is intolerable. Grabbing kitchen roll and a fistful of cutlery I go back outside... Napkins would be overdoing it, so I rip off paper sheets and fold them into triangles, weighing them down with a knife and fork.

"Here you go," says Martin, holding a sparkling flute.

"Oh well—why not?"

He sits heavily in the nearest chair, a sandalled foot resting on one brown knee. I make a thing of admiring my glass's moussant.

"Cheers!" he says. He looks downcast all the same. I flip to mother-hen mode.

"What are you having? I'm doing salad, but there'll be too much for me if you want to—"

He shakes his head. "I'll have a sandwich in a bit. Big lunch at the pub."

Cass comes looking for the salt grinder. I direct him to Georgie's shelf. Strewn with mouse-turd coffee grounds, it is where everything AWOL in the kitchen turns up eventually...

Once the atmosphere has cleared, I return to whizzing up oil and vinegar with a piquant seasoning. The boys finish cooking and plates are ferried outside. Ethan produces an ice bucket from a rarely opened cupboard and manages to wedge in both bottles.

"Let's finish mine first," says Martin.

Which won't take long.

Chapter 23

Sparrows skitter and fizz flows. A light breeze wafts the scent of honeysuckle over the fence from next door. My appetite eludes me and I find myself with half a lettuce on my plate. It feels like one of those summer days of childhood, when the evening went on forever. Except here, with my housemates and a discarded salad, it is laced with anticipation... Feels pivotal somehow and I don't know why.

"Here you go," says Cass, giving me a refill.

He ignores my palm, topping up everyone with the carefree abandon of a modest drinker.

Martin raises his glass in thanks. "Nice one, Cass. So, what does your promotion mean? More hours, more perks or both?"

"Probably, yeah. Hours anyway. Means I'm running the store when the boss is out, which she is a fair bit. Got her eye on Regional, so..."

Martin nods knowingly before launching into a story I have heard before; his Saturday job at the Our Price record shop in Colchester. Teenage Martin scored a coup, by arranging a personal appearance by the singer from Right Said Fred. The shop was mobbed with eager pop fans, keen to meet a face from the telly. Until the musician turned out to be a local flautist with the same name.

Cass laughs. He pauses just long enough before adding, "We've got Billie Eilish in next week..."

I am sharing a table with Ethan. Martin is on the other one with Cass, so any quiet asides must negotiate the patio umbrella shaft. Probably best I bide my time; let the convivial atmosphere dissipate, then offer myself as the mature sounding board he needs. The boys will be off when they've eaten, then it will be the two of us in the ebbing sunlight... This cava is slipping down very nicely. But it is a school day tomorrow, I should be sensible. Alternate any more with a glass of water... Which reminds me, I have a bottle of Lambrusco on my shelf—a typically mean-spirited gift from work. 'Elegantly frizzante' according to the label, which sounds unlikely but it's a useful fallback.

A hollow thud ricochets from the back door. Giggling and a crinkly clatter of shopping hitting the worktop herald further complication.

"Evening all!" says Lorenzo, striding across the lawn like a minor royal at a garden party. He is in his work clothes, cuffs folded to the elbow, pinstripe shirt tails liberated from his waistband. Too many buttons have been undone by someone, hopefully not on the train.

Georgie follows, brandishing another bottle of fizz. Both are barefoot.

"Great minds, eh?" she says. "What is it about a gorgeous English summer evening that makes you want to get absolutely smashed?"

"The novelty?" says Ethan. "It's a celebration in our case. Cass got a big fat pay rise!"

His boyfriend looks embarrassed, but it makes perfect sense to Lorenzo.

"Good on you, mate! Always nice to be appreciated." He disappears indoors, coming back with stools from the breakfast bar. Georgie tuts and takes them back, returning with the last two folding chairs.

"So," she cajoles, "good days all round? Fen? Martin?"

She is flushed, and by her standards brimming with bonhomie, suggesting recent sex or heavy drinking. I take a sip of cava and say nothing. Martin grunts, aware he is about to burst her bubble.

"Not so good in my case, George..."

He goes over the events of yesterday. The newcomers gape and shake heads appropriately. Georgie glances once at me, her only hint that the demise of Martin and Monique is anything but a blow.

"Bad luck, mate," says Lorenzo sitting back, his input complete. Georgie has more:

"What a nightmare, Martin. Are you okay? She was a nice sort, Monique..."

My jaw almost drops. I wait for Georgie to mention the children who are clearly caught up in this. Instead she says:

"Might it be salvageable? I mean, it's not easy, meeting someone you really like." Her bare toes find Lorenzo's. "And you guys were so good together..."

Is there no end to her duplicity? Empathy is all very well, but the last thing Martin needs is any doubt cast on his lucky escape! Horrifyingly, he is nodding.

"You're not wrong there, George. Monique was a catch."

(Yes, and so's smallpox!)

I catch my breath, double-checking the words didn't escape my head... I have had quite enough to drink. The booze prohibits me from framing a response, though I feel increasingly protective of Martin. He does not need the raw edges of his private life raked over in public.

He burps lightly. "Probably for the best. I should never have taken up with her, with all I've got going on."

Well, at least he is seeing sense...

"How did she take it?" asks Georgie. An irrelevance, to my mind.

He grimaces. "Didn't say much to be honest. I don't think she slept. Neither of us did. I felt horrible." He helps himself to another glass of fizz. "She's not had it easy, Monique."

I am off my chair. "Well, if we've all finished, I'll get these plates in the dishwasher—"

"How do you mean?" asks Cass. "Not prying, but..."

Martin sighs like hydraulic brakes. Frowning, I sit back down.

"She got married at nineteen. Nasty bastard, by the sound of it. Couldn't hold down a job, so she brought in the money and he was spending it down the bookies. Did a flit and left Monique with a load of debts... Took her years to track him down and divorce him. And all the while she was supporting her parents, while her mum was in and out of hospital. Had to turn off her life support in the end."

"Wow," says Cass. "Wouldn't wish that on anyone."

Martin hasn't finished. I sense his ramble is cathartic.

"Then she meets another bloke. Didn't marry this one, thank God. Turns out he had a wife and kids ten miles down the road! Tells Monique he's a commercial pilot, flying all over, when he's really playing happy families three nights a week... Nut-job or what?" It sounds like something out of the tabloids. Trouble has a way of following some people around.

"And that's why I feel so bad," says Martin. "She comes to London to make a fresh start and what does she get? Me, piling more grief on her!"

This I will not allow! If I could reach his arm, I would touch it.

"Martin, you weren't to know. We are not to blame for other people's baggage. I'm sure you told Monique your situation pretty quickly. She knew you were in a difficult position..."

Georgie nods. "Fen's right, Mart. We're all grown-ups. Past a certain age, we go into relationships with our eyes open."

"What age is that?" quips Lorenzo, who is younger than she is. "Am I excused or—*Oww!*"

She treads on his toes. Martin is looking sadly into his glass. He has had enough of the spotlight.

"Anyway," I say brightly, "in answer to your question, Georgie, I had a very good day! One of my juniors was on a course, which is usually a nuisance but meant I could crack on with commissioning articles for our next catalogue... I spent an hour on the phone to the arts critic of *The Sunday Times*, who I'm pretty sure will—"

"We were coming to your gallery next Sunday," interrupts Martin. "Me, Monique and the kids. Some history-of-animation thing?"

"Oh, *Popeye To Pixar*? Actually I was going to say, if you can bring the children in the week, I can comp you in. No point forking out fourteen pounds each when—"

He isn't listening. "I suppose, subconsciously, I was trying to get back what I lost with Trudie... What I'm depriving my kids of." His head lolls back, as if communing with an invisible presence above the sunshade. Lifting the hem of his tee shirt Martin scratches his navel. "I don't mean I'm depriving them of their mother. She's not going anywhere, 'cept maybe Downing Street... Just, you know, the family unit."

I sit back. This is the drink talking. Any man who takes up with a brassy piece like Monique is pleasing no one but himself. I am seeing another side to him tonight: delusional!

Delusional *and* confessional. I am still taken aback when men bear their souls like this. Reality television has a lot to answer for: instant fame, just for washing your dirty linen in public, silicone implants optional... Men of my father's generation would jump off a cliff before they aired their failed conquests. Now it's all about 'being open', the star of your own biopic! Sometimes I feel I am fighting a solo crusade for discretion. And if that makes me a stick in the mud, fine!

I am beginning to wonder if Martin is the man I thought he was. In fact, as of now, I'm not even sure why I fell for him at all... He is back on his train of thought:

"They say there's someone for everyone, don't they? *One*, mind. I need to remember that. Look at me, two marriages down, then jumping in feet-first with Monique..." He sniffs. "I should've held out for my soul mate."

A-ha.

Now I'm sure!

Chapter 24

Silence is punctuated by the dry whine of an electric mower a few doors down. Everyone chews, sips, or in Lorenzo's case picks a scab under his watch strap as we ruminate on this. Georgie is the first to speak.

"It's an idealised concept though, Martin. I mean, statistically it's bollocks obviously. If there was only one person on the planet for everyone, we'd be massively unlikely to meet them. Mine's probably in Uzbekistan or somewhere."

"Cheers," says Lorenzo, not looking up.

"I said *if!* Anyway, a relationship's not a failure just cos you don't end up spending your life with someone. I always learned from mine—even the dodgy ones. I tell you, I wouldn't wish myself on Lorenzo without my relationship history. Better I did my fuck-ups with Kieran Spratley when I was sixteen!" She reaches over to tousle his well-gelled hair. "You'd have ditched me by now, babe."

Ethan agrees. "Don't beat yourself up, Martin. George is right, we learn from our mistakes. And next time Monique meets someone, maybe she'll go a bit slower too. Takes two, doesn't it?"

I see their logic, but they've both left something unsaid... In which case, whether it is the three glasses of sparkling or just my innate sense of fairness, saying it falls to me:

"I think—whatever your view on relationships—there's always one thing you should ask yourself. And it isn't easy once the carnal urges come into play..." I acknowledge the variety of expressions this is prompting. "Well, it's simply—*Is this person right for me?*"

Now the words are out I can't decide if they sound profound or banal. From the utterly neutral reaction, I wonder if I made myself clear:

"I mean yes, Georgie's right. It's nonsense to think we all have one perfect partner, or that we can't have a worthwhile relationship with an imperfect partner." I am thinking of my parents. "But there has to be a... A base line!"

Cass slides a glance at Ethan before breaking into a guitar mime with plunking noises. Everyone laughs, but I am undeterred.

"We can all give into our urges when the situation arises. I've done it myself!" Eyebrows raise; "Yes, it's true. When I was at uni, I was on the verge of getting quite a reputation! *Any-Fella-Fenella*, I was christened by one wag. That was a wake-up call!" I haven't thought of that in years (—why am I telling them this?). "Anyway what I learned, and this isn't me being holier-than-thou because I haven't always kept to it... is that you stand more chance of a successful relationship by sticking to a few parameters."

I am looking at Martin who looks lost.

"Parameters, as in...?"

"She means like, standards," says Lorenzo, flicking a speck of something crusty onto the grass.

That is exactly what I mean, though I don't like the way he makes it sound.

"Not standards, exactly. But a couple need to share certain factors if it's going to work out. A similar outlook, say. Not on everything, but the basics."

Martin is nodding. "You're saying Monique and I didn't have enough in common?"

"In a way, yes."

"But we were in the same industry. Had mutual friends we'd worked with..."

"I'm talking more about—" I am out on a limb and I know it; "Background!"

Cass is trying not to smile. "Fen! You're not gonna say something racist, are you?"

"Of course I'm not!"

"—Just cos Monique's from the colonies doesn't mean she's any less—"

"I know! And that's not what I mean. It's nothing to do with where she's from." I tip the last of the booze between my lips.

"I get you," says Lorenzo. "You're saying she's punching above her weight with our-man-Mart... It's a compliment, mate!"

"Huh," laughs Martin. "I know I'm no Tom Hardy. And she's ten years younger than me. Loads of guys at the office fancy her... No, it's nice of you to say, Fen, but if anyone was slumming it, it's her."

This isn't coming across as I intended. I am not trying to massage Martin's ego, merely point out what is obvious to everyone. I look to Ethan and Georgie for help. We are all of a mind on this—why is it being left to me?

Georgie is muttering in Lorenzo's ear. Ethan feeds Cass the last cube of mango on a cocktail stick. In that case... So be it:

"Monique was too bloody common!"

The feeding stops. I plough on.

"I mean, look what happened at the museum! I don't know your wife, Martin, but could you honestly see that happening with her? Do you really want your children under the influence of someone like that?" Georgie bites a thumbnail; Ethan is engrossed in the pattern on the table. "Think what sweet little things they are now. Then imagine the teenagers they'd be after years of Monique's parenting!"

There, I've said it! Yet somewhere in the drunken fug inside me, the absolute certainty I am right is grappling with a suspicion I've gone too far.

"My dad was a builder, Fen," says Martin evenly. "I'm a working class lad myself."

His smile says sympathy. But is it for himself, or the drunken blabbermouth?

"Look, I don't even believe in the class system," I lie. "It has nothing to do with how we turn out, and nor does the country we're born in. I'm just saying, it's making a rod for your own back getting involved with someone who doesn't see the world as we do. As you do... *As one does!*"

I fiddle with the stem of my glass. The silence is disconcerting, and from some quarters downright traitorous. Foolishly I keep digging:

"I'm not saying it can't work. Just that it makes life harder all round."

I want to add "when children are involved", but that may be over-egging it coming from me. A feeling I have slightly lost control is passing over me, like the shadow of next door's outhouse... How does what I said stack up with those here present? Isn't Lorenzo a bit county for Georgie? And Cass is from Brixton, Ethan from Harpenden. Have I managed to offend everyone without even trying?

The only sound is the drone of the mower. Until Martin says: "You could be right."

I dare to look up. He is stretching, hands behind his head, the small of his back arched away from the chair. He seems surprised that I'm looking at him.

"No, fair-dos—I was being selfish. The wife gives me the heave-ho, ego in a state, and what do I do? Grab the first cracking bit of solace that comes along! And you're right about the kids, Fen. Barely got their heads round me and their mum splitting up, and I go and chuck Monique in the mix! Nathan didn't say much but it was obvious Freya didn't like her. She's too kind to say it, but I knew."

Now he is looking down, hands in his pockets. I have a horrid suspicion he is tearing up.

"Martin, I'm sorry if I made you feel—"

But he is out of his chair, face impossible to read in the dwindling light.

"I've got one last bottle of fizz somewhere, if anyone fancies it."

"I'll join you, squire!" says Lorenzo, waggling the wrong sort of wine glass. They arrived too late for flutes.

I am not about to drink another drop. Nor should Martin, though I won't say so. Safe to say, I have broadcast enough opinions for one day...

Chapter 25

The chatter and the evening move on. Sitting around like this feels highly convivial, like we're all closer friends than we are. The couples are becoming more tactile, heads on shoulders, fingers finding fingers. Martin is intent on getting sozzled. Again, I wish it were just the two of us.

"What you looking at?" Ethan asks Cass, who is peering over his shoulder. Both are toying with the half-glass of prosecco Martin pressed on them.

"Mrs What's-Her-Name. Burns?"

"Burnside, yeah. Don't worry, she doesn't come out at night."

I have never seen either of them tipsy before. Cass is swaying slightly, baffled and amused at once, as if the concept of a grave in the garden only just struck him as odd.

"Is it like, legal? You know, 'ealth and safety?"

He walks over to the sacred plot for a better look. Ethan, amazingly for the first time in an hour, consults his phone.

"Hang on, here we go... *Home burials are legal in Britain under the terms of the Burial Laws Amendment of 1880... As long as the bereaved party owns the freehold, it is not necessary to seek official permission.*" He scrolls down. "*However, there are some environmental restrictions governing home burials — e.g. bodies must not be interred near a body of water.*"

Martin grunts. "I thought all bodies were 70% water!"

Only I smile at his swipe at a joke. He is very drunk.

"*... In addition, corpses must be buried at least two feet below ground.*"

"Gawd," says Lorenzo, "I should hope so!" He is following Cass across the lawn. "Have you guys tested it?"

"Babe!" says Georgie looking unamused.

Lorenzo finds a garden cane at the edge of the border. He and Cass take turns stabbing it into the earth at forty-five degrees, manoeuvring it under the raised plinth.

"How's your Pythagoras?" asks Lorenzo.

But their combined efforts won't penetrate more than a couple of inches.

"Soil's baked solid," says Martin. "You need to get the hose on it."

Now he is up, a drunk on a mission, pushing at the shed door that opens outwards.

"*Guys!*" hisses Georgie. "That's someone's wife, for God's sake..."

She checks the adjacent upstairs windows for observers. I am glad not to be the killjoy for once. Lorenzo and Cass stop, looking sheepish. Martin stands in the shed door, hose-end dangling forlornly. His head is wobbling like a string puppet.

"You know what? I reckon I'll turn in."

Oblivion eludes me. My sleep pattern is ragged at the best of times, and this was never going to be a night I'd succumb easily. Luckily I have no need of the textbook eight-hours, and view those who do as slug-a-beds who'll believe any old nonsense.

I have also had far too much to drink. Lying down brings flashes of my Fresher's Ball at Exeter Uni; my first bed-spinner, when closing my eyes did nothing to stem the sensation of being strapped to a fairground ride. My poison that night was *creme de menthe*, the bulk of which reappeared tremulously in my hostel room sink at 4am with a lone, mulched *vol au vent*. A rite of passage that scarred me for life—I haven't touched green liquid soap since.

I won't be sick this time. A round of toast, a glass of milk and two of water have done the trick. I could not persuade Martin to eat. As everyone else tottered off to bed, he rebuffed my attempt to stall him, insisting he'd make himself a fry-up in the morning. He is an affable drunk; like a giddy, grizzly-bear cub. But there was an edge to him tonight. His expletive, as he misjudged the gap between his shoulder and the kitchen doorframe, said further cajoling was inadvisable.

The luminous hands of my alarm clock say five past two. Under the duvet, my own are across my chest like a carved angel. I have conditioned myself to embrace insomnia, and to believe that torpor of body and mind can be as regenerative as sleep. Tonight, my faculties won't cooperate.

I was too forthright!

The more I replay my words, the less they say what I meant them to. So when sleep finally nibbles at my psyche, it is with the sensation of seeping dread I only ever feel in the dark: tomorrow is a mountain, and its gradient all my own making.

I am on the verge of succumbing to Morpheus when I have an idea. I've got sausages and eggs, even a bag of those rather disappointing hash browns in the freezer... Reaching out, I fumble for the knob on the back of my alarm clock.

Six-thirty. That gives me ample time to cook a hearty breakfast for anyone who needs it.

"Oh, it's no bother!"

I am waving the spatula like a talent-show score paddle. Martin grunts as he slides a stool from the breakfast bar with a wince-inducing scrape.

"Fen, I'd puke, honestly."

He changes his mind about sitting near the frying pan and stumbles to the coffee maker. The light tracing of lines on his forehead are now furrows. He looks jowly, and the smudges below his half-open eyes are charcoal-dark. His vest is in situ, but the boxer shorts say negotiating pyjama bottoms was a conundrum too far.

I go back to the hob. My own sunny egg and single sausage are searing to perfection. I feel livelier than I deserve, given the amount I drank and four hours' sleep. Communal living has taught me this can irritate people who wallow in early-morning doldrums. I am careful to regulate my demeanour.

Martin is uncommunicative. Slotting together the components of the coffee machine is taking all his concentration. Once an espresso cup is under the nozzle he presses a button and stands, arms folded.

"How's your head?" he asks at last.

Freshly brewed coffee spews forth. I wait for the gobbling noise to stop.

"Oh, bearable. That was an impromptu one, wasn't it—I planned on watching telly! You must be famished though. Slice of toast?"

He spoons sugars. "I'll have cereal in a bit. I'm going back to bed for half an hour, blame the trains."

As he passes I slop oil over my egg. Those boxers aren't offering the fullest coverage...

"Martin—"

He pauses, leaning the shoulder that didn't collide with the door against the wall (no visible bruising). "Fen?"

"Sorry if I was sticking my oar in—I *was* sticking my oar in. I'll mind my own business in future, I promise."

The furrows crinkle as he sips his coffee. For a moment I wonder if he was too drunk to remember. He sniffs, which seems to clear his thoughts.

"Fen, there are people who speak their mind, and people who don't. That's as true in this house as anywhere." Do I spy the tiniest twinkle in those sleep-crusted brown eyes? "Better out than in, I say."

I am lost for a response. Just watch, as his softly angled calves amble up the hall.

"Your sausage is burning," says Martin from halfway upstairs.

Chapter 26

The theatre is a converted perfume factory near London Bridge. The walk from Waterloo, against a tide of office workers heading home, takes nine minutes.

Avril is already at a table in the adjoining restaurant. My diminutive best friend is peering at the menu, immaculately dressed as ever in a style all her own. It has changed little since the 1990s.

"Good day?" she asks, half standing. We execute our single cheek-press-with-chirp.

"Interesting," I say, threading the jacket I could have left at work over the chair-back. It is another muggy evening, and the table is illuminated by a hot pool from the skylight. "I got an email from Lorraine Dawkins at Tate Mod. You remember, we met her at that private view for Damien Hirst—moaning about the Mayor's office putting the kibosh on his rhinestone suicide vest?"

Avril nods uncertainly.

"Anyway, she didn't say in as many words, but I think she's got me in mind for a job!"

"Gosh. Had you applied?"

"No. I hadn't considered I was in the market, but you don't look a gift horse in the proverbial... I'm meeting her for a drink on Thursday."

"Fancy..." Avril goes back to the menu. "I've ordered a bottle of Pinot Gridge. We can take it through in cups if we knock back half now."

I blanch. I have promised my liver the night off. Then again, that lunchtime tuna panini didn't do the trick, so a hair of the dog may be wise.

Showtime is in fifty-five minutes. We are still choosing when the waitress brings the wine. In the time it takes to pour two generous glasses, I plump for the whitebait and duchesse cottage pie.

"Cheers," says Avril.

We clink, sitting back in unison. These nights out—dinner, theatre or both—have been integral to our social lives for as long as I can remember. I first met Avril at a leaving do, quickly discovering our shared interests: the arts, and drinking too much wine. This was at Penguin, when I was toying with a life in publishing. Three years my senior, she had just begun her career in theatre, which would take her from tea-girl at the Camden Tricycle to her current, long-term position as P.A. and mistress to a lauded West-End impresario.

As twenty-somethings, for a matter of weeks only, we shared a flat in North London; an arrangement that proved less harmonious than I hoped. But we have remained friends, thanks partly to the steady stream of first-night invitations that come with Avril's job. Being concubine to a globally respected captain of the arts requires social invisibility. Thus, we fall into our roles as plus-ones whenever a hot-ticket show or must-see exhibition rolls into town.

"How's Soki?" I ask dutifully.

"No idea. He's in Monte Carlo. Where they don't have email apparently. Or FaceTime."

Last year we celebrated the seventy-fifth birthday of Sir Soki Papadakis at Claridge's, with dinner in a deluxe suite and a private aromatherapist. It was everything Avril could have wished for, bar the actual presence of her lover. I could accuse Soki of many things but stinginess isn't one of them.

"What's he up to this time? Meeting money-men from Broadway?"

She shakes her head. "Purely social, I think." Avril prises a paper napkin from the wodge in an earthenware pot. "As long as he's not jet-skiing, I don't care."

Over the years, their affair has become as much a part of Avril as her messy bun and the asymmetrical belts she thinks make her look taller than five foot one. What I once found quietly scandalous is now the aching norm. I have watched her mellow (less charitably, sag) from *femme fatale* to fond factotum. Avril's relationship with Soki, which for the first fifteen years she conveyed as passionate without exposing me to unwelcome detail, has lost its spark. This makes sense, given her Lothario's advancing years, and a recent bout of cancer requiring extensive chemotherapy. Yet, occasionally and triumphantly, she still implies their relationship breaches the boundaries of P.A./ mogul, thus exceeding that of Sir Soki and Lady Ruth... I, who can no longer see any of them as sexual beings, indulge her like a parent pandering to a six-year-old who earmarks a particular playmate as their 'boyfriend'.

"What else is new?" she asks. "How's the zoo?"

The soap-opera aspect of my living arrangements never ceases to amuse her. From her one-bed flat in Marble Arch, which Avril has occupied at a peppercorn rent since the last millennium, communal living is another world.

"Well, that's the other thing," I say, as our first course arrives. "Martin and Monique are no more."

Her mouth falls open. Through the steam billowing off her minestrone, she looks like a startled if stylish witch. "Hooray! Who gave who the push?"

I give her the rundown between spearings of whitebait, up to and including breakfast this morning. She smiles sagely.

"Always coming though, wasn't it? Poor Martin. Out of the frying pan, onto the barbie..."

Avril speaks of my housemates as if she is acquainted, though of the current intake she has met none. In fact, she has not crossed the threshold of No. 4, The Ridge since soon after I moved in; the night of a Eurovision party, foisted on the house by Scott, a muscular short-lived tenant whose bread was buttered the way of Ethan's... Chaos ensued when everyone grew bored of the scoring, and the male contingent, which was top-heavy in every sense, started stripping off their tee shirts to compare pectorals. A couple of the girls who Scott knew from nightclubbing joined in. Cue for the remaining residents to escape upstairs, and Avril, who planned to spend the night in my room, to order a murderously expensive cab. Since then, her forays south of the river have been limited to trips to Tate Modern, and my own gallery in Dulwich when she can bring herself to venture out of Zone One. Alternate summers, she also makes the foray to Wimbledon for the Men's Semi-finals. Soki, and to a lesser extent Lady Ruth, are fans and make use of their treasured debentures. But the tennis coincides with a Women's Pro-Celebrity Golf tournament in Texas of which Lady Ruth is patron. Hence, the spare tickets to Centre Court every other year. A treat I enjoy, while Avril gazes wistfully at everyone else as they lunch, quaff and cast a tipsy eye over the tennis with the one they love.

She winks mischievously. "So, he's single again! If you call it that before they're divorced..."

I rarely mention any man who catches my eye, even to her. But I have kept Avril abreast of events since the day Martin took the vacant bedroom, even producing a photo culled from a recruitment agency website. It was a few years old; his hair was longer, and his casual shirt said darts player more than graphic designer. She nodded without acknowledging his undeniable good looks. But then, when you're trapped in a futile relationship with an ageing bullfrog who owns half the West End, bitterness is to be expected.

I do not respond to her inference. Just finish my fish while she alternately blows and slurps. The restaurant is full, courtesy of the generous meal-deal tickets the paying public snap up first.

As with most of our nights out, Avril will pick up the tab for drinks, the only element that is not complimentary, and charge it to expenses along with her cabs to and from Marble Arch. Tonight is a preview rather than the premiere, so the crowd skews towards the young and cost-conscious. The play itself, which I looked up at the office, is a new musical fresh from Broadway. Something political and TONY-ed to the eyeballs, West End transfer all but guaranteed.

"Yes well, I'm keeping out of it," I say as our plates are lifted and replaced with main courses. I mean Martin.

"God, absolutely. You don't want to get involved now... His head'll be all over the place. Lawyers and children *and* bonking the bird from the office. Do they still work together?"

"I suppose. He says he's trying to get something else. It can't be fun with Monique giving him daggers every five minutes. Apparently she controls the rota, so she can make him work weekends when he doesn't want to."

"Men!" says Avril. "Brains in their trousers. Never learn, do they?"

This is a rhetorical question she has posed in various forms over the years, always irony-free. She reinforces her next point with a wave of a tartar sauce-smeared knife:

"I've told you what I think. Play the long game with *this* one." Her stress suggests I am in the habit of playing with men en masse. "It's no good making a move while he's hung up on someone else. I'm not even sure you should do it while you're living with him. You said it was temporary—Well, keep in touch when he moves out, then show him not every woman's a career-bitch or mouth-on-legs... Is your mince alright?"

"What? Oh, yes."

I contemplate my duchesse cottage pie. It has arrived as a two-tone pool, the fluted potato roof struggling to contain the gravy-heavy layer beneath. The garnish, lettuce and a worm-cast of grated carrot, is the same as Avril's plaice and chips. She is pouring wine.

"Come on, we need to polish off more of this. They only let you take a cupful."

They also let you keep it behind the bar for the interval. But this is not an option Avril favours, in case the show is toe-curling and she hears the siren-call of her Ovaltine from Seymour Mews. As bountiful provider of the evening's entertainment, she will have no qualms about leaving me to watch the second act alone.

I sip my Pinot, surprised to be keeping pace. Avril has her failings, but her judgement of people beats her instinct for a box-office hit. I am still not sure how to read what Martin said in the kitchen this morning… Either way, steaming in and making my feelings plain is likely to be a disaster. He needs time. And I need the right moment, if I am to tell him how I feel.

My gaze rests on another table. A man, sitting across from a pushed-back chair with a woman's cardigan draped over it. He is chewing thoughtfully, swirling a morsel of bread round his plate to mop up sauce. His date returns from the Ladies, saying something admonishing that makes him smile. He sits back, hands raised, playfully chastised… It reminds me of an evening at home with Martin, pre-Monique. Ribbing him for adding a shredded slice of white bread to my homemade tomato soup. He smiled and sat back in the exact same way, a picture of stung male innocence, enjoying a woman being assertive.

This man is not as handsome as Martin, but he shares his olive skin and thick brown hair. An open top shirt button reveals the same chest-thatch to which I was once indifferent and am now drawn when it appears opposite me on the train. A surprise; by and large bodily fetishes are a shallow response I associate with men only.

I fork up the last of my potatoey gloop. Avril, down to a blackened stump of tail, checks her watch.

"Better skip pud," she says, miming to the waitress for plastic cups.

If this is anything like the last play we saw here, we'll need them.

Chapter 27

Four days later it is all back on.

I am just getting used to having Martin around the house again. Little chats over tea; ribald quips as TV quizzes field the thickest possible contestants for our amusement. Everything is as before, thank goodness. No awkwardness.

Then he is gone two nights running. On the second I lay awake until midnight, staring at my phone and deleting half-written texts. I am not his mother. What he is up to is none of my business... But then if something *has* happened, who would know? If he doesn't turn up at work and they can't get hold of him, who is down as his next-of-kin? His wife, of course. And didn't he tell me Trudie's slack at picking up messages? One of many annoying habits dredged up over a bottle of wine...

Next morning, Georgie and I are making toast in our dressing gowns when Monique sails in. She is wearing one of Martin's shirts, and a pair of knickers cut too high for decency. Georgie's buttering halts mid-scrape.

"That kettle on?" demands a gravelly Monique, taking two mugs from the cupboard.

I nod dumbly. From on high, the bathroom door opens, followed by a drumroll of footsteps down the stairs. Martin, in a hurry.

"Morning, guys," he says with a nervous quaver. "Hope we didn't wake you coming in?"

He looks rougher than I've ever seen him, hair in all directions, eyes peeping from puffy little sacs like ravioli. Still no one speaks.

Monique sidles over. Flings her arms round his neck and presses her breasts against him as he smiles uneasily.

"We had a helluva night..."

I am not interested in the details. I take my toast up in silence, get ready for work and out of the house, all without running into anyone. I pound the pavement, onto my train and off again, a journey I endure in poker-faced fury.

By the time I reach the Picture Gallery, my breathing has subsided. I hurl myself into the results of a ticketing analysis from last summer's exhibition, a perfect-bound document long repurposed as a drip-mat for potted succulents.

Men! What absolute fucking idiots!

Even the ones you think have their heads screwed on! Then again, what do I really know about Martin? Was I as gullible as he is, to fall for his twinkly charms? I've only heard one side of the marital breakdown story. His wife may have bloody good reasons for throwing him out!

Avril was right. On current evidence, he may well be one of those men with fidelity issues... In which case, does his *volte-face* back into the arms of the same, blowsy tart actually speak in his favour?

Heads turn as I slam a desk drawer. I pluck a pen from the desk-tidy, like a dagger from a scabbard.

"You okay, Fen?" asks Cheryl. She has been in the sun, the results on display in one of her sleeveless smocks (... *If the Buddha wore a vest...*).

"Fine. Just deciding if these analytics people are worth the fortune we pay them."

Cheryl goes back to her crossword. For once, I am glad to see Millie and Tash paying me no attention. I am often irritated by the way they sideline me. Tash, who still regales the office with her music when it suits her, is playing Derek like a penny whistle. Quietly broadening her role from Marketing Assistant, via occasional dog-walker, into his unofficial adviser on youth culture; specifically, how to divert the flow of arty millennials in a ten-mile radius through the doors of the Picture Gallery... I fully appreciate the logic of tapping the capabilities of our department. What galls me is that I prepared a report on that very topic. It has been in Derek's inbox for months.

I am thumbing through the ticketing doc, flicking not reading, when the man himself emerges from his office.

"Morning, Fen. Everything alright?"

"Yes, thank you. Morning, Derek."

(Is there an *ANGRY* sign flashing over my head?)

For the second time today, I face a man who looks embarrassed.

"Good, good. Oh, quick heads-up, I'll be out this afternoon. Lunch with O'Grady from the Arts Council. Fear it'll drag on, so... Could you sit in on a meeting for me? Just the chaps from Southwark Planning, re our application to revamp the staff loos."

"Of course, Derek." *(Shall I scrub them out while I'm at it!)*

"Excellent..."

En route to his lair, he stops at Tash's desk. His next words are shamelessly audible.

"Cab at midday, Tash? Table's booked for twelve-thirty and we mustn't keep him waiting..."

Her answer is a lipsticky smile. Today's earrings, I note, are quite restrained.

That night I work late. Contrive to be out the next night too, by choosing a film from the three on offer at our local boutique cinema. A Woody Allen is out of the question, and I'm not up for something Chilean that sounds like Almodóvar with even more transexuals... In retrospect, a First World War epic is not a wise choice either. The lead is a lily-skinned actor with lips like a camel who gets nominated for everything. He carries off the khakis well enough, but two hours of trench-based tragedy do not lift my mood.

I am wishing I'd braved the sticky seats of the multiplex when another explosion leaves a batman and his horse with one and three legs respectively. My cue to leave.

It is spitting rain as I hit the street, the first time in weeks. The town-centre clock says twenty to nine. Still too early... The fast-food sushi place is open. I decide to pop in, since eating out means less exposure to the communal areas at home.

Inside, the crowd is bigger than I expect for an evening. I pick out a tray from the chill cabinet—rice medallions with a glossy hill of beans—and pay at the counter. Sliding into an empty booth, I separate my chopsticks with a wishbone snap and wonder if any other health-conscious diners are avoiding their own home. The thought sets me back in my seat... This is ridiculous! Like being back at uni, keeping away from halls until a chap I don't want to run into is safely off campus.

Games are not for grown-ups!

I dab a last oblong in the soy sauce, avoiding the pyramid of neon-green condiment that takes my head off. Snatching up my bag, I tip the tray of plastic detritus into the letterbox-bin and resume my walk home.

The rain, which is more of a mist, isn't dampening anyone's spirits. Any summer night is party night in Wimbledon town. Apart from in the holy fortnight itself when it all happens up in the village, where the bars are close enough to the All-England Club for those not too tiddly or sunburnt to indulge in more carousing... Tonight, a gaggle of smokers take up the row of bum-rests outside Pret a Manger. Across the street, the town's rusting sculpture of a giant stag is a backdrop for girls taking selfies. Our Council's nod to municipal art doubles as a display for lost sweatshirts, and at Christmas, Santa hats and wryly knotted scarves.

I turn off the main drag, into the warren of streets that wind up the hill. Past the Rotary Club, and the Christian Science Church with dour tracts in the window. Halfway along, a dead-end for motorists leads to a footpath; my favoured route up the hill when the low-hanging mulberry trees offer their fruits to the eagle-eyed.

Berries are not on my mind tonight. Turning into The Ridge, the gateposts of No. 4 come into view, just as the bonnet of Martin's Fiat edges out. As it swings in my direction I will myself to keep walking... Pretend not to notice until it's almost adjacent, and a raised hand and two inquisitive faces register at the corner of my eye. A glimpse, then gone in a flash, embarrassment averted.

As I close the front door the first voice I hear is Lorenzo's.

"Cheeky cow! What does she know about it?"

The words tumble out on a quaver of laughter, but he is not amused.

"Jesus," says Ethan, shaking his head. *"Jee-sus!"*

He is kneeling at the coffee table, looking for something in a pile of magazines. Georgie and Lorenzo are in a heap on the settee.

"Everything okay?" I breeze. Sometimes all you can do with an ants' nest is stir it.

"No it bloody isn't!" snaps Georgie. "That woman was just *so* rude to Lorenzo, I could've hit her!"

My fingers fly to the neck of my blouse.

"They asked about my day," explains Lorenzo, "so I said I'd been in and out of meetings, cos we had a run on Chinese conglomerates..."

Ethan retakes the armchair. "It was just Martin making conversation. He was as shocked as anyone!"

Lorenzo shrugs. "Then Monique launches into this diatribe, about how the Chinese are buying up half of Australia, gutting the mining industry so half her mates have lost their jobs and the other half are getting pay cuts. Like I'm to blame!"

Ethan flips open his magazine. "I reckon she'd had a few, to be fair."

"I see." I am thinking about Martin behind the wheel. "Were they both drinking?"

"Nope," says Georgie. "He wasn't expecting her. We'd all settled in for a quiet night when she turns up on the doorstep. Said she'd been for dinner with a friend down the road, and could she crash here?"

I pick my way through shoeless feet to the other armchair.

"And *Chinkies* she called them!" spits Georgie. "In this day and age!"

"Totally unacceptable," chips in Lorenzo. He frowns gallantly at Ethan who is trying not to laugh. Georgie leaps from the settee:

"Seriously, I don't need this. I've had the day from hell — bailing out two of our lads at Lewisham nick, then stuck on the train for an hour, plus I lost my Oyster card... Heart rate just back to normal when Marine-bloody-Le Pen walks in!" She sniffs, wiping an eye on her sleeve. "Stay down here if you want, Lorenzo. I'm going to bed."

He looks up from the television, slightly dazed. Snooker, I register for the first time.

"Can I watch it online?" he wheedles.

She nudges his calf with her heel. "If you use headphones, come on..."

He stands with some reluctance, shirt tails flapping over crumpled suit trousers. They are at the door when Georgie says:

"I mean it, guys — I'm not happy about this. If you're in, can we chat tomorrow night?"

This catches me off guard. "Yes, I think I —"

"Thing is," says Ethan, "chances are Martin will be in too. They've gone to hers tonight."

Georgie's fingers drum on the door. "Good call. Meet in The Umpire? Seven-ish?"

This is a turn-up! Our first-ever trip to the pub as a household, or three-quarters of it... The Umpire's Chair is on the high street, a block from the station. I have passed it twice a day for eight years but never been in at night. They do a passable Sunday lunch, which I took Mother to once when she was still mobile (—a debacle over flat Yorkshire puddings; we didn't go back).

I have a raft of questions now Ethan and I are alone. How did Martin react to Monique's outburst? Was she really as poisonous as they implied? And who decided they should go back to her place? I am about to launch in when his mobile chirps.

"Uh-oh, got to go," he says, stabbing a reply. A holdall appears from behind his chair. "Cass is working late and I'm staying at his. It's his birthday tomorrow." He chucks the magazine on the coffee table, disturbing an open yellow bag of sweets.

"But you'll be here tomorrow night? It sounds like we've a lot to discuss. Or Georgie has." Once again, I am happy not to be the one leading this.

"Sure," he says from the hall. "Cass is on lates so I'll defo be in the pub for seven."

"Good, see you there... Don't you want your sweets?"

His head reappears. "Eh? Oh, they're not mine." His expression is comedy-queasy. "Monique bought them for Martin. *Luurve* token! Help yourself—he won't care and she was in no state to count them!"

I am still staring at the shiny bag when the front door slams. M&Ms.

Peanuts, chocolate-coated or otherwise, make me cough. I am not tempted.

Chapter 28

The following evening, I am the one at the mercy of South-East Trains.

The line was shut for a month last winter while they replaced the track outside Earlsfield. A gross inconvenience to commuters like me, to whom the operators promised a vastly improved service. Only now my train is more delayed than ever. Excuse: the wrong sort of sleeper, problem to be rectified next February. Just when jostling for replacement buses with a horde smelling of bacon and aggressive body sprays is as miserable as it could be.

It is ten past seven when I arrive at The Umpire. I am still glad I hung around at work rather than brave the pub alone. Ethan spots me from a table by the fireplace.

"I'll get you one, Fen, what you having?"

He and Georgie have made inroads into their drinks already.

"G&T, thanks. Slimline if they've got it."

I slump on a stool beside Georgie who smiles through my tale of travel woes.

"You and me both, Fen. If I hadn't slipped out when the boss wasn't looking I'd never have made it..."

The pub is busy. Its name and the crossed wooden tennis rackets in the window suggest a tourist haunt, not that there are many of those outside The Fortnight. Elsewhere touches of memorabilia are discreet beyond the freestanding portrait in the hearth: a dripping Chris Evert, waving the Ladies' Singles salver like a serving dish she rescued from the *Titanic*.

Ethan returns with my gin. Unusually his own glass looks to contain more than orange juice.

"So," says Georgie. "Am I being petty? Does Monique grate on you guys, or is it just me?"

Haven't we already *had* this conversation?

"Well," I say, "obviously I wasn't there last night. But we've all voiced reservations before. Haven't we?" I am looking at Ethan.

"Yeah. I mean, Monique's not the kind of person I'd choose to hang around with but... Well, house-sharing—you take your chances, don't you?"

Georgie nods reluctantly.

"On the other hand," I say, "precedence must count for something. We've all been here longer. Surely we have a right to feel comfortable in our own home?"

The nodding stops.

"Are you saying we give Mart his marching orders?" says Georgie. "Contract-wise I'm not sure we can do that, and I don't want to involve old Burnside."

This is not what I am saying, nor am I keen to rope in the landlord. I sit back, the better to let her speak. This is her idea after all.

She takes a sip from her jumbo wine. "Look, I pride myself on getting along with anyone. I have to in my job. But when I get in at night, I want to relax... And I appreciate, when you share and you're seeing someone it's tricky. You've got to strike a balance. Lorenzo's in the same boat, but if I'm honest I prefer hanging out at ours. His housemates are alright, but they're a bit public-school. Not your full-on hunters-and-shooters, though one does own half a polo pony... I bet you think he's a real posh boy, but it's all a facade. Cos of the crowd he works with."

"Hey," says Ethan. "Lorenzo's cool. Good guy."

Georgie takes another sip. "Exactly. And he's lovely to me— as I'm sure you've noticed..."

I haven't, but say nothing. To my surprise her eyes are filling up.

"I tell you, I've had some rotten relationships. I know we've all been around but I'm talking *serious* errors of judgement.

That's why I want to make this one work. Me and Lorenzo are still getting to know each other and it really isn't conducive, being around someone who winds him up. You can see that, can't you?"

"Of course," I say. I have never been able to square Georgie's beau with her supposed Socialist principles. Then again, believing in a fairer sharing of wealth doesn't have to mean dating a pauper... She is still ruminating:

"Obviously, Martin's got his life to sort out. And I feel for him, I do. Family break-ups are the worst. Our Director of Outreach says divorce is like a war no one's fighting but you... But when Martin said he'd split with Monique, I was like *Yesss!* So if it's all on again I'm not sure I can bear being under the same roof."

"Shit, George!" says Ethan. "You can't let his gobby girlfriend drive you out of your home!"

He is right. I am nonplussed. No one finds Monique's presence more obnoxious than I do, but I won't let her get her claws into me. I'd have said Georgie was made of sterner stuff. But those are tears glistening on her eyelashes.

"What would you do?" I ask. "Find a place with Lorenzo?"

Her glass stalls. Her face says my suggestion is utterly left-field.

"After a couple of months? God no!"

My imagination, or is Ethan stifling a smirk too?

I can't win! No matter how I try to engage, I always miss the mark... In this age of instant hook-ups, how am I to know when shacking up is appropriate? Entire TV series are predicated on people marrying people they've only just met! Vows aren't promises any more—they're light entertainment!

I am starting to feel the strangeness of the evening. The three of us here, without the familiar focus of No. 4, The Ridge. I want to knock back my drink and head home. But the prospect of running into Martin and Monique appeals even less.

"Anyone else eating?" says Ethan. "I can't hang on till I get to Cass's."

Georgie grunts and he disappears to find menus. She reaches across and touches my arm.

"Sorry, Fen, I didn't mean to be rude. It's just, I've been caught like that before. Getting too serious, too soon. Won't get fooled again!"

Ethan returns with wipe-clean bar menus. A border of cheery cows, sheep and chickens suggests their delight at being part of the selection on offer. I'm not very hungry and all I can think about is the mini-quiche in the fridge, and bag of watercress that would go beautifully with the dressing I bought at the weekend. Nine pounds for a burger does not compare.

"They do a decent Sunday lunch," I say, giving the impression of pondering. "But I'm not sure I'm in the mood for pub-grub. Don't let me stop you, though..."

I can leave them to it. There's hours of daylight left, and if the peanut twins are home I can always grab my quiche and retreat to a corner of the garden.

"Oh, go on," says Georgie. "We can't let Ethan eat alone. I've nothing in anyway."

She plumps for a chicken burger, Ethan the veggie moussaka, and they agree to share fries. I have already put my menu down.

"Twist your arm?" she niggles playfully.

Well—I suppose if they really to want me to stay... "Alright, I'll have the fish finger sandwich. Do we order separately or—"

"I'll get them," says Ethan. "You wanna pay cash, yeah?"

Like the girls in the office he buys everything with his mobile. I feel a Luddite, reaching for my purse.

"Take thirty," I say, handing over a crinkle of notes. "And get another round..."

Chapter 29

Whilst I am not a fan of pubs, I have to say The Umpire is quite convivial. Aside from dutiful socials with work, I rarely set foot anywhere more louche than a wine bar. The restaurant area is separate, and the tables here are smaller so the plate sizes should be too.

None of the other punters are eating anything but crisps. They are older than the crowd in the street last night. Proper drinkers, here for the beer, not the Sky Sports other hostelries offer as a matter of course. Mostly male; office workers on their none-too-urgent way home, plus two old lags at the bar, eyes trained on the optics like strikers lining up a penalty. At the feet of one a small terrier lies patiently, a red bandana in place of a collar.

We settle back with our drinks and chat as we wait for the food. Ethan is surprisingly good company, after what are indeed a couple of single vodka-oranges. He tells a funny story about Cass's landlord, letting a room to a tenant with a gecko. It escaped and climbed onto the Victorian-high ceiling, from which no amount of tickling with an extendable cobweb brush would bring it down. Two days later they were about to call the fire brigade, when it lost its footing on the ceiling rose and landed in someone's salad.

"Probably spotted a slug," says Ethan. Georgie and I laugh.

Some people spend their lives like this: easy nights in easy company—there's a lot to be said for it. Aren't all jobs drudgery to a degree? Worthy of a drink and a giggle at the end of the day? All the more reason we deserve to feel happy at home... Which reminds me;

"Now, I don't want to split hairs. But when we were in the garden the other night, I did feel a bit unsupported." I can say this, we're all friends here. "You know, when Martin was talking about getting together with Monique. Given what we all thought—think of her—I was a bit surprised I was the only one expressing an opinion."

Georgie looks vague. "Were you? I mean, I was right behind you. You were spot on!"

I raise an eyebrow. Ethan is ready to meet me halfway.

"Actually, yeah. Cass did say he thought you were brave, sticking your neck out like that. Said it took guts, even if it was a bit..."

I assume he is skirting the word *tactless*. He is a kind boy, easy-going if prone to pussyfooting. He will learn it gets you nowhere.

"Ethan, there is a time for sensitivity. I'm all for household harmony, but sometimes you just have to say *Enough!*"

Georgie is about to reply when the first of our food appears—a burger for her and fries for them, at a speed that says they are not freshly prepared. I am starting to feel peckish, on the verge of giving in to a chip, when mine arrives. Three breadcrumbed sticks between doorsteps of lightly grained white bread, the very definition of a fish finger sandwich. It comes with tartare sauce, so I ask for ketchup which takes longer than everything else.

Ethan has drawn the short straw. His moussaka is served cold; rubbery and wrinkled at the edges, with lettuce leaves shredded to snot-coloured confetti.

"I'd send it back," I say.

But he risks botulism and digs in, pausing to sprinkle pepper and salt.

It is probably the gin, or the fact I only had a prawn salad for lunch, but my own dish is surprisingly tasty. I am transported to the Guy Fawkes' Nights of childhood. Walking home from fireworks in the park, to feast on sausages cooked in the hearth on the knitting needles Mother kept for the purpose... Fish finger sandwiches were another staple, served in baps with margarine and ketchup. She always went to town on the catering to compensate for Father, who forbade us a bonfire on account of a low-hanging sycamore.

"It's the rental dichotomy," says Georgie. "People are sharing for longer because they can't afford to buy. You try and make a home for yourself then end up walking on eggshells... Don't get me wrong, I love our place. The rent's bearable, Wimbledon's cool and you guys are great. And I've nothing against Martin as such. But if I was holding back about Monique—and yeah you're right, Fen, guilty—I guess I thought I had no choice. That it's the price we pay..." She's not finished. The wine is making her philosophical. "I see so much self-delusion in my job. People lying to themselves, and half the time it's cos of childhood stuff they never processed." She snorts, pinching up a chip. "This isn't America. We can't all go to shrinks. I'm trained to help these kids, and I'm good at it, but that doesn't make me immune. I'm as guilty as anyone."

She is down to a crescent of burger, slurring slightly. Two large glasses leave little change out of a bottle. She is not leaving Ethan many of those chips either. I am wondering whether to order more carbs as she says:

"My brother died when I was eleven. Car crash. He was nine."

My sandwich freezes an inch from my lips.

"—Second week of Jan. There was ice on the roads, and Mum was taking us into Milton Keynes in the Mini. We were all wearing seat belts, me in front, him in the back, when something ran out in the road. A cat, dog—we didn't see it. Mum hit the brakes and a car transporter slammed straight in the back of us. She and I got whiplash, bruises. But Jason..."

I clamp a hand over my mouth. Ethan's face says this is news to him too.

"Jesus, George. I can't believe it."

She is bolt upright, trance-like. Her eyes are dry now. At this distance there are no tears left. "All because I wanted the Westlife CD I didn't get for Christmas. Wouldn't let up about it, threatened to run away if I couldn't buy it with my pocket money! That's why we were in the car and that's why Jason died."

I want to hug her. Tell her she mustn't think like that... But this is something she has dealt with. The horror is only fresh to us.

"I've spent the rest of my life trying to make up for it."

I touch her arm. "You can't blame yourself, Georgie. You weren't to—"

"No, I know. You should see Mum if anyone tries to guilt-trip me, or her. We went through hell afterwards, for years, but we've come to terms as much as we can... And everything, job included, comes down to that. I've been trying to save people ever since." She sighs. "You only get one family. And they can be a total nightmare but take it from me, the alternative's worse."

"I feel terrible," I say. "All this time under the same roof, you've been carrying this round and I never knew!"

"But that's my point, Fen. We all need to feel safe in our own little world. We don't go volunteering the stuff that makes us feel like freaks. Grin-and-bear-it—us Brits are famous for it."

I'm not sure about that. Few people seem to think twice about letting it all hang out these days... But there is something old-fashioned in what Georgie is saying, something I rather like. I've always thought of her as a mite immature. Shows how wrong you can be!

"I know what you're saying, George," says Ethan. "Anything for a quiet life."

He finishes chewing and puts down his fork. He also has something to say.

"I always knew I was gay, but it took me years to come out to my parents. Tied myself in knots about it. My mum and dad are pretty traditional. Especially Mum."

Georgie nods. "I remember you saying."

I can't stop myself. Ethan catches my expression: *Silly old Fen, left out again.* He looks embarrassed.

"Oh, water under the bridge, Fen, honestly... Basically I got in trouble with the police. Not in a George Michael way—I'm not talking raid on the local Gents! I was back living in Harpenden after uni. Went for a lunchtime drink with this mate from school I always had the hots for... I was a proper drinker in those days, so of course one pint became five. Ended up telling him all the stuff I kept quiet at school, which surprise-surprise he was fine about... So we're staggering home, one thing leads to another, and we end up sneaking into someone's garage for a fumble! Next thing you know, a squad car roars up and we're getting hauled off down the cop shop. Someone dialled 999 cos they thought we were nicking a Saab!"

I am agog. Georgie is laughing.

Ethan shakes his head. "I was twenty-two. I mean, not a kid, so they wouldn't inform my parents. But Mum's friend Carol worked there—clerical not a copper, but sod's law she saw me waiting to be cautioned. Maybe she wouldn't have said anything but I couldn't risk it. I was nearly sick on the way home, thinking what I was going to tell them. Pathetic."

Well—*Still waters!* This evening hasn't turned out at all as I expected. I am rather enjoying it, if a little wary. Too long in the pub has a way of ending in a truth session, and eventually the spotlight will fall on me. I do not feel confessional—not that I can compete with these two. Even so, I'd rather not come across as a total bore...

"I suppose we all avoid the truth at times. It can be a very blunt instrument." I am looking from Georgie to Ethan. "And I am sorry for what you've both been through, truly. But all the more reason why you deserve to be happy now... Anyway, for better or worse I told Martin what we think of Monique—and now she's back on the scene, it's all blown up in our faces!"

By the bar the terrier wakes from its slumbers. Cocks an ear at its master, lifts its head from the parquet to do a mighty yawn, then slumps back to sleep...

Quite oblivious that, in the time it took to yawn, I have realised what I have to do next.

Chapter 30

"Don't fuss, Fenella! I'm not a complete—"

My face pulls her up short. "Invalid, Mother? That's exactly what you are. Eat this."

I slot the tray over her midriff and sit on the edge of the bed. She is propped up on pillows to make swallowing easier. Chicken soup is the most appropriate thing I found in her cupboard.

"The doctor says you have to eat. I'm getting a lift to the shops later so I can buy whatever you like..."

I picked up the message on my way into a meeting: Kath, Mother's joint person-at-arms, announcing breathlessly that Lillian is in an ambulance after falling in the kitchen. I make my excuses, draft in Derek to dig me out of a hole for once, and summon an Uber... When I arrive at the local A&E, Mother is on a trolley, with Kath and the redoubtable Bill on either side like they're manning a tombola. Since they can't agree on the doctor's exact words, I ignore them and go and find the horse's mouth.

"Nothing showing on the X-ray," says a man so young it is hard to believe he's sat his A-levels, let alone qualified. "But she's badly bruised. We've a bed free from four o'clock and I'd like her to stay in overnight. Can't be too careful with your mother's MS."

Well, at least he knows... But Mother will have none of it. She submits to a dressing on her hip, but nothing more. Twenty minutes later, Bill is wheeling her across the tarmac with her handbag on her knee.

Once we are all back at the bungalow, suggesting I would like some time alone with Mother gets me nowhere. Consequently I take a leaf out of her book: tell Bill and Kath to go because I'll be fine without them.

"That's no way to get along with people," chides Mother, as I hold out soup and a spoon. "Ordering them about!"

"I don't need to get on with them. They're your friends, and they don't like me anyway. Are you going to eat that or do I have to feed you?"

Silently she takes the bowl.

There is nothing to see on the kitchen floor. If she slipped on something, as Mother insists, it has dried up now. For as long as she can get out of her chair, there is always the danger she will come a cropper in her walking frame. More handrails are the sensible option, though I can hear her retort if I suggest it *("If I wanted to live in a ballet school, Fenella, I'd be wearing a tutu!")*.

Sparring is her way of fending off the sadness. Mother, in bed in broad daylight, is a glimpse of the future neither of us wants to see. Despite her new-found willingness to spend money, she resists having this room decorated. The walls are the beige my father painted them twenty years ago. It was never a cosy room and it hasn't changed since he died *("It's a place to sleep. Can't see the walls with my eyes shut, can I?")*. Perhaps she thinks sprucing it up will make it harder to leave; that soft carpet and prettier curtains will take on a life of their own, meshing like the forest around Sleeping Beauty's castle, trapping her forever.

The only decoration are two of Father's paintings: a waterfall, and the murmuration of starlings we saw on the Norfolk Broads when I was a girl. I can still remember it, weaving over the fields in a black tornado, stunning my parents to silence... And there is a photo of Father himself, on the side where he used to sleep. Not one of the better ones, when he was young and relatively dashing. My friends at school used to say he looked like one of the vets on a Sunday night TV show, though I couldn't see it. In this picture he is standing at the dining table, carving knife in one hand, steel in the other, ready to dissect the Sunday joint.

It was the year before he died and his smile is uncertain; of a man who finds a task he's found easy for a lifetime suddenly requires full concentration.

There is a conversation Mother and I need to have without the do-gooders. I have been researching options for help at home. Trained staff who'll come in morning and night, to get her ready for the day, then ready for bed again. The Council pays an allowance so she can buy whatever help she needs from a roster of private companies, all with reassuring websites. They are full of guff about background checks and photos of fair-haired young women tending to fair-haired old women, most of whom look far too perky to need their tea pouring. The prospect reassures me, but I have to pick my moment.

Soup is disappearing. I pretend not to notice Mother's hand shaking, or the way she only half-fills the spoon. The tea towel over her nightgown has slipped down her ski-slope chest. As I reposition it she brushes me away.

"Heaven's sake, Fenella! I'm not a child, I don't need a bib."

A moment later a creamy rivulet soaks into the duvet, a glance from Mother quick to apportion the blame.

No more is said until the spoon lies in the near-empty bowl. I am halfway to the kitchen with the tray when she calls:

"There's a postcard on the mantelpiece you might want to see…"

It is a verdant cone of a mountain, reflected in an azure sea. I turn it over. The card has been splashed with water but the handwriting is still legible. In fountain pen, fluent and precise:

Greetings from the sunny isle of St. Lucia. Just been ashore for lunch and picked up this card. It's the view from my balcony. Have been here before, and there ain't so much to recommend it to be honest. You seen one white sandy beach, you seen 'em all! Here's hoping it's sunny in Surrey. Hi to you and Fen both.
Your friend, Irving Jessop

Nice of him to stay in touch. I remember making the usual noises when we said goodbye on the ship, but I didn't know Mother gave him her address. Touching, in a way; another counterstrike as her world closes in... He was an odd one, Mr Jessop, with his nomadic life like the world's richest hobo. But the card radiates kindness, which I appreciate on her behalf.

The doorbell chimes as I stack the dishwasher. Two o'clock on the dot, which can only mean—

"Ready, Fenella?" says Kath. She beams on the doorstep, holding out something in a Sainsbury's bag. "I thought you might need a nightie, and what with Lillian being a size...?"

Neither of us cares to be drawn.

"Thank you," I say, taking it.

I catch a glimpse of tiny buttons on something the same insipid pink as Kath herself. In fairness, she is right: I am not prepared for overnighting. I've told work I am taking a day's compassionate leave, and will be in touch tomorrow.

I keep her on the mat while I make sure Mother has everything she needs.

"Back in half an hour," I say, peeking round the bedroom door. "If you had a little television in here, you could—"

"Nescafé, Fenella! And if they're doing two-for-one Battenbergs, get four. They freeze, you know..."

"So brave your mother, isn't she?"

We are at the lights by the Nepalese restaurant. When I don't reply, Kath jumps back in.

"And so much to contend with, yet she never complains. An example to us all!"

We have never been alone before. She is a few years younger than Mother, with unflattering glasses and a snowy, blunt-cut hairdo, like an ageing Cleopatra. Kath wears jeans and a nougat-coloured sweater, one of her famous home-knits Mother is scathing about. Her driving leaves a bit to be desired too, as we lurch over the crossing.

"I'm not convinced she's getting the best support from that clinic," I say, turning to matters practical. "They cancelled her last appointment, and the time before they mixed up her notes with someone else."

At the steering wheel Kath is wide-eyed. "I know, Bill gave them hell about that. You should have seen him!"

A casual remark, I wonder, or a dig at me for not being there? I wish she would drive a bit faster—the whiff of her butterfly air freshener reminds me of aeroplane sick bags... I focus on the topic in hand.

"That said, if Mother won't do the physio, it's not surprising her condition's deteriorating. Does she ever do her exercises?"

The laminated A4 sheet has been on the table by her armchair for a year. I have seen it used as a drinks coaster, a crumb-catcher and one stultifying day last summer, a makeshift fan.

"You see, I think they're too difficult for her," says Kath. "Your mother hasn't the joint-mobility they think she has. They're supposed to alleviate the stiffness, but I think they make her muscle spasms worse. According to the research I read, the worst thing you can do with Secondary Progressive MS is—"

"Nonsense!" I am not getting into a debate about who is more abreast of the latest scientific developments, because I will lose. "Oh, here we are..."

We pull into the supermarket car park. Crawl, as Kath peers around for an empty space. The people of Oxted like their shopping.

I know I should be grateful to her, and Bill. Her 'godsends', Mother calls them. Most widows in her position would be struggling to live independently; the likely progress of her disease means it won't last forever, even with good neighbours and a dedicated cleaner. Professional care is the only option. We are backing into a space by a snake of shopping trolleys when I decide to dip a toe:

"Depending how she recovers from this, I do think it's time Mother had some help. As in, carers."

At first Kath seems not to register... Carries on twisting in her seat, her concentration flicking between the back window and the rear-view mirror. Doesn't say a thing until she turns off the engine.

"I don't think your mother would take to strangers, Fen, do you?" Her hands are between her knees and she is staring at the dashboard.

"Well, she'll reach a point where she won't have a choice. And they're not strangers, Kath, they're healthcare professionals. Mother will get to know them."

She looks scornful. "Healthcare professionals? All they do is get them out of bed!"

This is one area where I am confident I have the better grasp. Keen as I am to get out of this car, it is time someone was put in their place:

"Actually, they offer a full range of services. Housework and making meals — and Mother won't be able to manage the shower much longer. That's another fall waiting to happen. Then there's the loo... Don't look at me like that, Kath. It takes her half an hour to get in and out as it is, and it'll only get worse... And yes, some of them offer nursing care too!"

She is simmering. Fingers twitch. People who won't say boo to a goose can be the worst to cross.

"Well, obviously that's for you and your mother to decide. Lillian knows Bill and I are always happy to pop in if she needs anything. *At all*... And Bill loves that garden. Says it's a pleasure to do. He'll tell you himself, his own isn't big enough!"

I nod graciously. "And I know Mother appreciates everything you do — as I do... Look, I haven't said anything yet, and I'd appreciate if you don't either. She needs to get back on her feet, so to speak, before she decides anything... Now, shall we do this shopping?"

Kath is out of the car without another word. She pauses at the boot for a brace of hessian carriers, which she tucks under one arm as we cross the car park. For the moment, hostilities cease.

"And I can tell *you*, Fenella, your mother really appreciates how much you keep in touch. She knows you're busy with your career, and she looks forward to your visits. Such a rigmarole for you, what with not driving. And those trains with their endless engineering works..."

I keep walking. Here in dull leafy Oxted, far removed from the city and my life at No. 4, The Ridge, I cannot shake off an inkling there is more to Kath's sympathy than meets the eye.

Chapter 31

Mother is back to what amounts to full fitness in a week—a little miracle. The fear with MS is that each step down makes it harder to climb up again. Disruption of the nerve messages travelling from her brain to her hands and feet causes a host of symptoms, from numbness to unexpected spasms. Sometimes her legs will go rigid without warning, feet rising to the horizontal in her chair as if buoyed by an invisible sea. If she is alone, all she can do is wait for it to pass; if a trusted other is present, she can guide them through the procedure of bracing an arm behind her knees and pressing down on her shins, gently pushing them back through ninety degrees. It looks brutal, especially in public, and earned us startled stares in the library.

In the interim, I make a point of speaking to her at the beginning and end of each working day. Phoning her mobile, rather than the landline which is often answered by Kath or Bill. Fully intending to return at the weekend, I warn Avril we may need to rain-check on our Benedict Cumberbatch movie pencilled for Saturday night. But Mother has other ideas:

"That's very kind of you, Fenella, but I'm absolutely fine. The district nurse has been in every morning. Nice girl, though she could warm her hands up... And I've had a delivery of two Japanese maples for the garden. They took a fortnight longer than it said, and I've told Bill if they're not in soon they won't get enough sun to do their business. I've been caught like that before... Remember that rhododendron your father ruined?"

The inference is that this is all too dull for me; that I will have better things to do with my weekend than watch an old gent digging in borders. It is Friday afternoon, but there have been hints of this all week which I ignored. When the call ends, I sit back from my desk and refuse to take it personally. I am glad she is feeling better, and Mother's stoicism is admirable. It is a quality we share.

Don't we?

The question catches me off guard as I refill my glass at the water cooler, causing a minor overflow... 'You're just like your mother' are words I have heard all my life with mixed feelings. True, there is a physical resemblance: the upright posture and jut of her chin, notable in old photos. But by the time Mother was my age she had gained weight, to a degree I am not about to emulate. We have parallels in our character too. In the home where I grew up, a spade was called a spade. I remember how other children reacted when they came to tea: little Helen Agnew, rendered catatonic with a mouthful of coronation chicken when Mother barked at me for the margarine. Just our way of doing things, but from the expression on poor Helen-the-Mouse, you'd think she had stumbled into a penal colony.

I mop up water from the carpet using khaki paper towels... Brusqueness can be self-perpetuating, as a way of skating over the unbearable. Mother and I are both guilty of this, reluctant to face her prognosis. Unless... I toss the sodden wodge in the recycling and freeze. Stare dead ahead, one hand in the air, like a darts player checking where the last shaft landed.

It's not brusqueness! *It's sheer bloody-minded bravery!*

Mother's bluster is an act—to protect me. I see it now, clear as day, simultaneously realising I knew all along. I have a vision of Mother as an ostrich: towering over her tiny chick, as she demonstrates the best way to bury one's head in the sand. Her look of fear as she shields junior from reality tells the whole truth.

I return to my desk. In half an hour I can decently make a move. Only the two girls and I are left in the office. Derek is WFH (more cover for driving down to the cottage with wife and dachshund). Cheryl has put her phone on divert and taken her laptop to the side garden, a spot rarely found by visitors which gets the afternoon sun. She goes there when Derek has scarpered and sometimes before. Overlooked by the Ladies toilets only, it is a safe haven for going through the motions of work whilst demolishing a white chocolate Magnum from the newsagents.

I try to think of an instance where I have been as brave as Mother. My own robust health seems to preclude it. Barring a misread mammogram, it has rarely given me cause for concern. In all honesty, I can only think of one instance when I was called upon to be brave: aged fourteen, walking home from school in the autumn term, when a woman in a blue Ford Capri pulled up outside the Post Office... She crossed the road to feed letters into the box, oblivious to her tyres losing their grip on the shallow gradient. A terrified toddler screamed in the back window, pounding fists lost to the passing traffic. Schoolgirl Fen, in the right place at the right time, threw open the passenger door and yanked at the handbrake, the way she'd seen Father do... My action earned me a commendation in school assembly and my photo in the local paper.

But that isn't normal. Life should be harder than this. Look at what Georgie went through with her brother. Oh, she has her quirks, but in the light of everything isn't she remarkably level-headed? And Ethan, walking home from the police station, impending parental confession looming over him like a Thomas Hardy storm cloud. Bravery takes many forms, but there are as many ways to avoid it... When I worked at the publishers in Hammersmith, my boss was gunning for me, finding fault where none existed; Miranda had a reputation for bulldozing the niceties of office politics, so I made note of her slights. My new friend Avril, to whom I relayed every twist over drinks in Covent Garden, knew a trainee solicitor. One drunken night at the Punch and Judy, he said I had a case for constructive dismissal and even offered to represent me. I was swept along in my starring role as the turning worm, nodding at every suggested show of defiance against workplace bullying... In fact I was already applying for jobs left, right and centre. Had secured one before my mettle was tested, moving into the art world via a high-end gallery in Chelsea. At my leaving drinks Miranda sang my praises, mascaraed eyes streaming with the gush of the guilty.

I shied away from confrontation then. Are my sinews any stronger now — or have I spent virtually my entire life outside a relationship for the same reason? In my teens, the presence of any boy I found attractive first captivated, then terrified me. At uni, too little confidence and too much cider saw the brief rise and sharper fall of *Any-Fella-Fenella*... Thus chastened, I embarked on a career in London, avoiding drugs and rarely staying out late. I wriggled out of any invitations where the life-raft of work might potentially be abandoned for a skinny-dip in the ocean of carnal possibility. Eventually, the invitations ceased.

So on, through my thirties and forties. While everyone I knew settled into the rut of marriage or dug their way out of it, I was in stasis; immersed in my work, with a vehemence usually reserved for a divine calling. That said, even the fallow years were not without sporadic blooming — promising buds that sprang out of nowhere, briefly to blossom and as swiftly burst. It was after one such incident I sold my flat and invested the nest egg... Living alone, I reasoned, had got me nowhere. I needed the stimulation of mixed company offered by a house-share. It was that or succumb to cats!

As I sit at my desk, watching the clock count down to the blessed half-hour, I reach the same conclusion I came to in the pub with Ethan and Georgie. Only this time, I am entirely sober and have the bonus of hindsight. Mother's fall has given me a new perspective — and it is high time my innate resilience came out to play!

I think back to that afternoon, walking along the Dorking road in my grey school uniform skirt, pleats as stiff as cardboard. Catching sight of the moppet's silent scream, the Capri's incongruous roll on the asphalt spurred me to action... Fenella Woodruff was no bystander that day. Briefly, she was a hero. And her return is long overdue.

Chapter 32

The forest of arms and legs in the aisle is sparser than usual for a Friday night. My carriage was quiet this morning too. It is only as I catch a headline on someone's paper—delays at Heathrow, fistfights at check-in—that I remember it's August Bank Holiday weekend. That explains the prattling of the girls at work, re the relative merits of Brighton versus sunbathing in Hyde Park... Now I think of it, Notting Hill was mentioned too. The Carnival has signalled summer's end in London for longer than most of us can remember. Avril and I braved it once in our younger days: the milling hordes and blaring processions, the police with loud hailers shunting you down side streets... Nowadays, queueing for Centre Court at the tennis feels arduous enough.

This calls for a recalibration. Georgie is catching the Eurostar to Paris. I don't know about Ethan, but I am sure Martin said he was around this weekend. He mentioned taking the children to Legoland on Sunday—so if his schedule runs to form, he will be home-alone tonight and out with the mouthy woman tomorrow...

I am a stop from home as my plan begins to form. Pulling out of Earlsfield, I whisk off a WhatsApp to Ethan. The train is at a standstill, waiting for a clear platform, as he replies:

Not for me thanks Fen. Staying in Brixton ;-) Cheers for the offer tho.

Phew. That might have looked odd, me volunteering to cater out of the blue. Hopefully he will put it down to our renewed spirit of bonhomie since the night at the pub. Either way, it suits me fine.

I stop off at Little Waitrose and grab a basket. My frugal streak precludes me shopping here for more than distress purchases, but I haven't time to go further, and in the circumstances... I zero in on lamb cutlets—Martin's favourite. They are even on offer or what passes for one here. I toss two packs in my basket, adding a tray of oven-ready roast potatoes. Now for something green... It is still hot outside, and the forecast is for a sticky night. Salad is the obvious option, though Martin is not a fan. I cast an eye along the truncated selection of veg. He can't abide broccoli either, so I opt for asparagus spears. Then swap them for a medley pack with mange tout and baby carrots, stalks trimmed to a fluorescent inch, and so clean they might have grown in vitro.

Are flowers overdoing it? Possibly, though a few of those gerbera heads would look lovely, floating in that bowl with the tea-light centrepiece I won in a raffle... No. A nice bottle of wine will make the evening special enough. I am almost at the checkout when I remember pud. Not for me, but Martin has a man's appetite with a sweet tooth to match. His body is not the temple it was, but that's what happens when you date a woman who eats Jaffa Cakes for breakfast... I spy Sticky Toffee Cheesecake and pop it in my basket. And a Ginger-Crumb Treacle Tart for good measure... Men like a choice, and I can always freeze one.

As I walk through the door of No. 4, The Ridge, letters on the doormat say I am first home. Twenty to seven. I've made good time. I slot away the shopping so that any catering looks spontaneous. Shutting the fridge I take a breath; this is still a long shot. Martin could be out all night with his mates. Worse still, turn up with her.

Can I justify opening the wine now? Dangerous; staying in control is everything.

I run upstairs and take off my work skirt and blouse. Sniff-check my underarms... No need to shower, and it is only tempting fate... Knee-length shorts from Whistles and my tee shirt with Aztec symbols strike the right note: casual, yet a woman of the world.

Repairing my lipstick, I examine the roots of my honey-blonde rinse... I am experimenting with a necklace when the front door thuds. Slipping into sandals, I regret not touching up my toenails.

"How was your day?" I breeze, on my nonchalant way to the kitchen.

Martin is in the living area. His freshly shed loafers are on the carpet. Only his stocking feet are visible, twitching over the settee arm like a magician's assistant awaiting the saw.

"Fair to middling," he says. "Thank God it's the weekend!"

There is a sound of stretching, and the high-pitched grunt I associate with a man relinquishing the burden of work. A sudden suspicion makes me peer over the settee... Unfounded. He is alone.

"Are you heading out tonight, or—?"

"Joking!" says Martin. "I'm thinking couple of beers in the garden, maybe a takeaway. How 'bout you?"

"Good idea. Mind you, I've got stuff that needs eating. Nothing special—just boring old cutlets and roasties. Can you bear them? I'm fine with a takeaway if not..."

Chapter 33

That evening the garden at No. 4, The Ridge is an English idyll. The lawns and beds are immaculate, refreshed from a downpour earlier in the week and revelling in an end-of-summer growth spurt.

We chat for an hour without mentioning Monique. He helps me in the kitchen, leaning on the breakfast bar, tea towel over one shoulder. I regret buying sanitised veg; good honest dirt would give him something to do... Two-thirds of the wine has slipped down before we take our plates outside, barefoot and slightly giddy across the crazy paving.

"How lucky is this," sighs Martin, slicing a chop. "When I was a lad, you could set your watch by the rain on August Bank Hol weekend... We had a caravan at Camber Sands—God, the misery! Playing dominoes on a plastic table, trying not to think about the first day of school..."

I roll my eyes. "We only went caravanning once. No room to swing a cat. My father misread the brochure and took feet for yards. Plus it was freezing, like spending a week in a meat safe!"

Martin's guffaw meets a generous bite of lamb coming the other way. He lurches over the table and coughs, his red face smiling in some discomfort. He points behind his neck and I take the hint, clapping him hard between the shoulder blades. Again. And again... Four strikes and it's out. He raises a hand in thanks, which might also be *Stop*, as I deliver the final wallop. The hollow, meaty sound of his torso is oddly addictive.

"Better?" I ask, panting too.

My own hand lies on his shoulder, consoling and in no rush to move. Martin takes a reviving swig of Shiraz.

"You're a star," he says, still catching his breath. "Second time that's happened this week!"

"Oh? Then you eat too fast. My mother used to say chew every mouthful twenty—"

"Not me, Monique. We were in a Greek place in Soho when an olive went the wrong way. Thought I was gonna have to do the old Heimlich manoeuvre..." His mime looks more like seppuku. "Turned out there was a doctor on the next table. From Melbourne, of all places. Honeymooners. We ended up chatting to them all night."

This I can believe; Monique as centre of attention, making sure she stays that way... A moment later Martin is back at his plate. The lamb is pink, the way he likes it, a shade that makes me queasy but means I can plead a small appetite and leave half for him. I concentrate on the roast spuds, flavoured with something I'd never have thought of. The veg is perfect too, though Martin insisted on chopping off the carrots' jaunty stubble of leaves ("Paid extra for that, you know!") as if he couldn't trust himself not to scoff the lot.

The evening sun has passed its peak but the air is still sultry. I sense activity on the other side of the fence. The family next door rarely use their garden with its ancient, verdigrised swing. Barbecues only ever happen on the other side, so with luck we are not about to be blasted by the whiff of frazzling meat. Teenage voices carry over:

"I've got it, it's here!"

"Eh?"

"It's here!"

"What do you want two for...?"

We rarely cross paths but the children of the house, boys, never look the same twice. Georgie thinks they foster, hence occasional glimpses of an Afro-Caribbean lad who could also be a visiting friend. It is another unspoken rule at No. 4, The Ridge that we make no effort to get to know the neighbours. People here rent happily without developing any of the attachments that go with owning a home. Carpets slip out from door-trims;

wallpapers lift and no one cares. Some residents (Ethan) don't even notice.

Another voice over the fence, this time the mother. Her I do see, hauling shopping from a Peugeot, on top of their Ocado delivery on Tuesday nights. She is tall, a Wimbledon-blonde, about my age, though less well preserved if I do say so myself... The man of the house works away, which may stymie Georgie's theory though he is around at weekends. With his sandpaper hair, polo shirts and belted chinos, he could pass for a colonel in the U.S. Marines if the Marines enlisted Mancunians.

Sitting here, watching Martin chase juices from his chop with the last of the asparagus, I am transported to another life. *The* other life: the dominant strain on The Ridge and a million roads like it... These houses were built for families of the nuclear kind, with parents of opposite sexes. Anything else, like our household or the more exotic parental combinations, goes against the grain. We are the human equivalent of wasps colonising a bird box, or mice appropriating a rusty watering can. We thrive in an environment not meant for us.

I drain my glass and wonder if Martin feels any of this. He is used to the other life, after all. If he acknowledges the difference, he will see himself as a casual visitor to the singleton world. He has never wrestled with the reality of a life like mine—tyrannised by the *we* word, treading the path alone. Perhaps he never will.

A buzzing curtails my thoughts. Throaty and ominous, close by yet location unknown. We both look around.

"There it is," says Martin. "He's out late!"

The bumblebee crawls through the slats of the table. It takes off, wending its way round the patio umbrella then alighting on the orange canvas. With the fading sun behind, it becomes a black thumbprint on the cloth. It's big for a bumble. A size that would have terrified me as a child, a fear since repelled by the endless environmental propaganda. Bees still make me wary. The little black legs, and the furry stripes that tease you into warming to them despite your better instincts. Like the make-up on a clown.

The black blot emits the occasional buzz as if drifting in and out of sleep. I try to ignore it. Martin has already forgotten. He takes our plates into the kitchen, reappearing with a bottle of prosecco and two flutes. His eyes follow mine.

"Not bothering you, is it?"

"What? No, I just... As you say, you don't often see them out late."

The fragrant lavender is a magnet for smaller bees, which spend high summer trampolining on its stems like gleeful children. But its spherical sea of fronds is too delicate for this one. A creature this size needs a robuster feeding station.

Martin holds the bottle to the underside of the umbrella. Twists the cork, coaxing it with both thumbs... It fires into the canvas an inch from the bee, which is airborne in an instant and off into the sunset.

"Naughty," I scold lightly. "It could have had a heart attack!"

He chuckles. I accept a generous glass as penance.

"Oh, and there's pudding. Choice of, in fact. Waitrose had a special on."

"In a bit, maybe," says Martin leaning back, sliding both hands over his stomach (another signature move). He nods to the kitchen. "I polished off your lamb. Couldn't waste it."

We sit contentedly. In silence, but for the jag of voices fading in and out from next door. And somewhere, someone is trimming a hedge... This moment has a perfection all its own, like reaching a longed-for destination after an arduous journey. I would like to trap it under a glass forever.

"Don't you wish you lived somewhere this warm all year round?" asks Martin.

I smile. We are thinking the same thing.

"Italy for me. Not the south, too dry. But the Amalfi Coast, with those blue skies and bluer seas…"

I have never been, but this is the Italy of my fantasy. With fabulous wines and rustic fare, and waiters in shirts that keep their sleeve-crease even under a broiling sun.

He sips thoughtfully. "I'd go for California cos it's nice all year round. I don't mean L.A. or a city—not with the kids. Just some little town that's got everything." He pauses for a surreptitious burp. "Drive them to school in the morning, then spend the day at home… Office in the back garden with a view of the vineyards, or just a verandah where I can doodle on me iPad. Pull in work from all over the world, then ping off me invoices and watch the money roll in… Weekends, we'd go camping in the desert, or take a chopper over the Grand Canyon. Maybe nip to Vegas."

I have never seen the appeal of America, but he makes it sound attractive apart from the last bit. Las Vegas is my idea of hell. Seedy replicas of the Pyramids and the Eiffel Tower, and the equally plastic pop legends churning out the hits for a burger-munching crowd. I didn't have Martin down as the gambling type. It is a flaw in a man with his responsibilities.

"I've only been to New York," I say. "The rest of America's a bit of a closed book."

"What, not even Florida?"

I shake my head. "I like the sun, but it takes more than a beach to make it worth my while."

"Oh right. My kids love it."

Of course. They would, wouldn't they? Theme parks are nirvana for families. I'm pretty sure I just sounded like a snob.

"Yes, I bet! It's so well geared to children, isn't it? I remember going to the American Museum of Natural History in Manhattan. They were streets ahead of us, even then. 3-D interactive displays, and… What's it called when you wear the goggles?"

"Virtual Reality?"

"Yes, and that was years ago. Cutting-edge. I'd never seen anything like it!"

The last bit is true. I hated the tech wizardry, and the smiley chap in a tee shirt who tried to cajole me into swimming like a turtle in the Hall of Ocean Life. I settled for watching others lie on their stomachs and flail about like idiots... I have never seen the merit in anything that creates a barrier between viewer and exhibit, virtually or otherwise. Nothing is interesting in itself anymore. It all needs dressing-up to make it palatable to the masses.

It also strikes me how easy it is to fabricate an opinion, when you've had a few drinks...

"Yeah," says Martin. "They get it right over there. For kids."

"Well, it's a different ethos, isn't it? The whole any-child-can-be-president thing. We say it here, but it's not true. You're still far more likely to be prime minister if you went to Eton. Fact."

Little Freya and Nathan! What parent wouldn't want them to fulfil their potential? Enjoy a happy life in a sunny clime? Oh, America has its dark side: the shooting sprees and drug cartels, the TV preachers dispensing salvation as they dupe their way to a fortune... But it *is* the land of opportunity. Not above electing slimy reprobates to high office, but still where the civilised world looks to for a lead.

I give the impression of weighing it up. "I still think there's too much I'd miss about England. Britain, I mean. But for children with their whole lives ahead, I see your point. I'm sure 99% of the time no one in America ever sees a gun... People exist in their own little bubbles, don't they? And their bubbles are good." I tip my glass at Martin's; "Like ours!"

He returns the chink. "I know what you mean. Life's what you make it, 'course it is, but it's easier in some places than others. Look at me, I'm no one's idea of a high achiever... No it's true, Fen—I'm Mr Average on the career front. But the way it's going, what chance have my kids got of a life as good as mine?"

It occurs to me how rarely he uses my name. Martin's face, half-turned to me, shows none of the happy-go-lucky optimism I associate with him. It is the face of a man with his guard down; a man who reveals his fears so rarely that you could live under the same roof for months and never catch a glimpse.

I am aware of my arm, snaking out behind his manly torso. As if I am observing it, rather than responsible for the manoeuvre. It feels entirely natural, though I am also aware it crosses a line, fracturing the reserve that is a part of our day-to-day cohabitation.

But at this moment, in this garden, it feels like exactly the right thing to do.

Chapter 34

To my surprise, Martin's body language mirrors mine. His arm slips over my shoulders. And here we are, huddled together in the warmth of the evening like children on a fairground ride.

"I dunno what I'm doing to them, Fen... My mum and dad stayed together, so I've nothing to compare it with. Me and my brother always said they should have split up. Daggers-drawn they were, for as long as I can remember... Did your folks stay together? Happily married, yeah?"

Goodness. I didn't anticipate this.

"Together, yes. Happily, not entirely. I was an only child so I had no one to discuss it with, but I probably felt the same as you. Anyway, every case is different. No point in—"

"No, I know... But deep down, I still think it's the right thing to do. Rock and a hard place, but I reckon the kids are better off if me and Trudie make fresh starts. And better while they're young. I know what it's like, growing up when there's bad blood... Holidays were the worst with our Mum and Dad. Cooped up in the car as they snarled at each other, smoking away. Miracle we didn't all get lung cancer."

He shakes his head at the memory.

"Has your brother got children?"

"No. Long-term girlfriend, but he's never married. Parents scarred him for life, I reckon. 'Course I went the other way—got hitched too soon to prove I could do it right. Big mistake... And by the time we left home Mum and Dad were too set in their ways. Talked-the-talk about splitting up and bickered to the bitter end... She's gone now." He scoffs; "The way Dad talks about her, you'd think it was forty-odd years of wedded bliss!"

"In that case I suppose I was lucky. There was always tension between my parents, but it rarely surfaced when I was around. Then Mother got ill and that was that. Cue Father, waiting on her hand and foot, long before she needed it. It was the making of them really. Probably when they were happiest."

The sun has slipped behind the shed. This intimacy, raking over family coals in the gathering dusk, is not something I have felt before. Perversely I have an urge to move; to click my shoulder which is at an awkward angle. Or do I just want to test him?

Reaching for the bottle with my free hand I take back my arm and fill our glasses. His is still there as I lean back.

"To parents," says Martin, raising his glass. "Where would we be without them? Now there's a question…"

We both sip.

"You'd have been a good mother," he says abruptly. "Not that I'm saying it's too late. I mean—" He is squirming unnecessarily.

"It's quite alright. Safe to say, I've missed the boat on that one! Not sure I agree though. Why do you think that?"

"Just the way you are with the kids. Freya loves you. Don't be surprised if you get 'Aunty Fen' next time she sees you!"

"Aw. Really?"

"She's been trying it out. There was a painting prog on telly last week. Where they all stand around painting portraits of celebs in a gallery. Freya goes, 'Is that where Aunty Fen works?' Didn't go down well with Monique, I can tell you."

We share a snigger behind his girlfriend's back.

"Do you think she—Sorry, none of my business."

"No, go on."

"I was just thinking, do you think Monique wants children? She's got plenty of time."

Martin's head rocks back an inch. He makes a noise like he's been winded. His arm disappears, then comes back again.

"I think we've both skirted round that one. I'm not sure she's mother material, but that may be cos she's…" (Is he trying not to say 'Australian'?) "Cos of how she is." He flicks a speck of fluff from his snug-fit tee shirt. "Truth is, I'm not seeing anything straight at the moment... It just kind of happened with Monique, and now I'm trying to keep everything on the rails. Dumb idea, introducing her to the kids. But at the time I just thought, if this is how it's gonna be, maybe we should all get used to it."

He is wrong on this, but I say nothing. It's another hint of a reckless streak I am inclined to be wary of. And yet...

"But if it all worked out, and she did want children?"

The idea does not sit comfortably. "I couldn't, Fen. That'd be a deal breaker. Look at me, I've been lucky. Got Freya and Nathan, boy and a girl, both fantastic kids... But they're for life, aren't they? I'll be paying for them for as long as I'm working. Dunno what I'd have done if Monique had kids of her own. I checked that, straight-off. There's only so much a man can take on board..."

Well, no denying the sense in that.

"And don't ask me if it's gonna work out, cos I've no idea. You guys must have thought I was behaving like a teenager, jumping at the first woman that comes along. Guess I'm in a funny place—'scuse the self-help speak... Some mornings I wake up and think, right, whose life shall I ruin today? I've screwed things up with my wife. I'm doing a pretty good job with the kids. I could hurt Monique too, if it all goes to pot."

I feel myself warming to him again, helped by the bodily contact. I lean in a fraction.

"But you never would intentionally, Martin, I know that. People are resilient, and from what I've seen your children are coming through it remarkably well. For many kids, it's just part of growing up. You know what they say. What doesn't kill you makes you stronger..." Now I want to up the stakes and bare my soul as he is doing. "Sometimes I think I've skirted the difficulties in my life. I took the safe option with my career, for one thing. But some people just dive in, don't they? Swim in the sea of all life has to offer, while the rest of us stand around watching from the shore."

"Very poetic, Fen. You missed your vocation."

My laugh is hollow. "Possibly, but I doubt it was poetry!"

In the mellow warmth of the garden, after a very passable dinner and surfeit of booze, I slump into a comfortable haze. My original intention for the evening, lost among the confessions and refills, comes back to me with a start: *My past persona, Fen the fence-sitter, is the enemy. And tonight is the night she is routed!*

"You talk like your life's over," says Martin. "You've decades ahead of you! No baggage, no ties; you could do anything, go anywhere. Okay there's your mum, I know that. But I tell you, one of these days you'll be looking the other way when a door opens and—"

His face is hot as I bob at it. Rough with stubble, smooth where my lips meet his...

Were I thinking at all, I would expect him to flinch, yet not a muscle twitches. The only movement is a faint rush of breath from Martin; what might be a gasp if my own face weren't acting as soundproofing. If his other arm encloses me now, I will reciprocate... It doesn't, for which I blame the element of surprise. Still I feel oddly, resolutely in control. As if every moment since he walked into No. 4, The Ridge has led to this... Tonight is the endgame in my strategy, and I have played well!

I exercise my composure by also being the one to break the kiss... Martin's eyes are those of a startled boy. His mouth closes, one corner rising with the corresponding eyebrow. A dimple I have not seen before appears in his cheek. I evidently amuse *and* intrigue him.

"Time for pud," I say, rising from the chair. "Sticky toffee or treacle tart?"

"I'm easy," says Martin. His expression gives nothing away.

In the kitchen, I serve up large and small wedges of indulgent loveliness, onto the blue boards more suited to al fresco dining than our cereal bowls. Spotting a tub of double cream in the fridge, I wonder if a dollop is overdoing it? I am wrestling with switching to bowls when I hear Martin's mobile ping.

We meet on the doorstep, a snapshot of domesticity: he in his untucked tee shirt, scratching his head; me, balancing pudding and pudding forks on either board. Both of us are swaying slightly, waiting for the other to speak.

"Monique," he says. "Coming up the road. And either her spelling's got worse or she's had a skinful..."

Chapter 35

"Jeez, Fen, you're a lifesaver!"

Monique's voice rings out like flatulence at a funeral. She is wolfing down sticky toffee cheesecake in the dim and silent garden. The neighbours have long since retreated indoors, and the only light illuminating the patio comes from the kitchen window.

"Don't mind me dropping over, do you, darl?" Her fingers are digging into the crevice between Martin's thighs. "Jenna's having another crisis with Perry. Said it'd only be one drink but you know what she's like. Then I thought of those bloody trains, and the changes..."

Martin has sobered up a little with her arrival. Her excuse may be true, but wherever she has been alcohol was not the only stimulant. Her perfume is mixed with a distinct herbal tang that also explains her appetite.

I simmer quietly. For once in my life I throw caution to the winds, and what happens? The one and only person guaranteed to upset my raft of possibilities turns up out of the blue!

He fishes out her hand before it goes walkabout, holding it firmly on his knee. Martin looks tired and slightly dazed. I check my watch; ten twenty-five... With any luck, they'll shuffle off to bed and this whole sorry mess can be forgotten. In the flurry of her arrival, my own pudding is still on the drainer. His made it outside but he has only managed a forkful.

Monique's eyes are like saucers. "You leaving that, darl?"

He shrugs, so she slides the wooden board her way, upsetting the fork which clatters to the paving slabs. Any chance of a quick end to proceedings evaporates as, between mouthfuls, she launches into the tale of her evening:

Chapter 35

"So yeah, Jenna finally found out for sure Perry's been playing away. Turns out his—*mmm, yum*—golfing weekends with the guys were anything but!"

I have a vague idea who she is talking about. Jenna is her friend from Brisbane, recently arrived in London with a boyfriend who is less keen to settle down than she is. Like a disproportionate number of the capital's Australians, they are living in Wimbledon.

"I feel for Jen. She can't half pick 'em. Same thing happened with the guy she was dating in Sydney. Mind, he was a total freak..." She pauses to lick caramel off her fingers. "At least Perry doesn't run around in her underwear when she's not looking. And she'd know—from the pics on his mobile he can barely keep his bloody trousers up! Jen's trouble is, she's too soft. I told her, blokes get one chance only. With Perry's sort, give 'em an inch and they're spreading it about like horse shit on roses..."

The diatribe continues while I am in the kitchen. If I nip off to bed they'll be none the wiser. I find my cheesecake and pick at a corner. Say what you like about Waitrose, they know their pâtisserie... Monique's arrival is amusing in its way, like a character from a bad farce parachuting into our back garden. What Martin sees in her is still a mystery, but given the evening's ludicrous turn her babbling fits the ambience.

Oh, what the hell!

Before I know it, I am reaching in the fridge for another of Martin's proseccos. I find an extra flute; Monique won't say no, and I am up for half a glass myself. With my plans derailed and an empty weekend stretching ahead of me, this is as close to fun as I'm going to get.

Back on the patio I thrust the chilly bottle at Martin. He takes it without a word, scrabbling at the foil. Monique has barely drawn breath:

215

"—On top of that, Jen's old lady's all over the place, cos her dad's being a pig about the divorce. Sorry, darl, you don't wanna hear all this..." Martin twitches as he pops the cork and focuses on pouring. "And now her younger brother says *he* won't live with their mum cos she's a slapper. Which is a bit strong, given what her dad's been up to..." She slides her board onto the table and nearly misses. "God, Fen, you must think it's no wonder Mon found herself a Brit, when every other Aussie's a walking sperm gun! Not true, there's plenty of decent blokes back home. It's just no one ever talks about 'em."

Mon; a diminutive! Slip of the tongue, or are we really on these terms?

Martin looks up from the glass he is holding morosely. "I think Fen's had enough of warring parents for one night. I was just telling her about mine."

His hint lands way off target.

"Exactly," says Monique, "they're bloody everywhere! Someone should do a study. I betcha there's more divorced parents among Aussies living overseas than anyone else. Can you blame us for scarpering as far as we can get?"

For someone who didn't want a full glass, I am surprised to see mine is already half empty.

"I knew your mother had a long illness," I say. "But I didn't realise your parents were divorced."

As far as I know Monique knows nothing about Mother, which could be a useful topic in the event of a lull.

"Eh? Oh yeah, no; they got along fine. I was lucky, I had nothing to run away from. In fact I had the opposite problem. Felt guilty about being away. Mum was ill for years, but once she was on the way out it was heartbreaking. When we Skyped I was never sure if she remembered me or not. Till the time she thought I was Nicole Kidman calling from Hollywood—then I knew I had to get over there."

Martin is refilling his glass; chin down, in a way that says he's heard it before. He is swaying again.

" — And once I said I was coming, I knew everything'd grind to halt. Dad couldn't cope. Mum needed to get into a hospice, sharpish. But my boss in London was an insensitive bastard — thick as a Boxing Day turd! Said I couldn't fly till a week later... Jeez, it breaks your heart, Fen, seeing your old mum like that. I'll spare you the deets, but Dad was refusing all help. He'd not been turning her in bed like he should, so..."

Her eyes are full of tears. Martin has floated off on his own thoughts. His hands are on his glass, when even I can see Monique needs an arm around her.

"Children, animals and old people. Hear them scream in pain and it's like a dagger in the gut, right? I was phoning for an ambulance before I'd put my bloody suitcase down. Longest thirty minutes of my life!" A big sigh; Monique is drinking the least of all of us. "When something like that happens, your feet don't touch. Fuck of a cure for jet lag!"

A tear runs down her cheek. Martin finally pulls her towards him as she knuckles away the flow. As a rule, tears make me feel awkward or angry, depending on whether I think they're justified. But Monique's words paint a stark picture, and her mother in Brisbane will be my mother one day... Not yet. But if her mental faculties go the way of the rest, it will only take someone not paying attention for tragedy to occur... What if I'm away, or if Bill and Kath no longer find her captivating? She will be at the mercy of strangers, and decisions based on budgets and time constraints. That will be the reality for Mother. Maybe for me one day...

In the deep shadow across the table Martin and Monique meld to a huddle. She blows her nose into a wad of papier-mâché with a pull-yourself-together sniffle.

"Jeez look at me, making a spectacle! The old girl's in a better place now, thank Christ. Yeah, go on — "

Martin is unsettled at the sight of any glass less than two-thirds full. Marshalling my thoughts through the fug of inebriation, I say nothing as he waves the bottle at me. He tops me up anyway.

"At least you were there, Monique," I say. "You went all that way when your parents needed you. Not everyone's so lucky."

"True. And I know what you're saying, Fen—What happens if we don't have kids and end up on our own?"

"Misery-guts!" says Martin with a dry chuckle.

She elbows him in the ribs. "Oh yeah, you'll be right! Freya and Nathan'll probably end up CEOs of their own company, with a nice little Grandad-pad for you. We don't all have a brood—and not every brood give a shit about their old folks when the time comes." She snorts a laugh. "The other week, me and Jen were saying how we're gonna buy a place in Gold Coast if we end up singletons. Well, why not? It's the trend, I'm telling you!"

Martin shakes his head. "Fair enough. I'm just laughing at the idea of you and Jenna aged eighty, terrorising the local OAPs in your bikinis. Oldest swingers in town!"

Monique cackles, hitching up her bust. "Lowest swingers more like! Seriously, eighty's the new sixty... Fancy joining us, Fen? See out your days in the Aussie sun, hot-and-cold running houseboys tending to your every need?"

"I don't think that's Fen's scene," says Martin. "She's more of a—"

"More of a what?" I ask.

People—*Men!* Always quick to pigeonhole! Hardly knows me, yet here he is making assumptions about how I want to live my life thirty years from now!

"I just meant, you know—with you not liking the beach."

"Oh. Well, I'm sure I could—"

"Bollocks," says Monique, "you gotta love the beach, Fen! Don't worry about the sun, only dickheads tan these days! Factor-up and you can stay white as a polar bear's arse!"

Now I'm laughing. Monique's lewdness can be quite amusing. I am seeing her in a different light... Hard to believe, but in some ways we are two of a kind; women of the world, making the best of it. True, she has come ten thousand miles, while I live an hour from where I was born. But aren't we both just negotiating the assault course life has thrown at us? And after a thousand twists and turns, haven't we ended up here, in the garden of No. 4, The Ridge, because we only have eyes for Martin? Although...

Now I'm not so sure. With his non-stop boozing and generalisations, I'm finding him slightly annoying. And there's something disturbing about the way he clings to that glass... No wonder I'm drinking more since he moved in, he's forever opening bottles! Has he had the same effect on Monique? Perhaps she is not a natural lush after all...

I can hardly believe I am thinking this: but might she and I have been friends? Hypothetically of course—but if we'd met in different circumstances, could this bluff, no-nonsense woman be a kindred spirit? Look beyond her brassy exterior, and right now I honestly feel more relaxed with her than anyone I work with... More than Ethan and Georgie, come to that. I can't see them floating the idea of a shared retirement with a bevy of Aussie surf bums!

"*Fuck!*"

Monique slams down her glass, slopping fizz on the table.

Martin jumps. "Mind out, Mon, you'll break it!"

I follow their gaze to the base of the flute as Martin's mobile throws a searchlight on the slats.

"*Urgh!*" shudders Monique. "Where the fuck did that come from?"

The bumblebee is visible through the circle of glass, mashed against the wood like the work of a blind taxidermist. One wing and a few legs are preserved, the rest is a daub of muddy-yellow unrecognisable as anything living before it was rendered to sludge. It must have landed on the table when no one was looking.

"That was... It can't be the same one, can it, Martin?" My voice trails away.

"Dunno. Didn't hear it come back... Probably sick. I said bees don't hang around in the dark."

Monique squirms as she lifts the glass, her disgust turning to ruefulness.

"Sorry, unnecessary carnage. I know they're the gardener's friend and all." She flicks what isn't stuck to the base through the slats then wipes it on the grass. "I go all knee-jerky around bugs. Blame a close encounter with a funnel-web at kindergarten!"

Martin's look is disapproving. "Yeah well, this isn't the Outback. Nothing's going to kill you round here."

Monique's angry doll-face glowers back. "I know, like I said—Reflex action, okay?"

I don't wish to watch them argue. As it is, this prosecco is going through me at a rate of knots... I mumble an excuse and nip indoors.

Chapter 36

The sloping cubbyhole under the stairs is a refuge at the centre of the house. Whatever the temperature, the air here is always cool. Bafflingly so, like the haunted room in a stately home. Yet there is nothing unsettling about the downstairs loo at No. 4, The Ridge. The smell of little-worn coats, overflow from the rack in the hall, says *escape*. Over the years I have developed a habit of diving in here when I need a moment to think. It's easily disguised as the call of nature, and less provocative than shutting myself away upstairs.

Now is just such a time. On an evening turned into a soup of unexpected emotions, Monique's brutality has made me tearful in a way I can't explain. As I crank the cistern I feel dizzy. Steady myself on the little shelf, and find myself examining the novelty knitted pot plant that stands there. Left as a joke three or four housemates ago, it is an object of amusement to visitors, a sort of Mrs-Burnside-lite. Thick with dust, since I can never decide whether to wash it or scrub it with the nailbrush, and do neither.

I rinse my fingers in the tiny sink and dab cold water on my face. I should go to bed. I am tired and drunk, and the evening will only get messier. Part of me wishes I'd gone up the first time instead of giving in to the lure of the unexpected. Yet, slipping the bolt on the door, I find myself turning left.

Back outside all is jollity. Like the curtain rising on the second act of a play, when the stabbing or betrayal that ended the first seems long forgotten. Martin is laughing at something Monique said. She is sitting demurely, calves crossed, hands miming strokes on a keyboard. Her impression of someone at work requires the approximation of a Scottish accent:

"—She said, '*Monique, would you se-eey that blouse is entirely approo-priate for the office?*'... I said, 'Yes Morag, I think it's totally appropriate, when it's thirty fucking degrees outside and the air con's fucked again!'"

Martin hoots.

"Actually I didn't say fuck. I wanted to say fuck, but I didn't say fuck..."

I retake my seat, numbly aware of the quiet. Of how voices carry in the dark, and the rule drummed into me as a child about raised voices in the garden. Oddly, I cannot bring myself to give a—

"Hey, Fen! Monique's had an idea." Martin nudges his girlfriend.

"Yeah, so I was saying... Let's do a round-robin where we all have to confess something we've never told anyone. As in, *anyone-ever!*" She punctuates this with staccato claps. "Can be something you're either ashamed or proud of. Though obviously ashamed's better!"

Martin's face is a picture of comedy-terror. "Hang on, if this story's going where I think it is, telling Morag the Toe-rag where to get off is nothing to be ashamed of. She had it coming, big time!"

Monique shrugs. "Best I can do off the top of me head... One of yous two have a go while I think of another." Her hand is back between his thighs. This time Martin does not divert it. "And I want something suitably X-rated from you, sleaze ball!"

I am hoping my expression isn't giving me away. *Not another boozy truth session!*

You expect this sort of thing from freshers at university, off the leash and giddy with freedom. People our age should know better—and yet... Looking at Martin and Monique, dead parents and pulverised insects forgotten, there is a gleefulness I envy. I feel strangely like I am observing them as specimens, unburdened by my yearning for Martin. He is still the same man; attractive with his compact shoulders, and that twinkle in his clear brown gaze like an advert for eye-drops... But now

I see him as he is: clutching his glass, cavorting with Monique, he is in his natural state. And I am no longer in thrall to him.

What he thinks of me no longer matters. So I will play their game—why not?

Martin's brow is a furrow, his mouth a molehill as he dredges up something confessional. A twice-married man with a mighty thirst and career in the creative industries will have stories aplenty, I'm sure. My little life can hardly compete. Though there's always—

"Okay, got one!" he says, slapping the table. "In my first job, I had the hots for this girl who worked in Despatch—you know, the post room, where they handle all the deliveries... Sandra had a reputation as a bit of a goer, but she never gave me the time of day. I was the office junior, which was great cos it meant if anyone needed anything collecting I could nip down and chat to Sandra... Anyway, one day my boss was expecting a load of polyboard for a pitch presentation. He was gay as a goose, and he liked me cos I was pretty in those days—"

"Still are, darl!"

"Thanks, babe, if only... Anyway, it was urgent and he was a right old snob. Didn't trust the post room peeps to call him when his parcel arrived, so he sends me down to wait for it. I'm there half the morning, and when it gets to lunchtime it's someone's birthday, so everyone's off down the pub. That leaves me and Sandra sitting there, when she brings out this bottle of tequila and says, 'Well, if they're all getting sloshed, we can have one little drink!' Now, I'd never done tequila, and we didn't have the lime and the salt, so it was pretty disgusting. We're in these chairs on castors at a table facing the door... Next thing you know, we're necking the bottle, playing strip poker under the desk! Dunno what the rules were, but I kept losing. Trainers and socks off, jeans round me ankles, and me boxers were next!"

Monique snorts. "You're making this up!"

"Swear to God! So, I'm like twenty-two, not very experienced with the fairer sex, and finding it all quite arousing. We're halfway down the tequila, giggling like school kids, when the door flies open and in walks my boss, wanting to know where his polyboard is! He starts hunting around, shifting stuff on the table. Me and Sandra are frozen in our seats, trying not to laugh. She's lost her shoes and knickers but still got her skirt on, so she looks decent to the casual eye... Then the boss clocks the tequila behind the fax machine. Looks from her to me and says, 'Come on, Martin, time you were back at your desk!'"

His prissy intonation provokes a peal of laughter from Monique, nearly upsetting her glass in the process. His hand darts out to steady it.

"Careful... So I'm sitting there grinning like a loon, bare legs under the table and a pan-handle in me boxers, thinking, 'What the fuck do I do now?' Boss won't take no for an answer when Sandra, bless her, drops something on the floor and pushes me Levis back up me legs! Recipe for disaster, cos she bangs her head and shouts *Shit!* at the top of her voice... The boss comes steaming round the table, yanks back my chair. And there's me in all me upstanding-glory!" He shakes his head, fighting back tears to deliver the punchline. "And he gives me this look and says, '*Martin, if I wanted a tent I'd have sent you to the camping shop!*'"

Now I too am quaking in silent mirth. Monique is first to recover, her cheeks speckled with mascara.

"And wha—*hrrh, hrrh*... What happened then?"

He shrugs. "End of the week I was out on my ear. Should've done tequila with him instead, I'd have got promoted!" Martin sits back, rewarding himself with a slurp of prosecco. "Who's next?"

Mustering the will to make my contribution, I take a breath—

"Okay, got another!" says Monique. "Jeez, I haven't thought about this in years! So, when I was seventeen, me and Bronwen Craddock drove her dad's ute down to Byron Bay. Only gonna stay for two nights, but we were bumming around for the summer so it ended up being four. Thing was, we'd run out of cash..." She settles back, enjoying the attention. "Third night, we slept on the flatbed of the truck. Got bitten to death by mozzies, so we were buggered if we're doing that again. We go to a bar, then another bar, then a club cos we're on the pull... Nada! Every guy we meet's too pissed or too skanky or both. So me and Bron end up down the beach, with the half-bottles of voddie we've had down our jeans all night. It's like, three in the morning and we're thinking, fuck it, let's crash in the dunes, when up rocks this major spunk Bron had her eye on in the club! Bikie-looking, but clean hair and nicely kitted out... Wouldn't give her the time o' day on the dance floor, but now he's all over her like white on rice! Anyway, they're chatting away and I give 'em space, go for a paddle or whatever. When I get back, Bron's blouse is round her waist and her hands are where I can't see 'em. So I'm thinking *aye-aye*, that's me on me lonesome in the ute tonight!"

Annoyingly I feel myself colour. I do not shock easily, and have a story of my own that will give Monique a run for her money. If I can ever get a word in...

"So I say, 'Give us the keys, Bron, and I'll see yous later!' Only now she's not feeling too clever, and doesn't want to be left alone with him... Cut a long story short, we all end up in the back of his Winnebago, rolling spliffs and listening to Whitesnake. He's got these dice, and we take turns chucking 'em across the rug. Whoever scores lowest does a forfeit. Only sometimes it's the highest score—He's making up the bloody rules, but frankly we're too out of it to care. Anyway Bronwen goes outside to chuck up, and while she's gone he rolls a four and says, 'Okay, final throw... If you win, you girls get the bed and I'm on the floor. If I win, you girls still get the bed *and I'm in with ya!*'"

"Weh-hey!" crows Martin. The standard reaction from a certain kind of man to any mention of a bed and two women (—I'd have hoped for better).

"So I'm like, all affronted! 'You dirty bastard, me and her are just good friends blah-blah!'... Bron staggers back in, pleading for mouthwash. I tell her what he just said, thinking she'll either laugh her socks off or punch his lights out. Bron was hockey goalie at school so you didn't mess with her... Instead, she picks up the dice *and rolls a bloody one!*"

Now they are both laughing. Martin whispers something I don't catch, which earns him an elbow in the chest.

"Behave! Anyway, that's it, end of story..."

"No-oo! C'mon!"

I have a vision of him on the terrace at West Ham.

"Aw what—you want the gory details? I bet Fen doesn't!"

I gesture in a way that says, "Don't mind me..."

Monique sighs theatrically. "Alright, twist my arm. So yeah, one thing leads to another... And actually it wasn't that bad!" A swig of flat prosecco. "Whatcha looking at me like that for?"

Martin closes his mouth. "No, I just—I didn't think you..."

"Yeah well, you thought wrong... I mean, I knew Bronwen dabbled. You don't grow up with no mum and three brothers *faarting* all through breakfast without yearning for a bit of female company! What's-his-face, Jon Bon Jovi, was well and truly getting off on it. Doing the whole voyeur thing, not even joining in. Playing with his little soldier while we tussled on his sleeping bag!"

Martin rubs his chin. "So, what exac—No, sorry!"

Monique lets rip another peal of laughter; elbows him again and shoots me a look. "Jeez—blokes! You can set your watch by 'em, right, Fen? *So* predictable!"

I agree, though part of me is wondering the same as Martin. Not for prurient reasons, just curiosity. People are fascinating... You make your observations, construct little lives for them, but you never really know if you're right.

"All I'm saying," says Monique, "is that it takes a woman to know a woman... No, don't get the hump, darl, I'm not complaining. You're very attentive! But with a lady it's more— *instinctual*. She automatically knows where she's going, whereas for a guy it's all uncharted territory..." She slides a finger into her tee shirt, scratching under a bra strap. "A bloke needs to learn the route before he can plant his flag pole. Am I right, Fen?"

"Yes," I agree without realising. "Well, it makes sense..."

Hang on, what am I saying? The flush visiting my cheeks has spread the length and breadth of me. I am tingling, my armpits are moist and my mouth feels like someone else's. As if everything I have drunk tonight has joined forces to make its presence felt.

"Go on, Fen," says Martin. "Your turn."

Chapter 37

I can't. Not after that.

The tale of me, Avril and a troupe of Belgian mime artists at the Tricycle Theatre Christmas party is staying under wraps. All rather juvenile and innocent (tipsy high jinks, involving a bottle opener and ball of twine) but if you are inclined to see the smut in everything... It won't compete with theirs, and anyway Monique is more than happy in the spotlight. Which becomes more apparent as she says:

"Tell you what. Who's for spicing it up a bit?"

There is a glint in her eye I have not seen before. She reaches into the handbag at her feet and pulls out a tiny Ziploc sachet containing something white.

Oh.

Martin's smile is half-embarrassment. But only half.

"Where'd you get that?"

"Jen," says Monique. "Says she needs her wits about her while Perry's being Mr Slippery, so she wanted rid. Who's for getting this party started?"

Martin's mouth opens then closes again. Fighting to remain impassive, my bare toes scrunch on the concrete.

"I won't, thank you. But don't let me stop you."

I check the surrounding houses. Sitting here tight to the wall, we are overlooked by neither No. 2 nor No. 6, The Ridge. Sight-lines from the property abutting our back fence are obscured by the bamboo. Except for their loft conversion which has uninterrupted views, and from where lights are burning at two windows.

Martin glances my way before he speaks. "I dunno, Mon. Maybe we should turn in."

But by his tone and the way he's leaning over the table he is persuadable.

Monique grunts. "Go on, one little line. I've had a bastard of a week!"

There is something incongruous about the scene unfolding. For all I know, it happens in thousands of homes every night of the year, yet it's the first time I've known it happen here. Our old housemate, Javier, smoked dope, but only in his room with the window wide. Even that gave me the heebie-jeebies. I once nipped out at midnight on a pretext of observing the Plough, to check how far the smell carried... Who knew what else he'd got stashed in his room? I would lie in bed envisioning raids by the drug squad. Visored brutes, baton-charging the front door and hurtling upstairs into every bedroom till they found the culprit... Javier didn't smoke often, but this was two days before Mr Burnside's annual inspection (a date I double-ringed on the calendar!). I took the liberty of strafing his room with an odour-neutralising spray while he was in the bathroom. An act for which I received no thanks, despite leaving the aerosol outside his bedroom door.

I feel uneasy as Monique takes a credit card and ten-pound note from her purse. Martin's eyes triangulate between us two and the tabletop.

"Best not do it out here, Mon. We should—"

"Flip that over," she snaps, meaning the blue board that briefly held her pudding.

Not a breath of air disturbs the garden as she tips powder onto the surface. I pray for a tornado as her M&S card chops it into lines, like the scratch marks of a three-toed beast. She rolls up the note lolly-stick thin, then angles the board at me:

"Go on, Fen. Be a devil why doncha?"

"I'm fine, Monique. Really."

She holds my gaze for a second. Then bends over the table and snorts with a practised sweep.

"Uu-*uuh*..."

She sits back, luxuriating in the buzz. Twitches once, then sniffs as a finger bows a tremolo on her septum. Monique hands the miniature baton to Martin... The act of hoovering a line of his own reveals the sparseness of his hair at the crown; something I have never noticed, though apparent in the light from the kitchen window. His head lolls unflatteringly as his spine smacks back in the chair, triggering a memory of the only time I ever saw my father drunk.

And then there is one. A single, white-crested wave on a royal blue sea, marking the divide between the party people on one side of the table and the party pooper on the other... I pour a drink I don't want and sip. I have a suspicion one or both of them is out to intimidate me. Not Martin, surely—though the way I've changed my mind about him tonight, I don't trust my own judgement... No doubt Monique thought I would scuttle off the moment she revealed her stash, but I am not about to wither at the sight of an illegal substance. I am quite capable of enjoying myself, regardless of the choices of others.

"Ever had a three-way, Fen?"

Monique's eyes bore into mine, or try to. Her gaze is slightly off-centre.

I am minded to reply, if only to deny her the satisfaction she has got one over on me. Martin's mouth opens but nothing comes out.

"Why do you ask, Monique? Are you trying to embarrass me?"

"Not at all! Genuine curiosity. We're getting to know each other a bit tonight, aren't we? Didn't mean to pry, no offence."

She recrosses her legs. I am not about to let her win.

"I have to say, a person's sexual history tends not to be what I find interesting about them. Perhaps I'm just old-fashioned. But to answer your question, Monique, no I haven't."

The other side of the table take a moment to absorb this, before nodding in unison like novelty dogs. Martin still hasn't spoken. Just fiddles with a nostril, as if pursuing a phantom dewdrop. Abruptly Monique rummages in her bag… I am ready for anything, up to and including tinfoil and a syringe. When her mobile appears she starts to scroll, muttering occasional expletives. Martin is watching over her shoulder.

"Oh no, Mon. Not out here…"

He makes a grab for it as a guitar track chugs out at an antisocial volume. Monique tuts, huffily turning it down from ear-splitting to an irritating thud.

Here I draw the line! It is dark, this is Wimbledon, and we are not fifteen years old. I snatch the phone and tap the offending arrow symbol. I also note the time.

"It's 11.02, Monique. People are asleep!"

I slide the mobile back across the table. With my ramrod posture and her burning glare coming the other way, I am a school teacher returning confiscated goods.

"*Christ!*" snarls Monique, back in her bag. This time earbuds appear, a white tangle that Martin tries to unpick. This is getting silly. If she is just going to sit here, bobbing to her music… I take a sip and let most of the booze slip back into the glass. Bed and a large glass of milk are calling. But I have lasted this long; exit will be on my own terms.

Martin hands over the earbuds. Monique takes three goes getting them in, then fiddles with the volume until the beats seep tinnily. Now she stands, edging round the table. He smiles like an indulgent parent.

"She wants to boogie, Fen. Always happens…"

I follow his eyes as the performance unfolds. His girlfriend is not a graceful mover. Her undulating dance has its roots in the pole variety. Without a whirligig clothes dryer, as at No. 8, The Ridge, our garden is mercifully prop-free.

Next I look, she is unbuttoning her blouse from the bottom up. I fear the worst, but her striptease stops with two to go. She is knotting the tails below her bust, holding Martin in a glare that is meant to be coquettish but evokes a knife-fight... He smiles in his chair, neck slack and legs akimbo, a posture I associate with my least favourite commuters. He is tumbling further in my estimation, yet none of this feels like a surprise. It's as if I am seeing him as I've always known him to be, unfiltered by the gauzy veil I created. With a last exaggerated nip at my glass I pick my moment:

"Well, I'll love you and leave you!"

I am vaguely aware of a different kind of exertion and a scrabbling sound beyond my vision. Martin snaps to attention. Wide-eyed, with a hand to his mouth, he is looking past me.

"Fuck a three-way!" yells Monique over her music. *"Let's make it four!"*

She is straddling Mrs Burnside like a bronco bull. Clinging to the obelisk for a pommel, rubbing the silver flower holder suggestively. Throwing back her head she shrieks with laughter. Her Ziploc sachet is out again. And a moment later she is bent over the plinth, snuffling up another line like a starving anteater.

"Uu-*uuuh!*" she grunts. Satiated, she sags back on the grave. "And that's what marble's *bloody made for!*"

Her eyes find mine. Then Martin's, whose face is fighting a smile.

Monique sees it. Her fingers are back at her blouse buttons.

"Come on, tiger, you always said you wanted a gang-bang. And I reckon Fen here's bursting to oblige!"

Chapter 38

On Sunday afternoon I meet Avril. As per her text, downstairs at Costa Coffee on Marylebone High Street.

Why here rather than her flat three streets away, I have no idea. She loves her apartment in Marble Arch, despite the Eighties decor and the doorman I half-expect to pull a revolver whenever I pass his desk... It takes me a minute to find her. Avril is obscured by one of the faux bookcases that lend this branch a Bohemian air.

Even in weekend-casuals she never looks less than immaculate. Yet today, the set of her shoulders and angle of her chin over a skinny flat white say something is amiss. She looks even smaller than usual.

"Hello there," I say cautiously, placing my cup and a fudge-topped muffin on the table.

She doesn't rise, requiring an awkward bend from me to press cheeks. My shoulder bag nearly sweeps the refreshments to the floor, but she doesn't notice.

I am in need of a sounding board myself though her text beat me to it. I spent most of Saturday in bed nursing a crushing hangover, the events of Friday night rolling around my head. Emerged only when my appetite demanded more than a gallon of tap water, and when I ventured downstairs the house was quiet. Of Martin and Monique there was neither hide nor hair, not counting the two brassy strands on the worktop I flushed down the sink without touching... By late afternoon, still exhausted but feeling semi-human, I was back in bed, nodding off to an old Graham Norton when I heard Ethan turn up with Cass.

An empty No. 4, The Ridge on Saturday presages a full house today, and since I am in no rush to confront Martin, I am glad to be out. But for Avril to summon me to the West End without lure of theatre tickets is unusual, which suggests something serious. She has clearly been crying. Her eyes are a filigree of veins from which no amount of premium eye dew can distract. Before I can so much as unskirt my muffin, she launches in:

"Soki's dumped me. Friday night at The Ivy. Just like that!" She looks shellshocked, paler than her foundation. "I should have guessed! Not our usual table but one at the back. In case I kicked up a fuss!"

I am aghast. In the pantheon of what constitutes news in Avril-World, this is seismic. It raises a dozen questions and a good few theories; in the British tradition of turning worms, not least a 'me-or-the-divorce-courts-ultimatum' from Lady Ruth... I sit back with my cake and wait. If she has dragged me all this way, I am about to get chapter and verse.

"The cancer's back," she says, heaving a sigh. "When he said he was in Monte Carlo, he wasn't. He was seeing the specialist in Hamburg."

Three years ago, Soki's colon was scrutinised by top-flight consultants in both hemispheres. He was allegedly given the all-clear, as Avril reported gleefully at the time. Life, and their clandestine affair resumed, though I had an inkling the outlook was less than rosy.

"Avril, I'm so sorry. But why—"

"He says he's got a year to live! That he's handing over the business to the two eldest. No more transatlantic board meetings, no more punch-ups with Cameron Mackintosh at the Savoy. Says he's spending what time he has left sailing in the Maldives with Lady Ruth and the grandkids. Thus," she simmers with rage, "I am surplus to requirements. With immediate effect!"

I don't know what to say. Avril and Soki's liaisons are, to put it kindly, intermittent. How often they see each other, outside of work and the odd cocktail at Claridge's, is debatable. But there is no denying the effect this will have on her life.

"So. The flat?"

Her cup stalls, shaking slightly, like an elevator in a power cut.

"A month's notice!"

"No! After everything? After all you've—"

It crash-lands in the saucer with a perilous chink. "Twenty-two years, Fen! *Twenty-two fucking years!*"

Heads turn. Ladies who shop try to watch without appearing to. Foreign students look up from mobiles, unless they hail from a culture where coffee and swearing go hand-in-hand. I shuffle my chair a quarter-turn and slip an arm round her quaking shoulders. These are exceptional circumstances.

Whatever the truth of Avril's relationship, her affair with Soki is the cable that tethers her to this world. I have often wondered what would become of her when the inevitable happens; notwithstanding his failing health, Soki is older by twenty-five years. Once or twice, on boozy nights when a show or exhibition was too stultifying to endure, I have been minded to speculate whether she features in his will. But Avril, who could always sense a conversation moving in that direction, would change course adroitly. Now it's something she will have to face. She blows her nose on a serviette.

"I hope you didn't mind meeting here. I feel like the walls are closing in at home... Anyway, there's to be *a settlement*. That's the word he used, all official—solicitors and signing things. He wants me out of the flat so he can rent it to someone else, then when he... When the time comes, there's no paper trail. No unwelcome surprises for the fragrant Lady Ruth when she's in charge of his estate... Christ! He owns two hundred properties—does he think she'll be going round collecting the rent personally?"

She takes a fortifying sip. I have never seen Avril so angry. Fear is driving this. She gave Soki the best years of her life and here she is, spurned and about to lose the roof over her head. Which reminds me:

"If he's retiring, what about your job?"

She scoffs. "Oh well, that's high on his list of priorities, obviously! Says he'll have a word with Ed and Daniel. See if they want to keep their father's ancient mistress on to do the photocopying! No, I'm on the scrap heap, Fen—personally and professionally. I might as well self-immolate on their welcome mat in Eaton Square. Give Lady Ruth's Colombians something to clear up. Like Soki chucking up his clams after the Oliviers!"

There is the hint of a smile. Avril has had thirty-six hours to cry, fulminate and process this. My own Friday-night debacle seems small fry by comparison. While she rakes over the wreckage of her life, I make short work of my muffin's fudge topping. The sugar is doing me good, and so is the caffeine. This is the liveliest I've felt all weekend.

All talked-out, she is staring into the smears of her coffee cup.

"Fancy another?" I ask.

Avril shakes her head. "It's gone three, I'd be bouncing off the walls. Anyway, enough of my woes. Did you go for that drink with Lorraine Dawkins?"

The overtures from Tate Modern's marketing chief have slipped my mind.

"No, she postponed. Childcare-mare. We've rescheduled for Wednesday. But she was a bit more forthcoming over the phone. I get the impression it's something on a project, rather than full-time basis."

"Ah. So not stable."

"No, but a foot in the door. The Tate's a bigger beast than the Picture Gallery. Could be worth getting in." I pick the last crumbs off the paper case. "Maybe you should take the plunge into freelance. Temping? People always need P.A.s, and it's a handy stopgap while you look around."

She grimaces. "I can't face it yet. To be honest, I'm more bothered where I'm going to live."

"I know, poor you. Be a lot cheaper if you get out of Marble Arch. God knows what the going rate is when you're actually paying for it…"

"Alright," she mugs. "Don't rub it in. Actually, I'm wondering if I should follow your lead. If living on my own is all it's cracked up to be. I mean, my little flat's fine, and cosy on the nights Soki stays over—*Stayed* over."

I don't interrogate the point. She laughs.

"Sorry, back to me again! Anyway, how's it going with Martin and his ghastly sheila?"

"Ah…" I drain my cup. "Therein lies a tale, though it's not a patch on yours."

"Go on, I need a diversion."

"I want another coffee first. Can't I tempt you? Herb tea or one of those flavoured waters?"

"I'll have fizzy. Get a shift on, I'm all ears…"

I wait at the foot of the stairs for a woman staggering down with a baby in a neoprene breastplate. At the counter, I mirror-read the hours on the glass door; open till six. Mindful of the caffeine issue myself, I plump for decaf and a chocolate-covered flapjack.

Five minutes later Avril is looking faintly comical, mouth agape over her mineral water.

"You—are—joking!"

I shake my head.

"Straddling the plinth in full view of the other houses? And when she said foursome, she meant…?"

"I assume so. We'd already established she swings both ways. Presumably exhibitionism and a bit of quasi-necrophilia are just further options on the menu."

"God, Fen! What happened then?"

"Well, like I say it's a bit of a blur. Martin was a deer in the headlights, with this vacant smile. Sort of horrified-but-game-if-I-was… I said something like 'Monique, this isn't

237

Brisbane!' or maybe I just thought that. Can you blame me in the circumstances?"

I puff my cheeks, story expended.

Avril is appalled but trying not to laugh. "And? Aftermath?"

"Nothing so far. I was dead to the world till lunchtime yesterday. By then they'd scarpered. I daresay Martin will turn up today—God knows what I'll say to him... But that's it. If I was carrying a torch, it's well and truly snuffed out now."

She sips from her bottle. "Well... The apples of both our eyes, gone on the very same day!"

Which is kind of her. The Soki affair may not have been the *grande passion* Avril likes to believe, but it was something. Unlike my flimsy obsession with Martin.

"So, how do you feel about living with him now? I guess these things blow over."

These things! You'd think Martin had left his dirty smalls in the landing, not snorted Class-A drugs in the garden and let his girlfriend desecrate a burial site! I take a breath before answering.

"I don't know how I feel. I half-expected a knock from the local plod yesterday... Is it tattle-tale-ing, if I tell Ethan and Georgie?"

"Hardly," says Avril. "They've a right to know. I suppose that's the thing with house-sharing—the more of you there are, the more chance someone won't gel."

"Hmm, well I don't think one complication in eight years is bad going. Moving in was right for me at the time; I never regretted it. You remember how bored I was in my flat, coming home to the telly every night?" It occurs to me this is a chance to give her a boost. "I tell you, moving out of your place could be the best thing you ever do. I don't know how you've stood it, living alone all these years. Except when Soki was there obviously..."

She looks noncommittal. "I wasn't thinking of a big house like yours. Something more manageable." She swirls her fizzy water. "Something *à deux*?"

Her stare fills in the blanks. I am taken aback, and it shows.

"Sorry, Fen. I didn't mean to put you on the spot. If you're happy as you are, fine."

I regroup. "Let's rain-check. See what sort of settlement Soki comes up with. You never know, he could change his mind tomorrow... Can you really see Lady Ruth, stuck on a yacht for a year? There's no Harrods in the Maldives, and what about her golf? The islands are one big bunker!"

Avril laughs along. But these are uncertain times for us both.

Chapter 39

It is nearly seven o'clock when I get in.

The Sunday trains are busier than I expect. I am standing until Clapham Junction, though I hardly notice. Too busy pondering the irony of my first sexual overture in years. On a grave in a suburban back garden, with the man of my dreams and a coked-up floozy.

You couldn't make it up!

Then I mull the permutations of what to say, to whichever combination of housemates is at home when I get there. In this, fate is on my side, or seems to be...

It's Groundhog Sunday in the living area. Georgie and Lorenzo are on the settee, knotted up like a Henry Moore; Ethan and Cass sit respectively on, and cross-legged in front of, the armchair nearest the TV.

"Yo, Fen!" says Lorenzo, the only one to acknowledge me.

The others grunt, engrossed in the verdict of a judging panel swinging their axe through the dreams of a wannabe pop star.

I go to make dinner. If I say anything, it will be to Ethan and Georgie only, which rules out tonight. My shelf in the fridge is uninspiring. I settle for cheese on toast and make a mental note to do a proper shop tomorrow. I am peering under the grill to check for burning when Georgie appears.

"Hey, Fen. Everything alright?"

The edge in her voice says she wasn't engrossed in the show after all.

"Fine. Just seeing a friend in town. How was your weekend?"

My question falls fallow.

"You've just missed Martin and the kids."

"Oh. Are they coming back?"

"No, they've gone to Monique's. I hear you had a wild one on Friday night..."

I absorb this. Was that a singular 'you' or plural?

"Yes. It all got a bit out of hand in my opinion." I yank the grill pan as the cheese turns from bubbling to brown.

"That's what Martin said." Her edge grows steely. "Fen—this can't go on."

Reaching for a plate on the drainer, I stop. "Sorry?"

Georgie's arms are folded. "Look, we all share this place. It doesn't belong to any one of us. I know you've been here the longest and you pay the most rent, but all that entitles you to is the biggest bedroom!"

"I've never thought any different... Georgie, if you'd been here, you'd have been as mortified as I was! That woman's behaviour was lewd and utterly inappropriate. And I for one am not comfortable with drug-taking in our garden. There are children living nearby. Anyone could have seen!"

Nothing about her face says she is persuaded. She suddenly looks young and immovable. I feel a gulf open between us.

"I know you've got your issues with Monique, Fen. I appreciate she's not your sort of—"

"No, and she's not yours either!"

Georgie raises a palm. She is in professional mode, as if calming a jumpy service-user.

"But it's no excuse for language like *that*."

At this I skip a beat. "I have no idea what language you're referring to, Georgie. Given the stuff she was coming out with, I hardly think I—"

Hands rest on the worktop. "*'You junkie rednecked slag.'* Was that it?"

Her expression invites a challenge. I am incensed.

"Liar! That's preposterous, I said nothing of the sort!"

Admittedly the end of the evening is the foggiest, but there is no way I said anything like that. Not even accounting for Chinese whispers, or the recollections of a drug-fugged mind.

Did I?

The more I think, the less sure I am... At that moment Lorenzo ambles in, all tanned calves and tee shirt askew. Taking a beer from the fridge, he catches Georgie's eye and ambles out again.

"Look, Fen, we're all grown-ups. Sharing a house means taking the rough with the smooth. But if I bring a friend back here, I don't want to think they're at risk of getting some jingoistic rant out of nowhere."

She makes it sound like I've got Tourette's! The sheer injustice makes my blood boil. This is nonsense, from start to finish!

"Georgie, whatever you've been told that's not what happened. Martin and Monique were away with the fairies! He was virtually insensible—she was writhing about on top of Mrs Burnside like something out of Dennis Wheatley!"

She looks blank.

"And I have no recollection of saying anything like that! I left them to it and went to bed."

(Am I imagining, or did someone just turn down the television?)

Her level gaze meets mine. "Fen, when we have a lot to drink, we don't always remember everything we say." Her voice is measured; an adult making a child see reason.

"I am aware of that, Georgie. But I am not misremembering, because I would never use words like that! I admit, I wasn't comfortable with what they were doing. I don't take drugs, but other people can do what the hell they like. I'd just prefer they be a bit discreet about it!"

At least she is listening. I am emboldened.

"I also think they should be able to handle them. Now I'm no expert, plainly, but I know drugs affect people in different ways... I should probably be grateful I only had to contend with Monique's rampaging sexuality! I don't know if you got the full story, but she was basically angling for a bisexual orgy in our back garden!" Here Georgie is staring at the floor; presumably embarrassment. "I'm no prude, as you know. Open-minded as the next person, but there is a limit."

"*It's not about being a prude, Fen!*"

I swing round. Ethan is standing in the doorway with Cass looking on behind.

" —I guess not everyone's comfortable with diversity. People living their lives differently…"

My mouth falls open. Not this!

"Ethan, I am all for diversity. This has nothing to do with that. You know I'd never—"

"Do with what, Fen?"

This is Cass. I have never seen him so serious. Two such slight, soft-spoken men, yet suddenly I feel intimidated.

"With what you're implying!"

Cass snorts, half turning away. Ethan looks sad;

"You can say the word, Fen. It's not the 1950s!"

"*Being gay!* I'm entirely comfortable around gays. Always have been! What I object to, is people who pressure others into doing something they're not comfortable with. It's common decency—a rule we all stick by, or society falls apart!" I whip my forgotten snack off the grill pan, onto a plate. They are all staring at me. "What?"

Ethan speaks first. "Fen, you can't put self-expression on a par with rape. The fact someone like Monique has to do drugs before she can be open about her sexuality's bad enough without you demonising her for it!"

I feel like I woke up in the middle of a student debate I've not prepared for. (Where the hell is this going!)

"Monique doesn't do drugs to be open about her sexuality, Ethan. *She does them because she's a lush!* And it isn't demonising someone to say the way they behave makes you feel uncomfortable!"

I turn to Georgie.

"Look, this cuts both ways. I've a right to feel that I and anyone I bring into this house is safe and welcome. What I will not accept is being pilloried for saying something I didn't—and holding views I don't have! I've lived here happily for eight years, rubbing along with as diverse a bunch of people as you could wish for... Martin's been here five minutes, and Monique doesn't even live here! He, incidentally, has made it abundantly clear this is just a stopgap till his divorce comes through. So why you're so worried about him, I don't know!"

One of Georgie's eyebrows has developed a tremor.

"Sour grapes, Fen?"

As it spreads to the corner of her mouth, chuckles emanate from the doorway.

No one looks at me directly. I open the cutlery drawer and take out a butter knife. Cut my slices of cheese-on-toast on the diagonal and take a bite.

So much for my clandestine operation, intimate evenings with Martin beneath the radar! Someone has clearly been more open about my entirely chaste advances than I have.

It is only now I realise how hungry I am... A second triangle of toast disappears before I know it, and the next is in motion while I'm still chewing.

"Fuck you," I say. *"Fuck the lot of you!"*

I double over the third piece and shove it in.

Chapter 40

I ride out the Bank Holiday Monday with an impromptu visit to Oxted.

Eschewing a taxi, I walk from the station to Mother's, for a morning of listening and nodding. Of making tea and cutting cake, which I take outside to admire Bill's latest handiwork: a trellis for her climbing fuchsia.

I am as grateful for Mother's incessant commentary as the half-arsed train service both ways. Everything takes longer than it should—yet I bypass my stop on the way home and stay on till Waterloo. From there I walk, hugging the riverbank on a detour to Tate Modern, for a listless troop around the Bridget Riley exhibition I've had a mind to see for months. It will stand me in good stead if I have that chat with Lorraine Dawkins, and the eye-popping murals chime with my sense of being trapped in a world folding in on itself.

By the time they're closing up, I am tired... Back in Wimbledon, I grab a snack at the only open shop, something I can eat in my room. I charge straight up the stairs at No. 4, The Ridge without recourse to the communal areas. Turn in early, and sleep more soundly than the previous three nights. Exhaustion, coupled with the sheer boredom of worrying over my predicament.

Waking on Tuesday, I am grateful for the return to work. Only Lorenzo shows his face as I stomp through my breakfast-and-bathroom routine. Am still in my dressing gown as we come face to face in the kitchen. My coffee mug and a teaspoon make hard landings in the sink, as he manages an embarrassed nod before bolting for the train.

Twelve minutes later I follow in his wake, slamming the front door on a house that no longer feels like home. There's a crisp bag snagged in the roots of the silver birch. I am fastidious about litter, and to pick it up and toss it in the wheelie bin is the work of a moment. For the first time in eight years, I resist... Similarly, in my train carriage as a Fanta can rolls about in the foot space like a diabolo, I step on the platform at North Dulwich and leave it for someone else.

It is an odd sensation: to realise the place you call home is nothing of the sort. I remember a fantasy I amused myself with as a girl, decades before Hollywood cottoned on to the same idea. I imagined my life was a sham and the world a simulation. My own mother and father were actors, and wherever I went—school, shops, the swimming pool—there was someone just around the corner, preparing their lines for the giant con everyone was in on but me.

When I think of it now I tut at my naivety, for conjuring such a coordinated effort to dupe one unremarkable little girl. Yet, arriving at the office today, I am touched by the same feeling: that my housemates have been playing a part. For how long, I can't say. Certainly since my grave misstep of airing my feelings about Monique... Or was it earlier, as I developed an eye for Martin over a bottle of wine? And was our secret affinity anything-but? Has he been reporting back to Ethan and Georgie about his evenings with giddy old Fen? Did they giggle at my eagerness to please, to pop my cork for any man I see as long as it's Martin? The same man who complimented me on handling his children, inferring I made a better job of it than his girlfriend?

What a bastard. What a fool I've been!

Reaching for the herbal teabags at the bottom of my pedestal, I wilt. Am tempted to stay like this; slot myself under the desk so my workstation seems empty.

"Morning, Fen."

Cheryl. Looking nervous and apologetic as she fiddles with the new, shorter hairstyle she debuted last week. A radical change for a woman who lives in smocks and alternates two pairs of deck shoes the entire summer.

"Sorry to barge in before you've had your tea. But Derek says, can you do his nine forty-five with De Groots? Shouldn't be too much of a pain. They're bringing in the paper samples he asked about for *Picasso in Wartime...*"

Our next exhibition but one. I sigh... On the first day of the week, it's always a toss-up whether Derek will make it in before mid-morning.

"Go on then."

She lets go of the spiky tuft over one ear and shuffles away. I unpick the string on a camomile teabag... Paper samples are a bone of contention. As Marketing Coordinator responsible for all publicity materials, this is my province. Derek's sudden interest baffled me; until I heard him tell Tash about his breakfast chat at the Wolseley with Sebastian Pilger... Windbag Pilger is Derek's oppo at The Serpentine Gallery, who have just won an award for their Frida Kahlo brochure. All down to the stock, according to Derek, and a cost-effective way with holographic laminates. He has never shown an interest in production processes before, so I suspect an attack of award-envy. The other boys are waving their trophies over the devilled-kidneys and now he wants one, too.

Ever-professional, I take ten minutes to sift through the email thread with the printers. Dry stuff, though I am minded to check the print run these figures are based on. Derek isn't clear, and ordering too many is money down the drain.

Five minutes in the Ladies to check my make-up and I'm ready. The account manager from De Groots is known to the department as 'Dez-with-a-Zed'. He is relatively new, replacing my old friend Trevor, when he relinquished his grip on the industry that was his livelihood for thirty-five years. Digital did for Trevor, as it will us all in the end. He and his second wife moved to the South of France, where I like to think of them cultivating his precious zucchini beneath a 100% cyan sky.

Dez is in the glass meeting room when I arrive with my laptop.

"Fen! How we doin' this bright and breezy Tuesday?"

He shakes my hand without rising. I take the seat two along and don't reply. Despite his well-cut suit and fine grooming, Dez's manners are like his consonants: intermittent. He is one of those confident young men of whom I am wary: alabaster-bodied from too much gym, with a gift for charming both sexes. By all accounts, he and Derek have built a rapport through a spate of one-on-one meetings that always end with them walking through the office, talking cricket. The fact Dez has me to deal with this morning is a disappointment he conceals manfully. He is rummaging in a leather document case for samples, but I am straight to business:

"Can we just go through the figures for this run?"

I tap on my keyboard, though the relevant document is already open. He puts down his man-bag and fiddles with an upright tablet, one of three devices he's brought to the meeting.

"Got 'em — 'ere!"

Annoyingly he slides it towards me. I am all for paperless in principle, but spreadsheets never fit the screen. Navigating columns is easier on a printout.

"Right," I say, finding the bottom line. "And this is cost-per-thousand, or the whole run?"

Dez looks unsure. "If I can jus' have a squizz..." He takes back the tablet, catching it mid-topple as it hits a groove in the table. "Yep. No-yeah, that's the total cost on furteen-fousand."

"Oh? But that's too low, surely? The run I mean."

The smaller of the figures I saw in Derek's email was *thirty* thousand. Elsewhere there was a reference to three hundred.

"Erm, I'm sure that's what Derek arksed for..."

A brace of lines form between his jet-black eyebrows, which like the rest of him receive far too much attention. I return to my laptop, scrolling to the email in question.

"Obviously I'm only standing in. But we'd never print as few as thirteen thousand in a B-format brochure. Not for a major show."

The lines deepen. "B-format? These bad boys is A."

Formats differ, depending on whether it's a simple leaflet to give away, or something more substantial to present to customers who buy a ticket. The idea of using expensive print for something that will end up trodden on the pavements of South London is madness. We are studying the email together when there is a tap on the transparent door.

"Sorry to disturb," says Tash, waving her mobile. "Just got a message from Derek—*Hi Dez!*"

"Hi Tash, how's your weekend?"

My face puts the pleasantries on hold. Tash is in one of her outfits, a cross between children's TV presenter and Miami hooker. She looks bleary, like she had a hard night.

"Well?" I say.

"May I?" The girl pulls up the chair on the other side of Dez, which seems unnecessary to relay a message. I develop a frown of my own as he pushes the tablet her way. Annoyingly, Tash slides through the data-rich tabs with ease.

"Great," she nods. "Cool!"

She sits back, smiling at Dez as if the matter is resolved.

My patience is waning. "And the message?"

"Oh sorry. Doesn't matter. It's just, Derek said to triple-check that the figures include a quote for spot-varnish. He thinks this one's an award winner. He loves my design!"

My eyes come to rest on her mobile (—why didn't Derek message me?). I flick back in the emails for the briefing document.

"*Your* design?"

I find the scribbled layout for the brochure De Groots is working to. The cover is a montage of works created by Picasso during the Second World War, with a distinctive bronze at the centre. The layout is a good deal rougher than the concepts I expect from our design agency.

"Did Silent Splash do this?"

Tash shakes her head. "Have you not seen it, Fen? I assumed Derek ran it by you."

"It's sound, Tash!" pipes Dez. "The highlight on that blue lady's kneecap's gonna pop 'em in the eyeball, I'm telling you."

I have missed something. Their familiarity says Derek's meetings with Dez were not as one-to-one as I imagined. With everything else going on, I've let him take the lead with this brochure. So why has he handed the design of our collateral to the office junior? I peer again at the sketch.

"I appreciate you haven't been with us long, Tash, but I am surprised Derek didn't point you to our brochure for *Parisian Murmurs*. A couple of years ago?" I drag a folder from the archive. "Here…"

A momentary impasse. Neither of us moves… Tash blinks first, sashaying round the table to slouch at my shoulder. The brochure cover features works by various artists, including Picasso's bronze in the same central position as on Tash's design.

She looks blankly from the screen to me and back again. "So?"

"Well, obviously it's important we differentiate our publicity as much as possible. If people think we're trotting out works they've seen before, they're not going to buy a ticket. As with— Hang on, we're not even showing *Still Life With Guitar*!"

Picasso's slabby oil is also prominent in Tash's cover.

"Fen, these are the *kind of things* in the exhibition." Tash's earrings, toddler-bright shapes kebabed onto fuse wire, bob in time with her words. "It's about creating an ambience, yeah? We don't need to be pedantic about everything. Do we?"

I bridle at this. "We don't. Nor do we need to dupe the public into believing they're coming to see something that they're not!"

Tash throws her weight on one heel. "Well, Derek doesn't have a problem. Like I say, he loves it. That's why we're chucking everything at the print job."

Now her tone is proprietorial. I feel my status as senior member of department being eroded. Not even the exemplary fit of his double-breasted jacket can stop Dez looking uncomfortable.

"An' we love it too, Tash. My guys are gonna smash it!" He shoots me an awkward glance.

Her tongue clicks as she smiles brightly. "Counting on ya, Dez. Don't let me down…"

The look passing between them is familiar from decades of people-watching. It says I am not in on the game and, in the catalogue of human expressions, one guaranteed to make my heart sink… I have spent a lifetime trying not to let it show. Often unsuccessfully.

I slap shut my laptop and stand from the table. With my eyes to the front and head held high, the reflection in the room's fish tank wall says I am through the door before the others have even noticed.

Chapter 41

I am still fuming as I march down the passage. Tash's attitude galls me, and that's on top of Derek's incompetence with the maths. Not to mention his vainglorious hijack of a job that is rightfully mine! I am furious at myself too; I took my eye off the ball.

My thoughts are in order as I reach his office. The blazer on his desk, yet to make it to the hanger, says he has just arrived.

"Morning, Fen," says Derek, pulling back his chair. "Everything alright?" This is his default greeting when I arrive before he does, and which I take to mean I have been in charge. "Sorry I dropped you in it with De Groots. Nightmare traffic on the M11..."

Years of working together has made us fluent in each other's body language. Mine says 'coiled spring'; Derek's, that whatever I am about to unleash it is too early. Still standing, laptop under my arm, I make no preamble:

"Derek, why are you letting a junior marketing exec design our brochure covers?"

"I'm not, Fen. I'm letting her design one of them."

Pedantry! Storm-shelter of the rumbled!

"But, as per the terms I negotiated, Silent Splash have first dibs on all our major print jobs for the duration of their contract."

"Exactly," he replies. "Clever of you to sneak in a bit of wiggle-room." Another of his phrases that never fails to make my teeth grind.

"Sorry, Derek?"

"*Major* print jobs. Bit moot, isn't it?"

"Moot? I don't follow."

He takes a breath. To his credit, Derek rarely loses his cool.

"Well, as long as they get the Season brochures, I don't think Silent Splash can complain. The Picassos are only hanging for eight weeks. It's not like it's the whole quarter."

This is true. A problem with the lending estate means five of the paintings are needed in St Petersburg by Christmas, forcing us to cut short the exhibition and sling up some Bruegels for the festivities.

"But that's hardly in the spirit of the agreement, Derek. Any day now, they'll ask me what's next in the pipeline. You're putting me in a very awkward position!"

He nods at the wall behind me. His time-buying nod.

"Life's difficult for all of us, Fen," he says eventually, "budgets stretched as they are... Actually, I've been meaning to talk to you about that. Anywhere we can trim the fat—got to be a good thing."

"I'm not sure Silent Splash's legal person will see a breach of contract as fat-trimming!" The needle on my sarcasm meter is climbing; I rein back. "That aside, I've just seen Tash's cover design for the first time, and it bears a startling resemblance to *Parisian Murmurs* from the summer before last."

Derek's eyes, in close proximity at the best of times, shrink to pinholes.

"Well, if it does I'm sure it was an accident. Personally, I think she's done a jolly professional job." His brows knit, an expression of concern. "We need to nurture our staff, Fen. I'd be wary of bandying around accusations of plagiarism, if that's what you're—"

"That is *not* what I'm saying, Derek. We have the copyright on all our collateral, we can hardly plagiarise ourselves!" Must I state the obvious? "Surely you can see it makes no sense, flagging up the same old works? We're at the bijou end of London galleries as it is. Why make ourselves look even smaller?"

That struck a nerve! For the sake of Derek's ego, I have learned to ration my marketing acumen. Now I fear I've overstepped the mark.

Apparently noticing his summer-weight blazer for the first time, he carries it to the back of the door. I take the opportunity to sit in the other chair, to appear less intimidating.

"There is another reason I let Tash have a crack at that cover," he says, retaking the seat of power.

Ah, this should be interesting! The hands on top of his head indicate imminent pontification.

"We can learn a lot from the young, Fen. And since we'll only grow our mailing list by appealing to the next generation, I believe we should view Tash and Millie as our oracle... Oracles." He fingers an ear before returning the hand to his crown. "They're two very switched-on young women—*people*... Tash in particular. Between you and me, I'm delighted she chose to work here rather than somewhere high-tech and glamorous!"

I am about to point out that we had four hundred applicants for their positions, most of them under 30. We could have filled them ten times over, in my opinion with candidates far better qualified than made Derek's final cut. But he is on a roll:

"—So it's vital we make them feel like valued members of department. And that means allowing them a degree of responsibility."

"Alright. But in line with their position, surely? Marketing's marketing. If Tash wants to be a designer, she's in the wrong job." (Something he might have picked up on before offering it!)

Derek develops a sudden interest in the padded arms of his chair.

"That's just it. In my view, going forward, we need to take a more *holistic approach*. Keep down the number of cost-centres by embracing a multitasking model... Fen, you know the budgetary pressures as well as I do. The more we can keep in-house, the better the bottom line. And the happier we make Southwark and the Arts Council, just when they're about to review our funding!"

I know to be wary when Derek slips into marketing-ese. It is usually a smokescreen.

"Yes, but it's a false economy if our leaflets look like something thrown together by a Year Three art class!" My voice rises despite myself. "What next? Do we let her have a crack at the paintings? Is Tash a whizz at Post-Impressionism, too?"

I close my eyes in disgust. Is this what they talk about at their Boys' Club breakfasts—how to wring more work out of the troops, while they scarf down the marketing budget and play My-Award's-Bigger-Than-Your-Award?

When I open my eyes, eight of Derek's fingertips are on the desk, like the opening chord of a doomy sonata.

"Fen, what I also appreciate in Tash and Millie is their can-do attitude. Rather than always, *always* dwelling on the negative..." I dare him to catch my eye. "And when we have deadlines to meet, they are more than willing to burn the midnight oil. Even popping in at weekends, if required."

My lips meet like Velcro. Something Cheryl said weeks ago comes back in a flash: *Derek, checking his parking space would be free if he came in on Sunday...* Something to do with an influx of restaurant receipts in his expenses...

"I have never shirked putting the hours in, Derek, and I resent the implication I have. I am also frequently the only person here at our official starting time of 9am—first day of the week included!" This barb I could have resisted. "Furthermore, I often work through my lunch hour, and I'm never out of here before five-thirty. Even on Fridays, when half the department's buggered off or down in the quad with an ice cream!"

He is about to speak. But probing tales of truancy will only highlight his own fluid attendance. He changes tack:

"Which is highly commendable, Fen. Your reliability is an asset to the Gallery... Having said that, a bit of flexibility's not a bad thing. We all need to adapt in this day and age, don't we? Before A.I. is doing our jobs for us. No holidays, no toilet breaks!"

I am stony-faced. I've had enough of people siding against me at home, but anything I say now will be viewed in a negative light.

"Call me naive, Derek, but I think that's a little way off. You won't find an arts organisation in London that doesn't value reliability. Somewhere down the line, working to a budget means meeting deadlines and getting the numbers right." Which reminds me; "On that subject—"

Knuckles rap smartly on the door. *Not again!*

Tash doesn't wait for a reply. "Hey, Derek, you'll never guess who—Oh! You're busy..."

"It's alright, Tash, we'll only be two minutes." A limbo moment passes between them. "You were saying, Fen?"

Derek avoids confrontation at all costs; he will be hoping Tash's appearance derails my thought process. Naturally I plough on:

"I couldn't help noticing a discrepancy in the figures De Groots are working to. Probably a twitchy finger on the zero key, but that way lies disaster, as we know." Every marketer has a tale of an error that cost someone their job. Oddly, never the head of department...

Tash has developed a twitch of her own. She is looking at me suspiciously.

"It's nothing to do with me, Derek! I checked the costing on the spot-varnish like you said. All factored in."

I stifle a groan at her perky eagerness to please. "No one is saying it's to do with you, Tash. You're not running the project single-handed. Yet."

"Oh, pardon me for breathing!"

Arms fold at two points in the room but I say nothing. Despite being her line manager, I will not overstep the mark again. Derek is the boss, he can handle this... I wait for him to speak but he is distracted by his computer. Tash's look of slack-jawed insolence says she knows she is on safe ground.

For the third time this morning, I pick up my laptop and walk silently from the room.

Chapter 42

I stop off at my desk to dump the hardware. Then keep on walking.

Three minutes later I am on a banquette in the East Gallery, staring at my favourite canvas of the permanent collection. Unlike Cheryl and her crafty ice cream sorties, I find the best way to slip under the radar is by sticking to the public areas.

Poussin's *The Nurture of Jupiter* and I have a history of contemplative moments. I was on this exact spot when Mother phoned to say they'd confirmed her MS diagnosis... And again, when I decided to take the plunge and follow my financial adviser's advice: sell the flat and invest the money, rather than buy somewhere new to wallow alone... There is something in the fortitude of the painting's brawny shepherd and dishevelled nymph, as they help the infant Jupiter suckle a goat's udder. Something bolstering in a crisis.

Experience has taught me I do not require solitude to reach a decision; the presence of others makes me feel less conspicuous. Today, a disconsolate-looking girl with A3 pad and a tray of oil pastels. She is sitting cross-legged on the floor, too focused on her task to care about eyes over her shoulder. It pleases me to see a young acolyte paying grubby-fingered homage to the Old Masters, even when there's a reasonably priced postcard in the shop.

She has done a decent job of the background, less so the central figures. Whilst I claim no artistic bent beyond picking out a paint swatch, even I can see where the problem lies... Her shepherd lacks the sinuous solidity of Poussin's original; his grip on the horns of the lactating nanny goat is unconvincing. And the sketcher has let shade fall across the nymph's exquisite chin, suggesting a five o'clock shadow.

It is the work of a moment to point out her errors. Yet if I have learnt one thing of late, it is that expressing my opinion can be a minefield. So, with a last, appreciative look at Poussin's highlight on the shepherd's sinuous forearm, I return to my desk.

From: Fenella Woodruff   *Today at 11.01*
To: Derek Fleming
Subject: FYI

Derek

This is to inform you I am handing in my notice with immediate effect. It is a personal decision that does not require picking-over, nor the involvement of HR.

I am also taking the five and a half days annual leave owing to me, starting now. Apologies for any inconvenience this causes you or the department. In the light of your words this morning, perhaps you can view this as another opportunity for Tash to demonstrate her famous flexibility. You seem very taken with it.

Sincerely
FW

I slip the few things I need from my desk drawers into my bag. The heat of the day means I haven't brought a jacket, which makes it easier to slip out without looking conspicuous. The mouse-click, pressing Send, is my final act before walking. The sluggishness of the Picture Gallery's outmoded servers means I have ninety seconds to get past Derek's office before my email plops into his inbox.

As the side door to the car park closes behind me, I have an inkling I hear my name coinciding with the clunk of the lock. I

am halfway to the gate when footsteps ring out on the gravel...
In the circumstances, goodbyes are to be avoided. And if it's
Derek, I have no desire to make this easy for him.

"Fen!"

It is Cheryl. Good-hearted, downtrodden, slave-to-puddings
Cheryl.

"You forgot your eleven-fifteen with Retail, didn't you?"

We face each other a few strides apart, like duellists reluctant
to draw.

"I won't make the meeting, Cheryl... Ask Derek, could you?
He owes me one."

She looks uneasy. "You'll be back for lunch though?
Mohammed's 60th, remember? We're going for pizza. I booked
a table."

Mohammed is the Picture Gallery's longest serving
attendant. For three decades he has stood on the threshold of
rooms, watching like a hawk for overstepping feet and laser-
powered flashguns. He is famous for spotting typos in the blurbs
accompanying new paintings. Discoveries he relays sheepishly
to our department, when he drops in with a mollifying tin of
homemade baklava. Though he neither drinks nor celebrates
Christmas, Mohammed is the life and soul of the works' party,
first on the dance floor and last to leave. He has never married,
which seems odd for a Muslim.

"Damn. I had forgotten. Sorry, Cheryl, change of plan. I
won't be in this afternoon, or next week. Need some time off."

"Oh, I didn't realise... You okay, Fen? Is it your mum again?"

I mumble noncommittally. "Tell Mohammed happy birthday
from me, and I'll catch him next time I'm —" (I was about to say
'in' — Why do I stumble over even inconsequential fibs?)

Cheryl's chin dips. "You're not happy are you, Fen? Look,
it's none of my business but I'm just saying, if you ever need a
chat. Those girls get on my wick too, you know. I dunno what's
going on, but Derek's been like a dog with two tails ever since

they started. Plus his wife's phoning more than she ever has, whatever that's about..."

Part of me wants to probe, but now is not the time. I straighten the bag on my shoulder and give her a sort of wave.

"Fen—"

(Will I ever escape!)

"If it is your mum, or even if it isn't, I just wanted to say, she's lucky to have you. I wish I'd been better with mine..." Her eyes are glistening. "I'm more of a daughter to my Eric's mum than I ever was to her. Well, it's easier when the kids don't need you every minute... We owe our parents everything, don't we? Then, when they get old and start needing us, we don't do enough." She sniffs. "Course it's worse for you, cos yours is ill."

I field her look of concern. Return it as gratitude, which makes her blush.

Cheryl thrusts fingers into the pockets of her smock. "Anyway, I don't know why I'm telling you this—you never miss a trick with anyone! Listen, I hope your week goes okay. See you when you're back, yeah?"

My trains are less frequent in the middle of the day. Sitting on the platform at North Dulwich, I have time to think as the minutes count down on the dot matrix.

Martin isn't Martin! Martin is a construct, kindled by the real thing, set alight by my own foolish imagination!

Flesh-and-blood Martin played a part, but the man I fell for doesn't live at No. 4, The Ridge, because he's never lived anywhere outside my head... What hurts most, is knowing everything that meant so much to me—every smile and chink of wine glass, every confidence shared in the moonlit garden—meant precisely nothing to him.

It takes me two stops to compose another email. This one requires less finesse but more thought, since I haven't drafted it ten times before at the end of a trying day... I sift through my phone's address book. Select JBurnside52@hotmail.co.uk. And send.

Done.

As my train arrives at Wimbledon, I step over the paws of a sprawling lurcher asleep or dead in the aisle. Make short work of the deserted platform as I skip up the steps. But instead of exiting through the ticket hall, I dart down another flight onto Platform Five, just as a train for Clapham Junction pulls in.

Plenty of seats. I consult my phone again...

Perfect. A connecting train to Oxted goes in sixteen minutes.

Part II:

Unfixed Abode

Chapter 43

Hooray. The last of the packing crates are gone.

I watch from the kitchen window as Bill directs the removal men out of the gate. Their lorry is in no danger of clipping his Renault but he is not about to chance it... Now he's on the pavement, waving his arms like an airfield marshal. Bill was made for ear protectors and a high-vis jerkin.

The date is December 23rd. We made it in for Christmas, not that I'm feeling festive. Nothing saps the yuletide spirit like selling one property and buying another. All in time for 'the big day', as Mother insists on calling it. Old age has made her sentimental. Unpacking only took a day, thanks to Bill and Kath, who also packed up the bungalow when a last-minute meeting kept me away. I have only my own stuff to see to, and since upstairs is my province finding a place for everything is a breeze.

True, some adjustments are still required. A stairlift has been mentioned, and while Mother's en suite will do for now, the door to the utility room is too tight for her new electric wheelchair. (*"I won't be barred from my own home, Fenella... I may wish to do my own washing!"*) But they can wait. What matters is that we are here, and we like it.

All in all fate has smiled, not counting a last-minute drama with the vendor's solicitor. Liquidating the bulk of my portfolio was straightforward, and quite empowering. I enjoyed my financial adviser's strangled expression when I told him to cash in nearly all but my pension. Mother's bungalow, which the kind estate agents drool over, attracted a range of interest. Their spec was awash with words like 'highly desirable' and 'immaculately kempt', which as she said made it sound like George Clooney. Then we found this place, the last of four on our second day of viewing... I have never seen myself living in a close, but there is something reassuring about moving into a relative new-build. The house is seven years old and the previous owner an invalid, hence the dining room converted to a bedroom with en suite. Truly, it was meant to be.

Bretherton Close is five minutes from Godstone high street and ten from the station—a boon for getting to London. I am now officially a non-metropolitan. Another bullet bitten, but the advantages of consolidating our lives under one roof are inarguable.

"All done," says Bill, clumping through the back door. "Anything else, Fenella? Shall I give you a hand with your mother's decorations? The box is on the sideboard."

I am smiling as I shake my head. "We'll be fine, thanks, Bill. She'll probably have a nap soon. Why don't you go and say goodbye?"

He has an eye on the kettle but I am not falling for that. In the moment of inertia that follows we are both weighing the dynamics of our new situation. Bill blinks first.

"Right-o..."

He slinks off to the sitting room as I arrange storage jars on my new slate worktop. The units in the kitchen and bathrooms are higher-spec than anywhere I've ever lived—No. 4, The Ridge included. There is no wave of nostalgia when I think of my old home. The month I endured there after giving notice is one to forget. Words were spoken, apologies made of a sort, but the spell was broken. Any time I couldn't spend outside the house, I passed in my room. On the morning I left, no one was around. My final act was in the back garden: slipping a sprig of late-flowering clematis into Mrs Burnside's silver flower holder. Closing my eyes, fingers pressed to her black marble, I whispered a few words. Not a prayer; a farewell. It was just me and the-lady-of-the-garden on the day I moved in, and the same today. The symmetry was sobering.

That was the emotional highpoint. Staring at the front door from my laden taxi, I felt nothing at all.

In the two months since, I have been in Oxted with Mother, another move I never foresaw. But the best option in the circumstances, and a prelude to the sea-change of living here... Looking back, I never enjoyed Christmas at No. 4, The Ridge. My housemates would largely spend December embroiled in festive fun elsewhere, until sloping off to their families. On Christmas Eve, I would lock the door on the empty house, the half-hearted tinsel and tin of Quality Street bought in a misplaced spirit of fun. Invariably I was the first back, too. Once the prospect of a week trapped in the aspic of the bungalow became unendurable, I'd feign meet-ups with friends in the dead days before New Year and return as soon as the trains were running.

How times change!

As the front door closes on Bill, at least for today, I fill the kettle. Slip two Hobnobs onto a plate, and the bag into Mother's mug first so her tea is the way she likes it. When I push the sitting room door, she has nodded off despite the blare of a game show. Her afternoon nap is another new station of the day—like the arrival of her carers first-thing, and again at bedtime. For this is the reality of her life now, one I have opted to share. Mother's independence means everything to her, and if living together is what it takes to keep her out of institutional living, so be it.

I pop a coaster over the mug to keep the heat in. The flicker from the muted television casts a glow on the carpet. By four o'clock it is almost dark outside. Those border plants will need replacing before spring... So much to do, and all to pass through the sieve of negotiations with Mother. Take this settee: her beige monstrosity has a claret stain hidden by one of Kath's throws, yet I sense it whenever I sit... Occasionally I ask myself if I'm stark, staring mad. But then, as I watch the rise and fall of Mother's chest and her head loll on the wing of her chair, *I know*.

My gaze flips to the window when a sudden flare over the fence sets next door's roof ablaze. On, then off, then on again, as it will be till tomorrow morning. The red and white lights sketch the outline of Santa's sleigh against the slates, though from this angle Dasher and Dancer, Dinger and Donger, are hidden from view.

With a stuttering breath Mother opens her eyes. One glimpse of this lurid tableau is enough to shut them again.

"Dear God, Fenella... We should've moved to Blackpool and be done with it! We could afford a castle up there..."

Her head turns the other way and she falls back to sleep.

Two mornings later, I awake to a familiar feeling in unfamiliar surroundings.

Nothing makes you feel like a child more than Christmas morning under the parental roof. It is a mould I have broken but once in forty-nine years: in the early Eighties, camping out at a friend's flat in Camberwell with people I hardly knew. We spent the day in pyjamas, drinking wine and eating sausages; the turkey wasn't cooked through till midnight. It was a salutary lesson I was never to repeat, and less so once two parents became one. I consider it my duty to keep Mother company at Christmas, despite the fact she is rarely alone. This year we have a houseful. Bill will be bringing the bird, ready-to-serve courtesy of an insulated thing that slips in the hatchback. And I have bought the veg, though somehow it's ended up that Kath is cooking it... Part of my reasoning for looking at properties in Godstone was the three healthy miles it put between Mother and her entourage. From now on there will be no more dropping round, willy-nilly. Tea, biscuits and lawn mowing will be by appointment only.

Then there's Avril, who hummed and hah-ed before finally accepting my invitation yesterday. A bit off, but I cut her some slack. She has been pondering her first singleton-Christmas for months, hatching a dozen plans and changing her mind on all of them. I insisted she was welcome to spend the day with us wherever we were. Stopped short of pointing out she'd never seen Soki on Christmas Day anyway, for the entire duration of their affair. Somehow coffee in Harrods on the twenty-third, or a walk in Hyde Park after Boxing Day, became equated with a fulsome celebration. Yet the termination of even this has been a knife to her heart, so when she called to say she would love to come tomorrow, I was sweetness and light. Put down the phone and charged off to Sainsbury's, who miraculously were still well-stocked for veg.

My bedroom and the upstairs bathroom have yet to lose the feel of a hotel. It will go when I am rid of these curtains. I allow myself a moment's pause before pulling them back to peer out on the garden, in case the forecasters got it wrong and night has wrought a snowy miracle... Not to be; the garden looks as drab as an un-iced Christmas cake. Its rose beds and rockery, complete with a hideous cement pig the vendors inexplicably left, have yet to feel the force of Mother's direction and the toil of others. All in good time.

I go down to make her tea and toast. I have thirty minutes to feed and water her before the carer arrives. Somehow ablutions, dressing, make-up and a good deal of chat from Mother all fit the fifty-minute slot. She has two regulars, Fatima and Ewa, who alternate mornings and evenings. When it came to choosing a new home, Mother was more concerned about staying within her care firm's catchment area than anything else. I can see why; the girls are polite and efficient, friendly when they need to be but otherwise silent, apart from the rasp of starched cotton as they whisk about the place.

Giving over her intimate care to strangers is a life-change for Mother. A second fall in September decided it, and now moving about under her own steam is no longer an option I have kitted her out with an electric wheelchair. A scooter is on order too, like the one on the cruise. It is due the second week of January, just in time to cut up Godstone's shoppers on the last day of the sales.

"Here you go, Mother. Happy Christmas!"

Once her bed is adjusted to a seating position, she allows herself to be kissed. Mother looks positively cheerful.

"Happy Christmas, Fenella. May it be the first of many!"

The red and green checked nightgown Ewa put her in last night looks thoroughly festive. I fit the tray table over her lap; Mother has been online-shopping for ergonomic gadgets, to a point where I've considered limiting her screen time. Undeniably this table is a good wheeze, though the monstrous, easy-grip kettle will stay in the cupboard for as long as I am here.

"Did Santa leave us anything?"

This has been the Woodruff Christmas-morning mantra since I was four years old. Rhetorical, for all but the first twelve years, after which I joined my parents in putting gifts under the tree before bedtime, promising to forget I'd ever seen them. For now I sit on the edge of her bed and take my own mug and slice of marmalade toast from the tray.

"I wonder who's got the short straw?" says Mother. "Fatima presumably, being Muslim. Mind you, Ewa's Polish Orthodox. They don't do Christmas till January, you know."

I try not to smile. Having carers has opened up the world to Mother in unexpected ways.

"I'll do us both stockings next year," I say, changing the subject. "It's the one thing from childhood I miss."

The framed photograph of Father catches my eye. I should have thought before speaking, but she doesn't seem offended:

"Good idea. But I'll do yours and you can do mine—I'm a whizz at the internet shopping now..."

I raise an eyebrow but say nothing.

Chapter 44

I am glad of Avril in the end. Despite their seasonal bonhomie, Bill and Kath are, and always will be, Team Lillian.

The Oxted contingent are early, turning up just after eleven. They march in and commandeer the kitchen, in a manoeuvre I could resent but don't. Cooking for more than two unnerves me at the best of times. Avril is late, her arrival announced by a grind of brakes, and a screeched reverse when her Mini finds Bill's car in the drive. The roads are dead on Christmas Day, so how she managed to get stuck behind an articulated lorry...

At least she's made an effort, I think, taking in her immaculate trousers and a silk blouse I haven't seen before. More on-trend than usual, but then chic is easier to pull off when you're small.

"These should be in the fridge!" she says merrily, whisking over her tardiness. "They've been shaken about a bit, so open with care!"

Two bottles of Dom Pérignon seem generous, particularly on a temping salary. Then I remember her drinks cabinet at the Marble Arch flat, with doors that couldn't close on the clutter within. Each bottle was a present from Soki, accompanied by flowers from all the times he cancelled dinner or stood her up on a tryst. The cabinet has moved with her to the new place, and even Avril won't stoop to guzzling champagne alone.

I pour everyone a sherry and sit with her and Mother in the lounge. She is in the armchair where Fatima deposited her. From now until evening, Mother will need supervising in her moves from A to B... It still troubles me, this giving over so much responsibility to strangers—but then what was the alternative? If she's happy, and it spares us both the Rubicon-crossing bathing/clean-underwear routine... Pans clunk in the kitchen. Having one's Christmas lunch prepared by outsiders is odd too, though with this I have made my peace. Bill and Kath insisted weeks ago they were happy to cook Christmas lunch wherever Lillian was living, and she was happy to let them. In another age, Mother would have made an excellent Lady of the Manor, overseeing operations from her drawing room as the servants went about their business.

"Cheers, girls," she says. "Compliments of the season!" She is in a relatively tasteful Christmas sweater: a reindeer with pearl-button eyes. "How's life treating you, Avril?"

"Well, thank you, Lillian. It's so nice to see you. I can't remember the last time we—"

Mother can. "Waterstones Piccadilly! When Fen was dabbling in publishing. We all went to a book-launch thing. Bill Bryson, or one of those travel writers, been around Australia on a motorbike. I distinctly remember a man with a didgeridoo..."

Avril nods uncertainly.

"She's right," I say. "Nothing wrong with Mother's memory."

I also remember them arguing over where to go for dinner. We ended up in Chinatown, a dingy basement with peeling wallpaper and waiters even grumpier than we were. Not a success; I wasn't minded to get them together again.

"Lovely decs!" says Avril, spotting the pinky-red tinsel snaking over the mantelpiece. It is bookended by the jolly Santas with bellies as round as plum puddings, the stars of our family Christmas for decades. They, and the artificial tree in the corner, are my half-hearted attempt at seasonal decor. Bill would doubtless have done better.

"And how are you, Lillian?" asks Avril, looking concerned. She glances at me, unsure how much she is meant to know.

"Oh, bearing up, thank you. The doctors are doing what they can, which isn't much. But I've got a lovely new home and wonderful friends... And my daughter here with me, so all things considered, I'm very lucky." The sherry glass is suspended under her chin; two rows of fingertips grip the stem, like a child holding a tulip. "Anyway, it's Christmas! No time to dwell. Has Fenella given you the guided tour?"

"Oh no—I'd love to see round!"

I stifle a sigh. I would have done this first, but opted to propel her to the lounge instead before Mother could say she was being ignored. I keep hold of my own glass as I shepherd Avril upstairs. She pauses politely on the dog-leg, admiring a muddy watercolour of Stiffkey Saltmarshes. I move her on to the master bedroom, with its view of the cul-de-sac that still makes my heart sink a little.

"Uh-huh," says Avril, which covers a range of opinions. She glances into every corner before declaring, "Very roomy. You'll be comfy here..."

The smallest bedroom is next, which I have earmarked as my office. It is currently home to the ironing board and contents of Mother's box room, and does not warrant crossing the threshold. Half this stuff belonged to Father: books and fishing tackle, boxes of die-cast toy soldiers we have sworn will finally get a sort-out... The second bedroom, essentially the spare, is furnished in a mix of knick-knacks from her bungalow and my old flat. The queen-sized double has seen better days, apparent only when you lie on it. The dressing table is the one from my childhood, where Mother sat reflected in the angled mirrors, like a logical rendering of van Dyck's *Charles I.*

I sit on the crocheted bedspread and watch Avril look around.

"So," I say, "who'd have thought six months ago we'd both be in pastures new by Christmas!"

She replaces the potpourri she's feigning interest in. "True. You've found a lovely place, Fen!"

I check for irony as she sits beside me. Not long after I left the Picture Gallery, over blinis as we scarpered early from an Emin retrospective, the idea of us living together was again mooted... In the bullish, grapey fug I was almost swayed. We pealed with laughter at memories of our short-lived share in Lisson Grove, a period of my life I look back on with brittle fondness, aware how time takes an eraser to the messier parts. Deep down, I know Avril and I are still friends because we don't live together. Happily, her plans moved on before the subject came up again.

"And how about you? Settled in?"

"Oh yes," she says. "It's nice and warm, and I've met the people downstairs. I'm not sure Camden Town is for me in the long term, but it's handy for the West End."

She has plumped for what in our younger days we called a bedsit: a studio flat in a Victorian terrace. It was a wrench for Avril to leave W1, but when the harsh reality of renting dawned, relocation was the only answer. Factoring in the deposit, two months down and an online finder's fee, the flat scraped in on budget. Any further out than Camden was unthinkable. As it is, the area has a gritty ambience.

With her brave face in place, she is keen to talk of something else.

"So, any Christmas card from Wimbledon? I bet Martin designs his own."

I sniff. "Not likely, seeing as I didn't leave a forwarding address. All in the hands of the Post Office. Not that anyone sends interesting mail these days."

A chuckle as Avril nudges my arm. "Talking of 'interesting males', I'm doing online dating!"

My mouth drops open. "You swore you never would! Said it was 'a digital innovation too far'!"

She sits back defensively. "That was years ago. It's a different world now, Fen. Sink or swim. Look, I'll show you my profile..."

A burst of culinary-related noise drifts up from below. We will soon be required at table. I watch as Avril navigates her mobile to a site called *helloyou.com*. She hands it over.

"There. What do you think of my pics?"

I swipe a row of selfies; her in a variety of blouses, all a decent likeness if you ignore the faint fish-eye effect of the focus. There is a hint of the It Girl, or Avril's idea of one, in the park bench shot with sunglasses and Soki's famous handbag that cost more than a night at the Ritz. No chihuahua, thank goodness... The first two lines of her profile are visible beneath the moniker AVRIL-UP-WEST. I glimpse the words *Cultured free spirit, footloose and ready for*—before the mobile is snatched away.

I am quietly impressed. "Good for you. Any takers?"

She leans back on one hand. "A flurry initially. To be expected, from what I hear—Fresh meat and all..."

I don't blink. "Right."

"Saturday before last, I was out for lunch *and* dinner. Mostly we just meet for a drink or a coffee. Quite nice some of them, though no one I've seen more than twice yet. I'm waiting to be bowled over, like with..."

I could never imagine Soki having that effect on any woman, short of sitting on them. But then, after twenty-plus years as a one-man woman, who knows what sort of beau Avril's taste runs to... Once or twice at launch-dos, we got very drunk and ended up in a corner appraising the waiters. Robustly built and slightly exotic seemed to be her thing, facial hair a bonus. Years ago, a sommelier called Salvador tried to slip her his phone number at the Hayward Gallery. She made a great show of letting him down gently, which she mentions to this day.

"You should give it a go," she says buoyantly. "I'm rather enjoying myself. It all works by GPS or something, so you could meet chaps from round here. They might be more—*you*."

I fail to suppress a glare. But this is not a comment I am about to pick apart at Christmas.

"Bathroom," I say, standing. Avril will admire my whisper-shut lavatory seat whether she likes it or not.

Chapter 45

Mother and I are seated at either end of the dining table. Bill's lunch is a military exercise. When he set the table with three lots of glasses, a perplexing lineage of cutlery and foil crackers from John Lewis, I half-expected him to pull out a tape measure. He and Kath have all but ignored Avril beyond a quick hello over a steaming colander. Appetising smells have been emanating from the kitchen for over an hour, but only now is he carving and she dishing up veg.

Seeing another man at this table, blade raised over a crispy carcass, reminds me of the photo in Mother's room. But Bill is more adept with the honing steel than Father ever was, shaving off slices with aplomb and pausing once for a crucial strop.

"Breast for you, Lillian? Do you want stuffing? Who's for leg?"

His pre-roasting of the turkey is a great success, as he has told us. The method involves a pepper and onion-salt rub, and a trick from Nigella with a skewered kumquat. Kath is beside him, in a pinny she brought from home along with her serving dishes. She is doling out mash, parsnips, and peas she is careful not to offer Mother. She picks up the navy-striped gravy boat (house's own).

"Shall I pop it on the bird or on the side, Lillian?" she coos.

There is a line between being mindful of Mother's wavering grip and plain patronising. Kath has yet to master it.

"As it comes," deadpans Mother.

Like us all, she is desperate to eat. The acerbic, unnecessary grapefruit sorbet starter, doled out to those not involved in the kitchen, did nothing to fill the hole. So, as the steaming plate lands on her placemat, I see her eyeing it.

"Don't wait for us, Mother..."

She ignores me, staring stoically ahead.

"What about you, April?" says Bill, mindful of protocol, serving the visitor next.

No one pulls him up on this slip, for fear of delaying things further. When he finally sits to the Jenga-style heap of meat on his own plate, I am actually salivating. As a rule, I consider turkey overrated; a festive staple to be endured, like glacé fruits and that tedious James Stewart film Mother adores. But it is tasty enough, moist without being greasy.

"This is lovely," says Avril, anointing a morsel of breast with Kath's homemade cranberry jelly. "Best I've had in years!"

"All in the prep!" says Bill. He finishes chewing. "Second week of Advent, you mix your salt-and-pepper rub in a jam jar. Add cloves and a sprig of rosemary in week three, turning the jar every other day. Chef's secret to a crispy skin!"

I try not to catch Mother's eye. We have both come to savour Bill's theories on issues great and small. Mother is fond of, and grateful to, Bill and Kath without being blind to their shortcomings. Not for the first time, I find her attachment slightly baffling.

After her sherry Avril is on the champagne; I make a mental note not to give her more since she is driving. As ever, the alcohol loosens her social stays.

"So," she says, looking from Kath to Bill, "how come you're not with your family today?"

The question hovers over the table with the steam off the carrots.

"Oh, we're not together," says Kath. "We used to be Lillian's neighbours. Independently, I mean. Different houses!"

Avril nods slowly, catching my scowl. "Oh. Yes I remember now..."

Bill and Kath have been conversational grist to our nights out for years. Did none of it go in?

"Kath hasn't got any children," explains Bill, inappropriately. "And my daughter Chloe's in Perth, with her two little girls." He helps himself to a puddle of bread sauce. "I tend to go over there in our summer. Too hot at Christmas. I video-called them this morning though, they'd just got in from the beach. Evie loved that necklace you chose, Lillian, did I say?"

Mother nods, engrossed in a drumstick. A cutlery set-of-three with chunky plastic handles recently appeared in the kitchen drawer. But the spoon and fork look like they belonged to Uri Geller and will not be making an appearance on Christmas Day. At home, and without embarrassment, Mother takes any opportunity to eat with her fingers.

"And you," asks Kath. "Are you on your own too?"

Her directness throws Avril. She rests the fork on her plate.

"I am. For the first time in a while, actually. I split up with my long-term partner a few months ago. My mum and brother live in Harrogate, which is lovely if a bit noisy. He's got three young children, so I'm going up for New Year's Eve instead. They'll be in bed."

The conversation rolls on through second helpings, and a polite division of the sprouts-with-almonds Kath finds under a pan lid. They have not been missed in any other sense, but we chew through our allotted trio.

"It's a wrench though, isn't it, Avril?" says Mother, out of nowhere. "Being single in later life?"

A sullen green meteorite is pinched between her fingers. My serviette shields a smile. Avril is decades younger than Mother was when Father passed away; typically, it's all the same to her.

"I see it as an opportunity, Lillian," she replies cheerily. "Plenty more fish in the—"

"Who was the chap you were courting, anyway? Fenella was always cagey about him."

The serviette drops to my lap. "Water under the bridge, Mother..."

Avril ignores the escape route. "He was in the theatre, on the corporate side. We had a wonderful relationship for many years, but ultimately... Well, it was time we both moved on."

"Oh," says Kath. "Married, was he?"

"Thought so," mumbles Mother through a parsnip.

I clear my throat a little too volubly. Bill looks uncomfortable, but neither woman seems to see anything amiss.

Avril gathers herself. "He was, as a matter of fact. Not happily, obviously. He was also quite a bit older than me. All in all, it's a blessing in disguise."

The moment is tempered by champagne. I feel for her.

Mother lifts her glass carefully to her lips, then pauses. "So how do you go about it? Pursuing these *opportunities*, as you call them?"

Now all eyes are on Avril. Her expression says this is not a subject she prepped for.

"Everyone finished?" I snap, with an involuntary clap. "Time for presents! Avril, would you ferry over that little pile?"

I am pointing under the tree, where four gifts remain from the stash Mother and I opened this morning. I whisk around the table, stacking dishes like Russian dolls while everyone passes plates to Kath. By the time I am back from the kitchen there is a present on everyone's placemat, including something cylindrical for me that appeared out of Avril's bag. A last present after the meal is one of my earliest Christmas memories: Father, with something behind his back, never failing to make me squeal by insisting mine had been eaten by a reindeer.

"*Shall I just—?*" Bill and Kath speak as one, hands darting towards Mother's gift despite the minimal use of Sellotape.

"No you shan't, I am perfectly capable!"

Her unresponsive fingers turn the parcel end over end, inadvertently dictating proceedings as everyone else takes a slow-motion age to unwrap theirs. Protocol around who gives what to whom is stage-managed so we each only stump up for one gift. Avril and I have bought each other's, while Mother bought Kath's. Then Bill for Mother and Kath for Bill; predictably the result of much negotiation, though it hasn't stopped Kath slipping Mother an aromatic candle when she thought I wasn't looking.

A pause in the fumbling. My friend's love-life is still on the agenda:

"But don't you feel vulnerable," says Mother. "Meeting men without knowing who they are?"

Avril's lips tighten. As a guest on Christmas Day, she is well and truly trapped.

"Not really, Lillian. The ones I've met so far have been very honest about themselves. And I always choose somewhere there's people about. It was a leap the first time, but after that..."

Mother's thumbnail snags up a corner of tape. "Hmm, but you hear such horror stories."

"*You* hear such horror stories, Mother," I scoff. "Too much daytime television!"

"No, I agree," says Bill. "The Internet is a curse as well as a blessing. Be the end of us all one day, you mark my words." His gift, the shape and size of a Terry's Chocolate Orange, still sits squarely on his mat.

"Me too, Lillian," chips in Kath. She is fiddling with her present wrapping without breaking in. It is a paisley-print scarf I bought with Mother's blessing. Kath's fondness for paisley is widely apparent, from the handkerchief tucked in her watch strap to the draped swags of her downstairs loo.

"Mind you," counters Mother, "it must work for some. Otherwise they'd not all be doing it. Well, I say *all*..."

I do not look up. Just slide a finger under the repeat pattern of robins, and rip.

"Oh, perfume. Thank you, Avril."

It is a generous bottle of the latest Calvin Klein. The sort she would choose for herself, and another hint I should move on from my trusty White Linen. Avril's quirky atomisers end up on top of my bathroom cabinet, from where they serve as emergency room-deodorisers. She has saved me a fortune over the years. The packaging of this particular fragrance is covered in brushstroke butterflies. I feign eagerness, slipping off its artisanal band.

"Don't chuck that," says Avril. "It's an extra little gift!"

Mother is huffing over a tub of Green Tea hand cream Kath is at pains to show an interest in; Bill is nonplussed by something like a plain Rubik's Cube that is a gadget for moulding sushi rice. Avril takes the woven circlet and adjusts the fastening, slipping it over my hand:

"There—It's a friendship band! They're not just for kids, you know. Look, I've got one too..."

She slides up her sleeve, exposing a child-like wrist. Hers is orange and yellow, mine crimson and blue, but the design is the same. They look like something hawkers peddle on Camden High Street... With gift-giving, Avril is a dab hand at the near-miss. True, I prefer bracelets to necklaces and rings, but I am not about to waltz around in a bit of old shoelace at my age.

"I just saw them and thought, why not? They're fun, aren't they? And we've been friends for all these years!"

She is holding onto my wrist, looking me in the eye. Unsettling on two glasses of wine. "Merry Christmas, Fen. Thank you for inviting me!"

Squeezing her hand, I extricate my own. I now feel guilty for putting so little thought into her present. "Go on, open yours."

As ever she tears the paper gleefully, a throwback to days when Soki had gifts delivered in lieu of himself. Over-exuberance was her way of camouflaging the disappointment. Inside the box is an envelope, the outer casing merely a disguise.

"What can it be?" she wonders, smile fixed. "It's a—*oh!*" The presentation card holds a rectangle of plastic. "Annual Membership of the Tate Galleries! Fen, that's very generous."

I fold my discarded wrapping. "Hope you like it. I just thought, now you don't have all those first-nights to go to, you might like to do something cultural. On top of all your..."

The last word goes unspoken but we both hear it.

Her smile ossifies. "Thank you."

I busy myself around the table so we're ready for pud, balling up everyone's paper and dunking it in the wastepaper basket. Even with my back to her, I know Avril's eyes are on me... Sounding judgemental, when it is the last thing a situation needs, is a curse I have grown to live with.

Chapter 46

By seven o'clock the interlopers have gone. Goodbyes are drawn out, and almost resume when Kath returns in a squeal of tyres with a sweating pan taken in error.

The only foreign presence now, so to speak, is Ewa. She is in the downstairs bedroom, looking for things to tidy while Mother finishes in her bathroom. I can hear the wheelchair being positioned, ready to ferry her back to the lounge. The evening's viewing warrants comfort, and she will retake her armchair forthwith.

"So," says Ewa, ten minutes later. "All ready for Christmas night!"

She stands back to admire Mother in situ. Looking like a queen on her Parker Knoll throne in the dressing gown I chose from The White Company.

"Anything more?" asks Ewa. She slides the wheelchair into a niche by the bureau, its spot when Mother wishes it out of sight. We have ten minutes of her slot left, but I am at a loss for anything more she can do. The cracker trimmings are binned and the dishwasher is sloshing in the kitchen, where Bill and Kath cleaned up after themselves with Presbyterian diligence. Sherlock Holmes would not detect they'd made a sandwich there, let alone a feast for five.

As Ewa slinks back into her duffle she makes a jovial show of wishing us Happy Christmas in two languages. When the front door shuts behind her Mother lets out a sigh, followed by *"Oh, botheration!"*

"What is it?"

She thumps the armrest. "I forgot to give her those pickles! They're on my dressing table!"

Her conviction that Poles live on boiled meat and cabbage solved the puzzle of what to gift her evening carer. We found the presentation multipacks doing the Sainsbury's shop online. I said nothing, even as Mother clicked on a second selection for Fatima *("You can't go wrong with condiments!")*. I missed the actual handover this morning, though not the kink in the girl's immaculate eyebrows as she scrutinised the label for Pink Pickled Rhubarb.

Evenings with Mother have become a ritual I enjoy. Whilst I've always been a homebody whatever form home takes, I was wary of the consequences a move to the sticks would have on my social life. Not enough to push me off the path I chose, that day I walked out on work—but anxious nonetheless. Looking back on the pantomime of evenings at No. 4, The Ridge (the stilted conversations; my glassy-eyed sufferance of the drivel on TV as I waited for Martin to show his face) I haven't sacrificed much. Once a fortnight, my new freelance life takes me into London for meetings at Tate Modern. Enough to keep up the dinners with Avril, though even those haven't the pull they once did. She still spends the time talking about Soki. All that's changed is the tense.

Whereas, thus far, evenings at home are a pleasure. The mother-daughter tensions, which characterised our relationship for most of my adult life, have eased. The enormity of what we agreed to that pivotal Sunday (casually, in a phone call, on a pretext of checking the right way with egg custard) was also a necessity for us both. Yet, sailing has been remarkably plain; these long winter evenings have the air of a holiday. My nightly change into slippers and a medium-weight fleece precedes the pouring of generous sundowners. And this particular evening is one we've anticipated with relish.

"When's *Strictly* on?" says Mother. "I suppose we've got to sit through this first..."

'This' is the *Doctor Who* Christmas Special, an alleged festive highlight the BBC has been trailing for weeks. The romp involves skulduggery in an interplanetary outpost of Hamleys, which the

Doctor and chums get locked into on Christmas Eve... I am no fan of the programme either, though I was mildly in childhood. The modern take is more frantic, with monsters too convincing to be a man in a rubber suit. The stories lack the charm and relative coherence of the originals. On the odd occasion I have watched they remind me of my Third Form physics lessons; despite staunch concentration, I am lost in minutes. Tonight's special features creepy, creeping elves and a malevolent teddy bear. There is a fairy on top of the tree, which I know from the preview has a face like the unbandaged remains of Nefertiti. For now, our viewing options amount to this, tattooed celebrities abseiling the turrets of Harry Potter World, or a Bruce Willis film along similar lines. The seasonal smorgasbord can only improve.

Mother's bottle of Amontillado stands on the bureau. For Christmas it has been joined by a bottle of ready-mixed Mojitos, a reminder of our nights aboard ship. Like mother like daughter, we have rationed ourselves to a single glass on week nights with optional top-ups at the weekend. Tonight, as last night, house rules have been relaxed.

I pour her another. "Say when."

She ignores me. "That all went smoothly, didn't it? I say it's the sign of a good house, when it can host a decent Christmas."

I wait for the barb as I replace the cap; a box containing the rest of Mother's festive heirlooms went AWOL in the move. Cue the local newsagents to the rescue. Their emergency tinsel included the strand of iridescent cerise, winding between the cards on the mantelpiece like an alien caterpillar from old-school *Doctor Who*. That it is not up to Mother's standards has been mentioned more than once, but for now seems forgotten.

"I wonder how many we've got left?"

Her voice is plaintive.

"How many what, Mother?"

"Christmases. Together. Here. Before I'm six feet under, or you've shunted me into a home for the gaga!"

"Do you have to ruin the spirit? Drink your Mojito."

I swig my sherry. Turn to the television so she can't see me dab an eye on my sleeve... Mother can drink what she likes, but there will be no more for me tonight. Christmas always makes me wistful. New Year is worse, hence my trick of sleeping through it. Now we are under one roof, for good and not just a flying visit, moments like this are too poignant for words.

I focus on the screen. The Doctor's companions are trapped inside what looks like a Lego dungeon, being menaced by the giant teddy.

"Avril looks older," says Mother abruptly.

Better. I know where I am when she's making personal comments.

"She is older, Mother. You haven't seen her in twenty years."

"I know that! I mean, she looks older than her age."

Does she? I always think of Avril as well preserved. She spends far more on lotions and Ayurvedic what-nots than I do. Dermal fillers were mentioned recently, even without Soki's Harrods credit card, which I ascribed to her leap into the dating-unknown.

I let slip a hollow laugh. "Well, I hope all these beaus she's meeting feel differently... I can't think of anything worse than making small talk with desperate strangers..."

Mother slaps the arm of her chair. "You're a coward, Fenella, that's your problem! There's no wrong way to meet someone—I don't know why you can't do it too!"

"Not now, Mother. And thank you, but I'm quite capable of conducting my private life without your input. I can meet people if I want to!"

She snorts. "How? Where? You never met anyone sharing that house with all and sundry! How are you going to do it stuck here with me?"

Toes curl in my moccasins. I feel the same colour rise in my cheeks as when Mother spotted me holding hands with Philip

Russell through the window of the Wimpy Bar. Fourteen or forty-nine—it makes not a jot of difference!

"As I say, I am perfectly—"

"I tell you, if it wasn't for this bloody disease I'd be jumping in with both feet. People still court at my age, and good luck to them! *I'm not dead down there yet, you know!*"

My eyes freeze on the screen: the Doctor, roasting individual chestnuts with his sonic screwdriver. On second thoughts, Mother isn't drinking another drop!

It is five past seven on Christmas night, and this is the single, most explicit reference to sex that has ever passed between us... It's the MS talking, obviously. Not directly—there is no evidence it's affected her mind—but this is breaching boundaries, breaking the fetters that make our relationship workable.

Is the Mother I have moved in with a loose cannon? Not the kindest metaphor for a large woman in a wheelchair, granted; but it chimes with something I read in the MS charity mag that lives in her bathroom with the Pam Ayres anthology.

"I didn't imagine you were, Mother! Many people keep up physical intimacy well into later life, even with your condition. You're living with MS, you're not—"

"Not dying with it? Thank you for that, Fenella. Merry Christmas to you too!"

To my relief she is chortling. Her sense of humour, which leans towards the gallows, is a godsend at times. Mother is hard to offend, no matter how far you put your foot in it... And Christmas is Christmas after all: a day out of time, when the world stops spinning and anyone with sense gets off until the 27th. I can feel it in the tinny, glittering oasis of this evening, with the curtains drawn and the lights on the tree throwing speckles on the ceiling. Boxed chocolates are on the bureau; nuts are in the fruit bowl, which Mother of old would have spent the evening cracking in her paper hat as Father looked on, bareheaded.

"Has it nearly finished?"

She is staring blankly at the screen. In a plot development that patently makes sense to everyone, Teddy is revealed as an avatar containing the DNA of Catherine the Great.

"Five minutes," I say, getting up. "Which chocolates shall I open?"

Her wave tells me to choose. I opt for Thornton's Classic Collection.

"You know," says Mother, "if you'd asked me twenty years ago, I'd have said it'd be gone by now. The urge, I mean... Be a lot less bother, wouldn't it?"

I am flipping through the little leaflet (*Sicilian Lemon Ganache—NEW!*)... Good grief, there's no stopping her tonight! She has been a widow ten years, and I never conceived of my parents setting the duvet alight on a regular basis. Surely she has come to terms with it by now?

"Well, like I say. Everyone's different."

This is meant to sound breezy. Now I am worried it sounds confessional. If Mother thinks my own sex drive is in abeyance, how do I stem the flow of unwelcome advice?

I needn't have worried. About that.

She sighs. "I've been lucky, really. Most women in my situation would have given up hope about the physical side of life... It's an itch though, isn't it? The more you scratch it, the more you want to scratch."

On the verge of giving her first dibs of the tray, I help myself to the Praline Crunch. "I'm not with you, Mother..."

"Sexual intercourse, Fenella! Love in the afternoon! *There's more to Bill than just fluffy roast spuds, you know!*"

Chapter 47

"Bill? *Urpp!*" I slurp back the soft trample of chocolate sliding from my mouth. "Mother, what are you saying!"

Her eyebrows lift. "Well, you can't be that surprised. Had you not put two and two together, after all this time?"

My mind is racing. "All *what* time? It's not been going on since Father died!"

She chortles again and holds out a hand for the chocolates.

"Oh, Fenella! I'd have told you years ago, but I thought you knew and didn't want to talk about it. Bill and I have been intimate since—oh, 1990-something. I forget, but John Major was prime minister and Cilla Black was never off the telly."

"Jesus, Mother!"

Beyond this, I am speechless. The woman sitting opposite is not the one I know. The idea of her carrying on an affair behind my father's back is unthinkable!

The parents of my childhood were like bookends: a steadying presence who worked best a distance apart. Father was rarely given to displays of affection. I have the vaguest memory of Mother on a picnic blanket, giddy on something from a thermos; her legs are bare, in a short skirt he keeps drawing attention to with a mix of disapproval and something I can't fathom... After he died, in a sombre moment musing the contradiction of his loss and the shallow impression he left behind, it occurred to me this was the closest I ever came to seeing him aroused.

"Your father wasn't terribly interested in sex," says Mother. "In case you didn't gather that either... I knew it when I married him. I was reticent myself in those days, more interested in getting away from home. That said, one little experiment led to you popping up, so marriage was the only option, short of Granny garrotting your father on the village green. I told myself we were slow-burners—that it would all click one day, like the

Indians say about arranged marriage..." She helps herself to the Honeycomb Baton. "But I loved him in my way, and he loved me. Or rather, he loved us—you, me, our house. Remember how happy he was in front of the telly? Getting him to go on holiday was a trial... His face, if I suggested anywhere further than Norfolk—you'd think I said root canal treatment!"

The *Strictly* Christmas theme plays out in a cavalcade of glitter and American Tan faces. Now it comes to it, neither of us is watching. I feel queasy and at odds with the world. It is Christmas Day. *Is this really happening?*

Mother stares. "What are you so shocked about? That I've got a sex life in my state, or that it's Bill?"

Cue a vision of the man himself from earlier today: bent over the open oven in his pinny, pricking the sausages he insisted on bringing as well as pigs-in-blankets... I take back the selection box before it's more plastic than chocolate.

"It's just... You can't blame me if I'm seeing you in a new light!"

Mother shrugs as she chews.

"—I mean, I know it wasn't the happiest marriage, but Father was affable enough. How did you... And when did you find the time, with Bill? Didn't he suspect anything?"

Swallowing, Mother says, "Oh, your father knew. He was all for it."

The Orange Crisp tingles on my tongue, synchronised with a burst of onscreen applause.

"—I say 'all for it'... 'Tacitly approving' would be fairer. He knew what I needed, and that he wasn't about to step up to the mark. Plus he liked Bill. Trusted him. Well, we go back forever, us and him. And Brenda."

I stop chewing. Brenda! How could I forget?

Bill and his wife were an intrinsic part of the Woodruff social circle throughout my childhood. Always there, at the New Year's Day drinks we hosted for friends and neighbours. And on the bridge evenings I remember for the bursts of Brenda's laughter that accompanied the aroma of cigars, drifting upstairs like a pungent spectre... Memories made doubly distant because Brenda died soon after I started at Cazenove School. Her illness was shrouded in whispers on one-sided phone calls; her funeral, my introduction to the pageant of death, years before my grandparents began their sequential drop from the perch... I still remember that day, with a sky to match the mood, as we filed to our pew in the parish church behind Bill and their daughter, Chloe. The service fascinated me. The coffin was my first outside sitcoms and news footage of IRA funerals; the grief held in all around me, a preview of the solemnity that seemed so much a part of adulthood. The tribal nature of different schools meant I never got to know Chloe (*'Poor Chloe'* as she was known ever after), but I felt for her that day. Bill kept his hand on her shoulder even though it made for awkward turning of the Order of Service. Two prayers in, he dropped his pamphlet to the carpeted bench and shared hers instead.

In the years that followed, he was a fixture of my parents' lives. Still a regular visitor when Chloe went to university, married and eventually emigrated to Australia. I never suspected him of any function beyond family friend — yet, even when Father was alive it was subtly apparent Bill was Mother's friend, not his. I saw this as my parents being rather progressive, though it jarred on Father's other traits — his dominion over Sunday lunch, and reluctance to carry so much as a gravy spoon to the kitchen sink. Now it makes perfect sense... I never told him, but I was deeply touched by the way he nursed Mother when she became ill. It touches me more, to know he did it as a cuckold. On this night of all nights I am seeing him in a new and noble light.

Unaskable questions re Mother and Bill keep surfacing. How did it begin? What form did it take then and, dare I think it, now?

But the weight of this is too much for tonight. *"Well!"* is all I can manage.

On the television, a retired cricketer with a blacked-up nose strides through the Paso Doble, his arms forming parentheses around plastic antlers. He draws his partner to him as if folding a tablecloth, clasping her with manly vigour. As they traverse a diagonal of the snowflake-patterned floor, I think of Father's funeral; how grateful I was to Bill for being a rock for Mother. Insisting on taking the widow's seat without her walking frame, she tottered up the aisle on Bill's arm, earning nods of condolence from family and friends. This image, once comforting, now sticks in my craw.

There is a chocolate in my mouth I have no memory of putting there. I push it aside;

"It's true what they say, then. Always the quiet ones!"

Mother's look is earnest. "I appreciate it's a lot to take in, Fenella. And I could have picked a better moment. Blame it on the booze!" The cricketer is now straddling his partner, one arm raised as if harpooning a whale. "Sorry if I shocked you. I know it's not your thing."

My mouth slackens... Sacrificing my freedom is one thing. Having my lifelong view of my parents' marriage blown apart beneath the tinsel is another. *But this is going too far!*

"Oh, get off your high horse, Mother! You talk to me like I'm still at school! You haven't the faintest idea what I do in my private life!"

"No reason I should, Fenella. It's none of my—"

"No it isn't! And yours is none of mine, so pardon me if I haven't spent years scrutinising you for signs of an illicit affair! There is a reason they say ignorance is bliss. How will I ever look at that man again?" I knock back sherry. "Some of us are quite happy, keeping our private lives to ourselves. A dying breed admittedly, but if you think I spent eight years sharing with a procession of red-blooded adults without tales of my own, you are much mistaken!"

"Good. Fenella, I didn't mean to—"

"That house was a hotbed!" My exasperation is in danger of besting the truth; although—"I've had my fair share of adventures, alright. Including the offer of a threesome *in my own back garden!*"

The words hang between us; aquiver and just a little tacky, like the gold foil fairies dangling from the ceiling light.

"There, that's you told. You can't shock me, Mother!"

Her face is a picture of surprise... Or is it something else?

"No, Fenella, nor you me! That's the trouble with every generation—they all think they invented sex! Right back to Adam and Eve, though in their case they may have a point..." She is casting around for her glass. "I think this conversation's gone far enough for one evening. Though I will say, for your information, Kath's talents stretch a good deal further than running up a polo neck!" Fingers find her glass. It is clipped between her knees, empty. "No, don't ask. That's my final word... Is there more in that bottle? Then for God's sake pour me another, it's Christmas!"

Chapter 48

An Uber. All the way to the coast.

How Mother manages to keep the trip from Bill, I don't know. As a rule, he is still there on the doorstep in his virtual chauffeur's cap, for any trip further than the postbox. She is being cagey with me, too. But on the first Saturday in January with nothing on my agenda, I am happy to join her magical mystery tour.

"Not long now," she says.

We pass the Southampton turn-off and carry on in the direction of Portsmouth. Our driver is Serbian, and less loquacious than a London cabbie. His nationality is all Mother has wheedled, and he hasn't spoken since Guildford. The fact we haven't packed luggage or passports confirms this as a day trip only. My best guess involves lunch—and since it is past midday, and my muesli and cup of Assam feel a very long time ago, I hope I am right.

As we round a last bend, the Solent opens out before us. Insipid sunlight glints off the sea separating us from the ribbon of land that is the Isle of Wight. I haven't been over the strait since I was at school; felt horribly sick on the hovercraft and spent the day dreading the return journey... Where the road runs parallel to the water, the houses are a step-up on the pebble-dashed semis we passed on the way. On the higher slopes, sprawling homes with glass walls and ingenious roof extensions say this is prime real estate. Anything overlooking the sea is worth a fortune, even when the architecture is less than regal. Satellite dishes and union flags mark this as a last bastion of England, and a first line of defence against alien invaders.

On the dashboard, a flash from the car's own outer space communicator indicates a turn ahead.

"We here," says the driver, pulling up in the nearest parking space to the entrance of The Sailor's Arms.

It is the first pub we've passed for miles. By the time I help Mother swivel her feet onto the gravel, our efficient little driver has her old-school wheelchair out of the boot, erected and ready to go. He produces a bag of what may well be his lunch and slams the hatchback.

"Are you sure we don't tip?" hisses Mother.

"It's not expected. Though I'm sure he won't object if you insist..."

Cue an embarrassing scrabble in her bag as she mistakes a glasses case for her purse. There is a nip in the air. I want to get her indoors, but there's no hurrying Mother on a mission.

The driver frowns as he takes the fiver. "We return three-thirty, yes? I wait here."

I say nothing as I shunt the wheelchair across the car park. As with everything about today, Mother has played the transport cards close to her chest. Her fingers can only manage the basics of her mobile now, so it is safe to assume this Uber is someone else's doing. Curiouser and curiouser.

The mystery evaporates once we are inside. Even this far out of season the pub is two-thirds full with diners. But there is no mistaking the elegantly dressed figure standing from a table at the window, waving his fedora in our direction.

"You made it!" says Irving Jessop, greeting each of us with a handshake and single kiss on the cheek. "My, it's good to see you!"

He takes charge of Mother, slipping her into a place setting with an uninterrupted view of the Solent. I hover, unable to settle until she is out of her coat with reading glasses on her nose and in easy reach of a menu.

"This is a surprise, Irving," I say with my best show of conviction. Pondering the conundrum on the way down from Godstone, process of elimination left him as most likely suspect. From his postcards, displayed intermittently on the mantelpiece, I knew he and Mother kept in touch. I also noted the absence of a Christmas card, though I helped her send him one, via a mailbox in Boston. Then something with a foreign stamp arrived on the 24th and immediately disappeared from sight.

"Well," says Irving. "With a day on shore between ships, I couldn't think of anything I'd rather do than catch up with the two nicest people I met last year. Seemed the perfect opportunity!"

Touching, though I can only wonder what horrors he encountered to put us top of his list... I feel myself relax. Irving has a way of making even the busiest restaurant seem like an old friend's dining room.

"What'll it be to begin? As I remember, you ladies have a penchant for cocktails. I'm not sure they run to a mixologist here, but I can ask..."

"Shall we stick to wine, Mother?" I say, to save any awkwardness. The staff look neat in their black shirts and pinnies, but I wouldn't trust them to know a daiquiri from a decaf. Aside from cutlery, the only things on the table are a ceramic jug and a split pebble holding the dessert options. A waitress appears and pours water. She is dispatched to bring glasses of wine while we all consult the big menu. One thing about a liaison with Irving Jessop: you are never short of conversation.

"So, where have you been lately?" I ask. "Or should I say, where haven't you been?"

He smiles politely. "Well, quite exciting actually, Fen... Beginning of December, I took the *Queen Mary 2* from Buenos Aires to Santiago. Round the tip of South America, then back up the west coast. Extraordinary — and stunning, apart from Port Stanley. Wow, what a cheerless two-horse town that is! Can't think why your Mrs Thatcher went to war over the Falklands, just sheep and seagulls!" He sips from his tumbler. "Then I took a few days in Santiago, Chile. Was gonna go puma tracking in Patagonia, or take a side trip to Easter Island to see the statues. But the weather closed in, so I stayed put and sampled some fine Chilean reds instead."

He spreads a napkin over his lap.

"And where were you for Christmas, Irving," asks Mother, letting him help with hers. "Did you get my card?"

"I did, dear lady, thank you. It was forwarded to my daughter's place in Boulder, Colorado. I spent Christmas Day watching the little ones practise their snowploughs and end up with facefuls of mush. Gave the skis a go myself too, first time in a while. Must be the old sea-legs, but my sense of balance was still pretty solid!"

There is no denying he looks in fine fettle. I am torn between pizza and the beef & ale pie. When the girl comes to take our order I plump for the *quattro stagioni*.

"And what brings you to chilly England?" I ask. "I'd have thought you'd fancy some sun after that."

"You're right there, Fen. I came over from New York yesterday, and tomorrow I board the *Cunard Utopia*. Next stop the Canaries followed by Cape Verde!"

Mother is shaking her head. "Your life, Irving! You're the luckiest man in the world. I hope you appreciate it!"

I flash her a warning. It is wrong to make a gentleman feel uncomfortable when he is buying you lunch... Irving doesn't mean to brag. Though his life of luxury, which was a shared novelty in the fjords, does feel faintly galling now.

"Don't I know it," he says, the half-smile implying a justification he is used to making. "Anyhow, I understand I'm not the only one with a change of circumstance. How are you both liking your new home?"

Not the fairest comparison but a nifty switch. I let Mother answer.

"We do, don't we, Fenella? It's warmer than my old bungalow, and the garden's more manageable." She leans in conspiratorially. "And I've an island in my kitchen, Irving. Not like a desert island—one of those free-standing units they have on the cookery shows. So I can do my chopping without knocking the saucepans off the hob. My cramped old kitchen drove me round the bend..."

I avert my eyes. Mother has not cooked in years. Even standing at her precious island is a trial now, but she insisted on a new beechwood knife block. Still soothing her lost independence by buying the things she's always wanted.

"Sounds grand," says Irving. "I swear, one of these days I'm gonna explore more of England. Get to Bath and York. See where the Brontës lived. And when I do, I'll be dropping in on you two for tea!"

"Oh, you must," says Mother. "You can stay as long as you like. We've a lovely spare room. Or will have, once we sort out the last of the boxes..."

The girl comes to tell us the kitchen is stretched and that our food will be another ten minutes. She leaves a complimentary baguette in a basket, with ramekins for dipping: balsamic vinegar and an olive oil the colour of troubling urine. Mother, spotting food she has to wrestle with, gives a sigh only I hear. Nodding through Irving's remarks about the blueness of the sky, I double-dip a segment and pop it on her plate.

"I'm fine with it dry," she hisses but eats it anyway, making heavy weather of soaking up droplets with the crust. Irving is careful not to notice.

"And did I hear your mom say you've changed jobs, Fen? Still in the art world?"

"Yes, and yes. I've gone freelance, which makes sense now I'm out of London. No point commuting if you can avoid it, and I like being my own boss. I just finished a project for Tate

Modern, and now there's a sniff of something at the V&A. Same old marketing nonsense, but I enjoy the variety."

Irving smiles. "There's a lot to be said for flexibility. I tell you, the longer I spent in the nine-to-five, the less I thought it got the best outta people. At least the big corporates are starting to let staff set their own hours. Makes them more productive and stops the good ones getting restless."

Mother flicks a thumb at the bread basket for another piece. "It's a different world now, Irving. When I started work, if I wanted to spend a penny more than twice a day I needed a doctor's note. Can you believe that?"

I chew my lip. Mother's stories about the typing pool at Harcourt & Brinley, Solicitors make the Sixties sound Dickensian. It will be 'Polishing the partner's brogues on Friday afternoon' next.

Irving wipes a crumb off his finger. "And all the more reason you should be enjoying a life of leisure now, Lillian... In fact, I have a suggestion for you. I was worried it might not be feasible, but now I know your situation, Fen..."

I look quizzical. Are we here for more than just a sociable new-year lunch?

At this moment the main courses arrive. Irving makes sure Mother has everything she needs before continuing:

"Remember I told you I collect reward points from the cruise lines? I've probably paid enough to keep the entire fleet in bed linen over the years, so I take their chi-chi little bonuses when they come along. Mostly bottles of champagne, or dinner with the Captain. Which, let me tell you, can be a deal less interesting than room service with a good book... So, cut a long story short, last month they had their Premium Cardholder Prize Draw. It's fleet-wide, so you gotta one-in-two-thousand chance of winning. *And blow me down if I didn't win first prize!*"

"Ooh!" squeals Mother. "See, I said you were lucky, Irving! What was it?"

Disconcertingly he frowns. "Just a little thing. A seventeen-week cruise on the *Imperial Star*. New York to San Francisco, via Cape Town, Sydney and Tokyo!"

I trace the route in my head. "That's around the world!"

"Yup. Sets sail from Manhattan on Feb 16th... Emperor Stateroom, complimentary excursions at all ports, and unlimited access to the Rainforest Spa." He slices into his battered cod. "And of course, it's for two."

He blows the steaming morsel on his fork. "So, I was thinking... Well, fact is I've done it all before. Francine and I did virtually the same route when I hung up my stethoscope. Plus I was in Tokyo last spring. *Plus* I've already booked myself Christmas in the Cape this year... And to cap it all, my ever-prodigal son's finally making a lady of his long suffering girlfriend at the end of April. The wedding's in Boston and frankly, the idea of flying halfway round the world to make sure my boy doesn't slip-rope at the altar is more than I can bear!" He is smiling like Santa Claus. "Do you ladies see where I'm going with this?"

Mother and I exchange a look. Her mouth is wide open.

"—Now, I appreciate it's a big bite outta your schedule. And maybe you've booked holidays already, in which case—"

"We haven't," I say. "But we couldn't, Irving. I mean, it's lovely of you to think of us. But aren't these things non-transferable? Won't they say you—"

He cuts me off with a hand on the table. I have an image of him, taking the initiative at a high-level cardiology conference. I am treating him like a fool.

"All cleared with the Exec Membership Secretary," he says evenly. "Who is a good friend of mine. We play gin rummy when I'm in New York."

I sit back, speechless. This is the opportunity of a lifetime and I'm talking myself out of it! That said, taking four months out from the work arena is a bit reckless. But then expenses would be minimal, if board, lodging and trips up Table Mountain are all included. No need to stump up for so much as a manicure from a glam Slovenian! Of course there's Mother to consider… We managed fine last time, with a little help from Irving and the Scooter From Nowhere. But that was a week—this is seventeen. Her mobility is worse now, and while she'll soon have a scooter of her own, what if something happened? Would our insurance even cover her for a trip as long as this?

I glance again at Mother who is equally dumbstruck. Until:

"Oh, I'd have loved that Irving. I've always wanted to see Australia, haven't I, Fenella? Unfortunately I have plans for Easter, so that's that. But thank you, you're very kind!"

"What plans?" I snap.

She dabs a scrap of pastry off her lip with the napkin. "Didn't I say? Bill and I are visiting his brother in Orkney. Been a bit of a to-do, because you have to fly via Aberdeen. We've paid the extra for wheelchair assistance, and I know for a fact it's non-refundable."

Three questions pop in my head at once. Mother is off again before I can voice one.

"You could always take Avril. She does contract work too, doesn't she? I bet she could swing it if you gave her a bit of notice."

"Mother—Irving doesn't know Avril! It is not for us to decide who he gives his prize to…"

"Now, look here," says Irving with an amused smile, "I don't need an answer now. Think it over and let me know in a week or so. You have my email, right Fen?" I don't, but Mother does. "Seriously, I can't take this trip and they don't offer an alternative. Pity, cos I love the idea of you two seeing the world in splendour... Anyways, it's there if you want it."

"Can't you give it to one of your children?" suggests Mother. "Honeymoon for your son?"

I spot an eyebrow twitch on Irving's ever-genial countenance. It is a warning, as when the male lion of the pride has his authority challenged.

"Like I said, Mother, what Irving does with his prize is his business!" I turn to him. "Thank you, that's a wonderful offer. I daresay we're both a bit in shock, but we won't keep you waiting long. Can we get back to you in a couple of days?"

"Fine by me, Fenella. Seriously, no rush."

We have all finished eating. When the waitress reappears, Irving says, "Now, why don't we see what they do for dessert?"

Chapter 49

The *Imperial Star* is a grander affair than the liner we sailed to the fjords. Even now, eleven weeks in, I notice the subtle differences in the way it is appointed, and particularly the level of service. At dinner it's all off-menu *amuse-bouches*, and hot towels at unexpected junctures. I can see how someone like Irving becomes a connoisseur of these little luxuries—and how even they could become tedious. The shine goes off scallops when eating out is just a part of every day, like taking a shower and flossing.

That sounds ungrateful, I think, picking a freshly dry-cleaned blouse from the wardrobe. Not the case; this cruise, this jewel of unimaginable opulence in the copper-plated setting of my life, is all I had hoped for and more. Worth the rush brochure job I accepted at the last minute, and the weeks of preparation getting Mother ready to ride out the time without me. The job was unnecessary; my bank balance, like my mother, is healthy enough in the circumstances. But like all freelancers I fear every offer of work is my last, and refusing one to go gallivanting around the world, just plain cavalier.

Mother was at first less, then more of an issue. Her insistence she would be fine with her battalion of official and unofficial carers wavered as departure day approached.

"You will stay in touch?" she said more than once. "Did we get a mobile signal on our ship? I can't remember…"

When it dawned on her she would miss my fiftieth birthday, she was doubly perturbed. I had been careful not to flag it, trusting her trip to Orkney with Bill was adequate distraction. Made sure she had clothes laundered for every meteorological consequence, from snow to a plague of frogs. And with the brace of hospital appointments that Kath leapt to oversee, I knew she'd be well looked after.

Naturally, I am as good as my word. Every day I take the mirror-glazed lift to the business suite on Starboard Level Five. My e-missives home follow a familiar pattern: what we've eaten, what we saw if we disembarked, and anything ribald I can impart about Avril. Mother reads emails on her tablet, replying with her handheld stylus. She has also learned emoji, a boon for when she finds the keyboard a fiddle. This recent correspondence is typical:

<<F.WoodruffMs@gmail.com>>

Hello Mother

We are adrift for another sea day. It's an odd feeling, casting off from some funny little two-croc town in Papua New Guinea. Life aboard ship feels altogether more civilised, yet supposedly it's us who are cut off from the world.

I don't regret not buying that seashell pot holder. A man told Avril in the pancake queue the islanders' so-called sustainable fishing isn't up to much, so I'd be fanning the flames of environmental destruction. Something like that anyway. He was Dutch.

FYI no repeat of the lobster debacle. Only prawn cocktail on the menu last night, so Avril was not let loose with the claw crackers. But she does seem more prone to making a spectacle of herself than ever. A psychiatrist would have a field day! I keep meaning to nip into her room and see how many pairs of shoes she really brought. Our little cleaner must think I am on holiday with Victoria Beckham.

Not much else to report. What they laughingly call a 24-hour news channel is 80% baseball. Though I did see something about storms in Europe, with an arrow pointing at East Anglia. Batten down the hatches if they reach you. And get Bill to double-check the shed, that door will wake you if it bangs.

More anon.

Love

FW

<<Motherwoodruff.Oxt@gmail.com>>
😄 🎎 🪦 🦵

On my birthday in the second week of March, she managed an entire row of cakes with candles. We were in the Indian Ocean at the time, en route to Réunion. I was keen to keep a lid on the celebrations despite Avril making a show of ordering Bollinger at dinner. I only just stopped her announcing my glorious half-centenary to the adjacent table, and fixing me a knickerbocker glory with sparklers. Personally, I did my best to absorb the significance of the day then forget about it.

This particular morning, I finish dressing and carry my breakfast tray into the lounge of our generously proportioned suite. Avril will be back from the Empire Restaurant soon. Sometimes I go with her, though I prefer coffee and toast delivered to the room. She still relishes swanning around the public areas, whereas for me rubbernecking the breakfast choices of others has palled. No matter; we are getting along fine. We give each other space in the day as required, and come together in the evening for dinner.

She and I have often been away before, though never for more than a week. In the Soki years, opportunities to travel with her beau were few and far between: mostly the odd business shindig, onto which a night at some secluded luxury resort could be tacked without arousing the suspicion of Lady Ruth. I sometimes found myself on trips coinciding with Soki's own holidays, thus maximising Avril's availability for whatever sops of time he made for her on his return. Eurostar breaks were a favourite; Paris for shopping, Lille for the proximity. And Avril favoured Bruges over Brussels or Antwerp, its brooding skies and watery cobbles ideal for wallowing in her Other-Woman woes. I learned to eke out the joys of weekending in such cultural havens, ready to feign a migraine if her navel-gazing became too preposterous.

As a consequence, this trip together was a punt. Also my only viable option with Mother out of the picture. It's a shame she is not here, though her going away with Bill was a blessing in one sense: it has helped me over the bigger hurdle of her having a sex life... Post-Christmas, her confession was still the unlikeliest of elephants in the room. Unsavoury, in the way anything carnal to do with one's parent is, not to mention galling for me. Against all the odds, sexually impoverished and turning fifty, I have exchanged one house where they're at it like knives for another! If Bill comes round on a Wednesday afternoon, I have learned to pop to the shops, or at the very least sit upstairs with a lively podcast... Yet somehow Bill and Mother's holiday plans have normalised their relations, as well as reminding me travel is an adventure, where anything can happen. So far not much has. But each day is a new day, and I am a single woman of the world, after all...

I am perusing today's itinerary on the chaise longue when I hear the soft click of a card in the lock. Avril has taken to strolling round the deck after breakfast.

"How was the view?" I ask gamely. "Any surprises?" Our little joke.

"It's a prettier blue than the Atlantic," she says. "And I did actually see a flying fish, or something that went *splosh*. Have you had breakfast?"

I indicate the tray on the coffee table next to the ship's newsletter.

"What shall we do today? According to the blurb, we dock in Sydney Harbour at quarter to seven tomorrow morning. I'd quite like to be up to get pictures from the balcony. So I'm thinking an early night, but other than that the day is ours."

Avril crosses the vast hand-knotted rug to the full-length windows. The Persian carpet was a topic of debate on our first night in the suite. Over the complimentary Moet which greeted us (along with a butler, two maids and a precarious mountain of fruit) we tried to interpret its artfully woven pattern. Two days later, long after we'd swapped the Manhattan backdrop for a glittery-blue nothing, it dawned: the design wasn't Sanskrit or anything symbolic of the ocean. Just the cruise line's initials, rendered in a florid font.

"I can't take any more photos," says Avril. "My phone's full and I've deleted everything I can bear to. You'll have to send me yours when we get home."

I shrug. "How about line-dancing? Level Two Colonnade, 11am. The instructor's called Torsten. Isn't he the one you had your eye on in Legs, Bums and Tums?"

Her gaze is firmly on the horizon. "Line-dancing? We'd be the youngest there..."

Like this cruise, Avril's fitness regime has appeared out of nowhere. In all the years I've known her, the closest she came to exercise was lugging her shopping up four flights of stairs. So, as we settled into the Emperor Suite, with its bound dossier of excursions and diversions for the next seventeen weeks, her interest in the fitness timetable was a surprise. I put it down to a well-meaning intention to give me space in what could be a claustrophobic setting. Yet astonishingly, she has stuck to it, attending classes daily even when we disembark. Where she finds the energy to hike up African hills after fifty-minutes of ABBA-Tack With Lars, is beyond me.

My mention of Torsten is deliberate, and ignored. Avril's regime is not the only facet of her new persona. Online dating was a typhoon that blew itself out just before the trip, the flashpoint by all accounts St Valentine's Day. Dinner arrangements were brokered, then broken, in ways that suggested the day held a mystic significance for the online amorati; like the Cup Final, or the Eurovision Song Contest for gays. She deleted her profile—a relief. I had visions of listening out from my state room boudoir, as Avril went in search of a mast to clamber for a phone signal. But she has stuck to her guns on that too, although a new persona has replaced Online-Avril: Onboard-Avril, who exhibits still greater self-confidence...

An immaculately groomed creature that strides about the salons like a diminutive queen, Onboard Avril exudes an easy grace that men notice, women note and waiters fall over themselves to ply with honey-roasted nuts... Dating lit a fire that even the runaround from Ross, the slippery mortgage adviser from Cheshunt, has not extinguished. I lost track of the details in the slew of holiday planning; we only met once between Christmas and our giddy reunion at the B.A. Business Class desk. But it was there, beneath the Clarins scowl of the check-in girl, that I glimpsed this new Avril. Her hair, in its first restyle since the Nineties, was now asymmetrical, like she'd caught a wig in the drawer. And whilst she previously favoured the simplest of in-transit footwear, she now wore medium-height heels in emerald leather with contrast piping. Statement shoes, at odds with her designer-practical outfit and the fleece that doubled as a neck pillow. To my irritation, the desk girl took the shoes to mean Avril, not I, was lead party on the booking... More wardrobe additions have appeared throughout the trip, but her spending has clearly concentrated on footwear. Today, gold gladiator sandals, low heeled, with a woven laurel centrepiece at the toe.

"What's showing at the cinema?" she asks, still looking out on the edge of the world. "I wouldn't mind seeing that new Richard Curtis if it's on again."

"Not today." I read out the film schedule, every one a sequel and a mite high-octane for us. "We could go ice skating?"

The rink is a feature of the ship's central piazza. It features heavily in the annoying little idents that pop up whenever I turn on the television. It is trumpeted as 'The World's Biggest Ocean-Going Ice Rink', which may not be saying much. Minus the clever camera work it is the size of a badminton court, and with half a dozen bodies careering round, only a head-high net could make it more lethal. Even so, it is one of a dwindling number of options I am keen to try. I was an avid skater in my youth, fuelled by a Torvill and Dean fixation. My adulation for Nottingham's most celebrated pairing since Robin and Marian, and especially their *Bolero* routine, is one I have never shaken. The strains of that truncated score, the swaying, swanlike opening executed by the golden duo on their shins, still provokes a shiver. I last skated two winters ago, on a works outing to Somerset House. Even then I was pleasantly startled by my feel for edges, the fearless way I could dig my toe-rake into the ice and scrape to a halt... I glowed inwardly at my own aplomb, while Derek, Cheryl and others clung to the rail like survivors groping their way out of a bomb crater.

"Go on then," says Avril. "I was quite nippy on the ice in my teens, though I'll be lucky if I can stand up now. You might need to hold my hand." Breaking her gaze from the foredeck eight levels below, she makes a beeline for her bedroom. A costume change is imminent.

"Now?" I call, a little reluctantly. I am twenty pages off the end of a vintage thriller I fancy finishing on the balcony; find out if the scullery maid was gassed by the son of the house or just fainted hiding a tiara in the oven.

"May as well," Avril calls back. "I've got Stretch & Tone With Stretchi Toni at eleven. I'll need it if I seize up halfway round..."

Chapter 50

I resist the temptation to point out that Avril omitted skates from her packing. Luckily there is a booth dispensing them, between the rink and the bijou parade of shops boasting two upmarket jewellers. The lace-up boots in ladies' sizes are white with a penguin stencilled on the ankle. Fitting, in the case of the three skaters waddling arm-in-arm on the rink.

Avril takes back her first pair, demanding a smaller size from the dapper Indian steward who smiles no matter how much sweaty footwear is thrust at him. She ties and unties a second till she is satisfied, then stands on the coconut matting flexing her knees, as if divining something crucial to her performance. I hand in my espadrilles and take to the ice... By some aural ingenuity the soundtrack from the speakers, currently a Motown medley, barely seeps beyond the confines of the rink.

Uninvited, Avril's elfin hand takes mine. I steel myself, core engaging as I find my centre of gravity... The once-familiar sensation of floating—of being serenely, supremely in control in the way that so often eludes me—comes back like riding a bike. Not even her wobbling and intermittent squeaks ("*Yeee!*") unbalance me.

"You're hurting my hand!" she protests, shaking loose to grip the rail.

"Sorry!" I toss over my shoulder.

Sweeping off into a circuit unencumbered, I cover the ice at speed. The penguin trio also retreat to the side, and I am reminded of the rare occasions I've swum in a public pool and been forced to make way for faster swimmers. Only here, the one with mastery of the medium is me... How wonderful it feels! I am in my own world, though conscious of Avril at the corner of my eye, her skates sliding back and forth as she tests her balance at the rail. As she teeters I skim, switching edges and flipping round to skate backwards. As *Baby Love* blends into *Tears of a Clown*, I even allow myself a few interpretive arm movements...

No one likes a show-off. But something about this freedom over the ice exhilarates me like nothing else. I am tempted to try a jump... All those years ago, the single toe-loop was the peak of my repertoire. In reality more of a hop, but to the uninitiated even the measured circular preparation before take-off looks impressive. Though my audience is negligible, I feel the urge to perform welling up inside. The penguins have waddled off. Avril is enthralled by her toes, and of the steady stream of passengers crossing the foyer only one or two turn their eyes to the rink. My prowess and adjacent window displays (a frosting of diamanté on velveteen body parts and emergency pop-socks) receive the same, cursory interest.

One more circuit... I reach the end of the rink for the maximum run up. Glance in all directions, like a well-drilled motorist exiting a junction... Then change my mind. Two more circles to pluck up courage, and I lean into the propelling momentum. Arms outstretched, I balance on one leg as the other swings in a pendulum motion. At a flash-recollection of the next manoeuvre—face away, drive toe-rake into the ice—muscle-memory takes over... That moment, as my blade leaves *terra gelida*, is when the spirit of Jayne Torvill enters me! An exquisite feeling, long forgotten, like giving into the bliss of a non-self-administered orgasm... I am Jayne beside an invisible Chris, at one with my man and the cosmos... It is decades since I smoked marijuana yet I long to now, for the sensation of elongated time that is my only benign memory of the drug... *Oh, to stay up in the air forever!*

The crack when it comes echoes solidly through me. An excruciating pain in my ankle eclipses another as my buttocks jar on the ice. I stare in a daze at my boots; my legs are a twist I cannot unpick... A yelp from across the rink is Avril. Moments later, she is by me on hands and knees, the method she used to get here... The next however-long is a jumble; of fear for what I've done to myself, and embarrassment at the swirl of unknown, concerned faces.

"Don't move it!" squawks Avril, pushing my hands away from the boot.

The Indian steward appears, skateless on soles that allow for effortless gliding. "Madame, madame, help is coming..."

"I can wiggle my toes," I say through gritted teeth. "So I haven't—*Fuck!!*"

Another man appears, followed by two braided jackets who skid to a halt behind him. They are carrying a stretcher. I take the man to be the ship's doctor, so masterfully does he assess me.

"Keep it braced and keep her boot on!" This to the stretcher bearers. He nods reassuringly, looking me in the eye. "You'll be alright."

British. A bit younger than me, with sandy hair and fulsome brows. Wearing frameless ghost-glasses that are barely there at all...

"Thank you," I say. "Yes, I'm sure I'll be—*ooof!*"

Strong arms are under and over me. On a count of three I take to the air as the stretcher rises from the ice. It is hard to say which hurts more: the throbbing below my calf, firm as a heartbeat in the tightening grip of my boot, or the gaze of gawpers as I sail past a display of zircon earrings at 30% off. You need to be Elizabeth I, to pull off being carted through crowds on a palanquin.

At first Avril totters alongside, still holding my hand. But as the matting gives way to shiny floor, her skates can go no further. Floating round a kink in the walkway by the 24-hour chocolate fountain, I glimpse her waving as she wrestles out of a boot. That's when I notice there is still a hand on mine. It belongs to the doctor-man, whom I now note is wearing highly unsurgical Bermuda shorts and flip-flops. A froth of ice is turning to droplets on the fair hairs of his kneecaps.

"If you could, sir?" says one of the stretcher stewards as we reach the lift.

The man presses the button. Other passengers stand silently aside, as if for a funeral cortege. Our stretcher party take the mirrored box alone, sweeping down, not up, to a level I have not explored. I am observing the four of us, reflected infinitely in the walls of the lift, when the doors slide open and the steward at my feet says:

"Madame, the Health Suite is just down here..."

French; reassuring and inappropriately seductive all at once. I cannot remember the last time three attractive men were focused on my well-being. At the end of the corridor the steward blips a panel by waving something on a lanyard.

"Our consulting room is rather small, sir," he says in beautifully inflected English, "but you are welcome to wait while the medics examine your wife."

"Oh, he's not—"

"She's not my—"

I blush. So does the non-doctor, though his colour is less marked thanks to a pleasing honey-coloured tan. We establish he is Gary from Bishop's Stortford, who now looks quirkily out of place in the anodyne grey-and-white capsule of the sick bay.

"Guess I just panicked," he explains, not that I asked. *"Déjà vu.* I was looking your way when you took a tumble and it all came flooding back. School outing when I was nine!"

He stands there, looking at his hands. The Frenchman and the other steward have disappeared, replaced by two of the smallest nurses I have ever seen. One female, one not, identically dressed and so alike they could be fraternal twins. They take my name and cabin number. Then the woman unlaces my boot, while the man checks my arms for sprains and bruising; I suspect diversionary tactics, which are not about to work on me. Listening to Gary, however, is some distraction from my searing ankle:

"We went skating for the end of Christmas term. Luton it was, or Romford... It's one of those things that stays with you. Me and Sarah Welsby, bobbling around arm in arm, trying to look cool even though we were holding each other up. We went over a couple of times, got straight back up. Then I got cocky and we went a bit faster, carried away like we're on the dodgems... All of a sudden she goes over, spiralling onto the ice till she's sat cross-legged. Starts crying, and I tell her not to be a wuss, cos we'll all have bruises in the morning... Go to yank her up, and that's when she screams — the exact same noise you made! Went straight through me, I can tell you..." Poor Gary; the memory is painfully dredged. "She was in plaster, hip to ankle till summer. Kneecap shattered like a crab-shell!"

At this, his cheekbones and the squareness of his shoulders lose their allure. I grunt bestially as my boot comes off, and both nurses switch to the far end of the bed. Polythene gloves appear. With the dry hum of the air con and the tiny porthole windows, I have a sensation of being whisked off in an alien space craft.

"Wiggle toes, madame?" says the lady nurse.

Warily I oblige.

"Now wiggle ankle, madame," instructs the other.

I suck a breath. The moment of truth...

The movement is tiny but I manage it without making a sound. Nurses nod. One applauds with a plasticky rustle and I half-expect a high-five.

"Unfortunately we don't have X-ray machine onboard, madame," says the male nurse.

"Only for luggage!" says the female.

They both laugh and so does Gary. Even I wince a smile, at the idea of sailing down the conveyor belt that checks our bags whenever we re-embark.

The nurse waits politely for the laughter to subside. "So we advise bed rest with ice pack, and keep foot elevated until the swelling goes down. We gonna strap it up for now."

I tut. Tomorrow is Sydney: a two-night stopover and a highlight of the trip. The last thing I want is to spend the day with my leg up!

"Have you got ice," asks Gary, "or shall we raid the cocktail lounge?"

So practical, I think, rather liking the 'we'.

While one nurse roots in a countertop fridge a commotion sounds outside. With a bleep the door opens. And there is Avril, accompanied by another lanyarded steward who looks defensive.

"Fen, tell him it's me!" she orders opaquely.

"It's alright, Avril. I'm in good hands."

But her gaze has already scooted past me, via the nurses, to Gary.

"Yes, I see," she says, holding out manicured talons and adding "Avril!" unnecessarily. "You were *such* a hero," she coos, "swooping in like someone out of *Holby City*! You've obviously had training."

"Only with the Scouts," says Gary, embarrassed to be the centre of such gimlet-eyed attention. "It's just cos of what happened when I was at school…"

A light pressure on my elbow tells me ministrations are over. A folding wheelchair appears from a closet. It is left to the nurses to help me into it while my civilian friends swap scarring, school-day reminiscences.

The male nurse hands me a clipboard. "Before you go, madame…"

The page is headed APPROPRIATION OF MEDICAL FEES.

"Everything is billed to your room. We lend you crutches free of charge, yeah? But if you can jus' fill in name of insurance company and sign here..."

I take the proffered Imperial Cruises pen.

As if missing out on Sydney wasn't bad enough!

Chapter 51

That afternoon my ankle is the size and colour of an unglazed Cornish pasty. I have spent the day with my leg on cushions, watching the ocean from the stateroom's chaise longue. By five o'clock I have passed through the valley of self-pity and out the other side. My focus now is the travel insurance policy that Avril dug out of the wardrobe safe.

Her skills around the sick bed are attentive if a little inept. Her obsession with keeping my fluids up has made bathroom trips a nuisance. She seems happiest with an errand to run, even when they could easily be delegated to our butler. As it is I have enough to read, and there is a limit how much I can eat between the meals that arrive on trollies strewn with dried petals. My greatest concern is whether ice skating counts as a winter sport; cover I, not unreasonably, left off my insurance for the sake of economy. My mind is boggling at the prospect of an American-style healthcare bill. I curse myself for taking the risk, but I am savvy now. The lady-nurse has phoned twice, offering further examinations and extra dressings. I insisted I am fine and will be in touch if my ankle deteriorates. Nothing short of gangrene will see medical personnel get through our door.

Unlike Avril, I have not been exercising this trip, beyond diligent walks around the vineyards, museums and whelk farms each landfall requires. My skirts and trousers doth protest, to the extent that the two pairs of cotton beach shorts I picked up in Durban have become indispensable. Not only can they pass for evening wear, with court shoes and the right blouse, but their elasticated waists are a lifesaver.

"I've brought you another sundae," says Avril brightly, reappearing after an unspecified absence. "You wolfed the last one!"

That was this morning, when I heaved myself into the chaise's plush embrace. The combination of injury and shock left me feeling exhausted, a condition Nurse Avril diagnosed as a sugar-low before trotting off to the all-you-can-eat gelateria. This time, the contents of the plastic goblet are more liquid than frigid.

"I ran into Gary," she says, handing me a tissue for a bib.

Unlikely, given the vastness of the ship and its payload of six thousand bodies, all currently aboard. I let it pass and wait.

"He says he'd love us to join him for dinner. He's going to that Brazilian barbecue place, by the nail studio. It's not in his package but he's got a voucher. Do you fancy it? I think he might be on his own, so…"

My eyes are on the sundae. "I'm not feeling particularly sociable, Avril. Probably just eat here, like lunchtime." I retrieve a tiny plastic spade from the marmalade-coloured slurry. "Don't let me stop you though."

"Oh, but I can't leave you on your own! What if you need something? What if there's a fire?"

"I wouldn't worry. It's not the Kon-Tiki."

Her doe-eyed concern morphs to a grateful smile that lasts all the way to her bedroom. I listen as she runs the bath, soon to be transformed into a swamp of bubbles with the unguents the maids replenish daily. Forty-five minutes later, in a little black dress with a chain-link bag I haven't seen since Soki days, she totters off on another pair of heels.

I spend the evening on the chaise. Keep movement to a minimum, alternating attention between my ankle, the small print of my insurance, and the darkening blue horizon. It is only as the butler comes to turn down the bed that I realise I've forgotten to eat dinner. I have half a mind to settle for his pillow-truffles and nuts from the mini bar, until I hear Mother's voice say an invalid needs to keep their strength up. I order a prawn baguette and hot chocolate, which appear within fifteen minutes.

"Anything more, madame?" asks our perma-smiling butler. He has placed everything in easy reach, including the clever little remote control. "You wan' see nurse before you go bed?"

Shaking my head nearly spills the chocolate.

"And you can leave those, thank you," I say, as he goes to close the curtains.

Like the lights, the air con and the TV, I can do them with the remote. For now I am happy to give the endless, empty ocean an uninterrupted view of my predicament. I surf the limited satellite channels and return to my travel policy.

I pass the night as I pass the day: with one heel higher than my heart. This is more challenging in bed, since keeping a foot on two cushions and staying asleep when it rolls off is all but impossible... My knee cramps, just as I am dozing off a second time, coinciding with a creak from the suite's outer door.

The digital clock says 02.28. One set of footsteps passes through the lounge, accompanied by the sound of a shoulder dragged along the wall, presumably to keep its owner upright. I am on the edge of oblivion when something jogs me again. The outer door this time, opening from the inside. Someone has knocked, hence the just-audible conversation and two timbres of laughter: Avril's signature giggle and something deeper that ends in a cough.

I freeze. Since leaving New York Harbor, my companion's commentary on any male crew members appreciably taller than she is (roughly half) tells me Cougar Avril is very much aboard. That said, our routine of languid sea days and trips ashore seems to have largely quenched her thirst to meet men.

Until Gary. Until now.

Further extravagant creeping about the lounge is punctuated by suppressed giggles. They are looking for something, and have presumably found it when Avril's door shuts with a thump. I lie still, eyes trained on the shadowy deco coving. I wait. And wait...

It is a leitmotif, destined to haunt me till the end of my days, like Captain Hook's ticking crocodile. It began at university, and carried on through my early flat-sharing days in London; Wandsworth, Balham and, most potently, the fortnight I spent next door to a brothel in Tulse Hill... Owning my own flat was a respite, bar the antics of a short-lived but dogged lodger upstairs. The soundproofing at No. 4, The Ridge was generally good; as tested by Connor, a flame-haired Irishman who had regular sleepovers with a girl who played hockey, though it could have been ten-pin bowling for the racket they made... Years later, the headboard percussion through which I steeled myself when Martin met Monique was one more movement in the soundtrack of my moribund sex life. Another is being added now.

Little sound carries between our suite's bedrooms, so Avril is clearly giving it some. She is also drunk, gasping volubly between chuckles... It is as if she has undergone a total character transformation: from a woman not unlike myself, who sees sex as something to engage in discreetly, to one who flaunts her libido like the star of a post-watershed reality show... Now she (they!) are getting a rhythmic squeak out of the queen-size mattress I'd have wagered was too premium for that.

"Respect," I tell the ceiling, then wince at the pain running from ankle to knee.

Were I not abominably tired I would be looking forward to breakfast. A contrite Avril, lip-twitchingly funny with a hangover, is a sight to behold. Layers of guilt, which have so far slipped off her like eggs from a quality frying pan, will emerge. When Gary came to my aid, she must have known his attention was directed at me... Had she not bumbled into the Health Centre, I'd have been the one sharing dinner with an eligible fellow traveller tonight. That's the thanks I get for bringing her on the cruise of a lifetime!

I lie there for what feels like hours, discomfited in body and mind. Eventually the racket ceases, replaced by tittering and a chink of crockery... The next I know, I am waking up, still on my back and surprisingly in daylight, with one foot up on its perch. I stretch, then limp gingerly to the en suite on a single crutch, which feels appropriate given the setting.

Five minutes later a man's voice says, *"Hey, morning!"*, as I jab open the door to the lounge. It is Gary, cross-legged on the chaise holding a cup. He is wearing his invisible glasses and a bed sheet as a sarong. His bare torso glints in the sun pouring in from what I now muzzily register is Sydney Harbour. I don't know where to look first... Before I can speak, Avril appears from her centre of nocturnal operations in ship's bathrobe and slippers. Her robe has been shortened by artful tucking at the waist, and her hair is piled on top of her head with a clip so that fronds dangle.

"Oh, Fen, I hope we didn't wake you. How's your poorly foot?"

"No worse." I refuse to blink. "Hard to say till I put weight on it."

"Wouldn't you like your other crutch? You look like Long John—"

"I'm fine, Avril. I'll have tea though."

She disappears as I keel over into the nearest armchair. I would prefer the chaise, but Gary has made himself at home and is not attuned to the problems low-level furnishings pose the invalid. He smiles; I smile back, grateful for my years at No. 4, The Ridge which prepared me for moments like this. Once upon a time, a semi-naked stranger reeking of sex would have sent me scurrying for a safe-space. Now I hold my ground.

My ground. Home territory. As this suite undeniably is.

"We were just saying," he says, peering at my ankle. "It's dead flat round Sydney Harbour. Be no problem taking you in the wheelchair. Avril's had a Google and the Opera House has got step-free access. And the Aquarium, if you fancy it? Baby manta rays apparently!"

I stare at this well-fed Mahatma Gandhi, holding court in my window with a backdrop of seagulls and the glassy peaks of downtown Sydney. Avril returns with a tea bag steeping in china.

"It's an hour till we disembark. We forgot to order breakfast, Fen, did you? I could drum up some pastries…"

She makes for the nearest phone but I shake my head. "I won't. And I don't feel like going ashore. I'll see how I am tomorrow."

"Aw!" she says, stamping a terry flip-flop. "But it won't be the same without you. We were so looking forward to Sydney, weren't we?"

More triumphal pouting. Almost enough to change my mind, just to ruin her day.

I also forgot to order breakfast, but now more than ever I am happy to eat alone. I sip my tea while Avril stands at the writing table in her shorty robe, holding the receiver like a character from an Eighties sitcom. Gary, getting up without dislodging his waistband, breaks the silence:

"Listen, I'll grab something later. I'm just gonna nip back to my, er…"

I sit up, craning through the window now the view is clear. Make a play of being too absorbed to hear the discussion behind me.

"—can't leave her…!"

"I'm not saying you should, I—"

"Sydney, though!"

"Well, we can go for a walk after lunch. See if she's…"

"—*think she's embarrassed about the chair! You know I said about her mother...*"

I have pretended not to hear enough. "Why don't you both put your clothes on and do some exploring? I'm sure you've done plenty with them off!"

Avril's mouth falls open. I shift in the chair so I am facing them both. A moment later I am pointing.

"Look, whatever your name is, Gary—I am delighted you feel at home here, but if you come again would you mind bringing a robe? There's a limit how much naked flesh I want to see paraded about before breakfast... Are you sharing?"

He looks like I've just slapped his legs. "Am I—?"

"Your cabin? Are you sharing a stateroom?"

He tweaks an ear. "Oh yeah. I'm here with a mate. It's his big Four-Oh in two days, so..."

"Is it. Well, if you are going to go swapping your mate for other people's, I can see it must be awkward entertaining in your own room."

"Sorry, I didn't mean to interfere. You guys'll have plans— I'll get my..."

As he pushes past Avril into the bedroom, she turns to me. Her eyes are like white-hot coals.

"Did you *have* to do that, Fen? Would it hurt to be civil?"

"I was perfectly civil!"

"Oh yes! Making him feel like a naughty schoolboy! You don't even know him."

I can't hold back the snort. "*I* don't even know him?"

Those eyes again; wider this time.

"Sometimes, Fen, I could just..."

Her next words are replaced by a shuddering grimace. Spinning on a cardboard heel, she slams the bedroom door behind her.

Chapter 52

Was I born at the wrong time? Am I better suited to a more buttoned-down age—the 1950s, say? When I watch those black-and-white Ealing potboilers, with factory girls dallying with chaps in raincoats, I am drawn to their clipped world of Sunday teas and sacrosanct bath nights... Where politicians still worked for the common good, and sportsmen were no more important than they should be. It feels like the last time everyone knew their place. Before the Sixties breached the ramparts, consigning solid British decency to history, along with the Empire and rickets.

More conformity, less *laissez-faire*. That's me all over.

On the other hand, a trip like this would have been purgatory in those days. Limited menus, the service as stiff as the sheets... It is nearly midday. I am on the Aft Observation Deck, looking out across Sydney Harbour and a sky of cerulean blue. With everyone ashore, the liner is almost deserted. Once Avril went off to meet Gary without a word I ordered a croissant and coffee, which pepped me up enough to try my ankle. I hobbled into the shower, and even got the strapping back on unassisted. At the bottom of my wardrobe I found a pair of mules with Velcro fastening. Slotting the left one over my still-swollen toes, I felt able to venture out with my crutch.

The Observation Deck is a glass bubble, two levels high. It billows out of the ship's side as if one more breath would burst it, and gives a sensation of being suspended over the water. Beyond the triple glazing, passenger ferries plough back and forth, the equivalent of London buses in their green and yellow livery. I can just make out the end of the Harbour Bridge, its shape like hookless coat hangers familiar from the magazine on our coffee table. Early in the voyage I passed here numerous times without entering. Now I am a regular, camping out for hours when Avril is elsewhere. It is air-conditioned like everywhere else, but the sun-loungers and transparent resin tables make it feel remarkably like being outdoors. There is something dreamlike about simultaneously floating in mid-air as you float upon the sea.

I ease back in my seat. I need this quiet. The vastness of the vista is helping me think. The bustling city, visible in panorama from all points on the other side of the ship, can wait. I will take a tour tomorrow if I'm up to it; The Royal Botanic Gardens perhaps, with its roosting fruit bats... Cruising teaches you to be selective. All the promotional puffery whets the appetite for things to do onshore. Wine tasting on the Cape, the night safari at Singapore Zoo... But when you are rarely in port for more than a day, there's a limit how much you can fit in. I'm not complaining. If you'd told me a year ago I'd be hosing down baby elephants in Sri Lanka, I'd have laughed. Not on my salary, trapped in the rat-run between No. 4, The Ridge and my desk at the Picture Gallery.

How far away that seems!

The strangest thing is how quickly even the most dramatic change of circumstance *becomes* your life. We have been aboard the *Imperial Star* less than three months, but it might as well be three years. And yet on a distant day in June, or rather night, we will slip into our berth at San Francisco. I will open the curtains and it'll all be over, bar a last trip to Alcatraz and the long flight home. Bill, following a three-line whip from Mother, will be at Gatwick looking at his watch. With a nod or a tentative pat, he will load my suitcase into the Renault Scenic for the terse drive home... Land will never have felt as dry as the M23 to Godstone.

Of course Avril will want a lift. We'll be friends again by then, the Gary incident forgotten. Or it won't, on the off-chance their fling has legs and he becomes an integral part of our rich, globetrotting tapestry. He may even turn out to be the one she seeks; my missed toe-loop, the life-changing moment that brought them together, the crux of reminiscences and a Best Man's speech I'm obliged to smile through over flattening champagne.

Life, like skating, takes the unlikeliest turns.

At the other end of the salon a boy appears, running ahead of his sister. There are few children on board, though that could alter at any moment. Passengers changeover at major ports as holidays end and began. The boy is about eight years old and well behaved. He moves quietly along the salon's glass circumference, examining the seascape ranged between the bay's peninsulas like a vast canvas. He pauses, lifting a pair of mini binoculars from his chest, while his big sister sinks onto a lounger and takes a touchscreen from her bag.

I try to imagine what an experience like this means to a child. Does seeing the world now change the life to come? I'd never been further than Liverpool till my second year at university, my impressions of the wider world gleaned from TV and what I read in the papers... How different my sphere of reference if I began life like this, instead of waiting till I was fifty!

I am watching a waitress stack cups like the Pisan tower as the boy appears beside me.

"My mommie has one like that."

American, or perhaps Canadian. He is looking at my wrist: the woven bracelet I didn't realise I was fiddling with. Instinctively I pull in my poorly foot, tucking it under the chair. Children are unpredictable. He could break into a can-can at any moment.

"Oh. Has she?"

He nods. "Daddy bought it in Madagascar. It was made by the *Anta-ka-rana* tribe." He picks his way through the word. "Which tribe made yours?"

I am at a loss. I assume Avril bought it off a stall selling sunglasses and caps with cannabis-leaf motifs. It's been on my wrist since Christmas, barring the first few days on ship when I secretly unpicked it... In the opulence of our suite it felt inappropriately studenty, and Avril would never notice (hers is still in situ, smothered in an inch of bangles). That was before I saw how many of the women with immaculate hair and Calvin Klein for all occasions sported a similar strip with their gold and platinum. In my bathroom, and with judicious use of teeth, I knotted it back on again.

"I'm not sure. Possibly the Celts. I like your binoculars, may I look?"

Solemnly the boy unhooks them. He shows me how they adjust to reach both my eyes. "If you focus them right you can see New Zealand. It's over that way."

The arc of the bay puts even the open ocean out of view, but I play along.

"Yes, I see... Aren't you going into Sydney? There's a very good aquarium. And a zoo."

"Sure we are. We're just waiting for Mom and Dad. The zoo's over this way." He points to a wooded hillside across the water. "Wanna come?"

I am touched by the way he is looking at me. Warmth, mixed with concern that I am here alone.

"Thank you, no. Actually I've hurt my foot, can you see?" I show him the bandage. "I'll probably go into Sydney tomorrow with my friend Avril. Funnily enough, she's the one who gave me the bracelet."

"Okay," he nods, taking back the binoculars. "Does she love you the way Daddy loves Mommie?" Small hands readjust the eyepieces. "Like how Auntie Sharon loves Auntie Celia?"

A low whistle from the other side of the Deck spares me the answer; his sister, pointing to the door where their parents are ferreting in a daypack.

"C'mon, champ!" calls Dad.

They are older than I expect, dressed in identikit cruise-wear with more pockets than a sneak thief. The boy scampers off with the girl in tow, still reading her tablet. As I watch them go I balk slightly at the worldliness of the young... His observation is grossly misplaced, and from a ballpark I wouldn't know existed till I was twice his age.

What a world we live in!

Where are u? Av x

Mobile coverage resumes stealthily in port, so her text makes me jump. I pick up my phone, then change my mind. The ship's warren of carpeted nooks and dens, themed around high-calorie treats, means one can avoid detection for hours. Finishing my pistachio sundae, I reply:

Sunny Sodas, Level 6 opposite casino. Good day?

No response before she appears five minutes later. Alone.

Avril pulls back a metal chair with a clatter. The chic chiffon sundress that floated from the cabin eight hours earlier is as limp as a wet tea towel. For what is allegedly autumn, the Aussie sun is strong. Her neckline reveals she forgot to reapply factor. Too distracted, no doubt... Something is up, but I am not about to be drawn.

"Did you go to the Opera House?" I ask pleasantly. "Was it crowded?"

"He disappeared!" snaps Avril. "There one minute, gone the next!"

My long-handled spoon finds a last drip of green. "Gary, you mean?"

"Of course bloody Gary!" She waves away the waiter's laminated options. "We got as far as Mrs Macquarie's Chair, then he said he needed the Gents and that was that—gone!" She is bristling like a tethered pit bull. "His phone's going straight to voicemail!"

"How extraordinary. Aren't there Harbour Police or someone you can speak to? Maybe he fell in the water. Can he swim, do you know? Or are you not on those sort of terms?"

My teeth clench back a smile. Avril squirms, blushes adding to her unnatural glow.

"Do you have to take quite such a pleasure in it, Fen? Just for once, can't you let me enjoy myself without all your—*all your bitterness seeping out?*"

My spoon hangs in mid-air. "Bitterness, Avril? And what do you mean, 'Just for once'?"

"Oh come on, it's your default setting, or it is with me! I could never so much as mention Soki without you looking like you'd smelt B.O.!"

My eyes narrow. "Rubbish! I was very supportive, with everything he put you through. *You* spent half your time moaning about him!"

"I did not!"

"You did! When he was off on his jaunts you hadn't a good word to say for him. Till he popped up waving tickets for some five-star resort, then he couldn't put a foot wrong!"

She addresses her aubergine fingertips, two of which have chipped since yesterday's manicure. "Of course, if you'd actually had any experience with men, you'd appreciate the reality of a relationship... 'Vicarious' hardly qualifies you to judge other people's. Does it?"

"I've had my share, thank you very much!"

"When!" scoffs Avril. "Who? Two nights with a paedo who dressed you up as Anne Boleyn? Come off it, Fen. Everything you know about making a man happy comes from magazine quizzes!"

I feel embarrassed for the waiter who has no other customers. The ship's architect themed this unit as an American diner, with polished-steel counter and an ornamental fire hydrant. Diplomatically, the waistcoated man has his back to us. He is watching in the mirror, running a cloth over syrup-dispensing optics... This is not a conversation I care to have in public, but my ankle hurts again and the lift is a five-minute hobble.

"Avril, twenty years playing concubine to an asthmatic egotist doesn't make you an expert either... And whilst I'd defend your personal freedom to the hilt, nor does putting it about like a sixth-former in Faliraki. As this episode proves!"

She rises an inch in her seat. "How I run my life is none of your business. At least I'm not afraid to live it! If you want the truth, I was glad to get away from Soki. I gave him more years than he deserved, and if I'm making up for it now, so what? I tell you, Fen, the older you get the more you remind me of what my Pa used to say about his maiden aunts... Sad old souls who never let themselves meet anyone. *'Went back to heaven unwrapped,'* he said! And that's you, as good as. I bet you don't remember what sex is like!"

I am speechless. The waiter dips under the counter to rummage, snigger or both.

"We don't all choose to broadcast our personal life to the world, Avril. What I do in private is my business!"

"Oh yes—as if you could resist telling me if you snared a man! I never heard the end of it with that Martin, and he was a load of nothing blown out of all proportion!"

She is worrying her sunburn with a finger. It is not like her to be belligerent. Has she been drinking?

"I never mentioned him unless you asked!"

"Huh! And besides, didn't you ever wonder why he chose that Aussie woman over you?"

This I do not expect.

"No... We're all entitled to our preferences. I don't feel demeaned, just because I wasn't Martin's type. Probably a compliment in a way!"

She shrugs ironically. "Rationalise it any way you like. If you ask me, he probably wanted someone he could have a bit of

fun with! You don't see it, Fen, but those sharp little edges—
they've..."

I sit back. What's coming now?

"—I used to think your snippiness was just the price for
spending time in your company. But as you've got older it's
taken over—the way a parasite chokes the life out of its host!
The bitterness has won, Fen. You've turned into a caricature of
yourself!"

Poor Avril; she will regret this.

But she's not done; "I don't blame Martin for not wanting to
wake up with a frigid killjoy like you! *Sucked-lemon face and all!*"

Her mouth purses on the last word. I feel as if someone
punched me in the head... Numb, I stand from the table.

"Fen, I—"

I push through her conciliatory arm like a turnstile. The last
thing I see is the waiter, bobbing up wide-eyed from the counter.

A dozen paces across the Central Colonnade I realise my
crutch is still leaning on the table. I don't need it.

Chapter 53

I walk and walk. Up deck and down deck, goaded on by a piercing rage.

Where's the gratitude? The understanding?

Avril and I have been friends for most of a lifetime. There for each other, through every stab of her cloak-and-dagger love life, every stage of my tribulations with Mother. And our respective menopauses ('Personal Summer' as she christened hers, an HRT-triggered spiral of sweats and brain-fog). What does that amount to now, as we sail the world in splendour with nothing to pay but the odd off-menu cocktail?

How dare she speak to me like that!

It dawns on me the green zigzag signs I've passed ten times a day indicate stairs. I nip through the nearest exit. If I take them slowly the pain in my leg is minimal and moving between floors comfortably disorientating. I avoid the lifts for the drama of their sliding doors—the chance of Avril leaping out like a penitent nun, all tears and handwringing... Off the stairwell, doors open onto malls and anonymous corridors, some empty, some milling with bodies clutching souvenir carriers.

By the third switch of deck, my anger is waning. I feel like a mouse in a Heath Robinson maze, intrigued where my twitching nose will pop out next. Another door leads to the citrus-hued lobby of the Rainforest Spa. Around that corner is the desk, manned by staff in pedal pushers and unisex Nehru jackets. Here, teak-effect sunbeds match the shelves stacked with towels and sea-green products laid out like art. My ankle is smarting. Time to take the weight off...

The spa is a favourite haunt of Avril's, but I am prepared to risk her dropping in for a conscience-soothing Mani-Pedi. Gently flexing my foot, I lever onto a lounger and settle into its quality-cotton embrace. Again, it strikes me how luxury loses its cachet once it becomes the norm. Like the boy spotting the naked Emperor, the illusion around me is apparent. Corners are scuffed if you care to notice; chipped veneers and cobwebs are no respecters of class. (How *do* spiders get aboard ships? Hitching a ride on the rats, presumably.)

It feels like sacrilege, but I will be glad when this is over. After Auckland, Tonga and Hawaii—all once dreamlike prospects that now promise the same excitement as ticking items off a shopping list... I will disembark and take my place on whatever tour I've booked myself. There will be heat and noise; views and buildings I have only seen in pictures will gain a third dimension, plus smells and people hawking things. All very mind-broadening. But aren't life's pleasures different for everyone? All this—the ship and the pampering, the bowing and scraping and thrice-cooked *pomme frites*—is only heaven if you're that sort of person... Is any of it intrinsically more satisfying than sitting down to a TV quiz with Mother and an uncut Battenberg?

"You waiting for terrapy, madame?" enquires a bird-like girl, stacking towels.

"No," I say. Though perhaps I should be.

More staff appear at intervals, asking after my day and offering a herbal infusion from the countertop samovar, which explains the aroma of bath salts. I sense an edge to their obsequiousness, as if my presence lends their oasis a vagrant air. True, I am out of place in my civvies, like a mad aunt turning up to a christening in her housecoat. Before they force me into monogrammed slippers and high-end terry, I ease myself off the lounger and out through the frosted doors.

Passing between pillars, I come to what the deck plan calls the Aft Corral. It mirrors a similarly vast space at the opposite end of the ship which I still confuse with this one. The brass railing sways back on itself, away from the chasm that drops nine levels to the Palm Court below. It is currently, distantly, hosting afternoon tea for passengers seated around the chequered floor like chess pieces. Aspidistras at each corner suggest thoughtfully placed sea anemones... I have a sudden urge to try an experiment; to see how long it takes an object tossed over the railing to reach the bottom, ideally into someone's Earl Grey. As ever I don't have my purse, and the only things in my pocket are a crumpled tissue and my key card, neither of which would pack a satisfying heft.

The only other object that springs to mind, is me.

The formula we were taught at school to calculate terminal velocity escapes me. But after eleven weeks of cruise ship cuisine, it seems safe to assume a plummeting Fen, whether limbs flailing or head-first for maximum ballistic impact, will take out more than a china teacup... The prospect feels eerily familiar, from the many on-screen dramas I have consumed over the years where people, often women, are shown jumping, tipped or otherwise propelled off balconies. As a rule this is filmed in balletic slow motion and from more angles than the tennis, rendering every drawn-out second in explicit detail. All except for the impact; which is, for want of a better word, fudged.

It troubles me how rationally I am considering this.

No, not considering. *Embracing.*

The prospect of leaving a mess, literal and otherwise, for Avril to clear up is perversely appealing. There will be issues to untangle with the authorities—the UK Foreign Office and Australian equivalent—and Mother to explain it to. I can see her now: a picture of tight-lipped devastation, glaring at Avril across an open grave. My demise will break only one of them, which is as it should be. Mother's world is shrinking. What life she has left, with or without me, she will focus ever more intently on herself. It is Avril I am out to ruin, with a grand finale that ensures she will remember her vile words of the soda bar till her dying day.

For such words, which are beyond forgiveness, should never be spoken.

Even if they're true.

I look around. The only other people in the Aft Corral are a family on the far side, reminiscent of the one on the Observation Deck. Mother, father, and this time two boys, sifting tee shirts on a rail outside an outlet called Treasure Trove... Daddy is in rather good shape, with well-defined calves that probably spend eleven months a year concealed in navy suiting. Even he could not sprint from the clothes rail to the balcony in the time it takes me to flip first one, then the other leg over... That means hanging on with at least one hand until the manoeuvre is complete. And hanging on means letting go, the precise moment film-makers exploit for full dramatic potential: Will she do it? Has she the guts, or is this just another desperate woman's cry for help?

The alternative is a slow and elegant bow. Close my eyes and bend at the waist, like a performer taking leave of their audience. But instead of returning to vertical, to smile at the thunderous applause, I will lean further and further to the limit of my hamstrings. Then, with the grace of a high diver, lift my heels and topple away in pike position... End over end like a boomerang, as the gaping depths swallow me up.

One gulp. Gone.

I open my eyes. The Aft Corral takes a moment to reform, like a carousel shunting to a stop. My hand gropes for the brass rail, missing at the first attempt... How long I have stood here I cannot say, but the family are gone. I am about to step back from the edge when my eyes snag on something in the Palm Court.

Avril. Unmistakable even at a distance in that skirt, sitting by a planter of faux orange blooms. Her body language, hands on crossed knees, head nodding to one side, says she is in conversation. The lip of the corral conceals the other side of her table. I lean carefully to see who she's talking to... A glimpse that sets me rocking on my heels, then scissoring three steps to the left for a better view.

My ankle twinges as I half-hobble, half-run to the lift. Jab at the call button, its luminous red circle mocking the agitation in my stomach. The pause between the *bong* and the perfunctory slide of doors lasts a long breath. At first the only company is my own puffy reflection. Panic escalates with every opening swish, as bodies pile in, press buttons, and tut when we descend against their wishes.

"Level...Two," announces the soporific Tannoy. *"For the Palm Court, Dynasty Lounge and Empress Arcade."*

I am through the doors before they are fully open. Adrift for a moment, at a different point on the chessboard floor than I expected. There are only a dozen tables here, half of them obscured by vigorous pseudo-vegetation. I round a second bank of succulents—And there they are.

"Talk of the devil!" says Avril. "Here she is!"

Not a flash of remorse. Not a hint of recognition she has wounded me to the core... I know that expression only too well. Her chin, angled like a greetings-card spaniel, says, 'I will stop at nothing to be irresistible.'

When I don't respond my so-called friend shifts in her wicker chair.

"Of course, you know—"

Irving Jessop, smartly suited and as gallant as ever, stands. He opens his arms with a single word of greeting. "Surprise."

How can this be? How is he here, on the other side of the world!

He smiles. "Hope you don't mind my turning up like this, Fen. I took the liberty of joining your tour this morning. Don't worry, I won't be in your way. Just thought it might be nice to have dinner sometime?"

Perhaps it is the turmoil of the day, but his old-world courtesy makes me melt a little. That and his eyes, as he pulls up a chair between Avril's and his own. I tremble as I sit.

"Isn't this lovely?" she says, keen to be remembered. "When I got back to the suite, Fen, there was a note under the door. Addressed to both of us!"

"Of course," says Irving.

"He said he'd be waiting down here, and it didn't seem right to leave him dangling... Actually, Irving and I were just discussing what to do... Whether to get reception to put a call out for you, or if he should hide away till dinner time, then surprise you in the restaurant!"

I am not taking in a word. "I can't believe it, Irving. It's so good to see you. And oh, I can't thank you enough for everything. This trip has been—"

"Yes," chimes Avril, "I was just saying, the experience of a lifetime! You've opened up the world to me, Irving. To us, I mean. All the places we've seen!"

She leans over the glass-topped table, and the pot of tea I haven't noticed. There is an extra cup and saucer, though conspicuously no complimentary cakes, which suggests someone is feeling self-conscious. Avril pours a cup and slides it to me.

"I say *we've* seen. Poor Fen twisted her ankle on the ice rink yesterday. Didn't you? Missed out on Sydney today, which was such a shame... Marvellous city, isn't it, Irving? I bet you know it well."

Irving sips from his own cup and saucer. "I do. And it is... Sorry to hear that, Fen. Have you had it looked at? The medical team are pretty good on here. I know the main guy if it's still giving you trouble..."

I shake my head. "Thank you, but it's a lot better today. And yes, the nurses were very professional. I'm hoping to go ashore tomorrow. I can't come all this way and not see the Opera House!"

"Aha," says Irving. "You took the words out of my mouth..." He reaches into his jacket, producing an envelope. "Just so happens I have two tickets for tomorrow's matinee. The Los Angeles Opera company doing *Madame Butterfly*... Now, not a problem if you ladies wanna go sightseeing, or get out in the Sydney sunshine instead of being indoors." His eyes are on me. "On the other hand, if you don't feel like walking too far..."

This man is nothing short of an angel. What have I done to deserve this?

"Irving, I'd be delighted. Thank you."

"Yes, thank you!" parrots Avril. "That would be lovely!"

A flicker of uncertainty passes round the table.

"Actually, ma'am—Avril—I was thinking I'd escort your friend myself. Seems like she could do with a treat, don't you think? And if you fancy lunch first, Fen, I know a great little sushi place in the CBD..."

"Oh," fidgets Avril. "Of course..." She frees her skirt from a cane splinter. "Though you should probably see how you feel tomorrow, Fen. You can't be too careful with ankles. If you're not up to it, I can always—" She back-pedals as I catch her eye. "Fen and I are theatregoing chums of old, Irving. If there's one thing we can't abide, it's a wasted ticket!"

"Won't you be seeing Gary?" I ask pointedly. "He may have plans for you tomorrow."

Irving rests his tea on the table. "Who's Gary? Do I detect romance on the high seas?" There is just a hint of satisfaction in his good-natured smile.

"Oh, never a dull moment with Avril, Irving," I say, shoring up our pincer movement with a smile of my own. "I sometimes worry I'm cramping her style!"

And with that I sit back and finish my cup. Avril is chattering but I am not listening; too busy wondering where we should eat tonight, which of my modest selection of dresses to wear, and whether to nip to the Business Centre before I change for dinner. *Wait till I tell Mother I'm going to the opera with Irving Jessop!*

Two minutes later he pushes back his chair. "Anyways, I'll let you ladies enjoy the rest of your afternoon. No pressure, but if you fancy meeting for a cocktail later I'm in stateroom 785..."

Avril splutters. But as he takes leave of us with his characteristic tact, it is not her his gaze is trained upon. I resist the urge to break out of his spotlight. Then, with a nod and a smile, he is off. Crossing the foyer with its great glass panels, as the first lights of evening come on around Sydney Harbour.

For a citizen of the world, Irving Jessop has a remarkable way of making me feel at home precisely anywhere. I am looking forward to tomorrow already. Lunching on sushi; discovering the Opera House with its extraordinary architecture, like nuns in a high wind...

Travel is like life. It is a gift. Literally, in this case, though it's different for everyone. Whatever became of the mysterious Gary, for Avril I suspect Sydney is tainted forever. While for me, it is just the next stop on an open road.

One where everything lies ahead.

About the Author

Chris Chalmers was born in Lancashire and lives in south-west London with his partner, a quite famous concert pianist. He has been the understudy on *Mastermind*, visited 40 different countries and swum with iguanas. After many years of creating advertising campaigns for everything from *The Economist* to ballet shoes, he took the plunge into contemporary fiction. Aside from his novels, his proudest literary achievement is making Martina Navratilova ROFLAO on Twitter.

You can find him on Facebook @chrischalmersnovelist, Twitter @CCsw19 and Instagram @ccsw19.

By the Same Author

Dinner at the Happy Skeleton

Dan is the kind of gay man for whom the Noughties might have been named. Warm, witty and serially promiscuous, his heart melts at the sight of a chocolate brown Labrador—but with men, it's a different matter. He's thirty-nine and as single as ever, not counting the couple he just met online. An arrangement that looks oddly like it's going somewhere, until Dan gets fired from his job in advertising. With time out and a payoff in his pocket, summer presents a world of possibilities; just as memories surface of the ex he blames for the thinly veiled chaos of his life.

From London to Ljubljana, a yen for closure sets Dan on the trail of the man who fed his ego into a shredder. Through an eerie encounter at the home of the Olympiad and a sleepover at the Dutch Embassy, run-ins with a fading porn star and the celestial manifestation of Margaret Thatcher, he ultimately confronts his past. Until, with his Big Four-O rapidly approaching, destiny beckons from where he least expects it.

"The perfect novel for a sunny afternoon. Full of charm and vim and sauce—I wolfed it down."
Philip Hensher, Man Booker Prize nominee, critic and journalist

"An eye-opening, always entertaining romp through modern sexual mores, with a sweet, beating heart of true feeling at its core."
Suzi Feay, literary critic

"Full of wit, comedy and unflinching honesty... Like reading a gay Nick Hornby. This is clever contemporary fiction at its finest."
Bleach House Library

Five to One

Winner of the Wink Publishing Debut Novel Competition
Nominated for the Polari First Book Award

Every moment starts somewhere
A care assistant with a secret. A gardener with an eye for more than greenfly. An estate agent and an itinerant Kiwi, both facing a relationship crisis. And a pilot with nowhere to land.

At twelve fifty-five on a sunny afternoon, five lives converge in a moment of terror as a helicopter crashes on Clapham Common. It's a day that will change them all forever—and for some, will be their last.

"A funny, often painfully honest and moving story about the absurdity of modern life and the concerns that propel us. Chalmers writes with a sensitivity and wit that recalls Armistead Maupin's Tales of the City.*"*
Penny Hancock, bestselling author of *Tideline*

"A charming novel that's cleverly structured and consistently engaging."
Matt Cain, novelist and broadcaster

"A poignant study of genuine love in a big and fantastically diverse city."
Justine Solomons, BytetheBook.com

Light From Other Windows

How many secrets can a family hide?

Nineteen-year-old Josh Maitland is at the end of a gap-year trip round the world when the tsunami hits the Canary Islands. His family are devastated at the loss of someone they thought would outlive them all: mother Diana, advertising executive and shatterer of glass ceilings; older siblings Rachel and Jem, each contemplating a serious relationship after years of sidestepped commitment; and stepfather Colin, no stranger to loss, who finds himself frozen out by his wife's grief.

Only with the discovery of the private blog Josh was writing for his friends does the significance of his travels become clear. It reveals secrets he knew about everyone in his family—and one about himself that will change the way they think of him forever.

"Chris Chalmers combines sensitivity and wit in his observation of human behaviour with a cracking storyline. Unputdownable."
Penny Hancock, bestselling author of *Tideline*

"Chalmers can bring tears to your eyes on one page and make you laugh on the next. He deftly skewers the pretensions of contemporary urban life, and his dialogue is unfailingly sharp and witty."
Suzi Feay, literary critic

"A wonderful examination of human nature and relationships... The timing of the writing pulled me into the lives of the Maitland family and kept me turning page after page. A completely absorbing and entertaining read."
livemanylives.wordpress.com

The Last Lemming

TV naturalist 'Prof Leo' Sanders makes it to his deathbed without a whiff of scandal—then confesses his career-defining wildlife discovery was a hoax. A National Treasure shattering his own reputation on YouTube is enough to spark a media frenzy; and the curiosity of part-time journalism student Claire Webster, who makes him the subject of her dissertation.

Her investigations lead to Prof Leo's estranged family and a high-flying advertising guru he also slandered in the video. Ultimately Claire uncovers the truth behind the discovery of the Potley Hill Lemming, the first new species of British mammal in a century. It's a mystery spanning four decades— and a tale of greed, obsession and long-forgotten murder at a lonely beauty spot.

"A revered TV naturalist with a guilty secret, a cute critter, brand of stout and a lovelorn personal trainer all collide with tragic-comic results in this witty whydunnit. The Last Lemming *combines pathos, humour and mystery to irresistible effect."*
Suzi Feay, literary critic

*"*The Last Lemming *is a terrific romp of a read; witty, elegantly penned and thoroughly enjoyable."*
Alex Pearl, author of *Sleeping with the Blackbird* and *The Chair Man*

"A beguiling weave of storylines and vibrant characters that kept me enthralled and keen to savour every twist and turn. Really didn't want this to end... In fact I've written to the author to complain about it!"
P.J. Preston

Gillian Vermillion—Dream Detective

For children aged 6 to 8

Imagine you could see what people are dreaming...

Gillian Vermillion can, thanks to her dad's amazing invention—the Dream Detector.

Follow their adventures as Gillian, her brother Boris and little dog Redvers explore the world of dreams. Prepare to encounter knights and a chocolate-eating dragon... Sail a galleon full of kittens over storm-tossed seas... And tumble through outer space inside giant hats!

But the astonishing Dream Detector has even more surprises in store, including a way to solve the mystery of what dreams really mean! How many adventures can Gillian and her friends squeeze in, before it's time to return the machine to Dad's special cupboard?

"I bought this book for my son, who got so engrossed in it that he was awarded Star Reader of the Week at school by his teacher. His teacher praised the book citing it as the turning point in my son's interest in reading. A great narrative written in a way that clearly engages."

Taryn, UK reader

"A lovely read with lots of captivating imagery and characters. The author has a real way with description that strikes a chord with young readers."

Shenanagans, UK reader

"Inventive. Creative. Clever. Fun. Gripping. This book is great for children, and for adults reading to children learning to read. Highly recommended."

Brendan, Australian reader

Author's Note

Thank you for buying FENELLA'S FAIR SHARE. If you have a few moments, please post a quick review on your favourite online site. It's a big help and much appreciated.

If you'd like to find out more about my books, upcoming works and blog posts, please visit @chrischalmersnovelist on Facebook. And do say hi while you're there!

Chris Chalmers

ROUNDFIRE
BOOKS

FICTION

Put simply, we publish great stories. Whether it's literary or popular, a gentle tale or a pulsating thriller, the connecting theme in all Roundfire fiction titles is that once you pick them up you won't want to put them down.
If you have enjoyed this book, why not tell other readers by posting a review on your preferred book site.

Recent bestsellers from Roundfire are:

The Bookseller's Sonnets
Andi Rosenthal

The Bookseller's Sonnets intertwines three love stories with a tale of religious identity and mystery spanning five hundred years and three countries.

Paperback: 978-1-84694-342-3 ebook: 978-184694-626-4

Birds of the Nile
An Egyptian Adventure

N.E. David

Ex-diplomat Michael Blake wanted a quiet birding trip up the Nile – he wasn't expecting a revolution.

Paperback: 978-1-78279-158-4 ebook: 978-1-78279-157-7

Blood Profit$
The Lithium Conspiracy

J. Victor Tomaszek, James N. Patrick, Sr.

The blood of the many for the profits of the few... *Blood Profit$* will take you into the cigar-smoke-filled room where American policy and laws are really made.

Paperback: 978-1-78279-483-7 ebook: 978-1-78279-277-2

The Burden
A Family Saga

N.E. David

Frank will do anything to keep his mother and father apart. But he's carrying baggage – and it might just weigh him down ...

Paperback: 978-1-78279-936-8 ebook: 978-1-78279-937-5

The Cause
Roderick Vincent
The second American Revolution will be a fire lit from
an internal spark.
Paperback: 978-1-78279-763-0 ebook: 978-1-78279-762-3

Don't Drink and Fly
The Story of Bernice O'Hanlon: Part One
Cathie Devitt
Bernice is a witch living in Glasgow. She loses her way in her
life and wanders off the beaten track looking for the garden of
enlightenment.
Paperback: 978-1-78279-016-7 ebook: 978-1-78279-015-0

Gag
Melissa Unger
One rainy afternoon in a Brooklyn diner, Peter Howland
punctures an egg with his fork. Repulsed, Peter pushes the
plate away and never eats again.
Paperback: 978-1-78279-564-3 ebook: 978-1-78279-563-6

The Master Yeshua
The Undiscovered Gospel of Joseph
Joyce Luck
Jesus is not who you think he is. The year is 75 CE. Joseph
ben Jude is frail and ailing, but he has a prophecy to fulfil ...
Paperback: 978-1-78279-974-0 ebook: 978-1-78279-975-7

On the Far Side, There's a Boy
Paula Coston
Martine Haslett, a thirty-something 1980s woman, plays hard
on the fringes of the London drag club scene until one night
which prompts her to sign up to a charity. She writes to a
young Sri Lankan boy, with consequences far and long.
Paperback: 978-1-78279-574-2 ebook: 978-1-78279-573-5

Tuareg
Alberto Vazquez-Figueroa
With over 5 million copies sold worldwide, *Tuareg* is a classic
adventure story from best-selling author Alberto Vazquez-
Figueroa, about honour, revenge and a clash of cultures.
Paperback: 978-1-84694-192-4

Readers of ebooks can buy or view any of these bestsellers by
clicking on the live link in the title. Most titles are published
in paperback and as an ebook. Paperbacks are available in
traditional bookshops. Both print and ebook formats are
available online.

Find more titles and sign up to our readers' newsletter, visit:
www.collectiveinkbooks.com/fiction